WHISPERS

—from—

POMPEII

A NOVEL
LORRAINE BLUNDELL

authorHOUSE®

AuthorHouse™ UK Ltd.
1663 Liberty Drive
Bloomington, IN 47403 USA
www.authorhouse.co.uk
Phone: 0800.197.4150

Published by AuthorHouse 7/24/2013

ISBN: 978-1-4817-7521-2 (sc)
ISBN: 978-1-4817-7522-9 (e)

For Steve, Jenni and Lauren

Fabrizio Belleni guided me through a fascinating and emotionally moving tour of the archaeological site of Pompeii. His impressive depth of knowledge and obvious passion for the ancient city and its people was truly inspiring.

Nothing in the world can last forever

Pompeii
Graffiti scratched on a frescoed wall

ANCIENT POMPEII

1. Villa of the Mysteries
2. Villa of Diomedes
3. Herculaneum Gate
4. Suburban Bathhouse
5. Forum
6. Large theatre
7. Small theatre
8. Amphitheatre
9. Harbour
10. Temple of Venus

11. *Via delle Tombe*
12. *Via Consolare*
13. *Via del Vesuvio*
14. *Via di Nola*
15. *Vicolo del Centenario*
16. *Via Stabiana*
17. *Via Marina*
18. *Via dell' Abbondanza*
19. *Via dei Teatri*
20. *Via di Castricio*
21. *Via di Nocera*

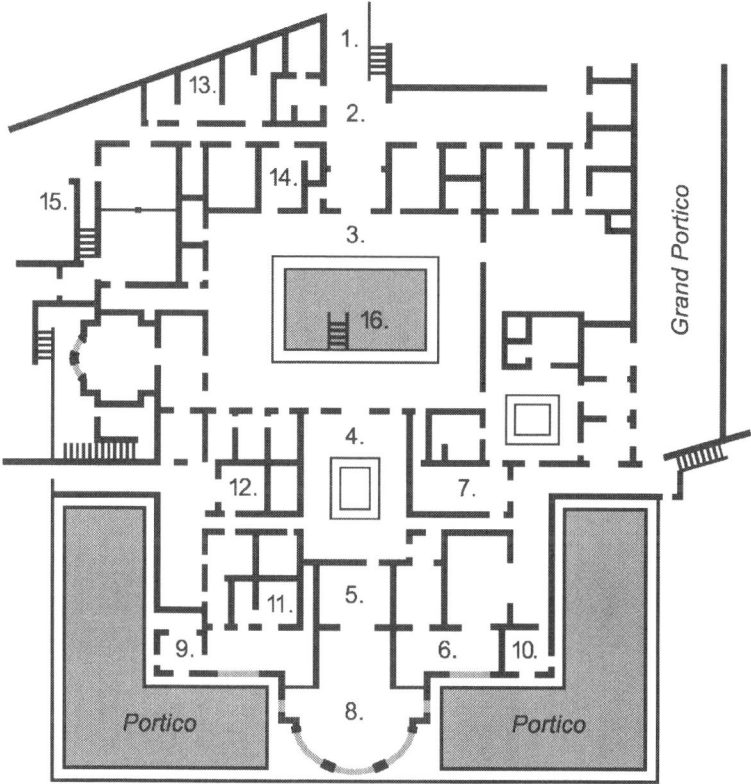

VILLA OF THE MYSTERIES

1. Entry
2. Vestibule
3. Peristyle
4. Atrium
5. Study
6. Initiation Room
7. Dining Room
8. Exedra
9. Day Room
10. Day Room
11. Bedroom - Alessia
12. Bedroom - Fabritio
13. Servants' Rooms
14. Kitchen
15. Wine Cellar
16. Crypt

Pompeii Site Locations

The locations below at the historic site of Pompeii are featured in *Whispers from Pompeii*. The names used here and on the map are those given by archaeologists. Street names in Pompeii, because they were unknown following the city's destruction, have also been chosen by the archaeologists.

Villa dei Misteri
(Lady Claudia's Villa)
The Villa of Diomedes

The House of the Centenary
The House of the Gilded Cupids
The House of Julia Felix
The House of the Lyre Player
The House of the Painter's Workshop
The House of the Perfumer
The House of the Surgeon
The House of the Tragic Poet

The Amphitheatre

The Bar of Fortunata
The Fullery of Stephanus
The Inn of Euxinus
The Thermopollium of
Vetutius Placidus

The Forum Baths
The Suburban Baths

The Forum

Temple of Bacchus
(Outside the Walls)
Temple of Isis
Temple of Venus

The Lupanare
The Street of Tombs

Villa Moregine
(Outside Pompeii)
Villa of Poppaea
(Oplontis)

Pompeii Characters

The following characters in *Whispers from Pompeii* are thought to have either lived in Pompeii or to have passed through the city. This conclusion is based on evidence from historical records, inscriptions, graffiti or personal possessions and business finds from the Pompeii excavations.

Dates are sometimes inexact other than the debated date of August or September of 79 A.D. when the city was destroyed by the eruption of Vesuvius. Major characters and their occupations are highlighted below.

Anicetus, Actius	Manager, theatre troupe
Astus	Gladiator (Murmillo)
Atimetus	**Gladiator (Thracian)**
Attice	**Prostitute**
Beryllos (Oplontis)	**Freedman, Villa of Poppaea**
Cassia	Owner, Villa of the Faun
Certus, Aulus Suettius	Owner, Gladiator Troupe
Diomedes, Marcus Arrius	**Owner, Villa of Diomedes**
Eumachia	Priestess, business woman
Euxinus	**Owner, Inn of Euxinus**
Felix, Julia	Wealthy female property owner
Grosphus, Gnaeus	Popeius Duumvir, (Senior Magistrate) 59 A.D.
Hinnulus	**Unknown**
Jucundus, Lucius Caecilius	**Banker. Owner, House of Jucundus**
Mesonius	Lanista
Nigidius, Gnaeus Allius	Real estate investor
Paris	**The leading pantomimist of his time**
Phoebus	**Perfumer**
Proculus, Paquius	Owner, House of Proculus
Regulus, Livineius	**Games Patron**
Rufus, Gnaeus Marcus	**Poet**
Scaurus, Umbricius	Garum (fish sauce) maker
Sorex, Norbanus	**Actor**
Stephanus	**Owner, Fullery**
Tibertinus	Poet
Verus, Tiberius Claudius	Duumvir. 61 A.D.
Vetutius, Lucius Placidus	Owner, street food shop

WHISPERS
FROM
POMPEII

LUCIUS

ALESSIA

THE POLITICIAN

THE PROSTITUTE

THE PAINTER

PROLOGUE

Baiae

(North West of Pompeii)

Nero's Royal Villa
64 A.D.

Alessia

It is made of pure gold.

The light from the oil lamp enhances its lustre drawing the eye to it. Lingeringly, I run my fingers over the curved bars finding them cool to the touch despite the heat of a summer's evening.

The cage is circular, curving inwards at its top to a finial. It is surprisingly strong, belying an initial impression of delicacy. Never in the time since my arrival have I ever entered the Emperor's bedroom, forbidden to all but the slave Anna. I'm waiting for Nero's return to his apartment for his morning music lesson, but curiosity has led me to wander. I glance around at the sumptuous bed, fine linens and antique furnishings. Frescoes of great beauty fill the walls with an explosion of colour and on the marble floor of the huge room lies an intricately woven, blood red carpet.

Impulsively, I allow one sandal to slip from my foot and slowly slide its bareness over the silken softness of the carpet's surface. Nearby, a lyre has been tossed casually onto a chair by the window.

Outside the room a cool breeze whispers in from the sea alleviating the heat, bringing with it the perfume of roses their pink and red petals also adorning the bed and scattered across the floor. I've heard it said that Nero loves beautiful things. After seeing this room, I believe it.

I dare not stay and risk discovery. I know only too well the penalty I would suffer if Nero found me in his bedroom. It's time I returned to the music room. A sound stops me dead in my tracks, an echo from the past that seems like a lifetime ago. The bird in the cage has begun to sing. Instantly I recognise its haunting melody. The prisoner in its cage is surely a nightingale. The sweetness of its singing is hypnotic, its piping and chirruping, unmistakable.

The last time I heard its magical voice was on another summer's evening, in Sicily. The bird is a small brown creature very plain to the eye. I have never actually seen one before, but as they hid in the trees above the azure waters of Tauromenium singing amidst the oleander and eucalyptus trees, they once filled my heart with joy.

Now, only longing remains. The years since I left Sicily with my brother, Fabritio, have been filled with both joy and fear. One thing is certain. We have a madman for an Emperor.

PART I

59 A.D.-61 A.D.

1

Sicily

Tauromenium
(Taormina)

59 A.D.

> *Flower, flower tell me do,*
> *Does he love me?*
> *Is he true?*

Petal by petal Alessia let them float gently in a pink scattering onto the ground at her feet. In a game as old as time she sought the answer to her question. She could still feel the intensity of Antonius' lips on hers from last night.

'Day dreaming again are you Lessi?' Her older brother, Fabritio, wore the same amused look on his face that had always infuriated her.

'That's none of your business!'

'He's not worth it, you know. Be careful, he likes to have the girls swooning over him.'

'I'm not swooning over him!' she snapped.

'Don't get serious about him, Lessi. I know him better than you do.' The expression on her brother's face changed from one of amusement to concern. 'Antonius will break your heart.' He placed his arm around her shoulders. She relented enough not to shrug it off. Their relationship was close. That was not surprising, as Fabritio had been both brother and father to Alessia since their arrival in Sicily. Then, she had been ten years old and he sixteen. Now she was the age he had been then. Life had been difficult.

Both of their parents had died from plague which had swept relentlessly through the city of Naples. The trading ships that brought all types of visitors, merchants and goods to the city also carried rats with fleas and with them, the plague.

Thousands of bodies were carried in lumbering carts to pits outside the city to be burned daily, until it reeked with the stench of death. Bread became scarcer with each passing day as the risk of contracting the disease increased. Young Fabritio Attilius was determined to get himself and his sister to safety. The citizens of Naples fortunate enough to have wealth or influence used it and scattered as far away as possible. Fabritio hurried himself and Alessia out of the city through the generosity of a friend's father who owned a fishing boat. They were set down in the nearest port to which he was travelling. They found themselves in Sicily.

Fabritio and Alessia made their way to the town of Tauromenium where he found work cleaning out the town's only sculpture workshop and running errands for the owner. As the years went by he grew tall and well muscled. The two young people barely survived in a cramped, dingy room with little food. As Fabritio grew older the owner, a dour man by the name of Dimitri, allowed him to use the workshop tools on some of the less important busts commissioned by his clients. For some reason the tough old man took a liking to the youngster and Fabritio became the son he'd never had. After that life became much easier.

A good looking young man with jet black hair and brown eyes the same as his sister's, Fabritio was also blessed with creative talent. Dimitri, recognising his ability and potential, trained him well. Soon he was reaping in the financial reward of Fabritio's work, some of which he used to increase the young sculptor's weekly salary.

Brother and sister sat together in companionable silence watching dusk settle over the magnificent Greek theatre. It perched high on a cliff looking out over the sea, and was itself overlooked by the snow capped peak of Aetna. The nightly performance began as the volcano glowered in showers of fiery, red fairy lights that spewed forth from its centre. The clean, astringent smell of eucalyptus mingled with the soft, subtly sweet fragrance of the oleander blossoms as they listened to the songs of the nightingales.

'We'll have to get ready to leave soon for Naples.'

Alessia kicked the fallen petals away with her foot. 'I know, Fabritio, you told me before. I'm glad I'm coming with you, I don't want to stay here alone.'

He glanced across at her serious face and realised how young and innocent she still was. 'I'd never leave you behind. You know that! Come on. It's time we went home.' Fabritio helped her up and they turned their backs on the theatre.

As the blackness of night thickened they walked down Theatre Street in silence, past the closed shops and gymnasium towards the centre of the town. Theatre Street, narrow, long and the main thoroughfare, had long felt the tread of many feet over countless centuries. Since the arrival of the Romans, inhabitants and visitors had included ordinary citizens, gladiators, actors, merchants, travellers and government officials.

A small detachment of Roman legionaries marched smartly past Alessia and Fabritio for the changeover of their shift, hob nailed boots clanking on the stone paved street. They kept watch diligently over those living on the inside of the sturdy town walls.

The city's main bathhouse loomed into view as a final few stragglers made their hasty way home hoping for a tasty dinner. Already, the aroma of chicken cooking reached them from a nearby worker's hut. Soon Fabritio and Alessia reached the small but pleasant house they'd rented for some time. Although tiny, it provided them with a bedroom each, kitchen and basic reception area. Alessia kept it neat and clean and learned to cook simple meals while Fabritio earned enough to keep them alive.

———∘∘∘)◉(∘∘∘———

Three weeks later

Tauromenium's climate was superb and the setting breathtakingly lovely. On a day like this with a blue sky and a slight breeze, Fabritio wondered, not for the first time, if they were doing the right thing by leaving. Still, he reasoned, they would have more of a future if they returned to Naples. He looked back to where Alessia still sat on the front step twisting strands of her long hair around her fingers as she watched him go. He was well aware that she was rapidly becoming a beautiful young woman. Along with her long dark hair, oval face, large brown eyes and curvaceous figure, she exuded an air of vulnerability. That combination, from his point of view as her male protector, was dynamite.

He waved and she smiled and waved back. He loved her dearly and her welfare was always uppermost in any decisions he made. At least that sod Antonius wouldn't get his hands on her! Fabritio had already warned him once and told him to shove off. If there was a next time things were likely to get ugly. As for his own romantic entanglements there had only really been one, and he had stepped away once he realised things were getting serious. The girl was pretty and he'd been attracted to her, but it was too soon for a long term commitment.

This final day at the workshop had come so rapidly that Fabritio was finding it difficult to adapt to the fact that he was really leaving. The workshop was located inside the city walls towards the southern fringes of the town, with its own protective wall and iron gates. It consisted of a small outer room and behind it, a much larger one where busts and statues were worked mostly in stone and sometimes in marble. There was a small yard mainly filled with rubble where Dimitri's dog, Drixus, roamed. A large, savage looking black mongrel of unknown parentage, it had been with Dimitri as long as anyone could remember. Few were observant enough to notice the intelligence in the dog's dark eyes. He provided security for the workshop and friendship for its owner.

This was not the place to be for anyone seeking peace and relaxation. The creation of the busts and statues was physically demanding. It was sweaty, dusty work as well as requiring a huge amount of patience and attention to detail. If the sculptor made a mistake he needed to be sufficiently talented to mask it or the work became unsaleable. There was no doubt, however, that completion of a beautiful piece was its own reward. Only gods, goddesses and elite members of the community warranted statues, especially in marble. Everyone else had to be content with a bust, hopefully made by a skilled artisan.

Fabritio held firmly to the heavy bag in his hands as he rounded the final bend, passing through the rusty, creaking gates to where Dimitri already stood working beside his bench. He grunted in his usual way as he saw Fabritio enter.

'Have you finished the bust of Aulus yet?' he asked gruffly without looking up.

'I finished it yesterday afternoon. I left it locked away in the back cupboard.' Fabritio placed his bag on the bench.

A young lad stood towards the rear of the room looking bewildered. Fabritio walked over to him.

'Are you starting work here?' he asked kindly.

'Y—es,' the boy stammered shyly, head bowed.

'Don't worry, it'll work out fine. Just you wait and see,' Fabritio reassured him.

'I thought I'd better replace you,' Dimitri said. 'That won't be easy!' Having finished the statue he was sculpting, he surveyed the younger man from under bushy eyebrows.

There was a moment of awkward silence. Taking off his apron, Dimitri limped arthritically over to the young sculptor who had come to mean so much to him. Experience, however, had taught him long ago that one thing, apart from death, was always certain and that was change.

'Lad, I'll miss you. Remember, if you ever need a place to go or a favour you know where to find me.' Unexpectedly he reached out and held Fabritio in a short, strong bear-hug.

This was the longest speech Fabritio had ever heard from him. Certainly, it was the most emotional. He picked up the bag from the bench were he'd placed it and handed it to Dimitri, who opened it carefully.

Inside was a lifelike, skilfully sculpted marble bust of the old man. It was a perfect size for a hall or bedside table.

'And this is a parting gift from me,' Dimitri muttered, turning aside to pick up a coin purse. Fabritio saw tears in his eyes. The old man, embarrassed, tried to wipe them away.

Fabritio opened it and was stunned at the amount of sesterces inside. His employer was now someone he could call a friend. Obviously, he'd been saving the money well in advance of this day so that he could give it to the talented young man who had touched his heart.

'Dimitri, I don't know how to thank you,' Fabritio said, overcome by his generosity.

'That's all right. Use them carefully, son, you'll need money where you're going. And don't forget, there are many who will try to take everything you have away from you.'

The two stood silently for a moment.

'Goodbye, Fabritio. May fortune smile on you. I wish you good luck!'

The young sculptor turned and walked away. Only time would tell if his decision had been the right one.

'Youngster, it's time we got to work!' Dimitri waved the new apprentice over to the work bench and handed him an apron.

Just as Fabritio had done years before, the boy wondered what lay ahead of him. It was just as well that he was unaware of the outstanding talent of the sculptor he was expected to replace.

Alessia

Everything's happening too fast. I long to stay in Tauromenium but I must trust Fabritio to know what's best for us. I remember Naples. It was so busy it scared me. I'd almost forgotten the noise and the crowds. Still, I'm older now, so perhaps it won't be so bad. At least I have one consolation, Fabritio will be with me.

Apparently we're to look for work as soon as we arrive. I hope it will be worth all of the upset. I didn't get to say goodbye to Antonius but Fabritio is right. If he'd really wanted to see me, he would've found a way before I left. Now it's too late.

—

2

Naples
(Neapolis)

It could be said that the city of Naples stood in the middle of hell on earth. Its citizens lived their lives unaware of the potential disaster all around them. They scoffed down the delicious wine produced from vines that thrived on the land of the Campi Flegrei. It consisted of four miles of a sunken volcanic field west of this, the 'Queen' city of the south and its leisure playgrounds. There, steam shooting upwards into the sky, and pools of boiling mud combined with poisonous sulphuric fumes to re-create man's vision of hades.

In nearby resorts up and down the coastline, Romans mistook danger for an opportunity to luxuriate in thermal baths. The hulking form of Vesuvius, a tiny area of the volcanic field, hung over Naples. Its high, fertile slopes were lush with vegetation and vineyards, its presence both dominating and familiar.

On this day the city awakened to the first rays of sunlight banishing the dark of night, inviting its people to live another day. Noisy, busy, grimy and ancient, the cosmopolitan city's narrow streets revelled in normal life with all its colour, smells, haste and needs. With its forum, theatre, baths, markets and temples, the city was little different from most other Roman cities of the time except for its bay.

The sweeping, breath-taking bay of Naples brought gasps of admiration from all who saw it. Nature had designed a visual feast impossible to improve upon. The water calmly lapping at the bay's edges was cool, clear and impossibly blue. On a fine day it shimmered in the sunlight inspiring joy and a feeling that it was good to be alive. Its waters, caressing the rocky shoreline, lay under the shadow of Vesuvius adjacent to the deadly fury of the Campi Flegrei.

---◦∘o⟩◈⟨o∘◦---

The Forum

Although not in any way a match for the glories of Rome's Forum, this major meeting place in Naples sported impressive marble statues and a decorative central fountain complete with naked nymphs spouting welcome gushes of cooling water. The large, paved square was devoted amongst other things to the selling of produce. It was always busy with the traffic of over-burdened donkeys and deliveries of olives as well as chickens hanging from poles carried by reluctant slaves. By its very nature it resounded with numerous conversations, commands and questions.

A variety of smells mingled together with tantalizing results. The aroma of freshly baked bread, the perfume of flowers, the earthy pungency of meat and fish, the odour of unwashed bodies, the pong of animal dung and the occasional, freshly groomed scents of well dressed passersby all found their way up human noses. Those attending the nearby Temple of the Dioscuri hurried piously to their destination, eager to arrive on time.

The day began with the shrieking of an angry vendor. It should be noted that this was not at all an unusual happening.

'Are you an absolute lunatic or what?' An angry cart owner yelled at another who had either purposely or otherwise knocked into his cart from behind, sending his cabbages sprawling across the ground.

'You stopped suddenly, you know you did you moron!'

The cabbage cart owner scrambled on his hands and knees across the filthy paving stones to retrieve his produce, providing unintended mirth for those watching. 'You old fool. You're so old you can't see straight,' he screeched.

The offending vendor's cart carried flowers collected from the Campania countryside. Deciding that the delicate load was too precious to risk, he turned and wiping away the sweat from his forehead with the back of his hand, trundled away to the other side of the forum muttering vulgarities under his breath.

'Apparently nothing has changed since the last time we were here.' Claudia Lucilla fanned herself as she watched in amusement from her litter.

'It never does. I don't think this place ever will.' Her housekeeper, Julia, looked around at the stall holders setting up for business, as slaves began to arrive to buy the day's fresh produce for households across the city.

Claudia's sharp eyes swept the quickly increasing chaos of the scene in front of her. 'Caius, do you see the young man with an even younger girl beside him? They're standing waiting to see the work hirers. Bring them here.' Claudia sat back relaxed, as her freedman approached to talk to them. She saw the hesitation in the stranger's manner as he looked towards the litter. Then he seemed to come to a decision and they made their way across to her.

'My name's Fabritio. You wish to speak to us, lady?'

Fabritio's voice was respectful. He saw before him a senior matron, elegantly dressed. She wore her silver hair swept up and back from her face, her veil now raised to reveal a kindly smile. She had little jewellery, but one look was enough to see that the pearl earrings and necklace she was wearing were enormously expensive. Her litter bearers were clean and well dressed and the man who had approached them introducing himself as Caius, head household supervisor for the lady Claudia, had been both pleasant and non-threatening.

'I'm Claudia Lucilla. I'm in need of staff for my villa in Pompeii. This young girl looks very much like someone who was dear to me when I was young, that's why I noticed her. What's your name, child?'

'I'm called Alessia,' she answered politely although somewhat annoyed at being addressed as *child*.

'You're citizens of which country?'

'Rome, lady. We've been living for many years in Tauromenium, having originally come from Naples,' Fabritio replied.

'As you were in line to visit the hirers, I assume that you're seeking work?'

'We are, preferably together. Alessia's my sister.'

'What are your qualifications?' Claudia looked thoughtful.

'I'm a sculptor. I carry with me a statement of recommendation and proof that I have fulfilled the requirements of my apprenticeship,' Fabritio answered. 'As for Alessia, she's yet to be trained in any particular type of work.' He handed over his written reference from Dimitri. For a few moments there was silence as Claudia read the scroll.

'This is highly complimentary regarding your service, and your skills. It appears that I've been most fortunate to find you.' She smiled and handed it back to him.

Claudia turned to speak once more to Alessia who was now gazing rather anxiously at her. 'Do you think you'd like to work for me at my villa in Pompeii? You'd be my personal maid and companion.'

Alessia was unsure. She glanced at her brother.

'Of course you'd be free to leave at any time if you weren't happy there,' Claudia continued.

'That's very kind.' Fabritio placed a reassuring arm around his sister. 'There's only one condition. We've always been together and I believe we need to stay that way. Alessia needs that security—at least to begin with.'

Claudia nodded understandingly. She approved of the caring relationship between brother and sister. She was inclined to believe that it was a positive indication of strength of character, and that was precisely what she needed from these two young people, especially the girl.

'I know my good friend Marcus Diomedes is presently in need of a quality sculptor. However, he'll have to wait. My own villa is currently undergoing renovation and I will be in need of your services first, Fabritio, for a short period of time. That should give Alessia the opportunity to settle in before you leave. In any case, the Diomedes' villa is just outside the Herculaneum Gate of Pompeii's city walls, not far from mine. Alessia could walk there easily if she wished. You will both be well paid and well treated. What do you think?'

She waited for their answer.

The nightingales hid in the trees at Tauromenium.

Naples

The Tavern of Capaneus

To: The Villa of Diomedes,
Via delle Tombe,
Pompeii

Dear Marcus
Greetings,

I trust that you've not been attempting to pull down that wall you were complaining about before I left! It will take at least another couple of men to help so that you don't injure yourself. We are neither of us young anymore.

I have both good news and bad news. Which would you like first? As you're not here to tell me and I can imagine you frowning with impatience as you read this, I'll give you the good news first. I've found you the most wonderful sculptor. He's young and fit and unless I'm much mistaken, extremely talented and reliable. Now for the bad news. That being the case, I've decided to keep him for myself, just for a while, to do work on my villa for me. I found him—so that's only fair!

Something else happened today though, Marcus, something that churned me up emotionally more than I could ever have expected. It's hard to explain, even to you, my old friend. I met a young woman, the sculptor's sister, who could have been Augusta she looked so much like her.

The girl's name is Alessia. Both she and her brother are most polite and respectful. They are Roman citizens who've been living for some years in Sicily. I know you'll say—'let it go. Augusta died many years ago.' But one never forgets a favourite sister! It's been lonely at times since I left Rome after Gaius died. I don't think I could have coped without your friendship.

When we lived in Rome I thought the Palatine was the most beautiful place in the world! It wasn't so much because of our lovely villa, although of course that was fantastic, as the feeling of being somewhere that was at the very pinnacle of the most awesome city in the world. I used to sit on the grass and gaze down on the Circus Maximus below. The action was all around us, and yet it could so easily be silenced, just by climbing up to our quiet paradise. Since then I've realised that my focus was somewhat narrow. After all, it's really the people who make a place what it is, isn't it?

A woman alone without a husband is often considered unnatural. At times it's only been my dedication to the 'Brides of Bacchus' and the group's closeness and caring for each other that has kept me going. I realise that I well and truly have more years behind me now, than I will ever have ahead. I wonder if young Alessia might be the companion and successor that I've been looking for?

Lorraine Blundell

Now I really must go, otherwise, I'll arrive back in Pompeii before you get this. Until then you have my affection as always.

Claudia

p.s. Marcus, I'd like to ask a favour. Please have my servants prepare two additional bedrooms. I will return home first with Caius, then Julia will follow a day or two later with the two newcomers. She's yet to complete buying a few luxuries for me that I've decided to allow myself.

3

Pompeii

Via delle Tombe

No moon. No moonlight.

The city's Herculaneum Gate seemed to loom upon her from nowhere before she was expecting it. Silly, really, she thought, considering she'd lived here all her life. Fabia hesitated just before the gate, peering down the long, narrow street of graves ahead of her. There was little to see in the darkness. Anyway, she knew where all the graves and shops were. She'd certainly walked along it often enough. It was just that somehow she'd never grown used to the unease she felt, especially at night, walking past people whose flesh lay putridly rotting or charred in urns in the realm of the dead. It was all so final, somehow.

A small rodent scuttled by just in front of her feet, scrabbling for a foothold on the uneven paving stones. Perhaps, she thought, she'd chosen the wrong spiritual path to follow. Apparently the Egyptian goddess Isis guaranteed a life after death to her followers. Not to mention that her temple was further away from the lonely roads of death outside the city gates.

Fabia smiled slightly to herself and began the long walk into a night as black as pitch. What was she thinking? She should be proud that she was now a priestess of purification. It had taken several years since her initiation into the cult to which she belonged to reach her present level. It was a small group entered into only by invitation. Its rites were shrouded in secrecy. Fabia glanced behind her and saw the outline of two veiled shapes approaching the gate, also probably hurrying to the same destination. It was considered very poor form to arrive late.

The evening was mild with thick, black clouds lying like a smothering blanket over the city. Later, there would probably be a storm. Shops along the road had long since closed and lay dark, the vendors having retreated to the back rooms in which they lived. It was late for any traveller to risk attempting to enter the town if they were strangers, as they would have little hope of finding their way. The street was utterly deserted except for the hurrying women.

Merchants slept soundly amongst the tombs in rooms clustered together inside entry archways at one side of the road of sepulchres, as their donkeys slumbered, tethered outside. The living and the dead slept side by side.

Fabia shivered as she passed the sepulchre of Quintus Clemens, a lover of the gladiator games. Dark cypress trees stood like silent sentinels over his final resting place. The Bestiarii pictured on his tomb would not have been skilled or quick enough to avoid death themselves, in the end. Clemens had died, apparently, on the very last day of the games of Ampliatus. That was rotten luck to say the least, if he'd hoped to collect on his bets—good luck if he'd suffered losses. Quickening her steps, Fabia reached the Villa of Cicero then that of Diomedes. It was only a short walk further to her destination.

She determined to calm herself in readiness to perform her duties. She must think of the young woman about to undergo one of the most important ceremonies of her life. Excited but afraid, she would be given no information about what was to come before the initiation began.

Reaching the villa she sought, Fabia entered the vestibule and walked to the atrium then into the portico. She trod quickly over the diamond patterned, black and white mosaic floor as she passed into the large, rectangular Initiation Room. Its high ceiling gave it a feeling of spaciousness. She entered a world of sisterhood, mystery and ritual. The head priestess nodded to her as she took her place amongst those already seated and removed her mantle.

Hands the colour of blood!

The initiand, Urbana, sat with her hands clasped on a table in front of her petrified with fear. In the dim light the candelabras cast prancing, liquid shapes onto the sacred, vivid crimson wall frescoes. A red flush fell over the young woman, her face pale in the candlelight. She struggled not to panic. The setting was unfamiliar to her as this was the first time she had ever been permitted to enter the room. Dressed in a simple, belted white tunic falling to her ankles, she sat shivering under the solemn gaze of the mistress of ceremonies, the head priestess, who was masked and wearing a long red robe edged with gold.

She signalled to Fabia who rose unhurriedly with a fluid grace and sat at the table beside Urbana. The incense, smelling evocatively of musk and amber permeated the room as the remaining women began a soft chanting. Several priestesses took their places at the front ready to begin the ceremony. Taking an amphora of water Fabia poured a small trickle over the girl's hands then dried them gently. The head priestess addressed the initiand, her voice ringing with authority throughout the room.

Urbana, you have come here to fulfil the secret rites for entry to the honoured society of the 'Brides of Bacchus.' Do you confirm that you are not yet married?
'I do.'
Tonight, you will pledge yourself to your spiritual husband, Bacchus, god of wine, fertility and the ecstasy of mystery. You have already been purified. You will progress through the remainder of the ceremony during which you will be shown the nature of the married state and purged of your sins.

The priestesses approached the girl. A lyre played softly in the background as Urbana's clothes were stripped from her body until she was semi-naked. The women's chanting increased in intensity as she was led to the centre of the room where a covered sculpture of a phallus had been placed.

Daughter, your time of fertility has come. Your progress from maidenhood to womanhood is almost complete. Tonight marks the spiritual end of that journey, Look upon the phallus, symbol of male fertility.

The high priestess uncovered the sculpture directing the innocent girl's gaze to it. Her eyes widened in a combination of confusion and fear. She realised that she'd seen this shape many times before on buildings and street paving stones as well as in gardens. She'd never known what it meant except that people seemed to think of it as a sign of good luck.

Turning away, Urbana stared at the life-sized figures on the frescoes, encased by friezes and classic borders. They seemed to be watching her and she felt mesmerised by their scrutiny. The moments passed.

Shaking, she was ordered to kneel, her head resting on the lap of a seated priestess who held her firmly. Urbana's alarm increased as she looked up and saw a whip raised in the hand of another. She screamed as twice she felt its sting so that her skin was broken and bleeding.

As suddenly as it had begun the chanting stopped and her ordeal was at an end. Urbana was led to an older matron who caringly washed away the blood and comforted her. Fabia stepped forward to clothe the young woman in a ceremonial robe and add a white veil.

There was a clash of cymbals as the head priestess removed her mask and kissed Urbana's cheek. 'Welcome, daughter, I will be here for you in times of sadness as well as happiness as will your new sisters.' A decorated silver cup holding wine the colour of rubies was pressed into the young girl's hands, as the women gathered around to congratulate her. She was now one of the spiritual 'Brides of Bacchus.'

Soon, she would wed the physical husband to whom she had recently become betrothed. Her journey to womanhood would be complete. The bond she had formed on this night with the sisterhood, would remain an unfailing source of affection and support throughout her life.

With the rising of the sun everything at the villa was quiet as if the night before had been a dream. Only the lacerations on the girl's back and the sculpture of the phallus, locked away in the room's cupboard along with the intricate silver cup, proved otherwise.

Claudia

After the trip to Naples and how well the ceremony went last night, I feel exhilarated as well as tired. I wonder what the future holds.

I feel as if I have every reason to be optimistic!

Soon, Julia will be here with Alessia and Fabritio. I can't wait to have the villa livened up with the energy and laughter of young people. They keep you young when you feel as if you're not anymore—that's what I always think.

It's best, I know, not to look too far ahead, but this is the first time for too long that I've felt genuinely happy. Now I really must settle down to deciding exactly what I want Fabritio to sculpt for me and what Alessia's duties will be.

4

Via Villa Dei Misteri

The Villa of the Mysteries
(Villa of Lady Claudia Lucilla)

Alessia opened her eyes and looked into the most enchanting blue she'd ever seen. She quickly closed then reopened them, unsure if what she'd seen had been real. Her bed faced a large, rectangular wall fresco. She lay gazing at it. The blue colour stood out from the others. It was a light rather than dark shade, but held within it a startling beauty, depth and vivacity. If asked, Alessia would have said it was the perfect colour for a girl's bedroom. She decided that she must remember to find out more about it. The picture centred around a wild boar, goatlike satyrs with pointed ears and cupids dancing in a frenzy, one of whom seemed to be looking straight at her with an impish grin. She wondered who'd painted it.

Alessia gazed around the room then jumped out of bed and ran quickly to the large, rectangular window. She pushed the wooden shutters and they swung outwards easily on their bronze hinges. The garden opened to view, displaying rosemary bushes, silvery olive trees and fig, lemon and orange trees.

'Oh, my!'

'Lessi, so you're finally awake!' Fabritio walked in and they stood together enjoying the view. 'You know, I think maybe we've been very lucky that Lady Claudia noticed us. Come on, my room's not far. You're not going to believe this!' Laughing, he pulled her after him into the portico then down two narrow hallways. The room Fabritio showed her was twice the size of Alessia's but not as pretty. Instead there was an alcove with a personal wash basin inside and above it, an upper, arched ceiling. Frescoes displaying classic pillars against a striking red and green background covered the walls. Alessia looked around in disbelief. It was a world away from the uninspiring, poor little house they'd lived in at Tauromenium.

'That's not all though.' Fabritio opened the sliding wooden door on the other side of the room. Through the portico was a sensational view of the ocean. It was so close Alessia gave a spontaneous squeal of delight.

'I don't believe it!'

'That's what I thought. I could live here forever,' Fabritio declared happily.

'That's good, but I'm not sure you'll be here quite that long, though.' Julia, Lady Claudia's housekeeper, had been watching them with an amused smile. They'd arrived at the villa late the night before and after showing them to their rooms, she'd left them to sleep after the long journey from Naples.

'I'm sorry. I hope we haven't done anything wrong?' Fabritio frowned.

'Of course not!' Julia's smile was reassuring. 'I'm sure Lady Claudia will be very happy that you like it here. She's asked me to give you a light breakfast then take you for a tour of the villa. After that, Alessia and I have other tasks to attend to. Fabritio, Lady Claudia has made arrangements for you to meet with Marcus Diomedes at his villa as you'll soon be working there. This afternoon, perhaps you might like to use the time to see something of Pompeii.'

Julia was silver haired, short, stout and capable. She was, perhaps, a decade or more younger than her employer. With a happy personality that invited everyone who met her to enjoy whatever they were doing at the time, it was easy to feel relaxed in her company. After a breakfast of freshly baked bread with honey and a selection of fruits, she took Fabritio and Alessia to the villa's entry.

'It's a very large villa as you can see, with porticoes on three sides and wonderful gardens located around it,' she explained as they began to walk. 'This is the front entry, through these graceful arches. The floor beyond that is made of lava stone so that the carts can go through to bring us what we need. They also take our produce to market for sale. Past this vestibule is the peristyle. If you go through that doorway at the side there,' she pointed, 'you'll find the family lararium. You're welcome to use it to pray at any time. There's also a crypt downstairs.'

That they were in a quiet, country setting was obvious. They were about to appreciate just how large and luxurious the villa itself really was.

The peristyle was so pretty that Alessia would love to have been able to sit down on the nearby bench to look around for a few minutes, but didn't like to ask. She thought it looked like a welcoming, green haven and hoped she would find time to walk and sit there in the future.

'Do you or Lady Claudia walk here often?' she asked.

'Both of us do when we have time. It's usually peaceful and a good place if you like to sit and read. There's plenty left for you to enjoy yet though,' Julia said, pleased by the younger woman's obvious interest.

'The servants' quarters are all at the back of the villa. Their rooms are smaller, but still comfortable. As for myself, as I have the major responsibility for the running of the villa, so I actually have a room in the main building. We'll have a quick look this morning at the library, dining room and some of the other bedrooms and I'll take you to the kitchen, cellar and gardens.'

As they walked they realised that nearly all of the living quarters enjoyed spectacular, unspoilt views of the sea. Several of the hallways were narrow, so much so, that Fabritio stretched his arms out to the sides and could easily touch the walls. They were painted in the most startling colour either of them had ever seen.

'Julia, what's this colour called?'

'Fabritio, I think of this as Pompeii's own special colour,' Julia replied appreciatively. 'It's a spectacular red, isn't it? I believe it's made from a pigment called Cinnabar. It comes from the mines of Almaden in Spain, owned by the Emperor. You'll find that colour all over Pompeii. We all love it. It's very passionate and I think has a zest for living that suits us.'

'I don't suppose many people live in the country, though,' Alessia commented.

'You might be surprised how close to the city walls we actually are rather than in the country, Alessia. But you're quite correct, most of the city's inhabitants don't have the good fortune to have so much land or peace and quiet. Now, here we are at the kitchen.'

She led them to a large space with an enormous oven and plenty of masonry work counters with room for servants to prepare food. In the corner opposite was a toilet.

'Good morning, cook.'

'Good morning, Julia. You've come to check on my cooking have you?'

'No, Azura, I wouldn't dream of it,' Julia laughed. 'You're quite capable of making enough mistakes without any help from me.'

The cook pulled a comic face. She was already hard at work using a large, pottery mortarium to grind up eggs and leeks for lunch. She nodded a greeting to the two visitors to her kitchen.

'Mind you don't take Julia too seriously. She expects high standards, but I have to admit she's easy to get on with,' she grinned.

'Azura, I'm sorry for the interruption. I'd like you to meet Alessia, Lady Claudia's new companion and Fabritio her sculptor. Now we'll leave you to get on with things otherwise I suppose we won't get any lunch.'

'Thanks, Julia. I must say it's busy today and Lady Claudia wants a special dessert made up for tonight.' She turned back to her task and the three of them walked away.

'We're fortunate she's a wonderful cook, just wait 'till you taste the meals here,' Julia whispered. 'Hopefully she hasn't heard me or I'll never hear the end of having praised her. She's got a wicked sense of humour.'

'We'll look forward to lunch then,' Alessia answered enthusiastically.

'Lady Claudia's a very generous employer. Unlike some others, she believes everyone should have good food. You won't find that the food here served to servants, is much different than that provided for guests or friends,' Julia told them. 'We may not eat at the same table but we're treated the same otherwise.'

The housekeeper's steps slowed as she led them to another doorway. 'As you can see, this is the dining room. Its decoration is quite outstanding. At least most people seem to think so.'

They stood admiring what was certainly a striking design. The room was a blaze of colour covering every wall. Not an inch seemed to have been left bare. Obviously, many hours of work by a talented painter and a great deal of money had gone into creating this masterpiece of a room.

'What a pretty garland of flowers!' Alessia's eyes were drawn to delicate, white flowers painted on one wall of the room.

'It certainly is,' Julia agreed. I should think that you'll be able to enjoy yourselves dining in here very soon.

'But, I thought we'd be eating with the servants?'

'No! You're a step up the social ladder from us, Alessia, even in a household as liberal as this one.'

Continuing on, they descended carefully down very steep, narrow stone steps to a deep, bottom level. It was well below the ground but was saved from being claustrophobic or musty by a very generously sized window with a view of the trees.

'The wines are kept in the cryptoporticus. I'm sure you'll be interested to know that the estate has its own vineyards. The presses are constantly in use. We supply all of our own needs as well as those of the local people.

'Do you have any left over to send to other places?' Fabritio looked around curiously.

'As you may know,' Julia continued, 'Sicily exports wine to other countries, even to Pompeii. As our wine is considered of excellent quality, we do the same.'

Ascending again to the upper level, they walked down the dozen or so steps that led on the opposite side to a pleasant garden exedra. Everywhere, the beauty of nature lay displayed before them.

23

'This place is incredible.' Fabritio was genuinely close to speechless.

'If you look inside that doorway there,' Julia waved her hand towards a room nearby, 'you'll see that it's set up with a daybed. Sometimes it's very pleasant to just take a short break on a hot day. There are several of these rooms and they all look out over the gardens. When you're not working please feel free to use any that aren't occupied whenever you'd like.'

They could see fluttering wings just outside the door as birds joyfully took their early morning dip in the classic birdbath. Julia had brought bread with her and scattered it on the grass for them. They devoured it eagerly.

'Now, here's the villa's crowning glory in my opinion.' She led them out into one of the main garden areas as proudly as if it had been her own and waited for their reaction.

Alessia's glimpse of the garden from her bedroom that morning, she now realised, had been simply a teasing sample. Persian fruits—red pomegranates, juicy peaches, apricots and sweet cherries as well as walnuts, chestnuts, hazelnuts, herbs and fig trees—she could see them all in front of her. A large fountain, the water gurgling cheerily from its central, demure statue of Venus, completed the picture.

Silence.

All three stood just taking in the peace, lushness and beauty. Julia understood. She'd reacted the same way the first time she'd seen it.

'There's something I have to tell you, though, that's of real importance.' Julia's expression became serious. 'There's one room in the villa that's entered only by permission from Lady Claudia. I very much doubt that you'll ever be allowed there and I'm not talking about her bedroom. I'm going to show you when we finish our tour where it is. The door to the room is kept locked. There's only one entry—through the portico that leads from the exedra. Lady Claudia's a warm, generous person. The only thing she asks of you is that you respect her wishes concerning that room. It's not easily reached from most other rooms in the villa, anyway. There's nothing sinister about it, it's just that it's her private room and she wants to keep it that way. If you disobey this instruction you'll almost certainly be asked to leave her employ.'

Fabritio and Alessia murmured their understanding.

'Julia, do you mind if I ask how you came to live here in Pompeii?' Alessia already had a feeling she would come to like the housekeeper as a friend. She hoped her curiosity was not a step too far, too early.

'Here, let's sit on the bench in the garden for a few minutes. You might as well know something about me,' Julia replied quietly. 'You see, Lady Claudia and her husband Gaius once owned a luxury villa in Rome. They were important, rich and entertained often. At the time I was working as a slave in another wealthy villa. I'm afraid my background before that will have to keep for another day. Anyway, one of the other slaves, a worker in the kitchens, had a violent argument one night with the master of the house, an aggressive, cruel man. The slave killed him. I don't know how much you know about the law, but there was no question of what he'd done, so we were all due to be executed.' The housekeeper gave a bitter laugh. 'It's sort of like getting rid of all the "bad" apples so it doesn't happen again.'

Julia shook her head. She had Fabritio and Alessia's full attention.

'Lady Claudia heard about it. She'd actually met me once before when she'd been a guest at the villa where I was working as a maid. She intervened through her husband's influence. I was reprieved and taken to work for them along with one of the young gardeners. She saved our lives. Later, when Gaius died we came here. She was terribly distraught and I wondered at times if she would ever recover. That was when she also gave me my freedom. Do you see that gardener working over there?' They looked in the direction she indicated. 'Atticus owes his life to Lady Claudia just like me.'

A young man was conscientiously trimming the rose bushes not far from them. Seeing them watching him, he gave them a friendly wave.

'But that's enough of the past.' Julia got up from the bench. 'We must get going or we'll all be late. Fabritio, ask Atticus to take you to the Diomedes' villa. Alessia, come with me. Lady Claudia would like us to look through your clothes to see what else you'll need while you're here. After that if we have time, we'll pick some flowers to freshen up the rooms. Move along now, we really must go. First, however, I'll walk you both past the locked room.'

Lorraine Blundell

Messenger—By hand

To: The House of Marcus Gnaeus Rufus
   Via delle Terme

Dearest Friend,

Do you have anything planned for tomorrow night? I know it's terribly short notice but I'd love you to come for dinner.

Do say you will! I have the nicest young man and his sister here with me and I'd like you to meet them, especially as he's a sculptor and you may want to consider having him work for you in the future, either here in town or at your country villa.

I'm going to invite Marcus and Valentina as well. So, shall we say at dusk? Let me know whether you'll be coming. Until then, I wish you well.

Your friend,
Claudia

5

Via di Nocera

The Perfumery of Phoebus
(House of the Perfumer)

Vexatio! Vexatio!

Tullia's pretty face was flushed with exertion and irritation. She wiped the sweat from her forehead and sniffed in annoyance. Immediately, she regretted it, as the strong odour of the reed perfume she'd been making went further up her cute nose. It was one thing, she supposed, to be poor. It was, however, quite another for women to choose to wear perfume that was downright disgusting!

She checked the batch she'd been working on. Finally, it was finished. Maybe now her father would let her make her favourite rose perfume this afternoon. If not, she would insist on the lilies or violets. With difficulty she pushed the large vats of olive oil used as a base for the perfumes over to one side of the room. She would prepare the roses later. Talking about roses—by walking into the long hallway she could see the garden outside the back door. It was a brilliantly sunny, blue-skied Pompeii day. She'd prefer to be working outside. Even if she was pulling out weeds or replanting it would be better than being indoors with the reeds.

The garden was large, providing enough space for hedges of myrtle and olive trees, as well as flowers for the perfumery and herbs for cooking, growing in neat rows. Tullia and her father also enjoyed the benefit of figs and chestnuts for their evening desserts. Fortunately, they flourished in the fertile soil. The boundary of their land lay adjacent to a large gymnasium and pool complex but noise was rarely a problem because of the high wall that surrounded it.

Tullia stood looking out at the triclinium built into the east wall of the garden dominated by a huge statue of the god, Hercules. Her eyes misted as she remembered her mother's light, carefree laughter during family meals there on summer evenings. It had taken her mother several months to die a painful, lingering death, tenderly nursed by her grieving husband.

It had also nearly ruined the business. That had been three years ago when Tullia was only fourteen. She didn't think that either she or her father had ever really recovered from her mother's death.

'Phoebus, how's business?' Tullia heard someone enter the fragrant, front shop with is well-filled counter displays where her father was serving customers. Sales had been brisk this morning. She couldn't quite place the newcomer's voice.

'I'm more convinced than ever that a second shop would be a good investment,' Phoebus replied. 'I'm so busy I've been run off my feet and my daughter, Tullia, can't help. She's out the back working. If this pace keeps up I'm going to have to hire someone.'

Paquus Proculus stood looking thoughtful for a few moments.

'Come by my place when you've closed for the day and we'll discuss this further,' he invited. 'In the meantime, Phoebus, if you can spare Tullia for a few minutes, would you have her drop off some samples of a few of your products for my wife to take a look at. She has a good eye for these types of items. Personally, it's a bit out of my area of expertise.' Paquius smiled but it didn't reach his eyes. He knew when he was following the scent of a good business investment. He was, without doubt, an ambitious business dealer who drove a hard bargain.

He gave Tullia's father a knowing wink. The two men talked amiably for a few minutes then Paquius left the shop.

Phoebus hurried into the back room. 'Tullia, quickly, get one of the fancy gift baskets.'

'What's going on, father?' She lifted one of the baskets off a side counter.

'Paquus Proculus might be willing to go into business with me. If I can get him to put in most of the funds, we may have a chance of finally making more money. Help me with the samples then you can take them over to his house on Abbondanza. Just hand them to his housekeeper.'

Together they carefully packed small, elegant Egyptian glass bottles filled with exquisite rose, basil, lily and violet perfumes.

'Here, father, put in a couple of jars of face masks underneath,' Tullia suggested. She chose one made of creamy honey and another of golden barley. 'Hopefully, his wife will like these.'

'That's a great idea, Tullia! Now take the basket over there while I mind the shop.'

'Yes, father.'

'Before you go though, you'd better wash the smell of that reed perfume off yourself as well as you can.' Phoebus smiled apologetically at his daughter as he left to attend to a customer at the front counter. If there was one thing they agreed upon, it was that there was no contest when it came to the difference between cheap and expensive, high quality perfumes.

Tullia decided there was only one way to remedy the situation. She took one of the remaining bottles of rose perfume from the batch prepared the day before, and doused herself liberally with its contents. Well, it was in a good cause, wasn't it?

———∘∘∘▷◁∘∘∘———

Via delle Tombe
The Villa of Diomedes

Fabritio walked along the footpath and up the steps from the street into the front porch. A servant answered his knock. He was led through a central peristyle with a small garden. A glance to each side as he followed the servant revealed a plunge pool on one, its back wall painted with a pleasant garden setting. On the other, a flight of stairs could be seen leading to a lower level.

'Come in, Fabritio. I'm in the library.' The voice came from a room at the back of the peristyle.

Fabritio walked on and found himself at the door of a room filled with scrolls and marble busts. Facing him sat a silver haired, distinguished looking man who stood to welcome him.

'Claudia told me you were coming this afternoon. It's a pleasure to meet you.'

'The pleasure is mine, Senator.'

'Please, call me Marcus. I'm a senator no longer. We tend, also, to be a little less formal with each other here than in Rome. Now I spend my days enjoying the gardens and the renovation of the villa. I admit, to keep my mind active, I also volunteered my advice as a part-time magistrate to the city duumvir, Pompeius Grosphus. Of course, whether he benefits from it is questionable.' Marcus laughed. It was the laugh of a man who is comfortable with himself and who enjoys life.

'Sir, it's good of you to agree to give me work.' Fabritio took an instant liking to the elderly man, whose charm and intelligence had apparently achieved so much in the way of beneficial policy and reform in Rome's Senate. He was of average height with a solid build and a winning smile.

'Come with me, Fabritio. I'll introduce you to the young man who's painting my frescoes. He's also highly talented, so perhaps you two will have something in common. In fact, you've probably seen some of his work already. He painted Claudia's walls for her. I believe he's working in the master bedroom here today.'

Marcus led the way through a long gallery and a passageway then into an ante room beyond which they found two men, one young, the other much older. The room curved out into the garden at one end, with a private bath area and views of both the gardens and the sea.

'Hinnulus, I'd like you to meet Fabritio, my new sculptor,' Marcus announced.

'By the way,' Marcus acknowledged the older man with his hand, 'this is Paulinus. He works for Hinnulus doing wall preparation and mixing pigments. Now I'll leave you two alone. When you're ready, why don't you get to know each other? Hinnulus, take Fabritio down to the town, will you? It's been a pleasure meeting you, young man. I'll no doubt see you again soon.' Marcus left to return to his study.

'So they're your creations I've been admiring at Lady Claudia's villa. I'm impressed,' Fabritio commented, 'and so is my sister.'

'That's good. I like painting on the walls of the large villas and both Lady Claudia and Magistrate Diomedes give me a free hand,' Hinnulus grinned. 'They pay pretty well too.' He took off his apron and shook hands with Fabritio.

'How many times have you layered the plaster and sand on the wall now?' Hinnulus turned to question Paulinus.

'Three so far, sir.'

'Do two more then you can go early today. Be back here at the usual time though, tomorrow.'

Hinnulus indicated that he and Fabritio should go, leaving the slave to finish his work. The two strolled down Via Consolare until they reached the Bar of Fortunata at the junction with Vicolo di Modesto. A water well stood in front and untidily scrawled in red onto the bar wall behind it was election advertising. Fabritio glanced at it with interest. Politics was obviously alive and well in Pompeii.

Vote for Helvius Sabinus for aedile

'This is my favourite bar. Let me buy you a drink.' Hinnulus led Fabritio inside. They passed through the narrow entryway to a long masonry counter on the right-hand side of the room. Cold snacks were provided for customers wanting more than a drink.

'Two cups of wine, the usual, thanks.' Hinnulus gave his order to the girl half asleep behind the counter. 'How long have you been a sculptor?' He turned to face Fabritio.

'For more years than I care to remember,' Fabritio answered him. 'And your painting?'

'It's much the same for me with the frescoes.' They stood companionably together. Fabritio looked around him. The place was small, surprisingly empty and somewhat run down.

'This one's a quiet place that's one reason I like it,' grinned Hinnulus, rubbing paint off that had fallen onto his skinny legs then picking his nose. 'Just about everyone's probably finished work earlier and gone to the baths by now. Actually, I've already made an arrangement to meet one of my friends later at the Stabian baths. I'll take you to my place while I gather up a few clean clothes, then you can head off and have a look at the amphitheatre or something, or if you'd like, you can come with me to the baths.'

They took a short-cut through Via della Fortuna to Via dell 'Abbondanza. It lay long and straight before them, with people hurrying about their business. Finally, they reached the house of Hinnulus at Vicolo dei Fuggiaschi, a narrow side street.

'You know what they say, it's not much, but at least I own it,' Hinnulus joked. He pushed open the door of a narrow fronted house with a long hallway inside opening into two good sized, rectangular rooms. The first was untidy, to say the least, with clothes strewn everywhere and rubbish yet to be tossed away. Hinnulus began to sort through bundles of clothing.

'Good. Here they are.' He held up a beige, woollen tunic and a pair of sandals. 'These will do for now. Follow me and I'll show you the other room before we go.'

When they entered the back room Fabritio could hardly believe his eyes. Hundreds of paint pots lay on, or tumbling over one another haphazardly in absolute chaos. Buckets for mixing pigments lay randomly against one wall. What really fascinated him, however, was that the whole thing looked like a rainbow gone mad. He stood staring in amazement.

Hardened remnants remained at the bottom of most of the pots and buckets, or where it had slopped over the sides. There was the fabulous red Cinnabar paint. Cerulian blue, the shade Alessia so loved in her bedroom, pale green, showy gold and the purple of royalty—all lay in pots or buckets discarded around the room.

'It's a great workroom, don't you think?' Hinnulus asked proudly.

'It's certainly different,' Fabritio replied diplomatically.

'Gotta go, Fabritio. You'll have to come by for a few drinks sometime.'

Hinnulus hustled them out the door. He left to make his way to the bathhouse. Fabritio wasn't quite sure where he was going, but it certainly wasn't to the bathhouse with Hinnulus.

———∞∘◦⦿◦∘∞———

Tullia grabbed the basket of samples and headed for the shop doorway. It shouldn't take long to reach Proculus' house, she thought.

'I'm going, father. I'll be back soon,' she called over her shoulder.

She'd barely taken two steps outside when she collided with someone. The impact sent her flying onto the pavement and the basket with her. Most of the light, smaller samples lay some distance away, a few of them, broken.

Fabritio hurried to help the girl who lay sprawled at his feet. Petite and weighing very little, she had taken the full force of the encounter. The face upturned to his was pretty with large, blue eyes. For a moment time seemed to stand still.

'I'm so sorry.' He looked across at the basket and samples scattered across the hard, basalt paving stones. Phoebus came to the doorway, taking in the scene in front of him.

'Tullia, are you hurt? How many times must I tell you not to rush around without looking?' he said, concern apparent on his face.

'No, father. I'm afraid it was my own fault. I was in such a rush I didn't look where I was going.'

'Sir, I see some of your bottles are broken. I'm happy to contribute to replacing them,' Fabritio offered.

Phoebus, a short, balding man, stood appraising the good looking young man who stood still holding his daughter's hand.

'Thank you, that's not necessary but I appreciate the offer,' he eventually responded.

'My name's Fabritio.'

'I don't think I've seen you here before?' Decimus raised an eyebrow.

'No, sir. My sister and I have just arrived from Sicily. We're employed by Lady Claudia and Magistrate Diomedes.'

'They are two of the most respected members of our community.' Phoebus nodded his approval while studying Fabritio more closely.

'It's a pleasure to meet you. I'm Phoebus and this is my daughter Tullia.'

She looked up shyly at him.

What was that marvellous scent? The rose perfume she wore surged over Fabritio. He released her hand but they were still standing close together.

All three bent to retrieve the samples and Fabritio was invited to enter the shop while the basket was repacked. He heard himself say—

'I'm sure my sister would like a bottle of your perfume. May I come back soon to buy one?'

'Of course. You'd be welcome,' Phoebus replied. He thought that the immediate chemistry between the two young people was obvious. Could it be that this was the beginning of something more significant?

Well, his daughter could have a worse future than one with a young, good looking man who was courteous, respectful and, of course, had wealthy, influential patrons.

Patient Case Notes

Pompeii

The House of the Surgeon
Via di Narcisso

Name of Patient: Paulinus
Age: Around 50 years
Status: Slave
Owner: Hinnulus the Fresco Painter
Payment: Owner

Date: 59 A.D.

The patient complains of handfuls of hair falling out over a period of a couple of years, causing baldness. He has several sores on his arms and these don't heal. I believe he's developed a reaction to poison from the fresco pigments he works with while mixing them, especially Cinnabar.

There is no cure.

Ointment has been prescribed in an attempt to heal the sores. It should at least ease the patient's discomfort.

6

Via delle Terme
(The House of the Tragic Poet)

A dark figure flitted from street to street like a bee from flower to flower, dodging the innocent shafts of moonlight that silvered and softened all they touched. He was the sole intruder into the solitude of the sleeping city as he darted furtively from street to street, then house to house.

Nervously, he clutched a bucket in one hand and a brush in the other. Finally, finding the wall he sought which stood between two narrow shop fronts, he took one last, searching look around to reassure himself of anonymity.

Rufus steals the ideas of others

The large, uneven words were daubed in red onto Rufus' front wall ready to greet the sun as it rose on the waking citizens of Pompeii. Not long after there was on knock on Rufus' front door.

'Hi, what brings you visiting so early, Sylvana?' The visitor was known to the servant who admitted her.

She was a middle aged friend of Rufus with short, dyed red hair, from a literary group to which they both belonged. Walking over the entry floor mosaic of a snarling guard dog and ignoring its cryptic warning, she strode briskly through the atrium past a variety of highly colourful wall masks and frescoes with theatrical scenes. She found the owner sitting in his library.

'Rufus, have you been outside yet this morning?'

'No. Should I have?'

'I just called in to say that I think you should look. I'm in a rush so I must go. I'll see you tomorrow.' She left him to his thoughts.

No doubt she heard the angry swearing that erupted a couple of minutes later, after Rufus stepped curiously out of his house and saw the words painted on his front wall. He was not a man known to be easy to anger or bad-tempered. This particular morning was an exception.

————∘∘∘—◦◯◦—∘∘∘————

Lady Claudia's Villa

'Alessia my dear, could you just sweep my hair back a little more from my face, please?'

Alessia carefully made the alteration. To complete Claudia's hairstyle she fixed a gold and pearl ornament into her hair.

'That's really glamorous. It's so much of a relief to finally have someone to help make me presentable when I'm entertaining.' Claudia looked at her elegant best, relaxed and every inch a patrician. She rose from her chair and smiled at her young companion encouragingly.

Alessia turned a becoming shade of pink.

'Thank you, Lady Claudia.'

'I think when there's just the two of us, you should call me Claudia—don't you? It's so much more pleasant and I do want you to be happy here. Now, let me have a look at you. Turn around.'

Alessia turned slowly in a circle as Claudia inspected her.

'I think you look beautiful tonight.'

Alessia's face lit up with pleasure.

She was wearing the only formal dress she owned. Claudia had presented her with a pair of gold earrings and a snake bracelet with glittering green eyes to wear on her upper arm. The expensive jewellery miraculously improved the plain, long beige robe.

'Julia tells me you could do with several new tunics and other items as you don't have much with you. Would you like to go into town with her and select them? I'll buy them as part of your payment as my companion.'

'Thank you, Claudia. I really feel so lucky.'

'It's wonderful to have you to help me here,' Claudia replied. 'And I have to say, you add a great deal of beauty and the enthusiasm of youth to our lives. Now, I believe it's time to go in to dinner.'

————∘∘∘—◦◯◦—∘∘∘————

Julia had outdone herself with the presentation of the dining room and especially the table. Silver candelabras provided subtle candlelight, softening the lines in the faces of the guests and chasing the shadows into retreat to the room's farthest corners. They stood within a circle of warmth, friendship and conviviality.

On the table, silverware gleamed amongst the flowers, the red flush of the pomegranates and scent of roses creating a setting of luxury and abundance. After being greeted by Julia and introduced to Fabritio, Claudia's guests stood waiting for her, discussing the events of the day.

'It's illegal. There's absolutely no doubt about it!' Rufus thundered, waving his arms about angrily. 'Tiburtinus isn't getting away with this. I intend to lodge a complaint with a magistrate. There are plenty of witnesses who saw the writing on my front wall!'

A short, somewhat plump man, Rufus' normally happy, carefree attitude had changed to one of anger, completely uncharacteristic of him. His face has become quite red.

'Yes, Rufus, I know, but did they see him paint it there? Almost certainly, he paid someone else to do it,' Marcus Diomedes pointed out, 'and you know I can't help you with such a complaint. I'm a friend so there would be a conflict of interest.'

'Of course,' Rufus replied. 'I wouldn't put you in that position, but don't you agree something should be done? He's simply taking revenge on me for beating him to the official title of City Poet. You know how furious he was.'

'My advice, for what it's worth,' Marcus continued, 'is to just remove it then simply ignore the whole thing. Don't give him the satisfaction of knowing that he's succeeded in making you angry.'

Rufus looked unconvinced.

'I have to agree with Marcus.' Valentina, the final one of their group looked thoughtful. 'If, however, you simply can't let it go, my advice would be to seek a private meeting with the mayor and leave the decision to him.'

'With Pompeius Grosphus? Really, Valentina? You can't be serious. You of all people know he's got no time for the arts. He tried to cut the city's contribution to the theatre staff's wages only a few months ago. I can't see him trying to help me.'

Valentina shrugged.

'I'm sorry, everyone,' Rufus grimaced, 'I'll think about your advice. In the meantime, I promise to forget about the incident, at least for this evening. I don't want to spoil dinner. Let's all have some more wine!'

'I see everyone's getting into the mood!' Claudia came in with Alessia. 'I'd like all of you to meet Fabritio's sister, Alessia. She's become my personal companion.'

Alessia accepted a cup of watered wine and smiled at each of the guests in turn. Fabritio was surprised at her level of composure. His little sister was growing up.

'Please, begin.' Valentina gestured to the lyre player who'd been patiently waiting in the background.

'Yes, Domina.'

Claudia's guests seated themselves comfortably to listen.

The girl was comely in appearance. Her forehead wrinkled in concentration, as she began to play and sing Sappho's 'Hymn to Aphrodite.' There was polite applause as she finished.

'Perhaps one more song, I think,' Claudia smiled at her.

Alessia closed her eyes, enjoying the sweetness of the music as the strains of 'Song of a Rose,' swept over her. The girl played well. It was a pity that her voice could hardly be heard.

'Thank you, Lucceia, that will be all for now.' Claudia dismissed the performer and turned back to her guests.

'Lucceia's improved considerably since I last heard her play,' Marcus remarked graciously.

'I agree,' Claudia replied. 'She's slowly gaining more confidence.'

'Claudia, grant me a favour please before dinner is served.' Rufus began to walk towards the atrium. 'Everyone, follow me.'

The atrium was huge, with Egyptian wall frescoes, a very high ceiling and a large impluvium. Enormous wooden doors separated it from the adjacent peristyle. Rufus walked over to one of the side walls. Guessing what was coming, everyone except Alessia and Fabritio laughed. 'I believe it's time,' he continued with a dramatic flourish, 'to update my portrait.' He added a laurel wreath to the forehead of a small drawing of a face on the wall.

Claudia gestured to Alessia and Fabritio. 'Look, our Rufus won the title of official City Poet recently. I believe he's quite proud of it.'

Rufus' whimsical face with its bulbous nose, jutting chin and twinkling eyes beneath a bald head, had been drawn onto the wall. Now his forehead sported a laurel wreath. There was much clapping and laughter. A talented, humorous and generous man, his win had been popular except with his competitors. That was particularly true, of course, of rival poet Tiburtinus.

A few days later, Claudia found Alessia sitting quietly in one of the daybed rooms, trying to play a lyre that had been left there. The sunlight played upon her young face emphasising its youth and innocence. It seemed to Claudia that her unspoilt beauty might well make her an ideal model for the new statue of Venus that she planned to have Fabritio create. Unseen, she watched curiously as the girl persisted for some time with very little luck then, disappointed, gently laid the instrument down.

'Would you like to learn how to play it?' Claudia asked, her entry surprising Alessia.

'I loved the music and the girl singing to it at the dinner,' she replied, embarrassed. 'I'm afraid I probably don't have the talent though.'

'Let's find out, shall we?'

Claudia made arrangements with Valentina for Alessia to visit her later that week. Valentina, a relative of the wealthy Popidius family who lived with them, was yet another of Claudia's group of friends who was exceptionally talented. A music teacher, she offered an annual scholarship to the winner of a competition to find the best of the city's young lyre players. They received Valentina's personal tuition and advice.

The nightingales hid in the trees at Tauromenium.

Lorraine Blundell

Vicolo del Lupanare

'Phoebus, I'm glad to see you.'

Attice led him through the door into the one room she owned where she 'entertained' selected male clients. The popular, double storey brothel building, the Lupanare, was a few doors away. It attracted a large clientele and their comings and goings made a certain amount of noise. At least her room was quieter and more personal.

'Attice, I've some really good news to tell you,' Phoebus blurted out. The prostitute patted the concrete bed beside her. A mattress filled with leaves and wool softened its discomfort.

'What's happened since I last saw you?'

'I've just done a great business deal with Paquus Proculus. Now I can expand my business and there should be enough money for me and Tullia to live comfortably.'

In the years since his wife had died Phoebus had been visiting Attice. They'd formed not only a business relationship, but also a friendship together. She was genuinely pleased for him.

'There's more good news to come, I think,' Phoebus put his hand over hers. 'I hope that Tullia's found a nice, young man. His name's Fabritio. He's been to visit the shop several times and now he's asked her to go to the theatre with him. It'll be a relief if I can feel that she's secure with someone.'

Attice's heart had warmed long ago to the genuine, honest man beside her. She hoped that even if it was only within their present relationship he would continue to be part of her life. Gratefully, she accepted the bottle of lily perfume Phoebus handed her. Anything was possible.

7

Rome

An Unnamed Guild Tavern

The stranger rubbed his hands together in anticipation, pleased that he'd been inspired some weeks before to start these 'adventures.' His eyes glittered with excitement. Night had fallen. He was beginning to feel the familiar tingle of adrenaline flooding through him.

A snatch of light from a flaring torch created grotesque shapes dancing across a filthy wall as it half lit the stranger's face. He approached the door of the guild tavern confidently and walked in unhindered. The gloomy interior smelled stale and musty. It already hosted a table of noisy soldiers playing dice as they nibbled cheese and nuts and three legally registered—or not-prostitutes, who knew? They lounged half drunkenly against the counter, tunics hitched up openly courting sexual approaches.

A couple of painters sat in animated conversation drinking at a table beside the wall under the tavern's one, dirt encrusted window, high up to stop thieves peering in. Perhaps they were discussing customers, their trade obvious from the paint on their work clothes.

'There's no way that's possible,' one of the soldiers half jokingly commented on the dice throw of his nearest companion. He peered at the dice in the half light.

'Are you accusing me of cheating?'

'Now boys, keep it friendly!' the tavern owner interrupted, 'otherwise you'll find yourselves out of here.' He had no intention of having the furniture wrecked by fighting legionaries.

On the far side of the room sitting well back into the shadows, a young male scruffily dressed, with a stubbled chin, sat cradling his one drink for the night. The stranger smiled to himself. There sat a runaway slave if ever he'd seen one. They never learned, did they, that their very fear gave them away. All of them reeked of it.

Several other customers drifted in. The stranger loved the noise, the excitement, the danger and the secrecy. He pulled his cloak more tightly about him and re-adjusted his dark wig.

'Get me a Falernian!' He raised his empty cup, waving it under the nose of the tavern keeper before thumping it down on the counter.

'You'll wait your turn!'

The stranger snarled an angry obscenity. His eyes narrowed and followed the owner as he served the soldiers nearby their refills, then returned to fill the cup.

The tavern wasn't far from the Forum on the fringes of the low-life Subura tenements. It stood beside a crossroads in a small nondescript lane barely lit by flares and stinking of excrement. By the time he'd sunk several more cups of wine the stranger, edgy and feeling uninhibited, decided it was time to move on. His excitement level was high and he hungered for action. He trotted happily out the door and into the laneway, sighting a careless drunk of a better class than usual, staggering alone in the dark. There was no one else in sight. At least, no one else he was going to have to worry about.

In a few steps he'd overtaken the wanderer and viciously stabbed him in the back with a gladius from under his cloak. The body slumped soundlessly to the ground, blood seeping slowly onto the paving stones. Ripping the victim's cloak off, the stranger also snatched his finger ring and purse then ran at full speed towards the Forum. He'd never felt more alive! He loved the feeling of the dagger sinking into the soft, yielding flesh. A small group of men nearby hustled after him.

As he reached the Forum he stopped and turned to rebuke those behind him. 'Too slow! Too slow!' he sniped. 'Perhaps a stint in the Carcer would wake you up!'

The undercover Praetorian Guard unit quickly hurried to the stranger's side. 'We have your back. Do you wish to return to the palace, Caesar?' Burrus, the Prefect of the Guards asked.

'Of course I do,' Nero snapped, 'unless you really expect me to stay out here all night! Imbeciles! Make sure that vermin's body is thrown into the sewer. And I want the tavern raided for runaway slaves—now!' He stabbed his finger aggressively into the Prefect's chest.

'Murdering bastard,' muttered Burrus after Nero had gone.

Praxus, the guard standing nearest to him heard the comment, one with which he found himself in complete agreement. Still, it didn't pay to openly criticise the Emperor.

The Royal Palace
One Week Later

Terpnus leaned casually against the nearest column, his wiry form and unkempt beard giving him a feral appearance. Lanky, black hair hung down his back, long and greasy. His eyes held veiled intelligence and cunning. He stared arrogantly at the Emperor, contemptuous of the inappropriate, unbelted silk dressing gown and scarf he was wearing. Nero's interviewing style was certainly different.

'Are you sure you have the skills to enhance my talent?' Nero questioned him abruptly, unimpressed by the Greek's attitude.

'That depends.'

'What do you mean *that depends*?' Nero's voice sharpened in irritation.

'Are you prepared to undertake the work required?' the Greek questioned, his tone arrogant.

Nero was somewhat taken by surprise. He was not used to being addressed in such a manner, especially by someone of the lower classes. He'd expected a more deferential approach from the man even if he was considered to be the best teacher of the lyre and singing anywhere. Still, he realised that he needed Terpnus' help if he was to reach his goal to perform successfully in public. That achievement meant everything to him—more than the Empire itself. He knew that he wanted to be the best artist of his time. If this irritating little Greek could help him to achieve that then he would allow him ample flexibility.

'Of course,' he finally replied.

Terpnus smirked. It had the effect of further strengthening his resemblance to a ferret. He was sure that he couldn't be so lucky as to have found a ruler who had real artistic talent, but no one was going to tell his pupil that. All he had to do was put up with Nero's 'noise' and keep him content. If he was successful, then he'd have the Emperor totally dependent upon him. The result would be more power and wealth than Terpnus had ever dreamed of and he knew it.

'Caesar, you've found yourself a teacher! Now, I would like to hear you sing.' Terpnus braced himself and sat down on a gilded couch nearby to listen.

Lorraine Blundell

Rome

Castra Praetoria
(Guard Barracks)

My dear brother Sextus
Via Gherardo
Ostia

Greetings,

It has to be one of the strangest things I've ever seen. An auction was held today in the grounds of the royal palace. There was a real mix of clothing on offer as well as daggers, swords, shoes and rings. It was all actually quite colourful. Some of the clothes were of good quality. Keep this quiet, but guess who owned them?—Nero.

Destroy this message once you've read it. Some of us are beginning to feel that things may get worse rather than better in regard to our safety from here on.

How, you may ask, did he get these items? He wanders the streets at night disguised, breaks into shops to steal, or takes them from the bodies of the men he kills. I have been unfortunate enough to belong to one of the units selected to work undercover to protect him, as he goes on his wild rampages.

It makes my blood run cold! Killing in battle or disposing of criminals is one thing—but randomly murdering innocent citizens is quite another! I hope my luck improves and he either gives up what he's doing, or I'm not selected for his night protection unit.

Apart from that, the city seems quiet enough. We have plenty to entertain us in the way of games and theatre performances. When are you visiting Rome again? I could do with a damned good night out getting drunk!' Make it soon!

Your brother,
Praxus

8

The Campus Martius

The caged cart careened around the corner lurching and swaying, threatening to run down anything in its path. It creaked and groaned throwing its occupants around like lifeless puppets. Sweating gladiators, their skin glistening their eyes glazed, stared through the thick, impenetrable bars that imprisoned them at the two toga clad young men who stood in their path.

Just in time the cart slowed a fraction allowing the senators to step aside. A few gladiators inside the cart watched uninterested, while others clung to the cage bars peering out like slaughterous animals as they continued on their way to the gladiator barracks.

The two young senators ignored the incident, a common enough occurrence in Rome's streets. They walked on with a grace and confidence known only to Rome's elite.

'Seneca loves the sound of his own voice,' Lucius complained irritably.

'How can you say such a thing?' Quintus feigned surprise at his friend's annoyance.

'Because it's damned obvious after listening to him squawk for three hours, that's how!'

'But I thought he was one of your father's closest friends?'

'You're right, but that doesn't make his speeches any less boring.' Lucius gave a wry smile.

They'd just walked from the Senate after a tedious morning listening to an address by Lucius Annaeus Seneca. As a long time advisor to the Emperor, as well as a respected philosopher and playwright, it was considered imperative that other senators attend when he chose to favour them with his wisdom. The two friends continued on their way to the Campus Martius to inspect the new wooden amphitheatre, nearly ready to hold an upcoming festival following a year's frantic preparations.

'Is your father coming up for the games?' Quintus asked, trying unsuccessfully to hold the hem of his toga out of the mud churned up by yesterday's rain, and the extra traffic from the construction work.

'I don't think he's made up his mind yet, he's obsessed at the moment with the villa's renovations. He might not come at all,' Lucius sighed. Since his father had been widowed and retired they had seen little of one another.

It was a pleasant enough day. The rain of the previous evening had disappeared with the morning, leaving only a damp smell in the air of approaching showers still to come. The two friends strolled across to where the finishing touches were being added to the amphitheatre. There was still chaos over the whole site. It was crowded and in disorder and the yelling of stressed supervisors under pressure to get work finished on time resounded across the field.

The senators were representative of upcoming young patricians succeeding fathers who had relinquished illustrious careers in the Senate, to take well deserved retirements living outside Rome. The ascendancy of Nero as Emperor had somewhat hurried those decisions along.

Lucius Diomedes and Quintus Attratinus were childhood friends. They shared hangovers following late night celebrations, mutual friends, life values in general and an attraction to similar types of women. Politically, they were considered conservatives loyal to the Emperor and traditional in their beliefs and Roman way of life.

Lucius was strikingly good looking, the mirror image of his father as a young man. He stood above average height with dark hair, green eyes and a face with a strong jawline. It was his smile, however, that set him apart. With a generous mouth as well as perfect teeth and a mischievous sense of humour, he caught the eye of many young women. Broad shouldered and fit, he would have done well in the legions or cut a fine figure in a praetorian's uniform had he not been fortunate enough to have been born into the moneyed, patrician class and a career in the Senate.

Quintus, thicker set in build and somewhat shorter, was himself far from physically unattractive. His hair was light brown, his eyes blue and his face honest and open. By nature he was quieter than his companion but no less blessed intellectually. When they were younger, it had not been unusual for Lucius to find himself blamed for some impulsive prank actually initiated by Quintus, deceptively appearing to be the less likely culprit of the two.

They stood casually watching the painters at work. The gladiators had disappeared into the adjacent barracks consisting of a cell block and training arena.

'You know, don't you, that Nero's list comes out in two days. Just pray to Jupiter that our names aren't on it,' Lucius grimaced.

'What I don't understand is why he's doing it,' Quintus frowned. 'What does he hope to achieve?'

'Control,' Lucius replied softly. 'Control and the enjoyment of watching us squirm.'

——ooo-⦇◎⦈-ooo——

Their names were not on the list.

Hundreds of other senators' names were. Many were influential and well known. The Emperor had decided that the games would not just be watched, but also participated in by the Senate. Its members would fight one another in the arena. Only one piece of information brought them any joy—the bouts would not be 'to the death.' At these games even criminals would receive a reprieve from the ultimate punishment. Embarrassed and physically afraid, Rome's senators were not impressed. By insisting that they fight in the arena, Nero had insulted their 'dignitas' by reducing them to the ranks of *infamia,* the lowest of the low. To say the least, Lucius and Quintus were relieved not to be competing.

Soon enough the first day of the games was upon them. Crowds flocked to the amphitheatre eager to find seats in their allocated sections. Women and slaves had a long slog up to the upper levels. Street food sellers mingled with the crowd tossing food to customers where they sat, their selection often finally reaching them after being passed hand to hand from one spectator to another. Savoury aromas drifted over the crowd.

The six Vestals sat quietly in a place of honour on the lower level at the front. Lucius and Quintus arrived and seated themselves in the senators' section just before the Emperor entered.

'This is going to be an interesting day.' Quintus stated the obvious.

'Just be grateful you're not down in the arena,' Lucius reminded him.

Nero arrived gaudily attired in Tyrian purple and gold. His popular wife, Octavia, followed quietly behind him. There was polite applause, taken by Nero as a compliment but no doubt meant instead for his wife. The Emperor was of average height with a thick neck. His hair was blond, set in curls and his features were somewhat pretty. These not very masculine characteristics were made more ineffectual by weak, blue eyes. An off-putting body odour was often complained about by those who were in close contact with him, leading them to wish fervently that they could hold their noses.

Nero looked around as the trumpets finished blaring. There was a good crowd today, he noted, pleased. His eyes flicked over the various groups that made up the spectators. If they needed to understand where any of them stood in relation to the power he wielded over them, their seating allocation would certainly have left none of them in any doubt.

'I noticed Seneca's name wasn't listed,' Quintus remarked conversationally.

'Of course not. There's no way Nero would risk an injury to him in the arena. Anyway, it looks like the action is about to get started.' Lucius turned his attention to those entering the arena below.

The morning's parade of animals began with a display of bears, panthers and lions followed by the Bestiarii—gladiators who skilfully fought the animals in a number of bouts. A variety of props had been dragged into the arena to provide a make believe jungle with rocky outcroppings.

The clowns came running into the arena next, dressed in multi colours and with fake weapons. Their tumbling and comic antics amused the crowd and they started to relax. Some of them fancied their comic talents and shouted insulting comments down to the competitors.

'I wouldn't want to meet you in a dark alley somewhere one night!'

'Maybe a bigger sword would help, but I don't think so!'

The water organ continued to grind on as they munched on their oyster snacks waiting for the real action to begin after the interval. Nero watched, amused, from the royal box.

'By all the gods, Octavia, what's wrong with you? Can't you even show some enthusiasm when I bring you to the best entertainment in Rome?' Nero glared at her with distaste. 'Put a smile on your face or I'll do it for you!'

Obediently, Octavia did as she was told. A smile, frozen in place, replaced her serious expression. Nervously she pulled her pale blue shawl more closely around her, plucking at it with nervous fingers. Nero, satisfied, looked away. She didn't like the games and would have much preferred to have been at the theatre. Her life seemed to be lived in constant fear of upsetting her demanding and unpredictable husband. She constantly felt as if she was walking on eggshells.

'Do you see any problems anywhere?' Nero turned questioningly to Burrus.

'No, Caesar. Your idea to hold these games was a master stroke.'

Nero nodded, his good humour restored. He settled back into his chair. No doubt the senators' fights would prove entertaining, even if, as he expected, there wouldn't be much blood spilled. Still, one never knew.

At least the humiliation should keep them in their places and cause them to think twice before opposing his wishes in the Senate.

'Who do you fancy in the first bout?' Nero asked Seneca who sat in the royal box with him, along with a couple of the Emperor's favoured ladies.

'I would think the Thracian might be expected to win,' he replied as the gates opened.

'And what about the senators? Which of them do you favour as the ultimate winner?' Nero was openly amused by Seneca's obvious discomfort at the question. He was not quite so enthralled by the philosopher's reply.

'Why they are all winners, of course, Caesar. For they will all have competed fairly under duress and with honour.'

Nero frowned. Lately he hadn't been impressed by some of the opinions of his long time tutor and advisor. Seneca would bear watching in the future. Nero brought his attention back to the entertainment.

Cheers rang out as the first gladiators entered the arena. The initial bout was between a Retiarius and a Thracian. The crowd gasped at the sight of the Retiarius, a gladiator in the prime of life with a physique for Roman matrons to sigh over, especially as he was wearing only a loincloth secured by a wide belt. He was the only type of gladiator to carry a net. The Thracian used a shield and a wicked looking curved sword. For additional protection he wore an intricately decorated, heavy visored helmet and leg protectors.

The pace of betting increased in intensity. Eager fans who hadn't already done so hurried to place bets on their favourite. The central referee stepped between the gladiators then withdrew, signalling the commencement of the action.

The crowd got their money's worth, with gladiatorial combat ferocious and unrelenting. Although he was by far the more experienced and better protected, the Thracian, the crowd's favourite, found himself flat on his back on the arena sand not long after the bout had commenced, after having failed to sidestep an attack by the Retiarius with his swirling net. Once an opponent became hopelessly entangled in it, the result was rarely in doubt. The two gladiators left the arena, no doubt the Thracian being relieved that no death blow would be delivered for his defeat. The crowd watched expectantly for the gates from the holding area beneath to open again, revealing the next competitors.

Slowly, the first group of senators, divided into pairs, walked upon the arena's sand for the first time, their white togas looking ridiculously out of place. Some gazed upwards in dazed disbelief at the spectators. They had the same view as any gladiator, freedman or criminal, who'd walked into the death pit before them.

There was an unusual hush as the crowd fell silent.

There had been murmurings of a special event on the program but this one was not something the people particularly enjoyed. They didn't like change unless it added extra excitement, especially if it meant change to the traditions of the arena and what went on there. They had a certain expectation of what they were about to see.

This was not it!

At first, heckling began from a few of the more vocal spectators, then catcalls and complaints spread to the rest of the crowd. These were directed not at the senators but at the Emperor.

'Sissy senators! Boring! Let's see some real men fight.'

'Call these contests? They're not worth shit. Look at that old fart over there—he can hardly stand up!'

'We want more gladiators. Where are they?'

'We want gladiators! We want gladiators!' Angrily, they stood and stamped their feet, yelling and throwing oyster shells or whatever else they could find.

'Stop this outrage!' Nero yelled. He stood abruptly, as if to subdue the crowd by the sheer force of his will. He turned to Burrus. 'How dare they defy me! Do something about it!'

'At once, Caesar.' Burrus barked out the order and Praetorian Guard reinforcements stationed outside the amphitheatre moved at a quick march to enter the main body of the crowd.

The hostility continued, quickly growing in intensity. Praetorians moved behind and around the spectators. As they caught sight of the dreaded red and gold uniforms and the glint of weapons being openly displayed, they fell silent. Each group of senators fought their bouts to an end, some sustaining injuries before they sullenly left the arena, their togas filthy and torn. Nero was furious as he departed the royal box.

Octavia's expression hinted at her fear of the violence she knew would follow, on their return to the royal palace on the Palatine. Her neck, well hidden under the clothing she wore, already bore ugly bruises resulting from her husband's uncontrollable aggression.

As she rose to leave she dropped her shawl. She bent to retrieve it but it was picked up first by a young praetorian guard standing nearby.

'Thank you, Praetorian.' She smiled into cool, grey eyes as their gaze met.

He snapped to attention. 'I'm honoured, Empress.' She bowed her acknowledgement and passed by him.

'I think it might be wise for us to see if there's anyone injured and if there's anything we can do.' Quintus left his seat hastily with Lucius following closely behind him. They hurried to the medical room out of sight behind the solid wooden arena door on the lower level.

There was a pungent smell of garlic in the treatment room as physicians worked cleaning wounds in an attempt to prevent infection. Only two of the group, Senator Scaevinus and Senator Natalis lay on benches, their gashes being stitched closed with long needles. Despite the poppy sedative they flinched with the stitching.

'We need you in the Senate,' Lucius told them. 'Make sure you both recover quickly. Good senators can be hard to find.'

'He hasn't heard the last of this,' Senator Natalis spat out the words. 'This won't be forgotten. Some of us have long memories!'

Lucius and Quintus made their way quickly to the nearest bathhouse each with his own thoughts. This day's events held a warning to be heeded for the future.

──∘∘∘⟨◉⟩∘∘∘──

The Forum Romanum

Later that afternoon the Vestals returned to their temple and convent in the Forum. They were preceded by lictors for protection and to maintain protocol. Those onlookers standing in their way stepped aside respectfully to allow the women to pass.

Spectators at the games were also returning, adding to the level of hubbub and chaos that signalled a return to normality. Many headed for the public baths and gymnasiums, still others to the taverns. Business was brisk except for the sellers of high end, luxury items in places like the Saepta. Vendors there usually found that customers preferred a more serious, cautious atmosphere in which to make decisions, when buying items that cost as much as theirs did.

Rubria, dressed in her white robe and veil, felt peace flow throughout her mind and body as she meditated deeply before Rome's precious flame, symbol of the city's security. The graceful temple of Vesta with its fluted columns was like an oasis amidst the Forum's chaos.

The curves of her shapely figure were obvious even under her robe. She was blessed with a serene, heart shaped face and long brown hair caught back at the nape of her neck. Rubria had conscientiously followed her pre-ordained path as a Vestal Virgin for more than ten years. Occasionally over that time, she'd felt her heart beat faster on noticing the glance of a particularly handsome man. There had never been a time, however, that

51

she had either regretted the path laid out for her as the child of patrician parents, or been tempted to break her vows. Perhaps another life would open up for her when she reached the age of thirty, and retired with a generous pension from a grateful Rome. In any case, the punishment for breaking her vows was death. She had no intention of risking being entombed alive at the Campus Sceleratis at the Colline Gate because of some love affair.

Rubria looked across at the Vestal's convent. She was fortunate, she knew, to be able to live the life of peace and serenity that she enjoyed. Her room was homely and comfortable and she had ample leisure time to enjoy walking by the rectangular pools, their shy, pink water lilies peeping above the surface of the water. The convent's gardens were laden with the heady scent of roses wafting their intoxication over the Vestals. Their colours and tranquillity seemed a world away from the odours, spruiking and noise outside.

Rubria spent the remainder of the afternoon carefully tending to the wills of Rome's citizens. She decided that Vesta had indeed been good to her. No doubt her life was progressing as it should.

Rome

To: Marcus Diomedes

The Villa of Diomedes
Via delle Tombe
Pompeii

My Esteemed Father,
Greetings!

I trust that you're well and that the villa renovations are underway and progressing to your satisfaction. Perhaps you've heard the latest news from Rome about the games? Anyway, I'll pass it on in case word hasn't yet reached you. I believe it's fortunate that you decided against attending.

There were ugly scenes at the amphitheatre. I should tell you firstly, that I was not involved in the events below and nor was Quintus for that matter. The Emperor decreed that selected senators were required to fight in the arena during the games. Although it wasn't 'to the death' the senators named were outraged as you can imagine. The crowd was intensely hostile at being deprived of some of their gladiator bouts. Perhaps our family name and reputation saved me from the humiliation of competing.

I look forward to seeing you again. It may, however, be some time before I do, as there's a great deal of business before the Senate. My intuition tells me that this is not politically a good time to be away from Rome. Please take good care of yourself.

I remain your loving son,
Lucius

9

The Palatine
Domus Transitoria
(The Royal Palace)

Nero strode impatiently up and down in his apartment, a determined look on his face. Where was he to get the money he needed to build a palace so magnificent it would be the envy of emperors down the ages? There must be a way. He just had to use his imagination. Thoughtfully, he fingered his purple robes. Then a glimmer of inspiration came to him. Of course!

'Call for Burrus. I want him here immediately.' A few minutes later the Prefect of the Guard hurried into the royal apartment where he found Nero strumming his fingers impatiently on a side table top.

'It's busy today in the Forum,' Nero stated, 'is it not?'

'I believe so, Caesar.'

'Then you have work to do. Arrange for a couple of freedmen, use Phaon as one of them, he has excellent powers of persuasion. They are to sell a few ounces of Tyrian purple dye to various dealers around the Forum and Palatine areas today.'

'But, Caesar, the use of the dye is forbidden, except for your royal self,' Burrus answered, surprised.

'I know, Burrus, just have it done!' Nero looked smug. 'Then you can return. I have a couple of other plans to put into operation. Now go!'

The Prefect made a hasty retreat. Nothing much surprised him anymore where Nero was concerned. What devious ideas had the Emperor thought up now, he wondered. Someone was sure to be either dead or to wish he was before the day was much older. That much was certain.

—∘∘∘—◦◦◦—

Arsenius fastidiously straightened up a few of the samples on the table as he looked up and down the aisle waiting for customers. The Porticus Margaritaria, a covered marketplace of shops, was a place of cool, marble floors and refined buyers with deep pockets. The range of goods on sale varied ranging from perfume, jewellery, gold and flowers, to cloth of both domestic and imported quality. The complex had recently been reconstructed by Nero from older buildings and tended to be considerably quieter and more elite than the other Forum shopping venues.

Arsenius really liked the location. Brick partitions between shops allowed for at least some privacy. Much of his stock was of the highest quality, whether local or imported. Just the sight of the vibrant colours drew the eye of the more discerning buyers. The shop's rental was expensive, but worth it. He smiled as he saw two Roman matrons advancing towards him.

'Good morning. Would you care to look at the latest in materials from Egypt and China?' he offered, smiling. The two women stopped. 'I have a particularly lovely fabric that's just arrived.' He picked it up and unrolled it onto the countertop, displaying it to perfection.

'Look at the colour!' one of the women gasped in admiration.

'Yes, lady. It's beautiful isn't it? This one's from China. It's a luxury silk and the colour gleams like gold, don't you think?' Arsenius continued his sales pitch as he held out the silk for her to feel its softness. She ran her fingers over it admiringly.

'I really must have some of this for Maia!'

'It's glorious. I don't think you'll do any better than this,' her companion agreed.

That was an easy sale, thought Arsenius, as the two women walked happily away afterwards chattering and laughing. He looked up in surprise at a young man who approached his stall, a small, grubby bag firmly grasped in his hand. He was surprised because the usual customers were either young girls shopping with a chaperone, or Roman matrons exactly like the two who had just left. They came to inspect the cloth he showed them then take it to their dressmakers, where it was fashioned into stolas or other luxury clothing. Arsenius was well known as having some of the most desirable stock of any shop in the Forum.

'I have something special to sell you.' The young man lent over the front counter, whispering to him. 'This will make you rich.'

'What are you talking about?' Arsenius asked, intrigued, and automatically lowering his voice.

'Something you can use to give your materials a unique quality,' Phaon answered. 'Here, look.' He checked to make sure no one else was nearby then opened the top of the bag. Arsenius bent forward, curious. He drew back with a sharp intake of breath.

'The use of royal Tyrian dye is forbidden,' he answered abruptly. He shook his head. 'I daren't buy it from you.'

'You can always say it's not the real thing if anyone who looks official comes asking,' Phaon coaxed. 'Perhaps it's just something similar made by creatures other than sea snails?' Both were silent as a couple of young women passed by with a chaperone.

Arsenius was tempted. Already the mark-ups he could add to the prices of his fabrics floated before his eyes. Maybe, just maybe he could get away with it. He was no longer young and if he fell ill had no family to run his business. He knew he must save as many sesterces as possible for the time when he could no longer work.

'All right. Just the one bag then,' he replied cautiously. They agreed on a price and Phaon left. Arsenius was unaware at the time that this ploy was repeated with a number of other vendors that same afternoon.

As closing time came that day, the shop owners in that vicinity were all raided. Unsurprisingly, many including Arsenius, were found to have Tyrian dye. The huge fines imposed on them forced the sale of their stall fittings and stock. Each lost his livelihood.

Later that day Aresenius walked out of Rome alone along the Via Appia. He hanged himself from a tree beside the tombs of the already dead.

'I seem to remember,' Nero mused as Burrus reported the profits to him at the end of the day, 'that Marcus Sempronius did not seem particularly grateful when I excused the inappropriate comment he made about me some time ago. Perhaps I was overly hasty. His insult really was very personal. Perhaps I should rectify the situation.'

'Caesar, Marcus died several days ago.'

'I know. That's why I remembered him. I believe, even so, that some punishment is in order. Therefore, I wish to see his will. It may be that the treasury coffers should have some recompense. Summon the Vestal who prepared the will. I would like to talk to her here tonight. She's to bring the will with her.'

Nero dismissed Burrus, pleased with his own resourcefulness. He'd found another source of the funds that he so desperately needed to build his spectacular, future palace—the Domus Aurea.

When Rubria received Nero's royal order she took it straight to the senior Vestal, Cornelia. The older woman rose from her work table and turning her back to Rubria, gazed out over the gardens, her face troubled. She was silent for some time. 'This is a real problem,' she said finally. 'Of course, you have no option but to go. You'll take an attendant with you and I'll arrange for lictors to accompany you to the palace.'

'Do you forsee difficulties then?' Rubria asked.

'I don't like it that you've been summoned at all, but especially at night and with Marcus Sempronius' will. Rubria, you have a sworn duty you must keep. Even if Nero demands it, you cannot either divulge the contents of a will until it is publicly read, or certainly, in any way alter that will. I can do little to protect you daughter, but remember you can always return here for refuge no matter what happens. No one would dare violate the sanctity of the Vestal quarters!'

Cornelia looked anxiously at her favourite Vestal to whom she felt a responsibility. She was also exceedingly fond of her.

'First, I will make an attempt to avoid this situation. I'll send a message to the palace asking if Nero will see me instead. Then we can only wait for his answer.'

The reply was received two hours later. It was as expected.

Rubria will attend the Emperor at the required time and place. She will bring with her the will of Marcus Sempronius.

———∘∘∘◦◄◙►◦∘∘∘———

Rubria covered her face with her veil. She realised that her hands were shaking. Cooler weather had begun in Rome and rain swept over the already sodden Palatine gardens. The remaining flowers drooped and dripped in a sad acceptance of a final flowering, as the heat of summer gave way to the cooler season. It was very quiet except for the splashing of numerous fountains.

Rubria clutched the will of Marcus Sempronius tightly in her hand, vainly attempting to protect it from the rain by placing it within the folds of her robe. It was early evening and growing dark quickly as she approached the royal palace with her attendant, Camia. Their escort of lictors led them to the front entry to the palace, then marched smartly away leaving the two Vestals alone.

'Come in please. May I have your names?' A guard held the door open, standing aside to allow the women to enter.

'I'm Rubria and my companion is Camia.'

'I have orders,' the guard brushed away an insect that had landed above his eye, 'to escort the Vestal, Rubria, to an audience with the Emperor. Camia, your presence is no longer required. I'll recall the lictors to return with you to the temple.'

'This cannot be!' Rubria protested. 'I'm not permitted to be alone with any man.' Shocked, Rubria and Camia stood momentarily speechless.

'Nonetheless, those are my orders,' the guard replied. He took her arm and she had no option but to accompany him further into the atrium as Camia looked on, alarmed.

The opulence of the surroundings was lost on Rubria who was becoming distraught. Across a vast expanse of gleaming marble flooring they walked, past exquisite sculptures and antique furnishings. Frescoes featuring singers and musicians adorned the walls and doors opened to the gardens and stadium beyond. Pine trees stood starkly silent in the gardens watching over the priceless classical statues placed at intervals amongst them. Eventually, Rubria and the guard reached a sitting room and were told to enter.

Nero sat casually strumming a lyre. As they came into the room the music tutor, Terpnus, rose and left with his nose in the air. They stood silently for a few minutes until Nero acknowledged their presence with a glance in their direction. His gaze travelled slowly from the top of Rubria's head down to her toes.

'The Vestal, Rubria, Caesar!' the guard announced.

'Ah, yes. I've noticed you before in the Vestals' seats at the games. Here, come sit on the chair opposite.'

'Yes, Caesar.' She forced herself to walk to the chair indicated and seated herself stiffly on the edge.

'Would you care for a cup of wine?' Nero asked pleasantly.

'No, thank you.' Rubria's mouth was so dry she would gladly have drunk water from the Tiber, tainted as it often was by dead bodies, but she wanted only to get this over with.

'You've brought the will with you?'

'I have, Caesar.'

'I should like to read it.' Nero stretched out his arm, his hand open to receive the document.

'I regret, Caesar, that my vows do not permit me to give you the will as it hasn't yet been publicly read,' Rubria managed to answer softly.

There was a frosty silence as Nero carefully and almost in slow motion, it seemed to Rubria, set down his silver wine cup on a side table.

'In that case, I presume that you would also be unwilling to oblige your Emperor by making a few "subtle" changes should I require you to do so?' he asked icily.

'I regret that is so,' Rubria replied.

'You regret!' Nero roared, his face red with fury. 'Guard, remove the will from her hand.'

Rubria shrank back in her chair. The guard moved to the Vestal snatching away the document which he handed to the Emperor.

'That will be all,' Nero ordered. The praetorian left the room closing the door behind him.

Rubria's face was white. She was well aware of the Emperor's reputation and the danger she faced. Silently, she prayed, her eyes tightly shut.

Please, Vesta, don't let him touch me!

Nero placed the will on the table beside him. Slowly and deliberately he undressed her once more with his eyes. She began to shake.

Without warning he was upon her. Grabbing her wrists he dragged her into the adjoining room and slung her hard onto the bed. Rubria cowered in fear as he stood over her.

'I haven't had the pleasure of getting to know a Vestal intimately before,' Nero leered in anticipation. 'You should feel honoured to be the first!'

Rubria's night of hell had begun.

The nightingales hid in the trees at Tauromenium.

Lorraine Blundell

Publius Catullus
(Tribune, Urban Cohorts)

It lay lightly upon the water as silky as a spider's gossamer threads. Pure white and filmy, it rocked in a gentle, lilting motion as the Tiber responded to the slight breeze drifting towards the Aventine. I realised that I was looking at a woman's veil.

My stomach felt suddenly queasy, as I arrived at the loading dock at the back of a complex of waterfront warehouses that received and stored Rome's luxuries and everyday merchandise. It was still early morning and workers were just beginning to arrive for their day's work.

A couple of vigiles lounged against a tree on the riverbank beside the candlemaker who had discovered the woman's body. He looked about as happy to be there as I was. The vigiles were chirpy now that they knew the tribune of the cohorts had turned up. Isn't that always the case though, once they have someone of authority so they can pass on the mess!

They had dragged the woman onto the bank. She wore a long white robe. What could be seen of her body showed obvious signs of massive bruising. Around her neck was a necklace with an image of Vesta. Unless I was very wrong, this woman was a Vestal Virgin who had met with foul play, then probably committed suicide. Obviously, her death by drowning was not the whole story.

'Sir, it appears the woman's been in the water for some time. We've sent for the doctor.'

'OK—Hop it boys! 'I'll see to things from here,' I grunted. They readily hurried away, no doubt to get a cup of strong wine from the nearest tavern. I would gladly have gone with them.

By Apollo's lyre! What sort of a mess had I landed myself in? One thing I was sure of—a suicide like this one would be hushed up at any cost. This had the stink of power about it. I just hoped I wouldn't end up posted to Britannia!

10

Whispers
  Whispers
    Whispers

Rubria the Vestal was seen leaving the royal palace in the dark of night. She hasn't been seen since.

The Emperor has ravished one of the handmaidens of Vesta.

Her white robe was bloodied, her hair flowing loose and her manner hysterical.

Scandalous!!

How the rumours flew! They quickly multiplied and were colourfully embellished in inns, villas, bathhouses, shops, hairdressers, gymnasiums and even temples. Only the silent graveyards that sheltered the dead escaped the murmurings.

Rubria had been seen fleeing from the royal palace, and it was known that she had attended the Emperor by his command, at night, her attendant having been sent away. Could it be that Nero had raped one of the Vestal Virgins?

The night before, the hours had gone by slowly as Cornelia paced the convent unsure what was happening to Rubria. She feared the worst but hoped for the best. As morning neared she called the other vestals to her and suggested that they pray to Vesta, as she suspected that Rubria might be in need of assistance. She drew one of the girls aside after the others had gone.

'Livia, please inform the priest that I wish to see him urgently,' the head Vestal asked anxiously.

The girl left. It wasn't long before the priest arrived at Cornelia's office door. She ushered him inside.

'Vesta's blessings be upon you, sister. I believe you requested my assistance?'

'I'm afraid so,' Cornelia confirmed. 'Would you please prepare a sacrifice and read the auspices. I fear that one of our Vestals, Rubria, may be in danger. Let me know the result as soon as possible.'

'Certainly. The hour is near that will be favourable for a reading.' The priest turned away, walking quickly back the way he had come through the Vestal convent gardens.

Cornelia prayed until she heard the old man return. One look at his ashen face told her all she needed to know. Nonetheless, she tried to calm herself to hear his words.

'I'm sorry. I bear grave news. Rarely have I seen such unfavourable portents. I fear you must ready yourself for something terrible yet to come. Have strength, sister.'

Cornelia stood in silence for some moments after he had gone. Then she closed the door and falling to her knees she wept as if her heart would break.

Not Rubria! Please Vesta, not Rubria!

———∘∘∘◦❁◦∘∘∘———

The towering portico of Octavia ornate and impressive did justice to the lady after whom it had been renamed—the sister of the Emperor Augustus. Behind the facade of the complex graced with her name, lay temples to Jupiter and Juno as well as shaded walks and a library. It had been built very close to the banks of the Tiber, almost opposite Tiber Island and adjacent to the magnificent Teatro di Marcello.

The Theatre of Marcellus, begun by Julius Caesar and completed by Augustus, dominated the landscape. Its archways rose gloriously above its surrounds, a monument to Rome and the skill of its engineers.

Lucius and Quintus sauntered down the slight gradient of the entry path shivering in the cool breeze off the river. They entered one of the multiple entry arches, themselves leading into inner archways, until they found the appropriate approach to the seats set aside for patrons of their rank. It really was a pleasure enjoying such an incredible venue for theatre performances in this stunning location. The theatre shone with marble and afforded every possible comfort to its patrons. Long gone were the days when going to the theatre meant necessarily sitting through some Greek tragedy such as *Oedipus,* only to re-emerge gloomier than one had arrived. Pantomime was scheduled for today's audience. At least plenty of comedy would be certain, most of it political.

'I could do with something to give me a few laughs,' Lucius remarked. He'd found life far more serious both in the Senate and outside it recently than previously expected.

'I know.' Quintus shifted uneasily in his seat. 'Things are not exactly going well.'

The two left the theatre at the end of the performance and lounged casually by the riverbank close by. Despite an afternoon of entertainment it had failed to completely dispel their gloom.

'Do you really think that Nero raped Rubria?' Quintus asked softly. 'You know there are rumours, there's nothing definite yet, that her body was found in the river.' He gazed at the water in front of him with distaste.

'It wouldn't surprise me at all,' Lucius replied angrily. 'The poor girl must have been devastated.'

'There's more of a problem here than is obvious though,' Quintus pondered thoughtfully. 'Her vows of chastity have almost certainly been broken, no matter who is to blame. Surely she couldn't be given the ultimate penalty?'

'You know the law, Quintus. If she isn't, then Rome's security is no longer guaranteed. She's one of the city's guardians. If she's impure, then the city is responsible for the offence and the gods will withhold their protection.'

Shadows were lengthening at the end of a perfect Roman winter's day. Rain clouds had moved in hanging low, threatening a bleak tomorrow.

There was no one nearby. These days it was necessary to guard against being overheard and accused of treason. There were many willing to point the finger to gain financially from palace bribes.

'Perhaps some kind of purification ceremony could be carried out by the head priest?'

'She'll certainly need an outstanding advocate, if she's ever found alive. That in itself is something I find most unlikely.' Lucius stood, picked up a stone, walked to the river's edge and skimmed it across the murky water.

'I don't like her chances,' Quintus said gravely. 'Even if she turns up again, who would have the courage to either defend her or to accuse the Emperor of raping her? He becomes more volatile with every day that passes. Nero's barely sane enough to rule.'

'One day someone may have to do something about that. For now I'll bide my time,' Lucius replied.

———∘∘∘─❋─∘∘∘———

The Royal Palace

Agrippina swept into the palace triclinium as slaves scattered right and left ahead of her. She was a tall woman who held herself ramrod straight.

Her hair was plainly dressed and her clothing simple. She had about her an undeniable air of authority as well as restraint that automatically demanded respect. Agrippina stood silently for a few moments looking down sourly at her son where he lounged on one of the couches. Empty and half empty dishes and cups lay discarded on a long table. Nero's lap was occupied by a woman who was not his wife.

'Get out!' Agrippina clapped her hands. The slaves ran. She glared at the young woman draped across her son, a newcomer to the court by the name of Poppaea.

'I'm going,' the woman replied in an insolent tone. She rose languidly and sidled silently out the door, a pout appearing on her pretty face.

Agrippina waited until Poppaea had gone.

'What the hell did you think you were doing forcing yourself on the Vestal?' Agippina demanded of Nero. 'Have you no sense of propriety whatever? Don't you realise the damage you've done to our reputation? Surely you already have enough boys and women to keep you satisfied, not to mention your slave girl, Acte? Rumours are circulating that Rubria is no longer at the temple and even that she is dead. That would make you the murderer of a Vestal wouldn't it?'

Over the last couple of years, Nero had just about had enough of his mother's constant monitoring of everything he did. Most of all he loathed the scathing criticism she levelled at him.

'She was asking for it! I'm the ultimate power in Rome. She should have known not to refuse my command,' he said defensively. 'I must admit, though, that I enjoyed taking my time with her. Rubria's a delectable little piece of work. Handing out her "punishment" was a real pleasure. As for anything that happened to her after that, why should you care?'

Agrippina drew back her arm and struck a stinging blow across Nero's face. Furious, he grabbed her and punched her forcefully, sending her spinning across the table and onto the floor where she landed heavily.

'Well, mother, what an interesting position we find ourselves in,' he sneered. She lay amongst the shattered shards of pottery and remnants of wine and uneaten food, a look of utter defiance on her face.

'Now you know where you stand. Well, perhaps given your present situation, that's an unfortunate choice of words. You will never again question what I do!' Nero stalked from the room and spent the afternoon sulking in his apartment. Spilt Falernian stained the milk white, mosaic floor the colour of fire flames.

Most of the slaves had fled as far away as possible. Some sidled into the kitchen, while others suddenly found work to do in bedrooms or public areas. There were still a few, however, who hung around in the hope of hearing some juicy morsel of gossip. Poppaea made her way to one of the peristyles where she sat thinking, a slight smile on her face.

Agrippina left the palace that day and never returned. She said nothing to anyone, simply retreating to the royal estate at Tusculum. From then on it was obvious that her power was at an end. Servants, however, have ears. They also have voices. *Whispers. Whispers. Whispers.*

Lorraine Blundell

Rome

To: *Farzana*
   The Villa of Poppaea
   Oplontis (Near Pompeii)

My darling Farzana,

Greetings! I absolutely had to write and let you know what's been going on at the palace. You simply wouldn't believe it! Everything is pretty much working out as planned. There are some things, though, that have been completely unexpected.

I've certainly managed to catch the eye of the Emperor. It only took a few weeks after arriving on the scene before I noticed his gaze lingering on me whenever he looked in my direction. I'm well on the way to having him exactly where I want him. However, there's certainly a lot of competition from other women at court. I was wheedling my way into his affections when Agrippina walked in the other day. I never need to worry about Nero's bland little wife, Octavia, but his mother—now that's a different matter entirely.

Anyway, she threw a real royal tantrum about his rumoured attack on the missing Vestal, Rubria. I couldn't believe it when I heard later, that apparently Nero had knocked Agrippina onto her backside on the floor during the argument. She was seen later brushing chunks of chicken and sauce out of her hair. I'd have given anything to have been invisible in the shadows watching that. Now she's left the palace. Things couldn't have worked out better.

I'll write and let you know when I have more news. Before long, hopefully, we'll have all the money we should ever need, no matter what happens. That, dear Farzana, also includes enough to buy clothes and jewellery. Nero continues to tire of Octavia. It shouldn't take much to get rid of her. Soon I will be Empress of Rome. Wish me luck!

Your dearest,
Poppaea

11

IV Urban Cohorts Barracks
(Near the Baths of Caracalla)

It had been one of those days. Publius Catullus knew it couldn't get any worse. Or could it? The morning had begun badly with some kind of severe stomach upset depleting the number of men available for duty. This necessitated the rearrangement of the week's rosters, resulting in grumbling and a decided lack of co-operation from the men under Publius' control.

'The Prefect wants to see you immediately in his office,' one of the junior centurions advised him, as he sat trying to work out a way for thirty men to do the work of fifty. Frustrated, he swatted away a fly attempting a landing on his breakfast pastry and followed the soldier out of his untidy, less than hygienically clean office.

'Come in Publius,' Prefect Macer signalled to him to take a seat. Publius noted that there was no welcoming smile.

'I don't know what you've been up to, but apparently you've really upset someone and that someone has enough power to have you demoted and transferred.'

Publius sat dumbfounded. Nothing could have been further from his mind when he'd walked in the door.

'I'm really sorry. You're one of the best tribunes I've ever had. You'll be missed. Your new orders are here, look for yourself.' Macer sat back looking puzzled.

Publius held out a trembling hand.

Written on a scroll and bearing the Emperor's seal, his orders reassigned him from Rome's Urban Cohort to the Vigiles in the port city of Ostia.

'Publius, what did you do?' Macer asked curiously. 'It's an unusual case because nothing at all relating to this has crossed my desk until now.'

Publius looked directly into the eyes of the Prefect.

'Sir, I know exactly what I did. I did my duty. The 'problem' apparently, is that I've begun an unwanted investigation. I found the body of a murdered Vestal in the Tiber,' Publius replied.

The silence of understanding lay heavily between them.

---∘∘∘ ❦ ∘∘∘---

The Esquiline Hill
Villa of Senator Natalis

Lucius sat enjoying a quiet autumn afternoon with Clodia, daughter of Senator Natalis. Their home high on fashionable Esquiline Hill in the elite quarter overlooked and stood aloof from the chaos of the life led by plebs and the busy streets that became the home of pimps, thieves and murderers after night fell. The villa was expensively furnished with good taste. Expensive mosaics covered the floors with heavy curtains falling gracefully onto them. This was obviously the home of a family very accustomed to wealth and privilege. The ancient nature of their social lineage was not in question.

'Would you like another cup of wine, Senator?' Clodia, tall, good looking and cooly sophisticated was the perfect hostess. Her brown hair was caught up in a bun and she wore a pale blue stola edged with gold. There was about her an air of entitlement to the social position she enjoyed. That Clodia would unquestioningly accede to his wishes as her husband should he marry her, Lucius had no doubt.

'That would be welcome, please.' Lucius watched her as she walked gracefully away, a well brought up, traditional, young Roman woman. He'd been attracted to her for some time and had approached her father for permission to see her at their home. Was it too soon to consider making her his wife?

Lucius was ready to settle down with a woman for whom he felt a physical attraction and with whom he had interests in common. And yet? He felt that his compatibility with Clodia had something missing. What was it? Something just didn't seem quite right. He'd wait a little longer to be sure he had made the right decision.

'I'm glad that fiasco in the arena is over.' Her father joined Lucius, cup in hand. 'What did you make of it?'

'I'm not sure, Antonius,' Lucius answered carefully. 'I believe we need to wait and see what the near future brings.'

'The Senate seems to be in a more vulnerable position as time goes on from what I can see of it,' Natalis continued. 'There are certainly rumblings of mounting discontent. Nero has little respect for Rome's traditional social order and especially for the Senate.'

Natalis began to pace the room. His steps were quick and he moved as a man does when highly agitated.

'I can say to you, Lucius, in confidence that I fear for the future. I believe it may be your generation rather than mine that will have to contend with the worst of things. Do you know what Quintus thinks about all this?'

Lucius paused for a few moments. When he spoke he chose his words with great care.

'Quintus is in a difficult position. He's unlikely to be able to take any action that might jeopardise the welfare of his family. His parents are far from in good health, especially his father and he must support his younger sister. Her husband died in the recent plague outbreak leaving her alone with a child to support. He's presently left Rome to visit his parent's home indefinitely in Misenum.

'That's unfortunate. His position is, of course, perfectly understandable. Still, it's early days yet and there are others to take his place. Enough said for now, Lucius. One thing I can promise you, though, is that our discussions will always remain confidential.'

Not if Nero's torturers get hold of you, Lucius thought.

Clodia returned with his wine as he rose to leave. He smiled at her apologetically.

'Must you go so soon, Senator?' she asked, her disappointment transparent.

'I'm afraid so, Clodia. Also, I may not see you for some time. I've promised to visit my father in Pompeii and I've left it far longer now than I should have.' Lucius smiled his goodbyes.

Clodia watched him go. She found Lucius an incredibly attractive man. Her opinion was no doubt that of women both young and old who knew him. She'd felt on a couple of occasions that he'd been on the verge of suggesting that he speak to her father about a marriage proposal, but for some reason had faltered. She had the strangest feeling that now the opportunity had been lost.

As the shadows lengthened leading into evening and the sun lost its warmth, a tinge of coldness crept into the air. After taking his leave, Lucius walked home deep in thought. He was unknowing and uncaring that the trees had turned the city brown and gold, spreading autumn's colours in a rich tapestry under his feet. Perhaps it was time very soon to seek his father's counsel in Pompeii.

Lorraine Blundell

Rome

To: Marcus Diomedes

The Villa of Diomedes
Via delle Tombe
Pompeii

My Esteemed Father,
Greetings!

I hope that you remain in good health. I received your letter with news of the arrival of the new sculptor and his sister and the progress made with the frescoes by Hinnulus.

I wouldn't worry too much, father, about Claudia becoming too close to the new young woman, the sculptor's sister. Even if she does remind her of Augusta, Claudia knows what she's doing I'm sure.

I'm pleased to let you know that you can expect me there very soon. I will send a message as to the exact time. I look forward to seeing you. There is much to discuss.

I remain your loving son,
Lucius

12

Pompeii
Lady Claudia's Villa

Mmm, a rose scented love message!
'Fabritio, it's addressed to you!' Alessia held a scroll in her hand that she'd just taken from the messenger. She made a point of sniffing it.

'Give me that Lessi!'

'No!'

'I'm warning you, give it to me!'

'Maybe you should come and get it?'

Alessia took off as fast as she could towards the far end of the rosemary bushes.

Fabritio took off after her.

Brother and sister chased each other round and round, Fabritio gaining a little with every turn. Alessia's dark hair streamed behind her as she held the scroll up like a trophy. Her eyes sparkled and her feet flew as the garden rang with peels of laughter. They'd played this game for other stakes many times before, so Fabritio knew that he would eventually catch up with her. So did she.

Finally, he caught her by the arm and reached for the scroll. She struggled then stiffened, her gaze riveted on something in the distance. Fabritio knew that at least on this occasion, she wasn't faking.

He turned to see what she was staring at. Claudia stood on the portico, smiling. Beside her stood a stranger, a good looking young man wearing a white toga with a purple stripe. He was grinning broadly and obviously enjoying the spectacle.

Meekly, Alessia handed Fabritio the scroll as they waited with some embarrassment for Claudia and the visitor, who were now walking towards them. Alessia didn't know which way to look. She supposed that her behaviour could be seen as somewhat unseemly. Still, she hadn't known they were being observed, especially by a stranger. She was acutely aware of being hot and dishevelled.

'I wondered where you two were.' Claudia looked as if she was having difficulty suppressing her amusement. 'I knew you'd finished work for the day, Fabritio, so I thought both of you would be here together somewhere.'

'Yes, Lady Claudia. We were "enjoying" the garden.' Fabritio stole a meaningful, sideways look at Alessia.

'I'd like both of you to meet Marcus' son. This is Lucius Diomedes.' She glanced across at him fondly.

'I've heard of you both.' Lucius shook Fabritio's hand. 'I'm taking a safe guess, then, that you must be Alessia.' He turned to acknowledge her.

'I am.' She found herself looking into earnest green eyes that smiled into hers. For some unaccountable reason she felt herself drawn to him. There was also a sensation in the pit of her stomach that she'd never felt before.

'Lucius, if you have time, we'll all go in for a drink and you can tell us what you've been doing in Rome,' Claudia suggested.

He nodded his acceptance. They walked towards the portico together, Fabritio and Alessia exchanging glances behind the other two.

'Would you mind if I have a look first at the statue Fabritio's working on, Claudia, before we sit down for a chat?' Lucius requested as they reached it.

Fabritio's face showed his surprise that Lucius would be interested. He studied the newcomer more closely.

'That's a good idea,' Claudia replied. 'We'll all go. I haven't seen it yet myself. In fact, we'll be the first to view it.' She led the way to a workroom just off the anteroom near the vestibule, and Fabritio removed the covering from his almost completed marble creation.

Standing before them was a statue of the goddess that almost defied description. Fabritio knew it was the best work he'd ever done. He stood watching their reaction with considerable interest as well as nervousness.

The figure was that of a young woman. She balanced gracefully on a circular pedestal, draped where necessary to preserve her modesty as she gazed at the flowers in her hand. They were brilliantly coloured as was the edging on the clothing of the goddess. It was her face, however, that immediately drew all eyes. As Claudia had requested, it was Alessia's face that looked back at them. Fabritio heard her intake of breath as his sister gazed at the figure. Venus' countenance had a sweet, gentle expression but in her eyes and her half smile, Fabritio had caught something of his sister's carefree happiness and love of life. It was unique.

For a few moments there was silence.

'May I congratulate you? Fabritio, this is absolutely superb!' Lucius was the first to speak and did so in a way that made it clear his words were sincere.

'The waiting was worth every minute, Fabritio. You're a brilliant sculptor.' Claudia was clearly delighted.

'And what do you think Alessia?' Lucius asked her.

'I think I'm honoured,' she replied quietly and simply. She gazed up at her brother, her face shining with sisterly love and pride in his accomplishment.

Fabritio managed to appear suitably humble.

Lucius looked thoughtfully at Alessia.

So, this is how she loves, he thought—*with all her heart.*

Lorraine Blundell

By Messenger

From: The Perfumery
Via Nocera

To: Fabritio
Lady Claudia's Villa
ViaVilla dei Misteri

Dear Fabritio,

I had a wonderful time at the theatre with you yesterday afternoon. I don't think I've ever laughed so much before! Father said that he has no problem with your suggestion for us to go to the games together, provided that you promise to look after me. Apparently things can get a bit rough there sometimes.

The shop's extremely busy, but father seems very pleased these days. Have you shown anyone your statue of Venus yet? I'm sure everyone will like it. Alessia sounds nice. Do you think I could meet her one day?

Tullia

13

Black turned, minute by minute, to a rich shade of midnight blue as dawn came to Pompeii. The sun's rays suffused the cloudless sky with a luminous light, growing stronger and brighter until, finally, the miracle of morning revealed a sky of the most glorious mid-blue. It was a joyful day to thank the gods simply for being alive.

They entered through the Vesuvius Gate at first light—the wine makers with their amphorae of sweet temptation. Cart after cart trundled down Via Vesuvio creaking, groaning and resisting as their wheels turned upon the uneven stone road.

The merchants also came after dawn with goods from Rome, hurrying through the Herculaneum Gate and along Via Consolare. The items they carried were many and varied. Pottery, footware, cloth and spices arrived to enhance the lives of the city's dwellers.

From the surrounding valleys heavily loaded carts of farm produce hustled into the city. Produce from the carts was taken into the forum to fill the vendors' stalls with all the goodness and vivid colours of nature. Fruits, nuts and vegetables awaited the inspection of local cooks from the best villas and women from the houses of the working class, as well as the poor, especially those without their own large gardens who lived in the insulae.

In the Macellum, fish and meat sellers set up their offerings for the day on their counters as well as on hooks hanging above their stalls. The bloody aprons of the latter proclaimed their trade. And still, there were more offerings to satisfy the insatiable demand of customers. The garum stall of Umbricium Scaurus was amongst the most popular, the savoury fish sauce selling quickly as a queue of customers formed, each person waiting for his turn.

Further along the forum the markets of Eumachia, the largest in the city, provided a huge choice of locally made woollen goods for purchase supplemented by items made of felt. As large exporters, the family dominated this segment of the trade. Customers simply followed their noses to the building's entrance where urinals had been built at the side to encourage locals to donate. Essential as part of the cleaning process, the urine's stink was not necessarily always appreciated, especially on a hot day.

The market was ready. Soon, customers would bring the scene to life.

―∘∘⊱❦⊰∘∘―

Claudia stood waiting in the villa vestibule becoming somewhat impatient as time went by.

'Alessia, it's time to go!' she called.

'I'm sorry, Claudia.' Alessia tore into the room looking as if she had a thousand demons chasing her. 'I was sorting out your scrolls and I wanted to finish them. Did you know that the poetry was all mixed up with those on philosophy?'

Claudia was stunned.

'I didn't know you understood that sort of thing. Where did you learn?'

'I don't know all that much, actually, but in Tauromenium, Fabritio insisted that we manage to find enough money for me to have a session occasionally with the local school teacher. Otherwise, he said, I'd never amount to anything and he wasn't going to have that.'

Claudia shook her head, bemused. These two young people never ceased to amaze her. Day by day her respect for Fabritio grew as she discovered more about him. As for Alessia—she sighed. It was as if her younger sister, Augusta, had been reincarnated. She felt so lucky to have found this delightful young woman.

'You're not angry with me are you, Claudia? I promise to be ready next time.'

'Of course not, my dear. A few minutes are nothing in the overall scheme of things.' Claudia gave the younger woman a fond hug. 'But now we really must go!'

They left the villa, walking down the sloping, quiet lane leading to Via delle Tombe. They'd barely reached it when Alessia stopped suddenly. Stepping onto the narrow footpath she reached out her hand to touch the pink blossoms on one of the trees lining the road.

'Alessia, wait!'

Her hand halted in mid-air as she turned back, surprised, to Claudia.

'That's an oleander tree. Its sap is poisonous. Be careful how you handle its flowers!'

'I know,' Alessia smiled. 'I can't believe you have them here. I thought I'd never see one again. Claudia, we had these trees in Tauromenium.'

For the first time it occurred to Claudia that Alessia might be homesick. She felt ashamed that in her own joy at finding this girl, she hadn't considered something so obvious.

'Do you miss your home very much?' she asked gently.

'Only sometimes, but still, seeing something again that I loved there brings back memories.'

'Are you happy here?'

'Oh, yes, Claudia. I just hope you'll let us stay!'

'Of course I will!'

They both laughed.

As they reached Via delle Tombe Claudia began to point out various tombs and places of interest until, without realising it, they'd come to the Herculaneum Gate. They passed through one of the small, side pedestrian archways. The large, central one towering over the street carried cart traffic.

When they reached Via Consolare Claudia decided it was time for Alessia to visit the forum for the first time. After that, they'd walk past Valentina's house to show Alessia where to go for her music lessons and then to the fullery. Today would be busy to say the least.

∘∘∘⧉∘∘∘

At the magistrate's court in the impressive, vividly coloured Basilica building at the far end of the forum, an interesting case was underway concerning a complaint brought by the City Poet, Rufus, against Tiburtinus, who was also a poet. The two literary men sat glaring at each other, prevented from coming to blows only by the presence of the magistrate. Even if they had, little harm would have almost certainly have come from it, as neither of them could exactly have been described as young and athletic. They could easily have had a physical confrontation without physical damage of any kind being suffered.

Rufus was furious to see that someone had scrawled a poem by Tiburtinus onto the Basilica wall. It was inferior rubbish that was true, but just reading it made his blood boil.

> *What happened? After having drawn me helplessly into the fire,*
> *O my eyes, now your cheeks run with tears.*
> *But the tears cannot put out the flames*
> *They spread across your face and darkness comes*
> *into the spirit.*
>
> Tiburtinus.

77

Interested on-lookers straggled through any and all of the five large doors with wooden shutters, leading to the huge indoor hall with its soaring columns, nave and two aisles. Rufus and Tiburtinus were standing at the far end in front of the platform, on which sat the presiding magistrate. Rufus recognised some of those entering many of whom waved or gave victory signs. Their murmurings quietened as the verdict was about to be given.

'I'm of the opinion, gentlemen,' the Magistrate looked sternly at the two poets, 'that you've both wasted the court's time. You should know better than to behave like spoilt children.

Therefore, this is my judgement:

Tiburtinus, your dislike and jealousy of the other party to this case is well known. I hereby order that you are not to engage

any person to do harm to the person or property of Rufus. Nor will you deliberately approach within the length of half a street of him or his home. As you live on Via dell'Abbondanza, that shouldn't be too much of a problem for you.

Rufus, I'm surprised to see you here. I thought you had more common sense! I agree that you've provided witnesses to the fact that someone defaced your property. You have, however, been unable to prove that this was done by, or on behalf of, the defendant in this case. I am therefore unable to award you compensation.

You are each required to pay your own court costs for this proceeding. The case is hereby dismissed.'

The two men scowled. There were jeers from some of Rufus' supporters watching.

Marcus Diomedes had come to court to see what the outcome would be and to provide Rufus with moral support. The result was exactly as he'd anticipated. He concluded that both men were equally stubborn but he couldn't help seeing the humour in the situation. No doubt Rufus would get over it!

'Look, Claudia!' Alessia and Claudia had just reached the Basilica when they saw Marcus leaving it. Just behind him came Rufus his face looking like a thundercloud.

'Oh dear, I don't think things went well by the look of it,' Claudia commented.

'Hello! I have to tell you both that I'm afraid each of them got exactly what he deserved,' Marcus reported as he reached the women. 'I tried to tell Rufus but he wouldn't listen. Oh, well, at least that's an end to the matter.' He glanced across at the sundial as they drew closer to the remainder of the forum.

'We must move along too, I'm afraid,' Claudia said, noticing his glance. 'We have a few things to do before we leave.'

'I'll see you soon.' Marcus turned, heading back on Via del foro towards his villa.

The forum that opened before Alessia's gaze was an enormous area paved with tufa. For safety reasons and ease of movement it was only for those walking. Several steps prevented the entry of wheeled vehicles. A number of temporary, movable stalls had been set up where vendors spruiked their wares. Beside the double storey, shady colonnades that majestically rose to the sides more permanent structures could be seen.

It was busy and noisy.

'Is it always like this?' Alessia asked.

'Most of the time,' Claudia replied. 'Why?'

'It's just that it's so loud, how does anyone hear anything?'

Claudia laughed.

'Well, it *is* Saturday and that's market day here, so I guess it's a little more busy than usual. 'Let's see what they're selling, shall we?'

They passed sellers of shoes, sandals, pottery, incense, candles, clothing and firewood as well as fruit and vegetables, especially cabbages and onions. The latter were always in demand by visitors because of their high quality. There were also many other types of goods.

A swarthy skinned, colourfully dressed young woman whose clothes jangled and jingled with numerous adornments, danced in the way of the Egyptians. Her hips swayed hypnotically in a sensual invitation. Squatting behind her, a man of about the same age with the air of a predator about him, eagerly watched those who approached to scrutinise the jewellery displayed for sale. He was quick to encourage customers and take their money. The merchandise was of poor quality, and no doubt lasted barely as long as it took for the pair to put a safe distance between them and their buyers at the end of the day.

Further along, Claudia paid a denarius for wheat. It was weighed for them at a weights and measures stone table in the portico. Alessia watched as the wheat was poured into one of the nine containers. It then trickled out of the bottom through a small hole into an amphora.

Around her, lining the exterior of the porticoes, were the most magnificent marble statues she'd ever seen. They honoured the city's leading citizens. Alessia wondered if Fabritio had been here yet. If so, he hadn't said anything to her about it. They were such good quality she was sure he'd want to see them. Of course, excellent as they were, she had no doubt that her brother could have done better.

At the far end from the Basilica they came to the huge Macellum. They paused to read the public notices posted on the whitewashed wall facing the street, then walked inside through the double storey portico. There were several halls and shops at the side, most of them selling meat and fish. It was impossible to miss the distinctive smell especially as they got closer to the fish.

'These will do nicely,' Claudia declared, accepting three large fish from one of the sellers. She turned to Alessia. 'Usually Julia or one of the servants does the buying, but I thought I'd bring you here myself today.'

Alessia nodded. Her eyes were firmly fixed on the large temple adjacent to the Macellum.

'I see you're impressed,' Claudia said approvingly. 'I'm not surprised. That's the temple of Jupiter and it's the most magnificent and important temple in all of Pompeii. Perhaps the most loved, though, is the temple of Apollo. He's Pompeii's special god and he protects the city. Look, you can see his temple over there, the one with all the steps.'

She pointed to the Delphic temple on the far side. Priests were readying the area in front of the temple for the afternoon's sacrifice to the god. It took place in full view of worshippers who gathered around in a circle at the appointed time to watch.

'Is there a special goddess as well?' Alessia asked Claudia curiously.

'Very much so,' Claudia replied. 'Our patron goddess is Venus, goddess of love. You'll see statues and paintings of her all over Pompeii. Actually, I don't know if you noticed, but adjacent to the Basilica there's building work going on. The Emperor's paying for a new temple of Venus to be built there. My friend, Cassia, was saying only yesterday that it's likely that Emperor Nero will come here one day to check on how work's progressing. Perhaps we'll be lucky enough to catch a glimpse of him.'

Alessia nodded as she tried to take in all of the information, sights, smells and voices overwhelming her. 'And what about you, Claudia? Do you believe in a special god or goddess?'

Claudia hesitated.

'Let's just say that Venus is my favourite goddess,' she replied cautiously. 'Now I'll show you Valentina's house and then we must go to the fullery.'

A short walk brought them to Via Stabiana. Claudia indicated the intersection with Via dell'Abbondanza. 'Just up from the well, can you see the house with the cart in front of it? That's Valentina's.'

'At least it's easy to find, even I couldn't get lost.' Alessia breathed a sigh of relief.

As they walked along Via dell'Abbondanza a torrent of blue water gushed from one of the building doorways. Claudia took Alessia's arm and guided her across the road using the thick, raised stepping stones.

'Don't get that on the hem of your robe, it's got blue dye in it. There's every chance if you do, we won't be able to wash it out,' she warned.

The building turned out to be the fullery of Stephanus where Claudia had handed in a piece of cloth to be dyed red. The two women passed a slave working on the toga pressing machine at the front of the shop and walked over to the counter.

'Lady Claudia,' Stephanus grimaced.

'What's wrong?'

'I'm afraid the dye for your cloth was late coming in. We've only just received it so your order won't be ready for pick up for at least another couple of days. I'm sorry.'

'Just be sure it's no longer than that,' Claudia said firmly. 'I'm waiting on it for something special.'

'Certainly, Lady Claudia. I give you my word.' Stephanus drew her attention to the slaves working at the large vat of urine, cleaning laundry. 'As you can see we're incredibly busy. However, as you're one of my best customers I'll make sure that the order is ready when you return. Would you care for refreshments from our food bar before you go?'

'Thank you. No. Goodbye, Stephanus.'

Claudia and Alessia left the shop to go back to the villa. They stopped at the bakery on Via delle Terme to buy fresh bread. Donkeys were doggedly pulling grinding poles in the heat in tedious and continuous circles to grind the wheat. Above the huge oven Alessia read an inscription bestowing good luck on all those who entered.

Good fortune lives here

Lorraine Blundell

In the forum portico

'Spider Legs!' *The two boys giggled as one of them wrote the students' favourite 'name' for the teacher on the finished drawing on his waxed tablet. The sketch looked like a thin, long legged spider but with a head on top, long hair and an arm holding a waxed tablet.*

A group of students sat on the ground at the end of one of the forum porticoes facing a tall, gangly looking man with a mop of long, silver hair. The two boys were amongst about twenty others.

'Silence!' the school teacher roared, his voice surprisingly strong and resonant given his scrawny appearance. 'Today you will attempt once more to master the grammatical construction of the ancient, classical language of Greek. So far, your attempts have been pathetic!'

There was a pause for affect.

He looked down at the two giggling boys at the back of the group, heads lowered, engaged in something that judging by their level of enjoyment was definitely not Greek. Striding quickly through the other students, he appeared suddenly beside them much to their dismay. Picking up the tablet he stared at the crude sketch without amusement. So, this was how they showed respect! He would teach them what their parents had apparently neglected to instil in them at home.

Lifting the tablet's owner up by the top of his tunic, he marched him to the front of the group. 'Lift him and hold him, you and you!' he pointed to two of the other boys.

Picking up the cane that was always ready nearby, the object of the boy's derision laid several strong strokes onto the offending student's backside. Several students turned their gaze away.

The boy shrieked with pain and embarrassment.

'Get back to your place!' the irate teacher ordered firmly. 'By the way, I have a message for your father. Come and see me after class. Be sure to give it to him.'

The boy walked slowly back to where he'd previously been sitting. Lessons continued until noon when the group was dismissed. The teacher shook his head in frustration. What were young people coming to these days? They had no respect and little ambition, not to mention no discipline from their parents at home. He feared that this one would be a generation of illiterates and layabouts.

To: Vetutius Placidus

Thermopollium
Via dell'Abbondanza

Sir, I have no option but to remind you that the school fees for the attendance of your son, due four weeks ago, have still not been paid. It would be appreciated if you would rectify this situation as a matter of urgency. School teachers also have to pay for food and shelter.

I also wish to advise you that your boy remains disobedient and disruptive in class. I consider that your attention to reminding him of his obligation in this regard remains imperative.

Alcibiades
Teacher of Classics

14

Via di Nola

The Gentlemen's Club
(House of the Centenary)

The eye was fixed and staring.
Deep brown, its lashes unseen, it was opened wide its focus determined by the small hole that surrounded it. Standing on a bench outside the room, the watcher shifted into a more comfortable position. The bedroom was small with a painted, classical wall fresco of Hercules and another of a couple engaging in sex. The couple on the bed were intent on reproducing the action on the wall and seemed to be succeeding rather well.

The prostitute was naked except for a tight, narrow piece of cloth bound around her breasts. The man, sturdily built, was covered in a mass of coarse, black hair. The watcher licked his lips in rising excitement as the couple's activity reached its inevitable conclusion. He then jumped lithely off the bench, retreating quickly down the narrow hallway, through the triclinium and antechamber and away from the isolated room.

So, that's how the rich and powerful had sex! It was considerably rougher than he'd imagined. He presumed that what he'd just seen was much the same for others of wealth and influence. They were obviously not much different, he thought, from anyone else when it came to life's necessities. Still, the interlude had proved interesting. This was the first time since being upgraded to the position of manager that he'd had a chance to see the club's brothel in action. It didn't worry him at all that the peep hole was meant to be used at times of suspected trouble—not for voyeurism.

'I may wish to book you again,' her client told the girl as his session with her came to an end. 'I'll let the manager know when I've time to come back.' He gave her a hard slap on the rump as he pushed her away and swung his legs off the bed.

Livineius Regulus was a wealthy man. He was also somewhat of a social pariah. Two misfortunes accounted for this inconvenient state of affairs. The first, was that he'd managed to get himself publicly expelled from Rome's Senate amidst rumours of unacceptable and illegal self enrichment. This resulted in his decision to reside in Pompeii. Unfortunately for him his reputation preceded him to that city.

The second, was that Regulus was considered overpoweringly arrogant by anyone who'd had the misfortune to meet him. Word soon spread.

He was presently sponsoring gladiatorial games, in which a troupe of gladiators representing Pompeii was to compete against those from Nuceria. Pompeii's citizens supported the gladiators wholeheartedly, but it had no affect on their negative assessment of Regulus.

Unaware that he'd been spied upon as he enjoyed the girl's body, Regulus made his way to the members' reception room. The gentlemen's club to which he belonged, with membership offered by invitation only, provided not only luxurious surroundings but just about any service a member requested. As evidenced by the intrusive spying by the club's manager, however, complete discretion was not always guaranteed. Regulus had been very lucky to be accepted. Only enthusiastic lobbying by a fellow Roman patrician now living in the city, pushed his membership application through.

Contented after his session with the prostitute and fortified by wine, Regulus made his way to the peristyle to stretch his legs a little. Should he take a swim in the club's private pool? No. He couldn't be bothered. It would probably be refreshing but he felt too lazy to go to the trouble.

Finding a bench amongst greenery pleasantly shaded from the sun, he sat in the garden gazing at the well stocked fish pond and nymphaeum. Encircling its four walls was painted a realistic scene of fish, birds and lizards. A real fountain stood in front, its finish resembling marble. It was certainly a most relaxing place to waste an hour or so.

He watched as a couple of overweight politicians waddled by. Obviously pampered and well fed from the public purse, their pleasurable afternoons and evenings well and truly compensated for any hard working mornings they were forced to endure. He allowed himself a small smile as he imagined them bobbing up and down in the club pool like buoys in the ocean.

Maybe life in Pompeii wasn't so bad.

As he moved inside to the reception area he ordered another cup of wine while the club's manager smirked knowingly nearby. Regulus studied a fresco of the numerous vineyards on the nearby mountain, as he considered the likely overall result of the bouts between Pompeii's gladiators and those from Nuceria. Presenting the upcoming games was costing him a bucket load of money in an effort to promote himself within the community. Little did he suspect that the good citizens of Pompeii had already made up their minds about him and their opinion wasn't going to change, regardless of how much money he threw around.

The major advertisements for the games had been painted onto the walls of buildings on major streets and even on some of the tombs outside the city wall. He'd even demanded the portrayal of exotic foreign animals snarling out at passersby, their yellow eyes wild and haunted. All he needed now were the pamphlets he'd ordered from the best known of the city's scribes. They were overdue. So where were they?

——ooo◦❧◦ooo——

The Gladiator Barracks
(Off Via dei Teatri)

The city's gladiator barracks occupied a prime position next to the large theatre and odeion complex. They were a considerable improvement on the former accommodation, now in disuse following damage from an earthquake. Only a short walk from the amphitheatre, they provided small but comfortable cells surrounded by a graceful colonnade.

At one end were cells for those gladiators who were considered prisoners and at risk of escape. Unsurprisingly, these were equipped with manacles. All exits to the barracks were closed except for the main door that gave entry to the common areas and the forty cells. In front of it was a large, open area suitable for training or lounging in the sun.

With the games coming up soon, serious training was well underway for the troupe of gladiators from Pompeii belonging to Aulus Suettius Certus. They were seasoned competitors with no novices amongst them. Some had been trained originally in Capua, some overseas and others locally in Pompeii. It was, however, still a diverse group, not only ethnically but in terms of age.

They were just as diverse in their particular gladiatorial skills. Thracians, Secutors, Retiarii and Murmillos were amongst their numbers. At this particular games, however, there would be no gladiators fighting on horseback or in chariots as they did in Rome.

Local girls often passed by on the shaded hill overlooking the barracks hoping for a glimpse of gladiators whose fine physiques they'd admired at the arena. If they were lucky there was a practice session underway and they could watch from a distance.

'What about we walk over to the Lupanare?' The Thracian was already heading out of the barracks following their latest workout. A small group joined him and they made their way down Via dell'Abbondanza towards the brothel.

'Which position are you trying today?' Astus the Murmillo asked his companion curiously.

The Retiarius punched him playfully as they walked. 'I'm not sure yet,' he replied, 'but I bet I'll have a lot more choice than you! That's if the owner doesn't want a dead girl on his hands. You weigh a ton!'

Astus roared with laughter.

They reached the brothel on Vicolo del Lupanare. Squeezing through the front entry into the tight space in the hallway, they studied the colourful, erotic pictures above the small cubicles to see what type of sex they wanted. Having made a selection and holding the fee of one denarius in his hand, Astus pulled aside the curtain. He entered a hot, tiny room with a stone bench and mattress. He didn't even bother to remove his sandals.

Then things got pleasurably even hotter.

Lorraine Blundell

Via Stabiana
The House/Shop of the Scribe Vibius

The last ten!

    I can't believe I've almost finished. My fingers are so cramped from holding the stylus it's a wonder they're not permanently curled in that position. As for the ink stains, they've been there for as long as I can remember.

    How will I earn enough to keep myself going if I can't continue to write? The gods know I can only see now when the light's really good. It sets me back by hours trying to meet customers' deadlines. Regulus will be sending some of his thugs over here to hurry me along if I don't get these pamphlets to him fast.

    I've lived more years than I had any right to expect. Perhaps I don't have many left, anyway. All I can do is to take life day by day.

    The last ten.

15

Piazzale Anfiteatro
The Amphitheatre

On a quiet Pompeii morning the umbrella pines so distinctive and familiar watched over him, as Numerius set up his small drinks stall under one of them. The trees with their tall, spindly trunks soared high above. No branches distracted the eye of the beholder until almost as a final thought gnarled, crooked offshoots sprang like arms and legs from the very top of the trunks. They were topped by greenery that was flat, drawing the fascinated eye of strangers to Campania.

Numerius always came very early so that other vendors didn't snatch the opportunity to steal his favourite spot. It was the best possible—near the outside double stairs into the arena, shaded from the sun by the tree he lent his back against. Turnover was always high as dusty, excited patrons quenched their thirst during the games and either bewailed their gladiators' losses or celebrated their victories afterwards.

His was the kind of business that wasn't much to look at and, in fact, no one looked at him twice except to buy cups of his watered down wine or chestnuts. In reality, the thin, middle aged man in his scruffy clothes made more money than many of his customers. Today would be a bumper one for him and other stall holders selling the usual souvenirs inside the exterior archways.

Actually, Numerius wondered at the amount of sesterces people were prepared to pay for tacky, cheaply made lamps, pottery cups, children's swords and any number of other goods, simply because they were shaped like gladiators or had pictures of them. The food and drinks he could understand. The rest of it was sheer waste from his point of view.

This was a 'home' games for Pompeii. Even Numerius' stall was painted in the city's rich, red colour. It had the necessary shelves to hold cups ready for use, with more stacked underneath in case he had a good day.

Temperatures were bound to rise as Pompeii's best troupe of gladiators battled Nuceria's. The two cities disagreed about almost everything but one fact was undisputed, Pompeii was larger and definitely more wealthy. They considered their neighbours from Nuceria more like country low-life than anything else. With an attitude like that, it was no wonder that everyone got somewhat heated whenever the two cities came up against one another in competition. As for the Nucerians, they were mostly of the opinion that Pompeians had their noses so far up their backsides they were suffering from an incurable superiority complex.

These irritations, however, only scratched the surface of the real reason for an entrenched hostility between the two communities. Politics played a large role, going back as far as the time of Pompeii's occupation by the Roman general, Sulla. Citizens of Nuceria and Pompeii simply didn't like one another's loyalties, attitudes, values or pretty much anything else.

The city's amphitheatre, the oldest in the Roman world built specifically for the purpose of gladiatorial combat, stood well away from the centre of the city on the outskirts, beside a large gymnasium complex. Even so, the noise on games day reverberated throughout Pompeii.

Numerius and the amphitheatre waited in silence, idling in the peaceful solitude. He heard the roar of the lions and panthers well before the carts carrying them appeared in time to provide animals for the combat to come.

'Numerius, if ever I get here on a games day and not find you here first waiting I'll know to worry about you!' Salvius grinned as he brought his cart to a standstill. 'So, what's the news since I've been away?'

'Nothing much. Just the usual stuff. Of course the temple of Venus is being rebuilt. Nero's been throwing his money around again. To be honest, I'll be happy when the noise and dirt from the construction's gone. You can hear it blocks away.'

'Sure. But I know how happy you'll be to be able to pray in such a fine temple,' Salvius replied sarcastically.

'That'll be the day,' Numerius spat. 'The whole thing's a bunch of crap if you ask me. I'll just look after my business and my money and hope that's enough for me to take care of myself. In the end we're all going to be dead anyway, aren't we!'

'You're not wrong about that today, that's for sure. Apparently some of the bouts are to the death. Poor bastards! I wouldn't want to be in their sandals. I'll see you later.' Salvius moved on with his cart.

Within minutes the whole atmosphere had changed. Carts full of gladiators arrived along with others carrying weapons, helmets and medical supplies. Under the eye of the lanista Mesonius, they swept past Numerius without a second glance, down into the depths of the dimly lit arena interior. They were followed by a group of musicians who straggled in ready to set up for the day.

At around the same time a thin, blue, ribbonlike line could be seen approaching the Nuceria Gate. By well before games' time the ribbon had turned into a huge swell of supporters all wearing the blue of Nuceria. They chattered, laughed and yelled the Nucerian cheer as they crowded into Pompeii.

Yes, it was going to be one hell of a day! As he saw them coming, Numerius rubbed his hands together with glee.

'Are you ready yet, Tullia?' Fabritio pushed the shop door back against the concrete doorstop and stuck his head around it.

'Coming, Fabritio!' She ran through the hallway to the
door, the basket on her arm swinging wildly from side to side.

'I see you're wearing red.' He stated the obvious. Even her earrings had small, red stones.

'Of course,' Tullia replied, and apparently someone warned you to wear it too.' She glanced at his waist.

'Hinnulus told me I might end up being lynched if I didn't. The best I could manage, though, at the last minute was this tunic cord. So I hope that's enough.'

'It should be. Just cheer loudly for the right gladiator, that's all!'

Phoebus came in and began to open the shop for the day. He nodded to Fabritio. 'I don't know why I even bother. I'll be lucky to get one or two customers at best today,' he grumbled, wiping non existent dust off the counter.

'Why not come with us to the amphitheatre,' Fabritio invited.

'No. You two go ahead. I think I'll have a quiet day here.' Phoebus settled himself on a bench near the door. 'I'll no doubt hear all about it when you get back.'

'Take care, father.'

'You too.'

Fabritio and Tullia reached Via dell'Abbondanza and found themselves amongst an already thickening throng of fellow Pompeian citizens. They came from every nook and cranny in the city following an inbuilt urge to see blood spilt and great victories. It was a happy, excited crowd that swarmed into the amphitheatre, outnumbering their opponents by two to one. They were already sure of their supremacy and an eventual, overall win at the end of the day against the pathetic Nucerians.

Would today be the day?

Atimetus wondered how long his luck would hold. Already he'd had nine wins. That was more than he'd expected. Would the end of the day see him with a tenth? He looked down at the helmet he held. Of the type worn by Thracians, it was heavy, highly decorated and fitted over his head leaving him with the feeling of a cage over his face.

He knew he shouldn't, but as he sat waiting on the bench behind the doors separating him from the arena, he allowed his thoughts to drift sadly to better days. He'd been captured in Carthage after a fight during which he'd attempted to stop an assault on a local girl by a Roman soldier. He'd been allowed to live by his Roman captors only because of his size and strength. He still remembered the words of the centurion entrusted with the task of sorting out those prisoners of worth from those to be slaughtered.

'Keep this one. He'll be good fodder for the games!'

Carthage, his beautiful city by the sea. He mourned the loss of his home and his freedom. If he closed his eyes he could just about remember what it looked like along the seashore where the ships came in to anchor and hear the waves breaking on the shore. And his mother? He knew her tears would never stop. He anguished that he couldn't reach out to tell her it was all right. Whatever his destiny was it was meant to be, Atimetus was sure that one day they'd be together again in spirit if nothing else.

The noise of the crowd brought him back to the present. Looking through a chink in the door he could see the colourful, painted panels with their gladiator scenes lining the boundary wall separating the crowd from the arena. It was such a small physical division, but it was often the difference between life and death.

Today he would do battle against Astus. Winner of fourteen bouts the older, more experienced Murmillo was a giant of a man and a cunning competitor. They were also close friends as they'd trained together at Capua. Astus fought for Pompeii, Atimetus for Nuceria. The gladiators themselves recognised these bouts as the worst. They pitted friend against friend. For that reason the majority had few friends. It was easier that way.

'Atimetus and Astus. You're next!'

Astus walked towards him and Atimetus held out his hand. They looked into each other's eyes sending a message with one promise. *Whoever wins will give the other a quick death.* Then they walked out through the doors.

The crowd roared.

It was said for years to come that this bout was one of the best ever seen in Pompeii. The Thracian and the Murmillo fought each other to a standstill. One had speed and quick reflexes—the other strength and weight. The advantage belonged to one then swung to his opponent, as each fought desperately for life.

The spectators, comfortable under the shade of the velarium, especially those in the elite boxes yelled themselves hoarse in between shoving drinks and snacks into their mouths. Atimetus, quick on his feet, attempted to use anticipation and recognition of the rhythm of his opponent's breathing to his advantage. Astus barged and on more than one occasion, managed to shove Atimetus off balance, placing him in danger of falling.

As the bout wore on, even the shouting spectators recognised the quality of the two gladiators they were watching. They stood and shouted for their favourite. Suddenly, it was all over. Atimetus was felled by the brute strength of the Murmillo. He tasted the metallic tang of blood in his mouth as he lay prostrate on the arena sand with Astus standing over him.

Atimetus raised his arm asking Regulus, the Pompeii games patron, for consideration of life. The crowd, even many Pompeii supporters, yelled for life for the fallen Nucerian gladiator, feeling that he'd competed heroically and deserved to live. It seemed as if in slow motion that Regulus, overcome by arrogance and seeking what he thought would be the increased goodwill of the home crowd—gave the verdict of death.

Astus made the kill quickly and cleanly.

The last words Atimetus ever heard as the killer blow gave him final peace were—'Forgive me.'

—∞◦◦◦|◎|◦◦◦—

The body of Atimetus was dragged into a cell at the end of one of the entrance ramps leading into the arena and the iron gate was slammed shut. Slaves whose job it was to clear the area threw him inside where he would be left until burial. When they returned the next morning they found that red roses had been thrown into the cell on top of his body.

'He didn't deserve death! You Pompeii mongrels are all the same. You bastards!' A spectator from Nuceria physically hurled a Pompeii supporter from his seat and onto the concrete steps nearby.

The whole crowd erupted as supporters of both teams began a fight that would be recorded and remembered for many years to come. The stadium was in turmoil.

'Tullia, hold on to me. We have to go!' Fabritio bodily picked her up and shouldered his way out of the stadium and into Via dell'Abbondanza as fast as he could. Her basket lay discarded where it had fallen.

Many were injured and some killed in the riot. The Nucerians came out of the situation the worst, many having to be taken for critical medical treatment.

By the time they reached the perfumery Phoebus was waiting for them anxiously. Word had spread even faster than Fabritio had managed to get Tullia home. She was so light he'd continued to carry her without any objection from his sweet smelling, willing companion.

'Thank the gods you're both safe!' Phoebus pulled them inside and locked the door. 'The world's gone mad!'

The nightingales hid in the trees at Tauromenium.

Rome

The Royal Palace

To: *The Duumvir*
  Pompeii

I will not wish you greetings as you deserve none!

The city of Pompeii is a disgrace! I've been made aware of the behaviour of the city's citizens which has been so lacking in any form of discipline, as to cause injury and death to dozens of both its own people and those from Nuceria at yesterday's games.

Death or injury to the infamia who compete in the arena is the normal state of affairs. However, I will not tolerate Roman citizens lowering themselves to the same base standards. Therefore, I have established an investigation which will report back to me.

Even so, it is already quite clear following the riot, that major blame must rest on the shoulders of the games' patron, Livineius Regulus. By the time I arrive in Pompeii again, my expectation is that he will have left, never to return. I have also exiled him from Rome.

Unless otherwise advised, gladiatorial games in your amphitheatre are hereby cancelled for a period of ten years. You will post this information immediately in all public places.

Caesar Nero

16

Lucius had enjoyed the week he'd been living at his father's villa. The cares of his senate responsibilities faded, to be replaced by a feeling of relaxation he hadn't known for a long time.

Seeing his father obviously at work with the door closed, he decided to postpone the discussions he'd planned to have with him this morning until later in the day. Lucius strolled casually towards Claudia's villa with no particular agenda in mind. The day was mild and eerily still. It was only a short distance from Pompeii's city walls to the serene country setting of the villa. He was enough of a realist to understand that the life his father lived in Pompeii was privileged and vastly different from the majority of the city's inhabitants. Many wealthy Romans also lived in luxurious villas along the Campania coastline. The poor in Pompeii managed without those luxuries of life the small percentage of wealthy Pompeians took for granted. Nonetheless, they got on with life with gusto.

'I just hope this piece is long enough.'

Lucius walked into the atrium to the sound of Claudia's voice. 'It's Lucius. Where are you Claudia?' he called.

'On the floor in the study,' came the muffled reply.

Slightly alarmed Lucius quickened his pace. What was she doing on the floor? Rounding the corner he saw her on her hands and knees with Julia beside her and a long, red piece of cloth spread out between them.

'You look like you've just had a shock, Lucius, if you don't mind my saying so,' Claudia laughed.

'It's not every day, you must admit,' Lucius defended himself, 'that I find you on the floor!'

Claudia stood. 'This was one of the few places with a clean floor where I could fully spread out this cloth I've just had dyed.'

'So I see.'

'It's good to see you. Are you enjoying your time and, hopefully, relaxing?

'I don't think I realised how tired and stressed I was before,' Lucius admitted. He turned as Alessia came to the door.

'Good morning, Alessia. How's your day been so far?'

'I'm not sure,' she frowned slightly. 'I'm still trying to find the missing Virgil scrolls for Claudia. Unfortunately, they haven't turned up yet so I shall have to go through the remainder in the study. I'm determined, though, that I'll find them!'

Lucius listened to Alessia's pleasant voice and to what she was saying. Indications were that she was intellectually bright as well as having a spirit of determination. Her naturally fresh, glowing skin was so different from the women of his social set in Rome that he found himself staring at her. Unquestionably, no man could fail to notice, either, that the curves of her body were well and truly in all the right places.

Their conversation continued.

Perhaps what he appreciated most, Lucius decided as he listened to her, was the unaffected ease she showed around others and the spontaneity of her laughter.

Claudia noticed the look on Lucius' face although Alessia seemed oblivious to it. So, she thought, unless she was much mistaken he was very much taken with Alessia indeed. Quickly she looked down at Julia who was continuing work on the cloth.

'Do you have any news, Lucius?' she finally interrupted, glancing up.

'Just that Fabritio has settled in well working with father,' Lucius replied. Fabritio had just been released by Claudia and much to Marcus' delight had begun to work on sculptures at his villa.

'Claudia, I think I'll extend my stay here. I need a longer break from Rome,' Lucius stated.

'That doesn't surprise me,' Claudia said ingenuously. Her reasons, however, were not quite those that Lucius might have expected so she kept them to herself.

———ooo-◈-ooo———

That afternoon after a relaxing lunch with excellent wine, Lucius and Marcus settled down comfortably for a long discussion. Marcus looked across at Lucius with fond indulgence. He was certainly aware that he was fortunate to have this young man as his son.

'I know you would've come to see me anyway, Lucius, but I'm not so unrealistic as to think that you would have hurried down here quite so quickly if there wasn't another reason as well.' Marcus looked questioningly at him and waited.

'As usual you're right.' Lucius gave a wry smile. 'It's bound up of course, with politics, or more precisely, with Nero.'

'I had a hunch it might've been.' Marcus settled into a comfortable position for the discussion to come.

'He's become increasingly hostile to the Senate. Rumours are well and truly gathering about a time and an opportunity in the short to medium term to remove him from power. His behaviour is totally unacceptable. He's unstable, unpredictable and sadistic. I don't want to worry you but it's impossible to know who he will murder or demand suicide of next.'

'I could have predicted this situation, Lucius. The man's certainly unstable and yet cunning and highly protective of his image. I've no doubt he eventually expects to be deified.'

'Father, he neglects the Empire those before him have spilt blood to expand and Romanise, and the gods only know how we will ever hold Londinium! His only interest is in becoming either a great singer, which he never will be, or a charioteer.' Lucius' frustration and concern was obvious from the tone of his voice.

'Stay out of his way whenever possible,' Marcus warned. 'I'm assuming he listens to the advice of very few who are wise enough to advise him well?'

'Seneca and Burrus have all but lost control over him.' Lucius got up and started to pace the room.

'Listen to me, son.' Marcus rose and placed his hand on his son's shoulder. 'You must carefully consider the future. The longer you spend around Nero, the more the chances are that you'll be caught up in the nightmare that surrounds him. You must try to find alternative options as to how you'll spend your life.'

'And what of the approaches already starting to be made to me of involvement in what is, in essence, a conspiracy to murder?'

'By Seneca?'

'No.'

'Stay away from them! This is a deadly game you cannot win, Lucius, if you become involved. Nero holds ultimate power. Even a sniff that you're connected with any conspiracy he uncovers would mean your death. Believe me the odds are well and truly stacked against any such action succeeding.' Marcus sat down heavily and drained his wine cup.

'I agree.' Lucius replied. The two men sat silently pondering the problem before them.

'Think on it while you're here and I'll do the same.' Marcus refilled both of their cups. 'For the present that's all we can do. Was there anything else?'

'Well . . .' Lucius hesitated. 'Actually, there is.'

'You'd better tell me then,' his father prompted.

'Father, what do you think of Clodia?'

'She seems to me to be a sophisticated, perfectly acceptable young woman. She's also good looking and would make a charming hostess,' Marcus replied, surprised by the question. He placed his cup down on the side table.

'That's pretty much what I thought you'd say,' Lucius answered.

'There's a problem or a proposition in the making?' his father probed.

'Something's happened. I've had doubts for quite a while whether Clodia and I are completely compatible so I've held back with any proposition,' Lucius explained.

'And . . .'

'There quite possibly may now be someone else,' Lucius admitted.

'I have to say I'm a little surprised.'

'Father, what if the girl isn't from our social class?' Lucius asked hesitantly. 'Would that necessarily make her unsuitable to be my wife?'

Marcus took his time before answering.

'It seems you've lost your heart son,' he smiled. 'The answer is no. High social status is by no means essential. I do, however, have questions for you.' He paused before continuing.

'Could she walk beside you with grace and dignity as she learned at your side?'

'I believe so.'

'She's younger than you are?'

'By quite a few years.'

'Do you love her?' Marcus studied his son's earnest face, watching the subtle changes of expression that passed over it.

'I believe so. I know that seems unlikely as I've known her such a short time, but I'll know for certain before I leave here. The answer for now is that I have never felt this way about a woman before.'

'Then I'd say that you may have just told me the identity of the young woman. If I'm correct then you have my blessing and my advice is to follow your heart. Alessia's a delight.'

Lucius clasped his father's hand and left the room with a lighter step than he'd entered it. Sometimes it really was true that wisdom came with age and his father was a good example of that.

They scampered and scurried throughout the city like rats on the trail of others' tasty leavings, clutching in their grubby hands the pamphlets shakily copied by Vibius from Nero's original decree. The recipients of the pamphlets, like walking stick insects, poor and starving, knew better than to pretend that a job not completed had been done as ordered. A supervisor would walk searchingly through the streets later checking that all public buildings and shops as well as any available walls had pamphlets on them.

Aulus put up the final one in his hand, gave a sigh of relief and went back towards the city centre. He was a tall man with hollowed out cheeks and thin lips pulled down at the corners. Heading over to Via dell Tempio D'Iside he lined up near the temple of Isis with the others of his class outside the charity bakery for the poor. The small but graceful temple with its fluted columns and carvings of strange, animal headed gods inside, stood in stark contrast to the 'down and outs' waiting nearby.

At the bakery he was given a ration of bread for the day. Made without yeast, it was unleavened and given daily to the poorest living in the city. It was tough and far from tasty but it was all that stood between them and starvation. Hungrily, he stuffed huge lumps of it into his mouth. Then he wearily joined another line waiting for the heavily watered cup of wine that was also on offer.

'I heard that we're waiting for nothing. They're not handing out wine tonight,'the skeletal figure in front of Aulus growled. 'I reckon we should do something about it. We need to let them know we won't put up with it!' He shook his fist in the air and began shouting the news as he ran along the long line to those waiting as well as to anyone else who'd listen.

'No wine tonight! Those wealthy loungers getting paid to feed us are eating and drinking in style while we go hungry and thirsty. I say we go to the forum and let them know we won't put up with it! Are you with me?'

'Yes! Let's go to the forum!'

The crowd quickly came together with a single purpose. Those waiting for food and drink found supporters amongst the other poor of the city as well as the usual troublemakers. Together, the ever swelling group headed for the forum.

Aulus sighed. I don't have the energy for all this, he thought. I could do with another cup of wine though. The few asses he'd receive later for the job he'd just completed would pay for a piece of fruit for his dinner. Still, that was tonight. What about tomorrow? He hurried to catch up with the rest of the rowdy mob.

Poverty was as unpalatable in Pompeii as anywhere else. Those who governed the city needed to be smart enough to understand that free bread, wine and sex could work marvels, but only if it was ongoing.

Via dell' Abbondanza
The Fullery of Stephanus

Whew! That was a close call!

If Lady Claudia had been just one hour earlier returning to pick up her dyed cloth I'd have been screwed. She's a good customer and she's nice enough, but not when things get stuffed up! The supplier will just have to do better. I know Lebanon's a long way from here, but Tyre's a big manufacturer of that red dye these days. The delay's inexcusable!

Cacat! Business isn't getting any easier. Eumachia's family stranglehold on business is becoming so strong it's getting more and more difficult to compete. It'd be nice too, if those dopey sheep farmers sitting on their backsides up on the mountain would supply me on time. What am I supposed to do without wool to dye?

'Amplicatus! Get out here and tip the rest of that piss into the vat out the back!'

17

T iberius Claudius Verus, the new duumvir of Pompeii, was feeling decidedly nauseous. A small man with a pot belly and short legs, he had the look of a nervous bird. His eyes constantly darted from side to side and he found it difficult to sit still for any period of time. His face was pleasant enough with round, large eyes and a weak chin, but it wasn't helped by the bald patch on top of his head. Although advised otherwise by friends, he persisted in trying to comb remaining strands of hair from the sides to cover the shiny, barren patch on the top. Needless to say it never worked. It simply made him look desperate.

The municipal buildings lay at the far, south end of the forum from the temple of Jupiter. They housed the magistrates and town councillors and provided storage for the city archives.

As senior city magistrate, Claudius Verus had allocated himself the largest and most palatial office with an outlook across the forum. Normally, it was a pleasing sight of busy and noisy prosperity.

He closed his door and sat staring into space. How in hell had he ever ended up in his current predicament, he wondered. First, the raucous crowd of last night had taken over the forum demanding wine and more food. They were lazy, a blot on society and they were never satisfied. That was the problem! Didn't the city provide the poorest with free bread, wine and even visits to brothels? Something only had to go wrong and they rioted. Well, he had to admit it hadn't actually been a riot, but what he had on his hands right now was fast turning into one.

This morning he'd arrived at his office to find the forum quickly filling with furious citizens. They'd torn down the posters from where they'd been posted on shops, walls and buildings and were now waving them with clenched fists towards his office.

The crowd, good naturedly jostling one another, swelled onto the footpaths, into the body of the forum, and spilt onto the outside roadway. They varied from scrawny and ragged to those dressed in typical everyday, decent garments. Here and there were a few scatterbrains treating the whole thing like an excuse to enjoy the moment, but they were few and far between.

'Move on! You can't just loiter here!' A variety of officials attempted to disperse the crowd but they were having none of it.

'Bugger off! We'll gather where we like!'

All ages and classes were represented as well as both men and women. Love of the games in Pompeii knew no social class or gender. Out on Via Marina random groups stood watching curiously wondering what would happen next.

Heavily laden carts attempted to make their way through the tightly packed gathering into the forum. The angry cursing of stall owners mingled with the jeers of the crowd.

No Games Ban! No Games Ban!

The thunderous roar was growing in intensity. Personally, Verus could see why everyone was so angry but why blame him? It was Nero who'd slapped the ten year ban on the city. Nero! His stomach felt even more queasy. The Emperor had made the decision sitting up there in Rome with games laid on whenever he wanted them. Generally speaking the people liked Nero, but that seemed to have been forgotten.

Verus wondered what would happen to him if the Emperor heard about this situation. He could only imagine the affect it would have if a second riot occurred, this time in the forum in the middle of Pompeii. He really didn't want to think about it. It seemed that Nero was already furious enough with Pompeii for the debacle in the amphitheatre. Why didn't he blame the Nucerians? It was their fault after all!

'Duumvir, the crowd are demanding to speak to you.' His young assistant, Samius, nervously opened the door a chink.

'Tell them I'll be out front soon,' Verus stalled for time. What to offer them to make them back off? That was the question. Then it came to him, like a shaft of light cutting through the darkness. Of course!

Verus stepped out of the building's front entrance and stationed himself on the top step leading into the portico. He stretched to get every inch of height he could manage in an attempt to appear more imposing and waited for calm.

Time went by on the nearby sundial.

Eventually, as the masses quietened, he raised his voice to address them. He knew he probably had only one chance to stop this situation from escalating.

Fellow citizens, listen to me!

I know why you're here today. I understand your anger at the decree that's been issued against the city. I also believe that the Emperor is unlikely to rescind it anytime soon. Obviously, Pompeii would struggle to cope without our games for ten years. I do, however, have a suggestion.

The crowd grew noticeably quieter.

We're not without other influence. It's come to my attention that our own Poppaea from Oplontis has been very favourably received at Rome's royal court. I will ask her to intercede with the Emperor for us. I believe this may be the answer to our dilemma.

For some moments success or failure hung in the balance. Then, appeased, people began to look to each other for confirmation of their own views. They milled around discussing the duumvir's suggestion. The forum was empty soon after, except for those going about their normal activities.

He'd won!

Verus found that he was shaking and completely spent. He'd certainly earned his pay for the day. He re-entered his office and slumped exhausted into his chair.

'Samius, get me the largest cup of unwatered wine you can find!'

Claudia

Lady Claudia's Villa
Cult of Bacchus Meeting

The Same Evening

I wonder how long I can go on doing this, but I must try. For the sake of the Alessia's of this world, I must try to increase and use women's influence. That's the only way forward I can see to reduce the cruelty and inequality all around us. As for Nero, he is the very embodiment of evil. I saw and heard enough of his doings in Rome to last a lifetime. We must be rid of him.

Our group is growing. The influence of the sisterhood's members on their husbands may be small, but it's increasing with every year that passes. Perhaps one day we'll have influence in our own right. I fear that day is either totally unreachable or lies in another time and world.

Unfortunately, my life is short in the overall scheme of things. Dedication to the god Bacchus gives these women and those in the ever growing groups spreading across the Empire a bond to hold them together. I pray it will be enough.

18

Rome

The Forum
The Temple of Vesta

Cornelia looked around her at the Vestals under her charge who were nervously gathered waiting for Nero's arrival. So, the Emperor was coming to the temple to seek Vesta's blessing for the start of his tour today to Alexandria! Cornelia felt like throwing up. The gall of the man! Did he really believe that the goddess would be unaware of the evil in him?

'You are to sit with as much dignity and serenity as possible as you watch the Emperor pray,' she told the priestesses. 'Under no circumstances will you speak unless spoken to. Do you all understand?'

There was a general murmur of assent.

'In the time remaining before the Emperor's arrival and that of the high priest, I suggest each of you offers a brief prayer to Vesta for the success of this occasion.' Cornelia gave the group a smile of encouragement and turned away to supervise the arrangement of the last of the flowers.

There was one seat the high priestess had ordered left vacant today. It would have been used by Rubria. Cornelia sighed. Was she the only one, she wondered, who still felt the young Vestal's presence in this holy shrine? Cornelia knew that in whatever sense, however, Rubria was indeed here.

A little later than expected Nero arrived with his entourage. A large, curious crowd had been following him through the Forum as he did the rounds of the other temples. He left the temple of Vesta until last, approaching somewhat hesitantly. Cornelia was far from surprised that he should feel uneasy in this particular temple.

After the bloody, sacrificial killing of a flower garlanded bull, an offering to Vesta for the success of the tour, the priest whispered the traditional prayers. Finally, Nero knelt to pray at the shrine. Rome's sacred flame flared strongly with the promise of good fortune for the city.

After a few minutes he rose and sat in the chair provided, to listen to a farewell speech from Seneca on behalf of the Senate.

'. . . We wish you fair winds and a safe journey as you venture to foreign shores,' *Seneca intoned. 'Your visit to Alexandria will certainly be an occasion for* *celebration and rejoicing by the Alexandrians. Farewell, Caesar, until you return* *to Rome.'*

Nero rose to leave. He tripped and almost fell as the hem of his robe caught on the chair leg and he lost his balance.

'I cannot see,' he shouted as he panicked and struggled to sit again, hands desperately kneading into his eyes.

'Why can't I see?'

Quickly he was helped from the temple and placed in a waiting litter. The crowd drifted away after he'd gone. The palace reported some time later in an official declaration, that the Emperor had fully regained his sight.

Cornelia looked on with interest. Vesta had sent Nero an unmistakable message. Had he heeded it? She was doubtful. His ego and vanity was such that he cared nothing for the warnings of anybody, even the divine.

The high priestess was not an impulsive person. Over the years, first as a Vestal and then as senior Vestal, she had long ago learned exceptional patience, compassion, a stillness of body and spirit and a deeper love for the goddess whose temple she served. Only some five years remained until she would be released from her vows and sent out into the world as an ideal example of a virtuous and highly respected Roman woman.

This, however, was not the extent of the senior Vestal's traits. Any member of her family could have verified, that she'd always had a stubborn streak allied to a personal values system that held the principle, 'do unto others as they do unto you.' In that sense, within her lay surprises of which others were unaware.

Born in Rome, she was a patrician in every sense of the word. Her father, recently deceased, had long been a respected member of the Senate. Her family had illustrious contacts of long standing, and Cornelia had been privy to many secrets. To these were added others told to her in confidence as a Vestal by those, some now dead, who came seeking consolation and advice. Cornelia held her counsel with a quiet dignity and discretion that gave little clue to her wealth of knowledge.

She slowly walked the peaceful convent garden praying that the decision she was about to make was both just and wise. She had no family except her elderly mother and those with whom she lived in the convent and for whom she felt a responsibility. Cornelia freely admitted to herself, however, that this was much, much more than a matter of responsibility.

How, exactly, had she felt about Rubria? Was it more like a motherly or a sisterly love? Either way, Cornelia knew it was deep and special. The snake that coiled around her heart demanded revenge for the death of the beautiful and virtuous young woman. Contacts had told her of a young woman's body in the Tiber. It was almost certainly that of Rubria.

Nero was evil through and through. She knew enough secrets to have no doubt of that. She looked again at the message she was sending to her father's old friend, Seneca. She had heard rumours of the gathering of evidence against Nero with a view to replacing him as Emperor. She would supply Seneca with ammunition. Cornelia had no doubt that Seneca would be instrumental in any coup that might be being contemplated. If so, he would need to watch his back, or he would be denounced by Nero's spies. They were everywhere and Nero was an all powerful, dangerous enemy.

Wills taken by force from the vestals and falsified to provide revenue for the Emperor, corruption and murder, were only the beginning of secrets that might in the near future see the light of day. Cornelia's face was set with determination as she called the messenger to her.

Greetings Seneca!

Please arrange a time suitable to you to meet me for consultation at the Vestal convent office. The matter is private and urgent.
May Vesta grant you her blessing,
Cornelia

---ooo-)◯(-ooo---

The Royal Palace

Nero lay on his bed pale and shaken. On returning from the ceremony at the Vestal temple he was slowly regaining his sight and his confidence. Courtiers hovered around him looking concerned. Amongst them was Burrus.

'Cancel the tour of Alexandria immediately!'

'Are you sure, Caesar? It may be that you'll feel well enough to go to the ship after a little more rest,' Burrus reassured him.

Nero glared. 'It's an omen of doom. You saw what happened at the temple. I couldn't possibly risk going to a country like Egypt now.' He kept to himself the visions of the Vestal Rubria that floated before his eyes increasing his anxiety. Was he to be punished for her fate? He simply couldn't take the risk.

'I said, cancel the tour. Do it!'

'Yes, Caesar.'

Then Nero had a flash of inspiration. Perhaps he should seek the blessing of another goddess in place of Vesta. Maybe he could play one off against the other.

'Instead, I will inspect progress on the restoration of the temple of Venus in Pompeii. It's costing me enough money. It's time I found out what they're doing down there. Make the arrangements.'

Burrus hastily left the chamber. He shook his head in frustration. First it was Alexandria now it was to be Pompeii. Talk about chaos! In an exasperated gesture typical of him he ran his hand through his wavy hair. There was one positive in all of this, though. At least they wouldn't have to put up with those bowing, conniving and totally corrupt, smarmy Alexandrian officials.

'Praxus, you're not going to believe this. Get ready and spread the word to the others. We're going to Pompeii.'

Egypt
Alexandria

The Prefect's Palace

By Messenger

To: *Sextus Afranius Burrus*
     Prefect, Praetorian Guard
     Rome

Greetings Prefect Burrus,

I received your message informing me that it has proved necessary to cancel Caesar Nero's tour here due to his ill health. Please extend to him my best wishes for a speedy recovery.

As I'm sure you're aware, Alexandrians will be disappointed not to have the opportunity to be able to demonstrate their loyalty and affection for the Emperor. Should he feel inclined, we would welcome a future tour at a date of his choosing.

I can reassure all concerned that security would be at a premium and the Jewish problem is well and truly under control.

Tiberius Claudius Balbilus
Prefect
Egypt

19

Naples

Clink, jingle. Clink, jingle. Clink, jingle.

The gleam of yellow gold shone in the sunshine as it swung to and fro from the wrists and around the necks of Nero's mounted attendants. Superb, swarthy horsemen from Morocco, they held their heads high, disdaining to even look into the eyes of those around them. White clad, bearded and dark eyed, they drew the awed gaze of the huge crowd who'd gathered to catch a fleeting glimpse of the Emperor as he began his journey to Pompeii.

'Seneca, were you avoiding me on the boat? Do you have a problem I should know about?' Nero's pale blue eyes bored into the philosopher's.

'No, Caesar. Should I have?'

'This Campania region is well known to you I believe?' Nero replied, avoiding the question.

'It is, Caesar.'

'What flea bitten hole of a hotel have they got me booked into in Pompeii?' Nero's mood had gradually soured as he was constantly delayed while the Praetorian Guard cleared the way ahead of his carriage. Wiping away the sweat from his face he glared ahead, ignoring the cheers and curious stares of onlookers.

'I believe, Caesar, that you're expected at the new luxury hotel that has only recently opened outside the city walls. I've heard that the Villa Moregine is as comfortable as anything to be found in Rome,' Seneca reassured him.

'I'll believe that when I see it,' Nero replied tersely.

The journey from Rome had been uneventful, no further ill omens having eventuated. The priests had decided that although the end destination had changed, visits already made to the various temples to solicit good fortune could still be considered valid, except of course, for that to the temple of Vesta which was conveniently ignored.

Burrus, waiting to lead the guards overland to Naples shook his head. So much of Nero's reign was a joke!

111

The voyage had been undertaken by boat in style, with Nero insisting on changes of clothing several times each day. They'd left Rome with the cheers of onlookers ringing in their ears. They'd gathered to stare at the festooned boat with Nero smiling and waving magnanimously, his hand flashing with gold finger rings. The destination might as well have been Egypt the way that pomp and ceremony was laid on, rather than a small hop down the coast to Naples.

What a farce!

The sea was calm and the weather fair. Nero had actually arrived in Naples in a good mood. It was a city that appealed to him for its predominantly Greek culture and theatre tradition.

Now, leaving the city one by one, the seemingly never ending line of carriages behind the Emperor's moved slowly forward. Numbering in the hundreds they followed, paying homage to Nero in the hope of gaining royal favour. With few exceptions, most would find themselves without accommodation in Pompeii suitable to their status.

Seneca glanced back at the pack mules following the Emperor's carriage. They were shod with silver and their handlers wore clothing made from the finest Canusium wool.

'I see that no expense has been spared in outfitting your entourage.' Seneca was not one of Nero's fawners who shielded their words in silken compliments.

'True gentlemen always throw their money about,' the Emperor boasted proudly. 'What would you have me do? Should I travel like a pauper?' His look was sullen.

'No. Just a little more modestly before the eyes of the people,' Seneca persisted.

The jangling beside them continued.

Nero laughed. 'By the way, doesn't one of our junior senators live in Pompeii? Now, who was it I heard about the other day?'

'There is no one I can think of,' Seneca replied, hoping that he wouldn't be pushed further to supply a name.

'No. Don't tell me!' Nero waved his hand as if swatting away an insect. 'You know I never forget a name.'

'I certainly do, Caesar,' Seneca replied reluctantly.

'I've got it! Lucius Diomedes. He lives there doesn't he?'

'No. I'm afraid you've been misinformed. His elderly, widowed father lives in Pompeii. I believe Senator Diomedes lives in Rome and rarely sees his father.'

Seemingly losing interest Nero turned away and began to doze. Seneca watched him, wondering if the question had been as innocent as it seemed. With Nero, you never really knew.

Lucius Diomedes' name was close to the top of a list Seneca had been compiling for some time, especially after his meeting with Cornelia. They were men of good character who had the welfare of Rome as their goal. He would need to count on every one of them if they were eventually to get rid of this despotic, corrupt and totally depraved Emperor.

───∘∘∘─◖◒◗─∘∘∘───

The Villa Moregine lay just outside Pompeii. Superbly located beside the cool, blue Sarno River it overlooked the stilt houses known as palafittes that stood at the river's mouth. Pompeii's rich, butterscotch coloured roofs could also easily be seen and admired from this hotel, built to accommodate the needs of wealthy businessmen and travellers of note. The villa gloried in its luxurious appointments and elite status.

Requests for accommodation were vetted carefully. It was not enough that an intending guest should be able to meet the considerable expense they would incur. Their social status was also scrutinised. Recently opened after completion of construction at huge cost to the rich banker who owned it, Villa Moregine, despite all of its sophistication, became completely awestruck at the thought of Nero's imminent presence.

Advised only a little over a week beforehand of the Emperor's intended arrival, staff and management at the Villa went into a panic. The owner was Lucius Caecilius Jucundus who also owned the Villa Pisanella, a villa and vineyard outside Pompeii. With a broad face and large nose he was seldom seen as handsome, but was known for his wealth and discretion. He arrived at the Villa not only in the hope of meeting Nero, but mainly to check that all was in readiness so as not to incur his wrath. Fortunately, he had no way of knowing that regardless of how well his establishment was prepared, it could never totally live up to the Emperor's inflated expectations.

With Nero's arrival expected any hour, Jucundus began a final inspection. The view, of course, was spectacular and needed no improvement. He walked along the circular approach and entered through the elaborately carved, wooden door. Dismissing the nervous staff he went through the Villa alone, one room after another, checking.

The floors were shining marble inlaid with classically themed mosaics. The walls came alive with vivid colour, especially Pompeii's unique red and tasteful curtains fell whispering softly onto the floors below. Antique furniture filled every room and for guests' enjoyment a luxurious, thermal baths gave privacy in a separate wing.

Jucundus paused for a few moments beside one particular fresco, still wet from the artists touch. Hinnulus had left only moments ago after working day and night to finish in time. On the wall he'd painted a youthful Apollo playing his lyre in front of a red background. He wore a laurel wreath and a flowing, delicate green cloak. As instructed, the artist had portrayed the face in the likeness of the Emperor. That was a nice touch, thought Jucundus. He'd had to pay Hinnulus a small fortune to get him to do the painting at all, nonetheless in the short time available.

Fixtures throughout were of marble and bronze. The smell of amber incense as well as flowers from the extensive gardens stimulated the noses of all entering in the most delightful way. Relaxed by the perfume and the sound of water falling from the many fountains, guests were in no doubt that they were in the best accommodation money could buy.

Finally, Jucundus inspected the private dining rooms. There were many of them and guests were offered every possible dish to tempt their palates as they lay on the plush couches. Jucundus felt exhilarated and flushed with the supremacy of his hotel and restaurant.

Villa Moregine was ready.

Rome

The Theatre of Marcellus

He was good!

No. He was so much more than that!

The crowd stood and stamped their feet as they yelled for more. Gaius Calpurnius Piso acknowledged their adoration with deep bows before finally relenting and performing another encore. His glorious, tenor voice rang truly through the great theatre, its acoustics enhancing the impact of its range, strength and quality.

When the enthusiastic audience finally allowed him to leave the stage and he'd reached his backstage room, he was greeted with jubilation by his friend Faenius Rufus.

'I hope Nero doesn't find out about this,' he warned, handing Piso a well earned drink. 'It's just as well he's left the city.'

'I'm just so damned tired of worrying about his ego. So he thinks he's the best performer ever on this earth. He already knows he's nowhere near my league. He just won't admit it,' Piso answered edgily.

'Be careful, he has a way of getting rid of competitors,' Rufus warned.

'Maybe someone will get rid of him first!'

Calpurnius Piso, wealthy, aristocratic and talented seemed to have the whole package. His fine physique, handsome face and amiable nature all added to his charisma. The only traits he seemed to have in common with Nero, his hated competitor, were his sexual appetites and love of ostentation and extravagance.

20

Pompeii

Via Stabiana

The House of Popidius
(The House of the Lyre Player)

How she loved this house!
Alessia halted at the entrance, her lyre held firmly under her arm, delaying the sensation of entering Valentina's home for a few more delicious seconds of anticipation.

She knocked softly.

'Hi, Alessia! Come on in. Valentina's waiting for you.'

'Thanks, Ameda.'

Alessia stepped through the narrow entrance. The huge atrium with its central impluvium opened out in front of her. Simultaneously, her senses reacted to the drifting, heady smell of incense and the musical tinkling of windchimes carried on a refreshing breeze. This huge house with its multiple gardens and peristyles was a place only fully appreciated by those with an artistic, creative spirit.

'Alessia, I'm just in the front peristyle.' Valentina's voice reached around the columns to her.

'I'm coming!'

'How are you, my dear?' Valentina rose from her chair.

'I'm well, thanks.'

'Would you like something to drink?' Valentina offered. 'The day's quite warm.' Her long, red hair was parted in the middle and tied back in a bun allowing the slight breeze to play around her neck and shoulders.

'Yes, that would cool me down a bit.'

Ameda left, returning minutes later with chilled wine and a bowl filled with segments of sweet, juicy oranges.

'So, what did you think of the last song I gave you?' Valentina asked as she sipped her wine. 'It's one that's considerably more difficult than any you've attempted so far.'

'I did have a few problems with some notes in the central section,' Alessia admitted.

'That's fine. We'll sort that out shortly. I thought we'd have the lesson out here today. It's too pleasant a day to miss any of it.' Valentina rose and pulled up a stool for Alessia to sit on next to her.

'I hope that Julius has been behaving himself!' Alessia glanced over towards the garden.

'Well, ever since you named him *Julius* he's been behaving remarkably well,' Valentina answered.

They walked over and peered at the stone, coiled snake that reared its head up beside the fish pond. Its body language and expression was highly aggressive and Alessia had been rather intimidated by it when she'd first begun lessons, even though she'd been told it was meant to bring good luck. In comparison she found the nearby, svelte statue of Apollo playing his lyre surprisingly reassuring.

'Alessia, don't worry too much if you make errors, but I'd like you to just play the song from beginning to end for me. Forget about the notes as much as you can and just enjoy the mood. Remember, it's a love song.'

Valentina sat down to listen. When the music had faded to its end she got up and walked a few paces away from Alessia, deep in reflection. The teacher turned back towards her pupil.

'When your technique matches your emotional input, then I believe you'll truly be an artist to contend with. We need to work on that. So far, Alessia, we've concentrated on your lyre playing. Today, let's move on to something else. What about that sweet song we practiced playing a couple of lessons ago. I'll play it today while you sing. It's your voice I'd like to hear now.'

'I'm a little nervous.'

'Don't be. We'll simply have fun with it.' Valentina sat and readied herself with her lyre. 'Alessia, just stand a few paces away facing me.'

The first lovely notes of the melody came from Valentina's lyre as Alessia waited. Then, she began to sing.

Valentina heard a voice so pure and a gift so natural that she almost doubted her own ears. The pitch of the voice was true and the tonal quality so sweet she was astounded. But most of all, it was the emotion permeating the song from a singer whose very spirit poured forth into it that enthralled Valentina. She'd never found a student yet, who could be taught that most precious of inherent qualities. It required an honesty and openness very few singers were ever willing to give.

The song ended.

Both teacher and student were still, Valentina with the sheer entranced shock of what she'd heard and Alessia still caught in the emotions of the song.

'Alessia, your true talent lies in your voice. I'd like to prepare you to compete in the city's music competition. It would take a great deal of practice but I believe you have the talent. What do you think?'

'I'd like to try if you're sure that I have some sort of chance. I wouldn't want to embarrass Lady Claudia.'

'If I thought that was a possibility I wouldn't even suggest such a thing,' Valentina reassured her. 'So, are we agreed?'

'We are.'

'Then I'll give Claudia a report on your progress so far and ask for her approval. Now, I think we need to have a look at that section of last week's practice piece that you said you struggled with.'

Alessia made her way home soon after. She was unaware of the delighted, surprised teacher she'd left behind.

———∞∞❧❦❧∞∞———

The Villa of Diomedes

'Fabritio, can you spare a few minutes?' Lucius found him working in the villa garden covered in dust from his sculpting.

'Of course.'

'Let's take a few paces around the garden,' Lucius suggested. Fabritio laid down his tools, dusted himself off and they began to walk.

'How are you finding the work here?'

'It's great. I'm enjoying the opportunity of sculpting these statues for the garden. It's always nice, too, to have the creative freedom that your father's given me.'

'I'm glad. I know how pleased father is and how much this villa means to him,' Lucius continued.

'I never thought in all the years Alessia and I spent in Tauromenium that I'd end up sculpting here,' Fabritio admitted. 'Something like this would've seemed like a dream.'

'It's Alessia I'd like to talk to you about, actually.' Lucius stopped walking and turned to face her brother.

'What about her?'

'Fabritio, I would have to be blind not to see how close you two are and how protective you are of her. That's as it should be and I respect you for it. I'm asking you to trust me.'

Fabritio looked somewhat puzzled.

'I don't need to tell you that your sister's special,' Lucius continued. 'I'd like your permission to find out if she can be rather more than that in my life. Will you do me the honour of allowing me to court your sister? I give you my word that I'll treat her with the utmost respect.' Lucius watched his face as Fabritio took in the impact of his words.

'There are few men in this world that I'd trust anywhere near my sister,' Fabritio anwered, 'but I believe you are one of them. I take you at your word.'

Fabritio and Lucius shook hands.

'Thank you for your trust. I'll ask her if she'll agree to go out with me.' Lucius turned and made his way back inside, leaving Fabritio watching thoughtfully after him.

The House of Popidius

To: *Lady Claudia Lucilla*
Via Villa dei Misteri

By Messenger

Greetings Claudia,

I hope this finds you well. I thought it was time I wrote to let you know how Alessia's progressing with her studies now she's been coming to me for some time.

As expected, she's an absolute pleasure to teach. Whatever I ask of her is always done and her commitment is total. She's turning out to be a more than adequate lyre player and I believe there's room for a great deal more improvement yet.

Today, however, I heard something totally unexpected. I decided to hear her sing. What a joy! What an exceptional talent she possesses! Rarely have I heard such a natural, gifted singer before.

Claudia, I told her that her strength of talent lay in her singing. I did not tell her, however, what I have told you. It's possible for a young woman such as Alessia, that it may place too much stress on her. I believe she must gradually come to recognise the depth of the gift that she possesses.

For the moment, she knows that I'm seeking your approval to prepare her to compete at the next Music Festival competition. May I do that with your blessing?

Love,
Valentina

The Villa dei Misteri

By Messenger

To: Valentina
  The House of Popidius
  Via Stabiana

Dearest Valentina,

Your message was such a surprise but a wonderful one. Who would have thought that Alessia was hiding such talent?

Of course I'd like you to go ahead and prepare her for the competition. Everyone's in for a huge surprise, I fancy, when they finally do get to hear her play and sing.

We must get together again soon. What do you think about next week? Perhaps, if you're free I can call on you at home?

Love,
Claudia

21

Villa Moregine
(Outside Pompeii)

They raged and cackled holding their flaring torches so close to him that he felt his hair sizzling and his nose screwed itself up with the smell of burning. Fire poked and probed his body until all the flames of Hades seemed to envelop it and he cried out in terror. Cursing and shrieking with the venom of demons the Furies pursued him. He ran to reach the river but they appeared in front of him barring his way.

Nero writhed and struggled until he was drenched in sweat. His eyes snapped open as he came out of the recurring nightmare that haunted his sleeping hours, and heard the same whispers he always did, as he returned to the world of reality.

You murdered your own mother.

He lay still, waiting to regain his composure.

Last night had been a pleasant surprise. The hotel really was outstanding and the food tempting. The women supplied for his pleasure were attractive and willing to sate his sexual appetite in whatever way he desired. The night had been good.

'See to my bath!' Nero shook off the remnants of his nightmare as he yelled for his attendants. Soon after, he was bathed, dressed and ready to face the day ahead.

On his arrival at Villa Moregine the night before he'd been given a tour of the hotel and restaurant by the owner then escorted to the most luxurious suite. He'd said little, simply listening and looking at what he was being shown. Now, he would have his say.

'We'll walk to the triclinium,' he stated.

Nero stood studying the fresco of Apollo. 'Get me the owner,' he demanded. Staff scurried everywhere. Within minutes Jucundus appeared at his side.

'As you're the owner of this hotel I presume you take responsibility for its faults?' he snapped.

'Yes, Caesar.'

'I have to say that this is one of the better places I've stayed in while travelling. There is one matter though,' he paused and the tension grew.

Jucundus wilted under Nero's glare.

'You have on this wall a painting of Apollo holding a lyre. His face bears my likeness.'

Jucundus nodded. He tried desperately to think why that could be a problem. He'd definitely meant it as a compliment.

'Make sure you have it altered. The lyre should be held with the other hand. Of course, you're aware, surely, that I'm left handed?'

Without another word Nero departed scowling, leaving the banker feeling both pleased and disappointed at the same time. Damn that fresco! If it hadn't been for that there would've been no fault to be found.

Jucundus still hadn't understood one important fact. Where Nero was concerned, there was always 'something.'

With the exception of Lucius and Marcus who purposely remained indoors out of sight all day, just about the whole city turned out to watch and welcome the Emperor. Even Alessia, Fabritio and Claudia walked down to Via dell'Abbondanza to catch a glimpse of him as he made his way towards the temple site.

As he drew level with them Alessia saw that Nero was a richly dressed young man some would call good looking. He waved languidly to the crowd without glancing in Alessia's direction as he passed. She caught only a momentary glimpse of him. His retinue was long and travelled in style. Amongst them she saw senators and a variety of courtiers and attendants. Nero passed by and continued the short distance to the construction site.

The consecration of this piece of earth was so very old. The prime, raised site still echoed to the worship of the ancient Samnite goddess of love, Mephitis. Long before the coming of Sulla in conquest, this land had been dedicated to a deity of love. The Roman goddess Venus inherited that mantle, becoming the patron goddess of Pompeii.

As the years passed, the temple suffered decay and fell into near ruin. It stood inside the Marine Gate beside Via Marina and adjacent to the huge Basilica, and could easily be seen by those approaching from the sea. As such, it was a powerful symbol of the city's wealth and artistic creativity. A plea for restoration funds had been answered by Nero, who responded with gold to rebuild the temple in marble.

To allow greater access to the temple, road widening had already been carried out on Via Marina inside the entry through the Marine Gate. This allowed greater ease of movement during special days of worship and for festivals.

Now Nero had come to assess what his money had achieved. Work had commenced early at the site on this day in the hope that the Emperor would be pleased to see the workers busy achieving his vision of the completed temple.

As the Emperor arrived, labourers toiled to lift the heavy marble blocks into position. Pompeii's new duumvir, Verus, welcomed Nero in a short speech of thanks then stood beside him on a raised dais as he watched the men working.

'Caesar, I trust that you're pleased with progress,' Verus ventured carefully, a small nerve twitching in his left eyelid.

'It's acceptable,' Nero replied grudgingly. 'How long will it take to finish?'

'The estimate is about another six months.'

'Just make sure that there's no tardiness amongst the workers,' Nero warned. 'I may very well wish to come down to worship here myself when the temple opens.'

'Yes, Caesar.'

'By the way, I trust that the amphitheatre is still closed to gladiatorial combat in accordance with my decree?'

'Yes, Caesar.'

'Good.'

Verus was pleased when the conversation stopped at that point and they stood silently watching. Suddenly, there was a screech nearby and they turned to see one of Nero's courtiers trapped by a large block of marble that had dropped from a pulley onto his foot. He'd strayed onto the construction site, and been unfortunate for an accident with the pulley to have occurred right where he was standing. Those responsible ran to help remove the block.

'Get that man a doctor!' Nero ordered. 'And arrest those workers!'

Chaos broke loose.

Verus looked on appalled. Everything happened so fast he barely had time to react. Before he knew it, the victim had been released and taken away, and the workers clamped in restraints and pushed into the back of a nearby caged cart.

Euxinus, a man standing in the crowd watched in horror as his son was manhandled away with the other workers. The young man looked desperately over his shoulder at his father one last time before he disappeared.

'Can you do nothing right in this city?' Nero thundered at Verus. He yelled for Burrus. 'We're returning to Rome immediately.' The two conversed briefly, with Burrus waving his arms around heatedly.

Watching, Seneca slipped away after a couple of minutes towards the back of the crowd. He followed the man he'd seen shouting to the prisoner he took to be his son. Eventually, as the cart disappeared and being unable to do anything to save him, Euxinus, highly alarmed, had decided to return to where he lived in order to decide what to do.

Seneca followed him to an inn. Satisfied, he returned quickly to the Emperor's retinue as it departed Pompeii. Exhaustive enquires and representations by Verus and others to the royal palace over several months, failed to locate the prisoners.

Several days after the event as Euxinus sat grieving the loss of his son, a messenger came to the inn. He waved a scroll in the air.

'I've a delivery for Euxinus.'

'That's me. What is it?'

'How should I know? Here, take it.'

When the man had gone, Euxinus sat down to open the sack. Inside he found a considerable sum of money and a message. It read:

From a friend who understands your grief. Use this money to search for your son.

It was unsigned.

Lorraine Blundell

Rome

Castra Praetoria
(Guard Barracks)

To: Sextus Lucceius
    Via Gherardo
    Ostia

Greetings Brother,

Pompeii's a strange kind of place.

I'm rather pleased to be back at the barracks, actually. It's good to sleep in my own bed again especially when the one I had down there was like trying to sleep on concrete it was that thin!

There's no doubt Pompeii's swimming in money with all its rich holiday villas and even the wealthy houses in the city. I could just about get used to living like that. Fat chance!

It's different from Rome, though. A few workmen got arrested—of course we copped that job—for dropping a block of marble on a stupid bastard who was on the site when he shouldn't have been. Of course, he was one of Nero's courtiers, wasn't he!

Anyway, the people just stood and gaped, even though not all of the workmen were slaves. They made no attempt to stop the poor bastards from being dragged away to end up the gods know where. If that was here, there would've at least been some attempt made to stop us taking them. Strange place! Maybe it's because it's basically a mix of holiday residents and those that really live there.

Afterwards, once we got back here, Nero ordered the prisoners to be taken to the Carcer. Looks like they'll be executed for treason within days. Seems a bit over the top to me considering what happened wasn't their fault. The way he's killing people off we won't have to worry about not having enough bread for everyone.

Your brother
Praxus

22

Lady Claudia's Villa

Ad astra!

Lucius paused as he reached the portico, watching Alessia who had her back to him. If he could only win her love, he had no doubt that this woman could take him from this world to the stars. The love he'd come to feel for her burned within him so intensely that now he couldn't envisage his world without her.

Claudia, having been informed of Lucius' intentions regarding Alessia, had wisely asked her to wait in the garden as Lucius was coming to see her. He watched as she stood holding her hand under the fountain's clear water trickling from Venus' amphora.

He'd really known from the first time he'd seen Alessia, that being with her had felt so right. It'd taken him some time to admit it even to himself, until he'd visited the villa several times after the conversation about her with his father.

'Alessia,' he greeted her, his voice friendly but casual. He wanted to make very sure that he didn't risk startling or frightening her in this initial stage of his courtship. It was obvious, that she was innocent in the way of girls who have not yet lost the outward presence that is forever changed by certain experiences.

Alessia turned and smiled.

'So here you are,' Lucius continued. 'I hope I haven't kept you waiting.'

'I've been here only a few minutes,' she smiled as he walked up to her. She wondered what he could possibly want. Claudia had steadfastly refused to tell her, saying that it would ruin a surprise.

'Do you spend much time here?' Lucius asked her, making casual conversation.

'Yes. I really like it. I enjoy watching the birds come to the birdbath each day.'

'Alessia, I've spoken to Fabritio. There's a special place I'd like to take you to see.'

'Now I'm curious,' she replied. 'Did he tell you that I'm not very good at waiting for surprises?'

Lucius laughed and walking to a nearby bench, beckoned to her to sit beside him. Claudia, unobtrusively watching nearby, thought how well he was handling the situation. She was absolutely delighted that her guess had been correct about his feelings for Alessia.

'No. But I take your word for it,' Lucius answered. 'Would you like to go out with me to see a unique place just outside the walls? Fabritio has no objection. That's if you're agreeable.' Older and far more experienced as he was, Lucius nonetheless found that he was holding his breath.

'I'd love to go with you. When will it be?' Alessia smiled.

Lucius relaxed.

'I thought in a couple of day's time. I'm sorry, but I can't stay right now. Father's waiting for me to go to the forum with him. I'll let Claudia know what time I'm coming for you.' They walked back together to the portico. Puzzled, Alessia stood watching his retreating back. Her stomach felt queasy. Why did Lucius want to take her on this outing? Did it mean something special or was he simply bored and looking for a companion? She already knew that she really liked him. Then she told herself to come back to reality. Why would a good looking, wealthy senator even look at her? The idea was insane. She decided that she'd try to simply enjoy what he'd offered—an opportunity to visit an interesting place.

That afternoon, Claudia interrupted Alessia as she was polishing the tables in the library. 'Alessia, please try this on and see if it fits would you?' Claudia held a silky soft, white, flowing robe on her arm. Attached to the shoulder was a three quarter length, diaphanous overlay of cerulean blue.

Alessia looked at Claudia enquiringly.

'Try it on first,' Claudia smiled, 'then I'll explain.'

Pre-warned of Lucius' intentions days before, Claudia had made certain arrangements. She'd taken a great deal of trouble to make sure the garment was perfectly cut. The robe fitted Alessia as if it'd been made for her—which it had. Softly feminine, it did little to hide the girl's curvy figure. Alessia had no way of knowing that what she wore had been carefully selected for a very important occasion.

'It's perfect!' Alessia exclaimed. 'How lovely!'

'Here's the veil.' Claudia placed it over the top of Alessia's hair just enough for it to stay in place when attached with a golden hair pin. It hung perfectly draped, displaying her face to perfection.

'I thought you might like something pretty to wear on your outing with Lucius,' Claudia explained. 'Also, he is a senator, after all. It wouldn't be seemly for you to wear something inappropriate.'

'Claudia, how can I ever thank you for all your kindness? Why have you been so wonderful to me?' Alessia asked.

'Because I think you're special, and I lost someone close to me once who was special too. I feel very fortunate to have you with me,' Claudia replied.

Alessia did what came naturally to her. She went to the older woman and embraced her. Claudia held her, her own face wet with tears.

———ooo-⦿-ooo———

Night was falling. The donkeys with their attendants, as well as four armed bodyguards waited on Via delle Tombe outside the Diomedes' villa. Although one of the Senators with no military experience, Lucius was capable of defending both himself and Alessia if it came to an altercation. He was carrying a weapon.

While still young, Marcus had employed an ex centurion to train Lucius in using a gladius and just generally being able to defend himself. The result was that he was very capable in that area. As he never bothered to mention it, however, very few were aware that he possessed those skills. On this evening he was taking no chances. He'd therefore engaged the services of bodyguards in the form of ex gladiators. Toughened by life and death combat in the arena, they were the best form of protection available.

'Fabritio, especially as it's a night visit, I wanted you to see the arrangements I've made,' Lucius told him as the two stood at the top of the steps.

'I hope you enjoy yourselves, I can't see any problems,' Fabritio assured him as he glanced down at the bodyguards.

'I'll go and pick her up then, and we'll be on our way.'

Lucius moved off with his retinue and they travelled the short distance in a leisurely fashion to Claudia's villa. Alessia waited somewhat nervously for their arrival.

'Don't worry, Alessia,' Claudia reassured her. 'I know you'll enjoy yourself!' She gave a shaky smile.

By the time Lucius arrived Alessia had composed herself and was looking forward to the evening. She was also rather curious as to what she was going to see that would need to be visited at night.

She walked towards Lucius as he stood waiting for her just inside the vestibule. She was still far enough away not to hear his sharp intake of breath, as he watched her approach. For the first time in his life, he felt his heart skip a beat at the sight of this beautiful woman.

The donkeys led them safely towards the city centre along Via della Fortuna. For some time after starting out, Lucius had been aware of the sweet scent of roses drifting across to him. He was unaware that Fabritio had given Alessia a bottle of Tullia's much loved rose perfume. He maintained that she didn't deserve it after the episode with the letter, but eventually, after some 'persuasion' on her part had handed the bottle over to her, saying that it was the most enticing perfume he'd ever smelt.

Now, Alessia sat on her donkey beside Lucius, unaware that it was affecting him in the same way that it had Fabritio. Aware that Alessia was not yet overly familiar with the city, Lucius pointed out several places of interest to her as they travelled.

'Are you going to tell me where we're going?' she asked eagerly as they turned onto Via Stabiana.

'No. I'm afraid you're going to have to wait to find out.' Lucius was amused when he saw the disappointment on her face. 'What I *can* tell you though is that it'll be worth waiting for.'

Down the dark, straight, long length of Via Stabiana they travelled, their way lit only by flares carried by their attendants. As they passed, she saw the ghostly walls and doors of numerous houses semi-lit by the flares. They cast a yellow glow throwing strange shapes among the shadows. The continuous clip clopping of the donkeys' hooves on the hard, basalt street paving stones sounded almost hypnotic.

Alessia began to think that the road would never end. Ahead of them she saw the shadowy outline of the arched Stabian Gate leading out of the city and before much longer they'd reached it.

'We'll stop here for a few minutes. Would you like a drink, Alessia?'

'No thank you.'

Lucius helped her off the donkey and led the way to the wall at the side of the arch. He beckoned to an attendant to hold his flare up. Alessia saw two wall niches, one small, the other above it, much larger. The interior of the largest had painted plaster and inside the niche stood the highly coloured statuette of a goddess.

'Who is that lady, Senator?' She peered closely at the figure.

'I think it's time you called me Lucius, don't you?' he smiled at her. 'To answer your question, this is the goddess Minerva. She stands here to protect the gate. There's actually an altar underneath the small niche, but you can't see it any more. It's been replaced by the larger one where people leave offerings. See, over here there are a couple of small bowls.

'I'm afraid I know little about that sort of thing Fabritio and I didn't really pray to the gods,' Alessia replied. She studied the offerings and statuette with interest. Personally, Lucius thought that that wasn't such a bad thing. She could always decide to do so if she wished in the future.

'You'll notice as we continue, too, that there are a number of graves here.'

'Are they what we've come to see?' Alessia asked, a little disappointed.

'No. We still have some way to go yet,' Lucius explained. He smiled to himself in the darkness at her impatience. That trait, one she herself had mentioned earlier, was now on display. 'We'd better move along or we'll be very late getting back again.' Lucius motioned to everyone to move forward.

They mounted the sleepy donkeys and rode on. As they travelled, the trees around them became more dense and the road, little more than a track. Eventually, they stopped.

'Come, Alessia,' Lucius held his hand out to her to dismount. 'I'll help you down.'

They made their way forward slowly. Lucius was pleased with his choice of this particular evening for the visit. It was still and utterly devoid of sound except for breaking twigs beneath the feet of their bodyguards. They followed in a circle around the couple just far enough away from them to allow privacy, but still close enough to successfully intervene should danger threaten. The sky was clear and sparkling with tiny stars and the moon had risen casting its cool, white light over the scene.

Lucius glanced sideways at Alessia's face as they entered the clearing. Their first sighting of the brilliantly coloured, perfectly formed Doric temple in the moonlight, held an ethereal quality. A temple to Bacchus had stood in this place for centuries.

'Alessia, this is the temple of Bacchus.'

'How incredibly beautiful it is!'

As she spoke Alessia turned, her face uplifted to him. It was possible that she'd never look more lovely than she did at that moment. The moonlight enhanced her natural beauty blended as it was with awe and innocence.

Lucius would have given everything he owned to kiss her as they stood together in front of the temple. With an inherent discipline he drew back, both out of deference to her as the woman he now hoped one day to marry and because he'd given his word to Fabritio.

They walked to the couches and tables set around a small altar in front of a ramp leading to the temple portico. Richly coloured grapes, a wine cup, a female figure and a panther, all symbols of the cult of Bacchus, decorated the pediment.

'Do people still worship here?' Alessia asked in a hushed voice.

'Yes, the temple is still in use, even quite often at night.'

'Is this a place, then, where I could learn to worship the gods?' Alessia was finding them quite interesting. Perhaps, she thought, she should learn more about them.

'I think this particular temple wouldn't be suitable,' Lucius replied, having in mind the emphasis he knew was placed on drinking and debauchery at this particular temple. It had been built outside the city walls for that reason. 'I'm sure, though, that there would be a place of worship just as impressive and more suitable for you elsewhere.'

He pointed out to her an ancient inscription worked into a mosaic on the ramp leading into the temple. It read:

Ovius Epidius, son of Ovius, and Trebius Mettius son of Trebius, aediles.

'Those are the patrons who funded the building of the temple,' he explained.

'Then they certainly succeeded in building one that's both graceful and inspiring.' Alessia knelt to run her hand slowly over the inscription. It was smooth to the touch, worn down by the tread of numerous feet.

'Alessia, I think we should go now,' Lucius suggested. He was finding his resolve running very low as to keeping his word to Fabritio. He took her hand and together they walked back to the donkeys. Both were silent for much of the return trip into the city, lost in their own thoughts.

'Did you enjoy yourself?' Lucius asked as they stood in the vestibule of Lady Claudia's villa.

'More than I could ever have imagined.'

'Alessia, I'm returning to Rome tomorrow. I'd like to stay longer, but I've already extended my holiday here as it is. I'm afraid I must return in time to sit in the Senate when it reconvenes. I'll come back at the earliest opportunity. In the meantime, would you mind if I write to you?'

'I'll look forward to it,' she replied, blushing.

Lucius bent to kiss her on the forehead. Then he turned and without looking back, left the villa.

By Messenger

To: The Innkeeper
The Inn of Euxinus
Via di Castricio
Pompeii.

Greetings Euxinus,

I write with a heavy heart to inform you that your son is dead. He was executed by Nero's order several days after being taken from Pompeii.

You have my profound sympathy for your loss. I felt that it was best that you should know, however, rather than living with false hope and continuing to search for him. If some of the funds I gave you still remain, please use the money for whatever purpose you wish.

A friend

PART II

62 A.D.-63 A.D.

23

Panataria

(Ventotene)
25 Miles South West of Rome

62 A.D.

Octavia first noticed the tiny speck far out on the horizon as dawn's rays broke night's darkness. She had been here for several days since Nero had exiled her for adultery. In truth, she knew he'd simply become bored with her. She hurried to her bedroom to replace her nightgown with one of the few possessions she'd been permitted to keep with her in exile. She removed the long, cream robe from the drawer, even now admiring the gold edging on its hem. It was her favourite.

She stared into a mirror, moving it from side to side to show the different angles of her face. The high cheekbones remained unchanged, but she looked much older now than her years. Her face was drawn, her eyes lifeless and her once shiny, long hair dull and drab. Quickly, she wound it up into a bun.

Octavia was aware that no one would probably ever know, but she cared that she should look her best on this day. Perhaps, it was because she was still until her death, Empress of Rome the greatest city the world had ever known and she had an inbuilt sense of duty and dignity.

In her heart she had known what her end would be when Nero had murdered their brother, Britannicus, by forcing the woman Locusta to poison his food. She had known then that the gods had not intended a long life for her, either. For a short time she'd been protected by the support of Agrippina, but even she ultimately could not control the madman who held ultimate power.

Apart from its location, Octavia had no complaint about the villa to which Nero had sent her. It was a delusional indulgence overlooking the ocean. Great care had been taken in establishing magnificent gardens and rolling lawns. The villa's marble floors swept out to the bathhouse that hung precariously over the very edge of the sea where the waves pounded

137

onto the rocks. Brick steps led down into the tepidarium the water's colour accentuated by its blue, mosaic floor tiles. Built by Augustus, the villa lacked nothing to ensure the pleasure of its guests.

Octavia saw that she'd been right. The faint speck had now become a boat. It was too small to be one of Rome's merchant ships. She very much doubted that visitors would have been given permission to visit Panataria and the likelihood of rescue was remote. That left only one possibility. This would be the last day of her life.

In one way it was almost a relief. She was imprisoned on Panataria Island just as surely as if she had been in a cell. It was a beautiful gilded cage, but no less a prison. She must compose herself before her executioners reached the island.

Octavia sat curled up on her favourite couch looking out to sea. She prayed for the courage to face the ordeal that would soon confront her. She would attempt to do so with dignity and acceptance. She rose, sat at her desk, picked up a stylus and began to write *'Testament . . .'*

—ooo◦)◦(◦ooo—

Silently they slipped into the small harbour of Panataria. As expected, they were completely alone.

'Decius, get your men together. We need to get going.'

'Yes, sir.'

Praxus and the four legionaries made their way towards the royal villa. He wasn't looking forward to doing his duty today. He'd been taken aside and informed that he'd been selected to carry out this task. Praxus found it both sickening and unnecessary.

The island had a wild beauty secluded and frequently pounded by wind and waves. Octavia and a single servant were the only present occupants. Panataria had a history of cruel executions and today would be no exception. The servant stood waiting for them as they reached the entry. As had to be expected, Octavia almost certainly would have seen them arrive. She was the type of woman he really liked. Regal, gracious and pretty, she was admired and respected by Rome's citizens for her generosity and obvious concern for their welfare. She didn't deserve this fate.

They entered a large atrium dominated by a huge marble statue of Augustus. No expense had been spared to lay floor tiles made of coloured marble from North Africa and marble busts lined the atrium. They progressed from room to room through the villa moving nearer and nearer to the sound of the sea.

'This is Lady Octavia's sitting room,' the servant told them, pointing at a closed wooden door. She withdrew, leaving them standing there.

'May I enter, Lady Octavia?' Praxus knocked at the door.

'You may enter.'

'Decius, keep the men here,' Praxus told the legionary. 'I'll call for you when I need you.' He opened the door, entered, then closed it behind him.

He found himself in a spacious, light room opening out towards a bathhouse. Octavia stood up from her chair as he came towards her.

'Do you know why I'm here?' Praxus asked her gently.

'I believe I do. The time has come has it not, for me to die?'

Praxus felt his throat tighten.

'My lady, I would have it otherwise, but you're correct. I must do my duty, but I will do so as quickly and painlessly as possible. You have my word.'

'How is it to be done?'

'I've been given orders to open your veins. Your blood will drain from your body until you are dead,' Praxus replied. 'Lady Octavia, may I be so bold as to offer to hold you for support while that is done?' Praxus' eyes revealed his pain at this crime of which he was to be a part.

'You're kind, please do. Also, here is a document I wish you to take back to Rome.' She handed him a scroll. 'Be assured, I do not hold what you are to do against either you or your men.'

'Thank you. Lady Octavia, I'll call them in. From now on I want you to look into my eyes and nowhere else. Do you understand?'

She nodded.

'Decius, bring the men with you,' Praxus ordered.

As they entered the room he turned Octavia to face him so they were standing close together, her arms stretched down by her side. He saw the flicker of fear in her eyes as she realised Decius had drawn his gladius.

'Remember, look at me. You'll feel the sting of the blade only briefly.' Praxus nodded to Decius then held her gaze with his. As she looked into his grey eyes Octavia had a fleeting feeling that she'd looked into those eyes before, but the sensation passed as quickly as it had come. She flinched as the cuts were made with the gladius. Praxus steadied her with his arm. As her lifeblood slowly drained away he eased her into the couch. Eventually, her eyes glazed over as her body slumped and her spirit left her. He found that he had tears in his eyes.

'Decius, do what you must do. I'll look for a suitable burial site,' Praxus ordered gruffly as he left the room. He found a shaded place under a cypress pine in the garden. She would have liked his choice, he hoped.

139

What Praxus had not told Octavia, was that the new, future Empress, Poppaea, had demanded that her head should be removed from her body and brought back to Poppaea in Rome. He also omitted to tell Octavia, or anyone else, that when she began to bleed but was still alive, he'd been ordered to suffocate her in a vat of boiling water. Since receiving his orders Praxus had always had absolutely no intention of carrying out that act of the drama. It was enough that an innocent woman had to die. He'd selected the four legionaries himself and knew that they wouldn't talk. No one else would ever know the details of her death.

The grisly task complete, Octavia's headless body was laid to rest. Praxus paused to murmur a prayer for the safe journey of her spirit then the executioners made their way back to the harbour. No one spoke. The slave had fled but would eventually die of starvation.

On the horizon the boat again became a small speck that finally completely disappeared, those on board grateful to have left the island of death. Octavia's scroll lay unread tucked into Praxus' uniform.

The nightingales hid in the trees at Tauromenium.

Panataria
9th June 62 A.D.

TESTAMENT

I, Claudia Octavia, direct that this Testament be given into the safekeeping of the senior Vestal Virgin and desire that that she carry out my wishes. I respectfully request that this document be read aloud on the Forum rostrum after my death.

First, I wish to state my love for Rome and its people. It has always been my honour to strive to uphold the dignity and wellbeing of the city and its citizens. I bear no ill will to those who have sought my destruction, for whatever reason. I can only believe that in some way I'm seen as a threat to them.

Second, I issue a warning to those who wield power over Rome's people. They need to be careful of the level of cruelty, corruption and self indulgence now evident, that threatens all that is good and worthwhile in Roman society. There is a more just, gentle and humane way.

Claudia Octavia

24

Rome

The Royal Palace

No! Stop! You stupid cow!
Poppaea's shrill shrieking sent her maid running from the room, bent low to avoid the glass perfume bottle that whizzed over her head, completely missed the door and smashed into the wall. The sweet smelling, golden contents dribbled slowly downwards like drizzled honey.

Poppaea rubbed at her scalp, her lovely face wearing an expression more suited to that of an old hag than a future empress. How hard could it be to dress her hair without digging pins into her head! How she missed Farzana. Her touch was so gentle, her manner so caring.

Poppaea smoothed her silk robe with her hands and considered the situation. She and Tigellinus might even eventually work well together sometime in the future. If ever he found his goals straying from those of Nero then who knew what could happen? She'd seen stranger alliances formed.

She could celebrate the fact that at the moment her future looked bright. It'd been Tigellinus who'd come up with the idea of using a charge of adultery to get rid of Octavia. Not that the people had bought it. But who cared what they thought, anyway. That naïve little 'butter wouldn't melt in her mouth' twit had been cooling her heels exiled on Panataria. Eventually, Nero had listened and ordered her death. Not without a great deal of cajoling—but he'd finally done it.

Octavia's head had been brought to her early this morning. What a ghastly object! She'd taken a look that was just sufficient to confirm whose head it was, then promptly ordered the bloody object burned.

The divorce was still to come. Nero considered it simply a formality. She knew that she was on the edge of a great victory which would put her within spitting distance of being Empress of Rome. She was determined that the only way she would be stopped now, was over her dead body.

—◦◦◦—◦◦—

Evening

'You may enter.' Poppaea looked ravishing in a long, green robe which highlighted her flame coloured hair. She wore at her neck a strand of priceless green emeralds, a present from Nero for this evening's banquet and matching emeralds swung from her ears.

'This has just arrived for you.' A servant bowed and handed her a scroll.

'Has the messenger gone yet?'

'Yes, Lady.'

'You may go.'

Poppaea opened the scroll and began to read its contents. She was surprised to see that it came from the duumvir of Pompeii. She was somewhat less surprised when she saw what he wanted. She tossed the opened scroll onto her table and left the apartment. After that little incident with Octavia's head this morning, she was more than ready for the evening's food and entertainment. There was one thing certain about Nero, he knew how to throw an incomparable banquet.

Roses, roses everywhere.

Roses in vases and petals all over the floor. Plush couches imitating their red, pink and white colours decorated the huge room. Hanging from the ceiling were numerous garlands and one wall had even been repainted so as to feature a large fresco with a rose garden setting.

Guests arriving for the evening were showered with petals as they reached the portico. They entered the banquet room to be further surprised by the highlight of the decor for the evening. In the centre of the room a huge replica of an open rose had been built. At its centre, enjoying the attention stood a young girl, naked. She smiled a welcome.

She'd been painted pink!

In her hand the girl held a basket of roses. She was already old enough to have inviting breasts. As time passed and she became tired she was replaced by a different girl—and so the evening went on.

Poppaea sidled up to Tigellinus who was watching as he lounged by a pillar. 'So, this is what five thousand gold pieces buys,' she whispered, referring to the un-named patron who'd sought Nero's favour by offering to pay for a special banquet. The unexpectedly extravagant cost had nearly financially ruined him.

'I wouldn't know,' Tigellinus replied, in a matter of fact tone. 'I don't concern myself with such trifles.'

Poppaea walked away towards a group of court ladies who fawned upon her as the Empress 'to be.' So, she thought, Tigellinus thinks he's too high and mighty to have discussions with me. One day, all that may change.

'Lady Poppaea, will you favour us with your presence at my house tomorrow morning? You may remember there's a Bona Dea gathering to raise clothing for the poor of the city,' pleaded one of the women.

'I'd be very pleased to attend but it may only be possible for a short time.'

A loud gong summoned guests to dinner, saving Poppaea from further discussion. She made her way to the royal couch walking unescorted, straight through the centre of the room as guests opened out before her like a retreating swell of water. She felt their eyes on her, greedily sizing up the richness of her robe and especially the emerald necklace she wore, as its brilliance winked in the light of the candelabras. Her presence oozed the confidence and authority appropriate to an Empress of Rome. This was Poppaea's moment. She used it well.

There was a fanfare of trumpets as Nero made his own ceremonial entry. Strolling to Poppaea's side as she was seated he whispered in her ear, 'who could have expected that something like this would be created? The day will come, I tell you, when I'll build a palace that will make this room look no better than a whore's brothel cell.'

All eyes were on Nero, as he turned and walked slowly away from her towards the girl in the rose at the centre of the room.

Poppaea gritted her teeth.

Taking the girl's face in his hands Nero kissed her roughly then ran his hands lingeringly over her body.

The night was still young.

Pompeii
Administration Offices

To: The Lady Poppaea
   The Royal palace
   Rome.

Greetings Lady Poppaea,

I send you best wishes and thoughts from the citizens of Pompeii. We trust that we'll soon see you back here for a visit to your home city.

I write in the hope that you might consider intervening, by using your favoured position with the Emperor, to lighten a punishment recently levied on Pompeii. I refer, of course, to the ten year ban on the holding of gladiatorial games.

You are the people's last hope. The loss of their games is a heavy price to pay and they're languishing under the burden.

I pray you will consider this request.

With Pompeii's best wishes,

Claudius Verus
Duumvir

Lorraine Blundell

Rome
The Royal Palace

The Apartment of Lady Poppaea
By Messenger

To: Duumvir Claudius Verus
Administration Building
Pompeii.

Greetings Duumvir,

How delightful it was to receive your message from the people of Pompeii. I miss the city and its citizens.

I have good news for you!

The Emperor has graciously consented, following my explanation to him of how grievously the ban has affected Pompeii, to modify the ban. In two years time you may once again hold gladiatorial games.

I trust that this development is of assistance. Please give my best wishes to all.

Poppaea

25

Praetorian Guard Barracks

Three drops of precious blood.

Sextus Afranius Burrus watched, riveted, as they fell onto the crumpled bed covering. It was almost as if they belonged to someone else. It had been such a small nick with his gladius.

He could end it all right now.

Maybe he should. Just a couple of quick slashes with the gladius across his wrists would be all it would take. The sword that had so many times saved his life could be enlisted to end it.

Which was better? He laughed hoarsely. It was a laugh of bitterness and anger. Should he allow the poison he was sure had been slipped to him under Nero's orders to take him to the gods or do it himself? One part of him wanted to slit his wrists to deny that murderous, insane monster the satisfaction of killing him. The other, wanted to fight for life to the very end. He wondered which course of action really took the most courage.

Burrus had no doubt that Nero was responsible. When he'd begun to feel ill his thoughts had turned immediately to recent events in Pompeii. He'd made the mistake of remonstrating with Nero after he'd ordered the arrest, let's be honest it would really be the deaths, of innocent workers at the temple of Venus. He should've known better. Now over sixty years old, he'd broken his own golden rule.

Keep your mouth shut!

His thoughts were interrupted by the sound of approaching footsteps. It wouldn't totally surprise him if Nero, deciding he was dying too slowly, had sent a lone assassin to finish him off. He looked expectantly towards the door.

'My dear friend, what has he done to you?' Seneca strode quickly to the bed, his face creased with lines of concern.

'I see you've come to the right conclusion,' Burrus answered sadly, grasping his hand.

'It wasn't difficult. I saw the incident in Pompeii. What does the surgeon say? Is there nothing to be done?'

'Only to finish myself off with my sword. I was debating that course of action just before you came in.'

'No! You've been too spirited a man and risen too many times to challenges defending Rome to take that course. Many may call it honourable. In this particular situation, I see it simply as an admission that you've acted improperly which most certainly, you have not. It's murder and nothing else. Let the record show it.' Seneca lifted a cup of water to Burrus' parched lips.

'I'll stay with you until the end. If I need to be absent for even brief periods I'll call my wife to remain with you. My friend you will not die alone!'

Burrus relaxed for the first time since he'd suspected his fate. He'd lived a long life. There were worse ways of dying than with a close friend by his side.

'Come. No more of this. We'll talk together of our visions for Rome. This city will still be here long after we're both gone. Now, tell me, what are your dreams for her?'

They talked until a veil of darkness began to descend on Burrus' beloved city. As he finally lay sleeping fitfully, Seneca sent a messenger and a litter to collect his wife. She kept watch while Seneca went to his bed for a few hours sleep.

The next morning Seneca was once again alone by his friend's side as he retched uncontrollably and writhed in pain. Early in the afternoon Burrus motioned to Seneca to bend towards him and murmured, *'all is well with me.'* Mercifully, soon after, he breathed his last.

The final barrier had been crossed. Seneca returned to his house and sitting at his desk wrote messages setting up a meeting, supposedly to discuss literature, with Calpurnius Piso, Faenius Rufus and his nephew, Marcus Lucanus.

Nomentum
(14 miles outside Rome)

Via Nomentana
Seneca's Country Estate

Seneca, his nephew Marcus Lucanus, Calpurnius Piso, and Faenius Rufus sat huddled together in the simple, farmhouse kitchen. Unlike some of his other luxurious estates, the house was basic, almost spartan in its furnishings and part of a farm with a small, unprofitable yield.

Dinner was cooking as the shadows deepened and Seneca's wife Paulina prepared a meal of stew and bread to be accompanied by wine of questionable quality for their guests. Seneca's tastes were basic but that wasn't an issue on this particular evening. He and his visitors had much more to worry about than the quality of wine from his vineyards.

Rufus had posted a lookout to look and listen for any sign that there were visitors approaching on the dark, lonely road. Not that the meeting would have looked like anything else other than friends coming together for a meal and a discussion on literature. Still, it always paid to be careful. A variety of literary scrolls lay on the table just in case of trouble.

Seneca got to his feet to speak. 'My friends, we mourn the passing of our good and noble friend, Afranius Burrus, but if our work here goes as planned he will not have died in vain. Faenius, your promotion to his post as Prefect of the Guard is a real stroke of luck! Your influence will be enormously helpful in achieving our goal. Marcus, my nephew, is known to all of you. He carries little weight politically but as a known poet, he does provide us with an additional shield for our activities as a literary group.'

They turned their eyes to Marcus Lucanus. He appeared calm and held their gaze with a look of determination.

'Calpurnius, as for yourself,' Seneca continued, 'I believe we all acknowledge that our goal is to offer you to the Senate and the people as a legitimate replacement for Nero once we can eliminate him. I believe we all realise the danger we face from this day forward. There is no dishonour in withdrawing now and your promise of silence will be respected. Does anyone wish to withdraw?'

No one moved or spoke.

'Let's move forward by choosing a code word. If you've no objection, I've chosen the word *Phoenix*. I believe it's appropriate. There are connections with the location I'm proposing as our meeting place from now on. Also, I believe it represents our goal. That is, of course, to raise from the ashes the dignity and pride of the Senate and people of Rome by dispatching Nero, who is obviously insane.

As for our meeting place—I believe I'll be able to cultivate a relationship I'm presently working on which will supply us with a safe, reliable and totally unsuspected base—in Pompeii.'

'Why Pompeii? Why not here in Rome?' Rufus queried.

'We won't meet often,' Seneca replied, 'but when we do it has to be somewhere none of us is known to have any prior connections. There is one man I'm hoping to recruit who may not meet those guidelines, however, he hasn't yet been approached and may not wish to participate. We must be extraordinarily careful with our recruiting. There's no rush, we must take our time. Already a number of senators have come to me proposing exactly what we're discussing tonight. So far, I've neither encouraged nor discouraged them. They include Senators Natalis, Quintianus, Araricus and Gratus but there are many more.'

'We need evidence of Nero's crimes, Seneca,' Piso said firmly. 'We must have sound facts to present to the people after the assassination.'

'An important role has been played in that regard by a brave and resourceful woman,' Seneca answered. 'Her name must not be spoken outside this room in connection with *Phoenix*. We must protect her at all costs. I speak of the senior Vestal, Cornelia.'

There were surprised looks from the other three.

'She's acted in accordance with her conscience by passing to me extensive, incriminating material against Nero. Her reputation is stainless. The evidence is solid and so repulsive that we'll have absolutely no problem convincing either the Senators or the people of the Emperor's guilt. More than that, I'm not prepared to say right now. I intend to resign from the Senate, which will remove me further from suspicion and Nero's gaze. Those of you who remain will be well able to co-ordinate those within that body.'

Seneca sat.

'For my part, there are certainly somewhere between six and ten guards close to me who'd commit to the cause and who could be totally trusted,' Rufus offered. 'Of importance is that most are of the rank of tribune or centurion.

'Good. Good,' Seneca murmured, pleased.

Calpurnius Piso stood to warm himself by the fire. He somehow managed to look at home in this setting, so different from the luxury and wealth of his usual environment. One of his positive attributes was that he had the common touch when necessary.

'If no one objects, I'd like to clarify the situation even more precisely,' Piso suggested. Rufus nodded to him to go on.

'The planning that must go into this if we're to have any hope of success is huge. There's much to be decided such as where Nero is to be assassinated, who'll do the job and what our actions will be immediately afterwards in terms of the people.'

'I agree completely.' Lucanus spoke for the first time. 'The two qualities we'll need in abundance are patience and silence. This venture won't happen overnight. If the slightest hint of this gets out in the meantime— we're dead men!'

'Rufus,' Seneca addressed him directly. 'More than the rest of us you have one particularly difficult problem. His name is Tigellinus.'

A sombre mood settled over the group.

Nero

Rome

The Royal Palace
Prefect Investiture Ceremony

This man, Tigellinus, will be my right hand.

Burrus certainly took his own sweet time about dying.

No one questions my decisions! No one!

He'd grown old and forgetful of his place. By the time this is all over, I will also wipe the cringing senators of this city from the face of the earth.

Tigellinus has been around long enough to know who his master is. He's greedy for wealth and ambitious for power, but I will tie his fate to mine with a bond so tight that he will cease to breathe should he dare to defy me. Today, I'll give him a taste of the success that comes with my favour, so he craves for more!

'Ofonius Tigellinus, I hereby promote you to the position of Prefect of the Praetorian Guard, to be held jointly with Prefect Faenius Rufus. Congratulations.'

26

Pompeii

Alessia sat on the grass in the garden reading Lucius' letter. It was the first one she'd received from him since he'd returned to Rome. She'd spent many an hour gazing up at the ceiling of her room, at the fresco on her wall, or out of the window since then, wondering just what his feelings were for her. She thought that this letter gave her reason for optimism that perhaps it really was more than just friendship. Did she dare hope?

Of course she would answer immediately. No. Maybe she should wait a few days? She wished that she'd had more experience in knowing what to do. There really was only one thing she knew how to do and that was to be herself.

Alessia may not have known it—but she'd chosen one of the very traits about her that was so attractive to Lucius. She read the letter again.

Rome

The House of Lucius Diomedes
The Caelian Hill

To: Alessia
The Villa of Lady Claudia
Via Villa dei Misteri
Pompeii

Dear Alessia,

I trust that you're still enjoying the birds coming each day to the birdbath! This is the first opportunity I've had to write as I've been so busy in the Senate and there hardly seems to be enough time even for sleep.

I trust that you're well. I'm sorry I had to rush away so quickly after our visit to the temple, but I hope you understand. Please write and tell me any news as to what you've been doing lately.

As there wasn't really time before I left, I'd like to tell you how unbelievably beautiful I thought you looked last time I saw you. If I shut my eyes I can see you now sitting on the donkey beside me. How are you progressing with your music lessons from Valentina?

It's the end of another long day so I must try to get some sleep. Do please write to me, dearest Alessia, so I have something to look forward to. I will return to Pompeii as soon as I can, but that may not be for a while yet.

With my affection,
Lucius

As Alessia sat down to write back to Lucius, she knew she was falling in love with him.

Lady *Claudia's Villa*
Via Villa dei Misteri
Pompeii.

To: Senator Lucius Diomedes
The Caelian Hill
Rome

Dear Lucius,

It was so wonderful to hear from you. It sounds as if you're really busy. Even if you enjoy what you're doing, it must be very tiring for you.

Thank you for what you said about how I looked on the trip to the temple. I'm sure most of it must have been the incredible dress I was wearing that Claudia gave me. She really has been like a mother to me. I'm so very fortunate. I had an incredible time that night.

Fabritio sends his best wishes. The music lessons are going really well. Valentina is now teaching me singing as well as how to play the lyre. I really love the days I go to music lessons and I especially love her house. It's amazing!

I met Tullia the other day. (I'm not sure if you know, but she's the girl Fabritio's been spending time with.) She seems to be a very sweet person, but she's always rushing here and there. She's even worse than I am!

Our cook, Azura, let me try my hand at cooking dinner the other day. I made stew but it was terrible! No one could eat it. Just as well she'd made something else so at least we didn't go hungry! She probably knew better than to trust my efforts! I can't think of any other news for now. It would be lovely to hear from you again soon.

With affection
Alessia

A smile of real pleasure lit Lucius' face as he read Alessia's reply. She was so genuinely unaware of her beauty and so honest. She was the only young woman he'd ever known who hadn't tried to 'play games' in an effort to lock him into a relationship. He was also really glad he hadn't been there to sample the stew. Would he have lied and eaten some of it to please her? Oh, yes!

Anyone could as well stop the winds from blowing and the waters from flowing as stop lovers from loving

Pompeii - Graffiti

27

Rome

Praxus hurried from the barracks and through Rome's streets, his red cloak swirling behind him. He had such a look of purpose that it caused others to step quickly out of his way. Why his errand was quite as important to him as it unquestionably was, he felt only in his heart. But there was no doubt that he had a sense within him that with the death of Burrus, the rise of Tigellinus and the increasing insanity of Nero, a watershed moment was fast approaching. What that would mean for him personally he wasn't too sure yet.

He did know that he hated Tigellinus. He had absolutely no doubt that the man would have knifed his own mother if it advanced his career. Hopefully, thought Praxus, he would be under the command not of Tigellinus, but of Faenius Rufus.

The future. Maybe that's what it was really all about. He'd seen too much—too much cruelty, too much killing, too much corruption. Was it time to find a different life for himself? Alone except for his brother in Ostia, so far he had no partner or even close friends in whom to confide. Burrus had come the closest to filling that role. Now he was gone. Praxus felt anger flow through him for the death of a man who'd done nothing but his duty.

It was time to think about the future.

The Forum baked in the sweltering heat. Water gushing and spraying out from the fountains did little to cool the street paving stones. People, animals and produce alike wilted under the sun's blistering, relentless blaze. Sweat ran from Praxus' armpits and down his back, soaking through his uniform. He pushed through the crowd and behind a vendor with squawking chickens desperate to escape from the furnace-like heat into the shade.

'Watch it! Push me again and I'll take you apart!' the vendor yelled irritably as Praxus pushed by him. The chicken owner turned to find himself looking into the steely eyes of the praetorian.

'I didn't see you,' he muttered, backing away.

Praxus ignored him.

On the next corner one of Rome's many street poets defied the heat in an effort to gain recognition, if not glory. Those of his kind seeking literary acclaim produced work of varying quality, ranging from utter drivel to the occasional poetic gem. Their spruiking was generally ignored or responded to with a rolling of the eyes.

Praxus turned into busy Via Argiletum and five minutes later entered the empty shop of a scribe. The man was a specialist in his trade. He was also a copyist. He looked up from his work as the praetorian entered.

'You've come at the right time,' the grey haired scribe commented briskly. 'I've just finished the work you ordered.' Rising, he drew a document from one of the pidgeon holes that lined the shop's walls.

'How much do I owe?' Praxus enquired.

'For a member of the Guard there's no fee,' the man answered.

'I insist that you charge me the usual fee.' Praxus held his hand out for the document which he unrolled on to the counter.

'Thank you.' The scribe was unsure what else to say. It was highly irregular. The praetorians always wanted work done for nothing.

'In that case, the fee is two sesterces.'

Praxus paid him.

'I do require *something* of you though,' Praxus told him as he re-rolled the scroll, satisfied with the copy.

'Yes?' The scribe cocked his head to one side.

'Forget that you've ever seen me and what you copied here today from the original.' Praxus' eyes held those of the scribe.

'I have already forgotten,' the older man told him.

Praxus left the shop, walking towards the centre of the Forum and the temple of Vesta. The doors to the Senate were closed but the doors to the temples were open, giving sanctuary from the heat to those who decided to enter. That is, all except the temple of Janus nearby. Nero had long ago ordered the doors closed which was normal practice during times of peace. Garlands of flowers had been hung across them.

'I'd like an audience with the senior Vestal,' Praxus requested of the young priestess who answered his knock at the temple of Vesta.

''I'll ask if she'll see you,' the girl replied. 'Please wait here. You may not enter further. What is your name?

'My name's Praxus of the Praetorian Guard. My business with her, however, is personal not public.'

Shortly afterwards, a slim, older Vestal, still of attractive appearance came towards him. She looked puzzled as she studied him curiously.

'May we speak privately?' Praxus asked.

'As you will know,' Cornelia replied, 'I may only speak to you within public view. Come over to the bench just here.' They sat within the public portico.

'My name is Cornelia. How may I assist you?'

'I'm here to keep a promise to someone I greatly respected,' Praxus began. 'Here is the will she wished to have handed to you.' He handed the copy of Octavia's will to Cornelia. 'Now, I have kept faith with her.'

Cornelia slowly read the will.

'There's only one way that could be the case.' Her eyes met his. 'I'm so sorry. Am I correct in assuming that you were present as she died?'

'I was.' Praxus looked away.

Cornelia, experienced with those carrying personal burdens, read the emotion in his face. 'I respected her greatly too,' she said softly. 'Be assured that I will carry out her wishes.'

'Thank you.' Praxus stood to leave.

'There's one more thing,' Cornelia asked. 'This is a copy. Where is the original?'

'With someone who'll forever remember her sweet face,' Praxus replied. His voice was so low that she barely heard him.

'Be at peace.' Cornelia laid her hand briefly on his arm as lightly as a butterfly—then left him.

The Castra Praetoria
(Praetorian Barracks)

'He's been a bit weird lately,' Gaius remarked to his fellow guard.

'I agree. You don't suppose do you that he's fallen in love with some rich widow somewhere?'

'Surely you're not serious!' his friend laughed. 'I suppose stranger things have happened, but he's so quiet and keeps to himself. I can't even imagine him socialising with a woman.'

'Well there's something wrong with Praxus and it'd be interesting to get to the bottom of it.'

'Ssh. Here he comes.'

Praxus walked past without even seeing the two guards, he was so lost in his own thoughts. As soon as he reached his room he hid Octavia's will under his mattress, along with the knife that was always there.

The Castra Praetoria stood close to the city's boundary. A large, high walled fort, it was the barracks for Rome's Praetorian Guard. Grey, forbidding and heavily guarded, it was both home and training facility for the men who were stationed there. With higher rates of pay than other soldiers and an intimidating reputation, these men considered themselves the most elite of the elite. For Praxus, it was home.

28

The Royal Palace

Lydos stood hesitantly on the top step leading to the lower level of the palace, listening to the distinctive sound of falling water. Earlier in the morning he'd received an official directive that he was required to attend at the art gallery for special duties. He walked slowly downwards, his movements athletic, so that his feet barely seemed to touch each step.

Dark haired, with features that rivalled those of the god Apollo, Lydos was strikingly good looking as well as intelligent. He found himself walking over marble flooring featuring a pattern of squares with borders outlined in the colour of the sea. The young Greek slave's eyes widened as his gaze was drawn upwards to the intricately decorated ceiling lavishly adorned with gold and lapis lazuli. One after another, masterpiece after masterpiece followed along the length of the frescoed walls. This art gallery took his breath away. It was also empty.

Steps faltering, he entered the next room into a world that reason told him couldn't exist, except that he knew he wasn't dreaming. The floor featured hand painted tiles decorated with brown and green leaves in nature's vibrant shades. However, it was one of the long side walls, seeming to go on forever that finally halted Lydos' steps. The wall curved with both strength and grace and along its length a fountain sent cascades of water tumbling down to a pool below. The huge room was completed by a lush, sunken garden and a small, twelve pillared summer pavilion.

'I'm glad you're on time!'

Lydos turned towards the sound of the voice. His heart sank as he recognised Terpnus, Nero's music tutor, striding towards him.

I know you're only new here,' Terpnus smiled. Reaching Lydos he ran his fingers lingeringly along the slave's arm, then caressingly through the younger man's luxuriant, wavy black hair.

'No doubt you'll be summoned to attend to the needs of the Emperor before long. I believe we should get to know one another now.' Terpnus' eyes travelled over the muscled physique in front of him as he savoured the idea of sampling such a delicious treat first, leaving Nero to take the 'leftovers.'

Lydos struggled to hide his revulsion as he was led into one of the bedrooms off the art gallery. The intoxication of aromatic Lebanese cedar wood pervaded the room which was richly decorated with intricately carved Moroccan turquoise painted artifacts. A variety of bottles of scented oils of varying sizes had been placed on a side table beside the bed. Terpnus closed the door and opening the top of a small, glass bottle containing an exotic oil from Damascus, sniffed its contents appreciatively. Removing his tunic he turned to the slave indicating that he should do the same.

'So, Lydos, shall we begin?'

Praxus prodded one of the malingerers with his gladius. 'Get your arse up the hill! While we're still young, pal—or in your case, still ugly!' The round-up of scruffy beggars and layabouts from around the steps of the Forum temples and public buildings continued. Nero had demanded the attendance of several dozen of them at his private stadium at the palace that afternoon. There would be hell to pay if Praxus and his three fellow guards didn't turn up with an audience. The many other citizens going about their business in the Forum no doubt appreciated the improved appearance of their surroundings, now free from the low-life who normally hung out there.

Dirty, half drunk and scowling the motley group of vagrants arrived to form part of a very unusual audience. Even the slaves waiting for them turned up their noses at the new arrivals. At least the palace slaves were reasonably clean. There was no doubt that most of the newcomers smelt appalling. They settled into place in seats offering the best view in Rome and began to titter and giggle stupidly behind their hands at the unexpected rise in their status.

Set into the natural hill of the Palatine, the seats overlooked the Emperor's private gardens and the Circus Maximus below. On the lawns covered with a carpet of wildflowers wealthy villas of the elite had been built near the palace, but at enough of a distance to allow for royal privacy. The guards took up their positions. Praxus was in no mood to play nursemaid to this lot. Having become right royally drunk with his brother the night before, he was nursing one hell of a hangover. His tongue felt disgustingly furry and his head had the thump of a dozen catapults roaring inside it. Anyway, how ridiculous was this situation? He'd be glad when it was over.

'Stand up!' The group stood on command as the Emperor ceremoniously exited one of the side doors of the palace dressed in the uniform of Rome's champion 'Greens' racing team. He headed for the chariot waiting for him in the gardens below, where he was aided by the freedman, Icelus, who held the horses steady. With an imperious raising of his arm to signal the start of the practice session, Nero took the reins, whipping the horses into action. They were a well matched team, the steadiest on the inside anchoring them, preventing the quickest and most volatile on the outside from veering off course. Nero had been around horses for many years and now, having enjoyed considerable practice, had become skilled. He was determined to race in the Circus. The crowd were shown baskets of free bread to be handed out later as a bribe to encourage them to cheer—loudly.

—ooo▪◖◉◗▪ooo—

Slowly now. Breathe In. One, two, three.
Hold. One, two three.
Breathe out. One, two, three.
Relax.

'How many more times?' Nero was growing frustrated and bored. The earlier practice session with his beloved horses had gone so well and to so much applause, that he'd been quite overwhelmed by it all. These ridiculous, constant singing exercises were annoying to say the least.

'Caesar, you said you wanted to be the best. This is the only way. I warned you that you would have to be willing to persist with the work,' Terpnus stated firmly. 'All great artists must pay a price for their gift. We've come so far it would be foolish to give up now.'

'So you think there's been improvement?' Nero asked, looking slightly mollified.

'Of course there has, Caesar. Do you think I would waste my time otherwise?'

Wasted was the last thing it had been, Terpnus thought, content after his morning with Lydos. His 'nest egg' was growing very nicely in one of the banks in the Clivus Argentarius while he lived a life of luxury. As for Nero's voice, it was of average volume at best and tended to have a husky tonal quality that was downright uninspiring. As far as he could hear, it had not improved at all despite the variety of exercises, diets and emetics used to solve the problems. That, however, was of no concern to the Greek.

'I think more fresh air would be good for your voice,' Terpnus suggested. 'Why don't you take the litter and give your subjects the pleasure of catching a glimpse of you?'

'An excellent suggestion,' Nero replied readily. 'That's just what I need.' He smiled broadly at his teacher who responded by bowing humbly. A few minutes later Nero was taken in the royal litter to the Forum by uniformed bearers, where he waved magnanimously to anyone who stood gawking nearby.

———∘∘∘-◆-∘∘∘———

The seer, Cleander, had been waiting for many days in all kinds of weather for an opportunity to get close to the Emperor. He couldn't believe his eyes. Unexpectedly, here was his opportunity. He could see the royal litter travelling towards him as he stood in front of the temple of Saturn. As the litter drew alongside, he held something out towards Nero who took it, more out of surprise than interest.

'Stop!' The litter bearers stopped instantly. 'Bring that man here!' Nero ordered sharply. The Praetorian Guards formed up around the litter their breastplates shining, each of them with his hand on his gladius, eyes alert for trouble. The old man was shabbily dressed, his beard untended and his hair scraggy. His eyes, however, were bright and animated.

'Caesar, beware of conspiracies. I bring you something to protect you,' the seer wheezed.

Nero studied the graceful ivory figure standing on its round base. Interesting.

'Let him go. He means no harm.' He pulled out several coins from his purse and pressed them into the old man's hand.

Cleander was bodily picked up and relocated unhurt a few feet away. The litter continued on, but the Emperor's interest was no longer on fresh air, greeting his subjects, or, surprisingly, on the seer's warning. The figure he held was that of a beautiful young woman with long hair and an honest, direct gaze that seemed to see inside him to his very core. Nero stared at it mesmerised.

The nightingales hid in the trees at Tauromenium.

Lorraine Blundell

Rome
The Royal Palace

To: Dareios
   Amnisos, Crete
   Greece

My dear brother,

I can only pray to Zeus that this message reaches you. I'll continue to send word whenever I have enough sesterces to pay for a messenger. I hope that you're well. I'm truly thankful that you weren't with me the day I was taken captive from the boat.

I can assure you that I'm in good health and fortunate at least, to be still working in the palace where there's ample food and somewhere to sleep. Today I have the unusual task of caring for a statuette of a lady. She's really exceptionally beautiful. There's something very pure and spiritual about her. She reminds me of the young women back home in Amnisos. My heart aches to be back there.

The Emperor's music teacher is a nightmare. How I wish he'd never noticed me, I'm sure you can guess the situation. I long for the gentleness of a woman's touch and to caress the curves of a woman's body, but I'll never have that here.

A shrine has been built in its own special room in the palace with marble, flowers and candles. Nothing but the most expensive frankincense is used. The Emperor comes three times daily to worship and sacrifice, sitting for long periods just gazing at the statuette. It seems to have some kind of a hold over him. I can't say I'm surprised—there's definitely something very special about whoever the sculptor used as a model. Nero believes, however, that she's not an ordinary woman but a goddess. Perhaps that's because I've heard it said he follows no other religion.

I hope that fish are still jumping into your nets! Please write when you can. One day I'll find my way to freedom. In the meantime, I'm determined that I'll do whatever I must to survive.

Your brother,
Lydos

29

Orange blossoms, jasmine and roses combined to perfume the air of the Palatine with a heady, indolent feeling of wellbeing on a perfect Roman day. It was late on a morning completely devoid of sound except for the musical gurgling of nearby water falling and the slight, pleasant hum of passing bees' wings.

Nero reclined in the pavilion looking sulky and displeased. Although Seneca was still far from absent in public life, he'd finally retired from the Senate. Nero saw less necessity these days to defer to his opinions in any way. The other thorn in his side, Burrus, was now also gone—permanently.

This morning, however, he'd found himself having to justify his judgement in relation to the mangy citizens of Rome. He chafed at the fact that he was forced to endure them from time to time. Poppaea and Tigellinus had joined forces to argue with him, that he should give the people a gift to celebrate the royal wedding. This, they said, would sweeten them up after their annoyance at the death of Octavia.

Why should he sweeten them up?

As far as he was concerned the people were there to do his bidding—not the other way around! Burrus had learned the hard way not to tell him what to do!

A soft breeze rustled through the gardens—otherwise, there was silence. Nero relaxed and looked around him with pleasure. This really was the closest place to paradise on earth. Not far from where he lay, a fountain several metres high its base decorated with crescent shaped shields, tossed cooling plumes of water into the air. It was surrounded by sweeping vistas of petunias so purple they were the colour of royalty.

Paradise.

He'd had terraces made covered with lush greenery that seemed to hang in the air before falling to earth as if defying gravity. Throughout the the gardens stood priceless marble sculptures placed to show them off to best advantage. For a while he drifted off into a light sleep.

Bang! Bang! Bang!

Nero jolted upright. Livid with anger, he went searching for the cause of the noise. He found it soon enough. Close by, in the direction of the Forum, workmen continued the building of the cryptoporticus he'd ordered.

He entered its gaping, black mouth.

'The Emperor. It's the Emperor!' The cry ran the length of the portion of the underground tunnel already completed.

The first section of the vault was wide and covered with fine, white stucco decorated with cupids. The tunnel was spacious enough for at least four people to walk abreast easily.

'You may keep working,' Nero ordered, somewhat mollified at the reason for the disturbance. These days he was becoming more and more concerned about his personal safety. When this tunnel was complete he would no longer have to publicly leave the Palatine to reach the Forum. Building it had been an excellent idea.

At the moment, the cryptoporticus was a bare shell, only partially complete. When it was finished its walls would be frescoed and its ceiling a soaring, vaulted delight. Nero left to get ready for an afternoon that he expected would not be quite so delightful.

---oo○❄❄○oo---

'Get out of there you sod!' The praetorian shoved a burly onlooker who was trying to break through the cordon.

He drew his gladius.

The man retreated.

The Forum was packed beyond its limit. Law advocates, vendors, merchants, inn keepers and vagrants all rubbed shoulders in the throng of curious onlookers. On the fringes of the crowd several litters were drawn up, their occupants watching proceedings in comfort. Sidling through the mob, vendors did good business selling their vinegary wine to thirsty, sweating spectators. The general atmosphere was neither one of celebration nor hostility, but rather of curiousity.

The Emperor had called for a post wedding celebration and all of Rome seemed to have turned up. Trumpets blared as Nero and Poppaea, surrounded by praetorians, stepped onto the Rostrum. Poppaea, her hair swept up, wore a long, golden robe and translucent veil. She drew herself up to her full height, looking every inch an Empress. A slight breeze played with the veil moving it gracefully around her, as gemstones worn at her neck and wrists caught the sunlight.

Groups of senators and courtiers stood to one side watching curiously and somewhat cynically. They knew only too well, that Nero was not given to displays of affection for Rome's citizens. He signalled for quiet, waiting until he had the crowd's full attention.

Fellow citizens of Rome!

I've called you here today to share the joy of the royal wedding. It is only fitting that my subjects should join in the celebrations!

Many faces in the throng were restless and surly. A muttering began and swelled. They chanted one word—

'Octavia.'

Nero continued, undaunted. When he had the desire, he wasn't lacking personal charm. On this occasion he used it to the full.

We remember with fondness sweet Octavia, who has now left us. It's time to look forward to the future. Look at the beautiful Empress who stands before you. How could you gaze upon her and not be moved by her grace and beauty? We must all work together to strengthen Rome and make her great. I have a surprise for you today so that you will always remember the wedding of Nero and Poppaea with joy!

The people, distracted, appeared somewhat appeased. A few watching more intently than others, had also noticed that from all of the high vantage points in the Forum, legionaries had positioned themselves with large bags. In front of and below each of them was a solid cordon of soldiers. At Nero's signal the bags were opened.

Silver, shining in the sunlight, rained down suddenly onto the people beneath. Handfuls of sesterces were thrown into the crowd some of whom were struck by the coins falling from a height. As soon as they realised what was happening they began to push and shove and to scramble and scrabble on their hands and knees on the Forum's filthy pavement stones.

The Forum could be a dangerous, even deadly place.

An area enclosed on one side by the Palatine, with restricted space due to large, crowded buildings and having few access points, the Forum allowed gatherings of large crowds little opportunity for escape. Bully boy thugs were often hired to cause trouble as well as injury. On this occasion, however, the main danger was about to result from the very human response of desperation, on the part of hungry, joyless people.

They screamed, laughed, shrieked or yelled with pain as they fought desperately for the coins. Many were trampled underfoot as the peaceful gathering turned into one of mass hysteria. A smile appeared on Nero's face. This was more fun than he'd anticipated. No one could say that he didn't look after the welfare of his people. It was rather enjoyable, though, he couldn't deny, seeing them down on their hands and knees. After all, that was exactly where they belonged!

Lorraine Blundell

After the spectacle was over the bodies of the dead men, women and children were dragged away. Many senators and courtiers remained, watching. Piso, Natalis, Lucan and others glanced at each other. The time to move on assassinating Nero was growing closer.

Mons Vaticanus
(Vatican Hill—dedicated to the goddess Vaticana)

Nero's Circus.

The obelisk reached forever upwards as if to touch the stars. In this place of ancient Etruscan settlement long since gone, a new group of people had gathered. Flares held by attendants cast flickering light not on Roman inscriptions, however, but on the symbols of ancient Egypt.

Towering above them standing majestically inviolable, that remnant of ancient civilisation, stolen by Caligula, looked down upon the new master of the world. A slit of a moon cut into the night sky threw an ethereal light on to the obelisk as it witnessed a madman's obsession.

'Hold the chariot steady!' Nero clad in the uniform of the 'Greens' strode to the team of horses and stepped into the chariot to take the reins. Several groups of attendants and praetorians stood nearby, watching.

'Now!'

Lydos dropped the white cloth.

The chariot hurtled forward down the long, first stretch of the circus, carrying Nero around the curve of the central spina. His eyes glittered as adrenaline pumped through him and his green cloak streamed behind him. The straining, sweating horses completed the practice laps without mishap.

Afterwards, they were led away to be pampered.

Nero stood acknowledging the cheers and applause of all present. The day and evening had been most enjoyable. He wondered why he'd ever worried about safety at all.

Everyone loved him—didn't they?

30

Pompeii

Pompeii didn't *do* ugly derelict and uninviting. It didn't know how, at least in the face that it presented to the world. Nothing could have emphasised that more to Fabritio than his first sighting of the city's large, commercial harbour. It looked like a slice of make believe snatched from a luxury dream world then gently set down at this spot on the Campania coastline.

Jetties lined along their length with gleaming, coloured statues jutted out into the water. He stood watching, fascinated. The port functioned not only to serve Pompeii, but also the towns of Nola and Nuceria. It was in constant chaos, teeming with life and noise. The babble of different languages mingled with the raucous cries of the fish mongers, hawkers and off key street musicians to produce a unique cacophony.

Numerous fishing boats had pulled into the harbour and were unloading their day's catch. Beside them larger boats rode at anchor with human and animal cargo as well as other merchandise.

The variety was endless.

Goods from the ships' holds ranged from reeking slaves who'd passed through markets such as those in Ephesus, to a variety of silks, frankincense and amphorae of luxury wines and grain from Sicily. Amber came from Gdansk to enhance the charms of upper class ladies and the highest quality olive oil from North Africa was also being unloaded.

Exotic birds squawked and preened displaying flamboyantly hued feathers of emerald greens, sunny yellows and fiery reds the colour of flames. The city's merchants made a fortune from their sale to elite villa owners from the Campania coast who proudly displayed them in cages to admiring dinner guests.

Pompeii was not just an importer of goods. Those exported from the city also reached around the Empire. The Eumachius family as well as other successful entrepreneurs, exported garum and fine wool as well as wines in considerable quantities from estate vineyards such as those of the Villa Regina.

Fabritio stood idly watching for a while then made his way to the office of the merchant he was seeking. Following Marcus' directions he soon found it nearby. The building was one of the better maintained on the docks, located not far from the official tax collectors' booth where those in line waiting to pay taxes for importing goods coming into port were impatient. The two collectors calculated the tax, mindlessly stamped the necessary documents and took the money, then waved each merchant through. Rome's treasury officials had long ago worked out that taxing goods was a highly lucrative business. Time had proven them correct.

Fabritio strolled into the merchant's office nearby. He found the place busy and was ignored by its staff. 'I've been sent to pick up an order for Magistrate Marcus Diomedes. Where can I do that?' he questioned the nearest person who came past him.

'See that counter over near the desk? Ask there and they should be able to help you.'

'Thanks. I'll do that.' He went over to the counter indicated, where the clerk looked up wearily at him, eyes bleary.

'Wait there and I'll bring it out to you,' he responded when told of Fabritio's request. 'It arrived here earlier this morning.' He disappeared into the storage room, returning a few minutes later with a large crate.

'Thanks. That was quick,' Fabritio complimented him.

'Don't thank me,' he replied, 'it's our business policy when dealing with someone of the rank of Magistrate Diomedes to hop to it when they want something.' He lowered his head and went back to checking his lists. To all intents and purposes Fabritio had ceased to exist.

Marcus had warned him that the goods he was collecting would have to be carried by donkey, so he'd come prepared. The journey back to the villa on the other side of the city took him some time. It was a typical, pleasant Pompeii day. Occasionally, Fabritio wondered how on earth he and Alessia had ended up here. Life was never predictable! He set off and arrived at the villa just as Marcus was taking a break from his writing in the study.

'That's great, Fabritio,' Marcus thanked him. 'Can you spare a few moments from your work on the Apollo statue? I'd like to discuss something with you.'

'Of course.'

'Come into the study and take a seat.' Marcus led the way. 'It's quite a walk to the harbour and back. Would you like a drink before we begin?'

'Actually, that'd be welcome,' Fabritio replied gratefully as he settled into one of the couches.

They engaged in small talk for a few minutes. A servant arrived quickly with the cups and set them down in front of the two men.

'The statue of Apollo will be finished soon will it Fabritio?' Marcus enquired.

'Yes. I've not much more to do. Are you happy with it?'

'That's what I wanted to talk to you about,' Marcus replied.

A look of concern flitted across Fabritio's face.

'It's wonderful, there's no need to worry,' Marcus reassured him. 'In fact, it's so sublime that it's set me thinking about your future. Your work here for me is almost finished. Of course, there's some possibility that Rufus may have something for you at his country house. I've been meaning to ask him. However, I have a business idea to put to you.'

Fabritio listened with obvious relief.

'For a while now I've been thinking of investing in some sort of business venture here,' Marcus continued. 'In my opinion, Pompeii desperately needs a quality sculptor's workshop to cope with the needs of local and nearby estates. Until now, demand has basically had to be met by word of mouth, or giving work to those in your trade just passing through. I'm afraid most of the time the results have been less than satisfactory. Fabritio, if I supplied the funds to buy a vacant building, would you be interested in owning your own workshop? We would, of course, need to agree on a certain percentage of the profits to be paid to me as the investor.'

Marcus waited with interest for Fabritio's reply.

'I don't quite know what to say,' he finally blurted out. 'It's an opportunity I can't refuse. To say I'm grateful is hardly enough.'

'You deserve it. You're highly talented and the type of man I like to have around me. In the hope that you'd be agreeable,' Marcus continued, 'I've searched around the city and I think there's a suitable place on Vicolo delle Nozze d'Argento. That area is away from the major houses yet still close enough for customers to reach easily. Shall we walk over and take a look at it now so you can tell me if you like it?'

'I'd be glad to.' Fabritio's head was in a spin. In the space of one day, seemingly his life and fortunes had changed forever.

Marcus rose and held out his hand. 'It looks like I have myself a business partner. Let's take a walk.'

———∞o∘❋∘o∞———

It was with a sense of unreality that Fabritio took a slow, leisurely walk with Marcus on the way to what could well turn out to be his own sculptor's workshop. After reaching Via Vesuvio they turned into the small, offshoot of a road where the promised building stood.

The first thing that met his eye was a painted advertisement on the wall for other property, obviously also for tenancy, by the owner of this building they'd come to inspect.

The Arrius Pollio Apartment Complex
Owned by Gnaeus Allius Nigidius Maius
FOR RENT from July 1st.
Streetfront shops with counter space,
Luxurious second-story apartments
And a townhouse.
Prospective renters, please make arrangements
With Primus, slave of Gnaeus Allius Nigidius.

Marcus unlocked the door of the house and they walked in through the narrow entryway into a long hallway off which was a small, but well lit room with a large window in the side wall.

'I thought this would make a good office or waiting room for your customers,' Marcus suggested.

'It's perfect. All it needs are chairs, a table and a couple of small couches,' Fabritio said, almost to himself.

The second room along the hallway was larger and obviously meant to be used as a bedroom. Fortunately, the ceiling was high, adding a spacious feel to the room. They continued on to the third and final room. It contained a small, neat kitchen with an oven and limited food preparation space, as well as a toilet area to one side.

'This could almost have been especially built for what I'd need,' Fabritio enthused, delighted with the layout.

'Out here's really what you need to see though,' Marcus told him enthusiastically as they walked to the back door. 'This is what really sold it as far as I'm concerned.'

The building had obviously been constructed not just as a house, but also as a live-in workshop of some kind. Exiting the back door, they came to a large, roofed area, perfect for Fabritio to do his sculpting.

There was a garden of sorts, but it was very small and probably only of use to hold an eating area and tiny fishpond. One solitary olive tree stood forlornly in the corner. Whoever lived here would not have the benefit of growing their own produce. Fabritio hoped that Tullia wouldn't mind that the garden was so small.

'Having a larger garden is the least of my concerns,' he commented. 'The main thing is that it has a good sized work space and pleasant living areas.'

'I'm glad you like it, Fabritio. Are you sure it meets your requirements? Once I buy it, there's no changing our minds,' Marcus warned him.

'That's one worry you won't have. Before you do, though, you need to tell me what the return to you will be. I'm a hard worker and I should be able to make good money.'

'We should go over now and see if we can make the purchase first before someone else does,' Marcus suggested, already walking towards the front door. 'After that we'll go back to the villa and I'm sure we can agree on a suitable arrangement.'

Fabritio could hardly believe his luck. He couldn't wait to tell Tullia.

Anataolia
Ephesus

The man was middle aged and stooped beyond his years. He gulped in huge mouthfuls of oxygen. After the reeking, hell hole of the ship's hold, the air of Ephesus was pure and lifegiving. He found himself on the ship's deck, blinking into the sunlight after a voyage that had been like a nightmare.

'Get moving! We're running out of time and time's money!' The overseer herded him along with the others towards the long, straight Arcadian Way leading into the centre of Ephesus. His bare feet felt the sting of the hot paving stones underfoot as they walked, it seemed forever, past the impressive gymnasium, until reaching Marble Street and the Great Theatre that loomed up before them.

He had to give the Romans their due. They knew how to build a city. The Great Theatre was one of the most impressive in the Empire but he knew that it wasn't their final destination. What awaited them wasn't entertainment.

Turning right, past the shops of the commercial forum, they walked by marble statues and fountains. They were starving and almost delirious from the smell of the food stalls.

'You first lot. Yes you! Get up here!'

They climbed onto a dais. They'd reached the slave market.

Inspected by those waiting, and displayed like animals, the bidding continued until almost all of the slaves had been sold. The man wondered what would happen to those who were obviously unwanted. He could take a good guess. He'd been bought by an agent who stood marking off the purchases on a list. No doubt he had several clients waiting to receive their ordered merchandise.

Sooner than he'd expected, the slave found himself back on a ship. This time it was bound for Pompeii. When he arrived he found himself in one of the many villas in that city. His value was not much more than that of a cog in a well oiled wheel.

31

Via di Castricio
The Inn of Euxinus

Pelting rain swept sideways by the gusting wind lashed the painted sign on the front wall of the inn. The storm had been coming since the darkening of the sky in the late afternoon. As evening fell, it ripped Pompeii's calm asunder with a howling fury unprecedented in its destruction and violence. The trunks of the umbrella pines swayed drunkenly, whipping to and fro in a satanic survival dance.

Euxinus, a big, thick set man, sat with his head in his hands oblivious to the mayhem outside the door. The last of his customers had taken his leave as the storm approached. The few rooms upstairs for visitors were unlet and Euxinus had the inn to himself. He was so engrossed in his thoughts that he'd lost track of time.

There was a sudden pounding on the inn door that startled him out of his melancholy musing. Wrenching open the door he found himself face to face with a hooded figure drenched from head to foot.

'Let me in before I drown out here!'

Euxinus stepped back quickly as the unknown visitor almost stumbled into the room. The innkeeper, remembering his duty to a customer, ran to get a covering to wrap around the woeful figure.

'Are we alone?' the visitor wanted to know.

'There's no one else here or upstairs,' Euxinus replied. 'Why do you ask?' He looked curiously at the wet form now revealed as an older man, tall and slender, with silver hair.

'It's time, I believe, Seneca answered, 'that you and I had a conversation. 'Could I have wine, please.'

Euxinus poured two cups of wine and put them on the table where Seneca was now sitting. He sat opposite him.

'I'm a friend,' Seneca began. 'You'll no doubt remember my messages and the money I sent you?'

'Of course I do and I'm grateful, but what I have never known,' Euxinus answered,' was why. Who are you?'

'Before I answer that, I'd like to know as honestly and as openly as possible, your opinion of our Emperor.'

'Surely, you can take a guess what my opinion is!' Euxinus exploded, jumping up from the bench. 'I didn't know it was possible to hate as completely and as intensely as I hate Nero. My son was innocent. Nero took his life with no more thought than the time it took to snap his fingers. I know it's not possible, but if it was, I'd crack him in two like a broken twig!'

Seneca smiled slightly.

'I believe I may be able to do something about that.'

Euxinus sat again.

'Would you be willing to be part of a group of patriotic Romans who are presently planning to dispatch Nero and replace him with someone more suitable?'

'By the gods, yes! He's taken away everything I had to live for. There's no one now to even pass this inn on to. At least that would give me some joy out of all this.' Euxinus buried his head momentarily in his hands once more.

Seneca patted his arm, the texture of the man's tunic feeling rough against his hand. 'Would my identity be safe with you?' he asked carefully.

'In view of your mission, I don't want to know your identity,' Euxinus replied. 'I can't tell your enemies, whoever they may be, what I don't know. It's better that way.'

Seneca regarded him with a new respect. 'Quite true,' he murmured. 'Euxinus, what I'm asking of you, is a meeting place at this inn for the men involved in our venture. We dare not meet again in Rome. As you'll understand that does, however, mean that you'd also be in imminent danger if our purpose here was discovered.'

'My life ended the day Nero took my son. This inn is yours to use as you see fit.'

'We would also need to be able, occasionally, to have several of our men lodge upstairs in your rooms,' Seneca continued. 'There would be, of course, more than adequate payment for the use of your facilities including the rooms. Do we have an agreement?'

'I don't know who you are, and I don't want to know,' Euxinus declared, 'but if you can successfully get rid of Nero, you'll have done this world a favour. You have my hand on it.'

'I don't suppose you'd have a room for tonight for an old man, would you? Seneca smiled. 'It's not a night to be out in.'

The innkeeper led him upstairs to his best room and having placed more wine on the table wished him good night.

———∘∘∘❧❦∘∘∘———

Seneca heard occasional, scattered showers against the shuttered window as he lay summoning the energy to face the day and an appointment with an old friend. His tiredness these days felt so ingrained it never really left him. When he emerged from the room he found Euxinus waiting downstairs for him, breakfast already laid out on the table.

'You slept well I trust, my friend?' the innkeeper enquired.

'Sometimes tiredness is overpowering enough to bring sleep's energising relief,' Seneca answered.

'You're welcome to remain here for as long as you like.'

'Thank you, but I must go, Euxinus. I'm grateful for your hospitality and support. I'll be in touch from time to time. Those who come here from me will always have the same code word.'

Euxinus looked up enquiringly.

'The code word is *Phoenix.*'

'So, you've seen the sign painted on the front wall of the inn,' Euxinus stated.

'I have indeed. A phoenix stands above two peacocks.'

'That's correct.'

'Then it shall be our code word. I find it exceedingly appropriate.' Seneca stood, shook hands with Euxinus and raising the hood of his outer garment, began the long walk across the city to meet a very dear friend.

The sky was gradually clearing of clouds. Much more comfortable now that his clothes had dried, Seneca unobtrusively walked through Pompeii's inner city streets apparently paying little heed to those around him. It was the start of a busy time of day with servants hurrying towards the vendors in the forum, workshops opening their doors and travellers entering or leaving the city. The noise level was escalating quickly.

Every one of Seneca's senses was alert, assessing if anyone was watching or following him. He bent once to re-adjust his shoe, glancing quickly around him, and a little further on in his journey, stopped suddenly to peer into the workshop of a lamp maker. He saw no one behind or beside him who appeared in any way suspicious.

Reaching Via del Vesuvio he passed through the Vesuvio Gate, pleased that he was almost at his destination. His aching bones told him that he wasn't getting any younger.

Euxinus

If I could turn back time I would.

The nightmare I wake to every morning of my life will never end. The pain of knowing I'll never see him again is bad enough, but guilt gnaws away at me. If only I hadn't insisted he take work at the temple he'd still be by my side.

My son! My precious son!

32

Pompeii's city wall had thirteen defensive towers. Marcus stopped, looked up at the nearest tower and corrected himself mentally. Actually, now there were really only twelve, one having recently fallen into disrepair. It had been many years since Pompeii had felt any need to worry about its defences. Roman rule had brought the city peace.

Marcus walked along Via delle Tombe and alongside the city wall not far from his villa. He stood waiting patiently for Seneca further along the pleasant, grassed pathway that led to the next tower, the Torre di Mercurio. His expression was troubled. He thought he knew why Seneca had asked to meet him. In the many years they'd known one another, he was anticipating that the meeting to come would be the only time he'd refuse a request from his old friend. That their friendship was strong enough to withstand the impact of his decision, he had no doubt.

Marcus was loyal to his few, true friends, to a fault. The one thing he would not give, however, was the life of his son. He watched as Seneca came into view. How much older he looked now, Marcus thought. This talented man whose intelligence, wit, oratory brilliance and literary works never ceased to awe him looked old and exhausted.

'My friend, it's been too long,' Marcus greeted Seneca as he reached him.

'You've often been in my thoughts though, Marcus,' the other replied as they embraced.

The two men smiled broadly. There was always between them a comfortable acceptance of one another that required little conversation—except today. This was a matter of no small consequence.

'Where should we talk? Is this safe?' Seneca enquired looking around him.

'We can rest our backs against the wall of the tower,' Marcus replied, glancing up at the high, limestone and lava tower beside them covered in white plaster. 'Standing where we are, we can't be approached or overheard without knowing about it.'

Seneca nodded his approval. From where they stood they looked down from a high vantage point and could also see open spaces beside and behind them. The rustic look of the countryside outside the defensive walls met with the noise and filth of the city within.

'We're at the start of a venture that I believe will gather momentum of its own accord from here,' Seneca began gravely.

'You're speaking of Nero, I presume?'

'Yes. He's a madman. There's been so much cruelty and murder and not one of us either feels, or is, safe. He's highly volatile.'

Marcus shook his head. 'My friend, are you sure of what you're undertaking?'

'If Nero's not replaced he'll virtually wipe out the whole Senate before he's finished.'

'I see.'

'Marcus, I know you must have misgivings but we don't intend to do this tomorrow. It'll be some time before all of the planning is complete. I'm not such a fool as to take unnecessary risks.'

'I know. Nonetheless, I feel it's too soon, even so. Too many of the people still admire him. They don't know who he really is. Without a majority of the people behind you, there's no hope of success.'

'You've been away from the Senate. You don't know what it's like now,' Seneca responded, his agitation obvious.

'Seneca, it's too soon!'

The two men stood silently together.

'Marcus, because of our years of friendship, I'm approaching you today for support in asking Lucius if he'll join us. Do I have that?'

'No. I'm sorry, you do not. As you must be aware from what I've said, I don't believe you can win. I can't stop you from approaching Lucius but I ask you not to. I don't want to lose my son.'

'Then your wish will be respected.' Seneca seemed to age by the minute. 'Should he come to us of his own accord, however, I can promise nothing.'

'That's all I ask,' Marcus replied. 'These are dangerous times.'

Both men, experienced and intelligent, saw before them a future full of the horrors of blood and death.

The nightingales hid in the trees at Tauromenium.

Lorraine Blundell

Via Marina,

The temple of Venus stood complete in all its gleaming magnificence. Its towering columns and elevated height above its surrounds, guaranteed its prominence in Pompeii.

Those who looked upwards towards it from below, or who gazed at it from afar across the harbour as they approached, were left in no doubt as to the wealth and artistic creativity of the city they were entering.

Having passed through the Marine Gate and drawn closer to the temple, travellers smelt the scent of roses, myrtle and laurel from the sacred temple surrounds. It delighted the senses even of the world weary and cynical. This place of worship was undoubtedly worthy of Pompeii's patron, Venus, the goddess of love. It had been paid for with Nero's wealth.

Its true, hidden cost could be counted in blood.

33

In the pale dawn light of an achingly cold winter's morning a lacklustre sun rose in a bleached-out sky. The city's inhabitants slept cosily in their shuttered houses warmed by braziers, unaware that death stalked them.

Phoebus, having woken early, shuffled out to open the door of the perfumery. His body felt stiff and sore. These days, he no longer enjoyed a good night's sleep. Finally, he realised, old age had caught up with him as, inevitably, it was always going to. He stood listening to the silence. It occurred to him that it was actually too silent. Strangely, he couldn't hear any birds singing. It was almost as if the city was holding its breath. He sniffed, detecting the hint of an unpleasant odour. Within seconds, he realised why.

Pompeii was shaking again.

A low rumbling began, accelerating to a roar as the ground ripped open in front of him. Reeking, sulphuric fumes rose from the rift in the earth. Phoebus watched in disbelief. This wasn't the usual shaking the city had experienced for years. This was something very different. He ran to get Tullia just as the first shockwave hit.

'Tullia! Get up!' She was already nearly at the door by the time he'd uttered his warning.

'Father, what is it?'

'I've never seen anything like this before!' Phoebus answered shakily, holding her close to him. 'We must try to get to a safer place!'

They ran.

At Marcus' villa the servants had already gathered in the front peristyle. They huddled together white faced as Fabritio ran through the gallery leading to the study, searching for Marcus. He was just leaving the room as Fabritio reached him.

'Where are the others?' Marcus asked as they heard the sound of smashing.

'In the peristyle,' Fabritio shouted as they hurried back the way he'd come.

'Get out of the villa!' Marcus ordered as they reached the servants.

Not sure where to go, everyone formed a group on the front footpath. Apart from severe shaking around them, the earth remained solid.

'For the moment we'll stay here,' Marcus decided. 'I believe we may be in the safest place. They looked around them in disbelief as their world turned to chaos. Flames rose in the distance from the area of the forum, municipal buildings and temple of Venus.

Not far away, there was no one left inside at Claudia's villa. She'd already ordered them all outside, where they stood uncertainly on the fringe of the track leading downwards towards Via delle Tombe. Fabritio found them there as he came running up the slope.

'Fabritio!' Alessia ran to him.

'Alessia, I think you're all safe here. I have to look for Tullia!' Hugging her quickly, he turned and headed for the forum.

'Don't worry. He'll come back safely,' Claudia reassured her as she stood watching his retreating back.

'I hope you're right!' Alessia sat down on the side of the path to pray to whatever god or goddess would listen to her.

The lop-sided hint of a smile remained on half a face. Eumachia's marble statue had fallen and shattered, leaving a jagged fragment of her face, eyes staring upwards at a dispassionate sky.

A hellish scene of utter destruction met Fabritio's eyes as he reached the junction of Via Stabiana and Via dell'Abbondanza. It was the screaming, smashing and sound of falling trees, combined with the dust and the stink of sulphur, however, that would always remain with him.

Nature had vented her full fury on the centre of the city with devastating results. The exterior walls of the huge Eumachia market had been extensively damaged, along with those of the municipal buildings nearby. Only rubble and debris was left of the internal walls, colonnade and shops of the Macellum, where so recently the fish mongers had proclaimed their day's catch. The triumphal arches of the forum had been badly damaged and everywhere, the echoes of voices once heard swirled through the dust as a memory.

The graceful colonnade of the temple of Apollo was graceful no longer. As for the temple of Jupiter, its central, holy cella lay in ruins as well as its marble pavement. The collapse of its roof was the final abomination.

On Via Marina the Suburban Bathhouse was badly damaged and remained only partially standing while nearby, the stunning, new temple of Venus had been almost totally obliterated. Its roof had collapsed and its perfumed garden was unrecognisable. A small statue of Minerva, having fallen from a niche in the wall of the adjacent Basilica, lay forlornly against the large fragment of a marble slab, miraculously, largely unbroken.

Shocked, Fabritio hurried on. Others passed him, running in panic, some covered in blood. Screams and shouts surrounded him as he made his way to the perfumery. He was relieved to find it largely intact, but deserted. Stopping temporarily, he tried to think where Tullia and Phoebus might have gone.

He bagan to search.

He reached the harbour where the water sizzled and bubbled like an evil brew in a witch's cauldron. The jetty, with its colourful statues, lay in chunks floating in a churning sea. There was no longer a tax collection kiosk for merchants to worry about and it would be some time before the fishing boats plyed their trade again.

Finally, Fabritio found them. Phoebus and Tullia were sheltering in the amphitheatre cell that not so long ago had held the body of the gladiator, Antimetus. Part of the arena had fallen in around them. Tullia couldn't stop shaking and her frightened face was caked with dirt streaked with her tears.

Having slowly but safely crossed the city the three dispirited, dirty figures made their way wearily upwards on the path to Claudia's villa. There they were bathed and put to bed after managing a few mouthfuls of hot food.

———◦◦◦◦{◦◦◦———

The scavangers came at night!

The scum and slime that made up the worst of Pompeii's underclass crawled out of their holes to loot and pillage. They wandered the streets fossicking through the rubble, as they searched for houses left unattended by their owners. Darkness hid their crimes as they circled like vultures, stealing the treasures of the earthquake's victims with their filthy hands. The culprits hid their faces behind masks made of old faded cloth. They ripped priceless frescoes from walls, removing sculptures, jewellery and coins from wherever they found them.

They knew no pity. They had a sense of entitlement to take from those who'd enjoyed life, while they'd struggled to survive.

Pompeii staggered under the enormity of the tragedy.

For several days the city suffered as the shaking continued, gradually becoming less violent. Rebuilding afterwards was slow and painstaking as well as expensive.

The initial clean-up was completed as quickly as possible to enable residents to return to some semblance of normality. Unfortunately, due to damage to the aqua castellum, water was available as a priority to the public city wells but not to fountains in private villas and houses. Pompeii had temporarily, at least, lost some of its aesthetic appeal.

Some said later that although the restoration had resulted in improvements, especially to the public areas and wealthy villas, the fact that the work took so long to complete across the whole city meant that Pompeii would never be quite the same again.

Three Days Later

'Alessia!'

She spun around at the sound of her name. Standing outside the day room at the far end of the portico, she heard Lucius' voice. He opened his arms to her and she ran to him down the length of the portico, her feet flying over the stone floor. He folded her in an embrace that said he would never let her go, kissing her with a passion that knew no inhibitions and left them both breathless.

'My darling girl,' he whispered, gently running his fingers over her cheek, 'I don't know what I'd have done if I'd lost you.'

'I knew you'd come,' Alessia whispered back. 'Lucius, I love you.'

'I promise that I will love you, Alessia, until my last breath,' he murmured.

He went down on one knee before her.

'Alessia, will you honour me by becoming my wife?'

'Lucius, you know the answer. I will, with all my heart.'

He saw the love that shone in her face as she looked down at him. It was a look that he realised he'd been waiting for, ever since the day of the unveiling of Fabritio's statue.

'You're my whole world!' He took her hand and brushed it with his lips. 'Alessia, there are matters, though, that you need to know,' He rose from his knees and walked her back to the day room at the far end of the portico. 'I must explain the situation to you. I've been reluctant to do so before, until I was sure that you returned my feelings.'

She looked at him with love as well as puzzlement.

'Alessia, these are dangerous times in Rome. For your own safety, I can only tell you that I have deliberately remained apart from those planning certain actions that I expect will soon take place. Even though I agree with their motivation, I believe, and so does my father, that it's too soon for them to be successful. Also, once I knew how I felt about you, I didn't wish to become involved in what I believe is a doomed venture.

After the event to come, everyone in the Senate will be suspected of treason until they're cleared, so it's imperative that you're not seen to be involved with me other than as a casual friend. For that reason, I hope that you'll understand our betrothal must be kept secret. Only my father, Fabritio and Claudia can be told. I'm afraid even Tullia must not know. I've spoken with your brother and he's in agreement that this is for the best.

My dearest, when this is all over we'll openly celebrate our betrothal and our love for each other. Will you trust me to do what I think is best?'

'Yes, Lucius. My only concern is that you're safe.'

'Then let's go and tell the others that you've agreed to be my wife.'

Their announcement to those privileged to share their secret, was received with genuine delight. It was also no real surprise to each of them.

That night the lovers enjoyed a celebration dinner in the most romantic setting that Claudia could create.

34

Via dei Teatri
The House of the Mask Maker

Three months later

Fantasy came at a price.

The glass cracked then smashed as it fell onto the floor at Ismene's feet, evading her outstretched hand.

It shattered into tiny pieces. She looked down in frustration, gave a deep sigh, then bent to gather up the fragments. It was a pretty, blue bauble and she had no more with which to replace it.

She could've done with help from someone to finish making the costumes and masks for the next production at the theatre. The committee members were totally unrealistic. They paid her practically nothing for her work and expected her not only to make costumes and masks to thrill audiences, but to have them done in too short a time. She was given little spending money to buy materials.

Sometimes she thought she'd tell them that she wasn't going to do it anymore. She really didn't have a choice, though, as the small amount of money she did earn, was the difference in keeping her very tiny home or ending up on the street. She had no option but to bow and scrape to them.

Yes, of course. That won't be any trouble at all!

Ismene heard her own voice in her ears telling them all what they wanted to hear and hating herself for it. It was pathetic! The only competent committee member who had any idea what they were doing was Valentina. However, she had little responsibility for the backstage work for the large theatre, as she now worked mainly in the Odeion, so Ismene couldn't go to her with any problems.

The next production was the most important of the year. It began the city's annual Music Festival and was always held on the first night. After that, a variety of other types of productions were staged and events also took place in the Odeion. The most popular of these was the singing and lyre competition.

Everyone made the same mistake every year as they prepared for the event. They never seemed to learn.

There's plenty of time left—they all said.

Of course, she'd heard that too many times before. There was never enough time to meet their demands for all of the masks and costumes. Last minute preparations were always frantic.

Ismene looked around the tiny room.

Brightly coloured ribbons spilled out of boxes alongside smaller containers overflowing with beads. Pushed into a corner of the room a bucket disappeared under a variety of beards. They were of many different types and textures, from wispy, straggly and luxuriant to small and nondescript. Their colours ranged from grey to silver and black.

Lying in stacks around the room lay costumes for female characters, resplendent with their glass baubles and fake gems. They were always made in brilliant colours to catch the eye no matter how far away from the stage someone in the audience was sitting. It was just a pity, she thought, that only men would be allowed to wear them—just like the masks she made. She sighed again and got up to inspect the large masks that sat on the shelves lining the wall. She had outdone herself this time both in number and quality.

There were fifteen of them.

They were life-sized, heavy and cumbersome. It had taken her hours of painstaking work to hand model the plaster into exaggerated expressions for their faces. She particularly liked the mask of the trickster. His sly smile and obvious craftiness perfectly portrayed the classic, much despised character.

She had more hours of work left to do to mould them into the lighter, more flexible, open-mouthed versions that would be worn by the actors. The colour of most was brown. A few were white, made to be worn by actors playing females.

Ismene had come to Pompeii when she was a small child with her parents. They were Greek and from a classical theatre background. It was natural for the child that she would be attracted to an occupation linked to their world. Her father had been a talented actor. Her mother was trained in the work Ismene now carried on in the same tradition. Both of her parents had been dead for some years.

There had been someone special to Ismene once. He was a travelling pantomimist who had lured the young Ismene with his dark good looks and charm into a relationship he'd later abandoned. Marriage was never mentioned, probably because there had been no child. At the time, she'd thought herself lucky to have attracted his attention. Of pleasant but not particularly striking appearance, Ismene had been flattered and naïve.

After that there had been no romantic interest in Ismene's life, perhaps because there'd been a few ugly whispers about the relationship, without a fully fledged scandal ever having taken hold. Life was lonely for the generous hearted, middle aged woman. She did have one passion, however, that would never leave her. She loved the theatre. Sometimes she'd sit in one of the back row seats watching the characters on stage that she'd helped to create. She listened to the musicians playing their flutes, tambourines and cymbals and was inspired by the beauty of the music and the artistry of her costumes.

It somehow made her existence more worthwhile.

———∘∘∘⦿∘∘∘———

As Ismene pondered her problems, casting auditions were taking place at the large theatre nearby. Nerves were on edge and tempers frayed as the actors presented themselves hoping for selection.

Norbanus Sorex, a Pompeii resident, was an experienced, supporting actor. He'd prepared thoroughly, hoping to move up to a lead role. His audition had just finished.

'Thank you. I'll let you know.' Actius Anicetus, manager of a major troupe and sole producer, smiled as he waved Sorex off the stage.

'Thank you.'

Norbanus'appearance wasn't particularly an advantage. He was middle aged with sparse, wavy hair, heavily lidded eyes and a large nose. He did, however, have considerable, innate talent. It was his misfortune to stand in the shadow of the leading actor of the day, Paris, who had more talent by far than Norbanus would ever have.

Maybe, this time, Paris won't come down here and I'll have a better chance, he thought, as he watched the next actor audition. Norbanus had also recently been honoured for his charitable works, with a bust in the temple of Isis. That had helped to bring his name into prominence. Maybe this time he would either be lucky enough for Paris to be absent, or good enough to be successful in his own right.

Having heard nothing two days after the end of the auditions, Norbanus went to see Anicetus at the theatre. It was early morning. He'd timed his visit well and found the producer readying himself for the day ahead. Norbanus walked up to him.

'My apologies for disturbing you, but I've heard nothing and wondered if you'd mind giving me the results of my audition?' he asked mildly.

'Norbanus, please take a seat. The results are going out to everyone this morning. You did very well. Your experience was obvious in your performance. I'm very pleased to tell you that I've given you the supporting role to the main lead. Congratulations!'

'Thank you.' Norbanus gave a weak smile. 'Would you mind telling me why I didn't get the leading role?'

'You'll forgive me, I trust, if I'm brutally honest,' Anicetus told him. 'I'm sure you know my reputation. I'm always direct and that can be difficult for actors but at least you know where you stand. I believe it also helps performers to improve their skills. Before I say more I'd like to ask you a question.'

'Yes?'

'Do you consider yourself of the same talent level as Paris?'

'Of course not,' Norbanus answered. 'I wouldn't dream of comparing myself to him.'

'When you can, come back and audition again for a leading role. Until then, good luck with the part your talent has won you.'

Norbanus decided to do just that. It was obvious he had gone as far as his talent and present experience could take him.

Lorraine Blundell

Tullia

The Perfumery

Fabritio's promised to take me to see Alessia compete at the Music Festival. He's so proud of her. I hope she wins!

He laughed when I told him about a couple of new ideas I had for the perfumery. It wasn't as if he was being unpleasant, he simply thought the whole thing was amusing. I don't know what I'd ever do if we weren't together. He's asked to see father tomorrow evening. All he'd tell me was that he'd made a business deal with Magistrate Diomedes. I'm impatient to know what's going on.

Anyway—to get back to my ideas for the shop.

I've managed to make up a new perfume using myrtle. It's not as nice as the rose one, of course, but it's very pleasant just the same. It's got a light floral smell. It's my second idea, though, that I believe could really sell well. I think we should make love potions. I've made one up already with rose petals, honey and wine.

Fabritio said he didn't need a love potion. Then he picked me up and swung me around in the air until everything became a blur of green and blue.

'I love you. Who needs a love potion?' he'd said. It was the first time he'd ever told me that he loved me.

That was sweet, wasn't it!

35

Naples

The Egyptian ship sleek as a pampered cat, glided across the bay, its oars barely disturbing the water's calm presence, its 'claws' muzzled, courtesy of the peace imposed by Rome. No longer would it and its kind harass the Roman fleet. Gone, also, were the purple sails of Cleopatra accompanied by sensual perfume drifting towards land. Its design and crew, however, still retained the ancient mystique that defined Egypt's very being.

Arriving from Alexandria on a mission of talks on commerce and diplomatic niceties, the ship proved to be a source of curiosity to the locals. They gathered at the dock watching the crew disembark eager to sample the cosmopolitan life of the city.

The harbour area teemed with life.

Fancy a woman, handsome?

Prostitutes plied their trade with distinctive propositions as old as time itself. Pimps hung back in the shadows, watching. Business was brisk—a combination of eager women and sex deprived seamen with money to spend.

The crew hungrily gorged themselves on offerings of fruit from the fresh food vendors, who gleefully attempted to mentally calculate how much profit the day would bring. Acrobats in multi coloured clothing performed tricks on the fringes, hoping for coins in return for their street entertainment. They tumbled, demonstrating their agility with cartwheels and somewhere amidst the throng, someone played a water organ. It was carnival time.

Into this melee royalty intruded.

'Tigellinus, what's going on here?' Nero asked testily, annoyed at having to pass through the chaos.

'It appears, Caesar, that a boat from Egypt has arrived,'

Tigellinus replied, calling more of the praetorians forward in a tighter cordon around the Emperor.

'Just get us out of this!' Nero demanded. 'We'll go straight to the theatre.'

As both locals and Egyptians gawked at the royal entourage, they extricated themselves from the scene. The fun continued once Nero had gone. It was as if nothing had interrupted the festivities.

————∘∘∘❦∘∘∘————

Attendants, courtiers and visitors from Rome walked down the long, arched entry corridor curious to see Nero's first public performance. Flares attached to the walls signalled the way. The whole atmosphere in the theatre changed with his arrival. He swept through the entry arch and across to the orchestra who had just settled themselves. Amidst a great flurry of introductions and bowing he stated loudly that this was one of the great moments of his life.

'Unheard melodies are never sweet!' Nero exclaimed grandly. 'I fully intend to give you all the benefit of my talent.' He smiled broadly.

The audience cheered and applauded.

'I'll warm up before we begin.' He turned and hurried through the door leading backstage, where he sat quietly for a few minutes before commencing the many scales and breathing exercises Terpnus had taught him. He wondered if they'd do him any good. He'd tired of the music tutor and ordered him not only to leave the palace, but never to show his face in Rome again. There was only one problem. Now he had no tutor.

Doubts began to race through his mind. His mouth was so dry all he wanted to do was to keep drinking the cups of wine that were constantly refilled for him. His hands sweated, his heart raced and he realised that he urgently needed to relieve himself. What was worse was that he'd started to shake.

It was some time before he felt he had his nerves under control enough to go on to the stage. He knew he couldn't sit backstage much longer. No doubt those in the audience were growing restive. It was time to perform. Nero entered the stage area to the sound of applause.

He had grave fears that he'd drop the lyre.

Seating himself, afraid to even clear his throat before beginning, he hesitantly began to play. He wasn't expecting what happened next.

The theatre began to shake.

Although only a minor earthquake seemed to be occurring, unlike the major one experienced not that long ago in Pompeii, it was frightening, nonetheless, to everyone in the theatre. That is, to everyone except Nero who continued to sing. He was determined that nothing was going to ruin this special occasion for him.

After a nervous start to his chosen music, a piece from an opera, he seemed to settle somewhat, even glancing out at the audience occasionally. He gave an acceptable if unspectacular performance.

'Nero's voice isn't exactly special,' one of the local Naple's residents in the audience whispered to his companion.

'I know. It's very feeble and husky, but don't say anything else. We don't want to end up in trouble,' his companion replied.

'Perhaps we should just leave?'

'That's a good idea. Let's quietly make our way out.'

They unobtrusively walked out into the corridor leading to the exit only to find themselves confronted by praetorian guards.

'Return to your seats!'

'Why?'

'By order of the Emperor,' one of the praetorians replied.

'No one is to leave while he's performing under any circumstances. If someone dies—the undertaker has orders to remove the body later.'

Suitably chastised they slunk back to their seats.

———∘∘∘◦◄◊►◦∘∘∘———

Afterwards, Nero stood bowing and smiling, relieved to have come through the experience virtually unscathed—or so he thought. At first the audience's response was somewhat listless. Then, a crescendo of applause began. There was something different about it though.

A rhythmic clapping and chanting was coming from the back of the theatre. A group of Alexandrians, having tired of the entertainment at the port, had decided to attend the theatre to hear the Emperor sing.

One, two—one, two, three! One, two—one, two, three!

Who is it we want to see!

The rhythm continued as Nero spun around to find out who was responsible. He waved and smiled his approval. The apparently spontaneous appreciation of his talent in public and in so unique a manner delighted him.

Feeling magnanimous, he walked amongst the audience clasping hands and accepting compliments. It was indeed a wonderful thing to be so admired!

That evening aboard the Egyptian ship, gently rocking at anchor in the bay of Naples, a high level meeting took place. A small group of those in command gathered with the door locked.

'The economic situation in Egypt has become a crisis. We have no alternative but to try to influence Nero himself, in order to get what we want,' the leader of the Egyptian group declared firmly.

'He'll listen to us now,' laughed one of the others around the table, 'he just won't be aware of who he's really listening to.'

'I can't say that I've ever seen such vanity before. Nero lapped up the praise and applause at the theatre pathetically. We might as well have been flattering a woman for her beauty in the hope of seducing her,' another so called 'seaman' added.

There was general laughter.

'It wouldn't have been so bad if he was talented. Unfortunately, the best thing that he could do is to go back to being an Emperor.'

'From what I've heard,' another member of the group added, 'he's not much good at that either!'

The Egyptians hadn't enjoyed themselves so much for a long time.

An official meeting had been arranged some months before, between court officials in Rome and Egyptian officials, liaising through Rome's tribune in Alexandria. Its purpose was to negotiate a trade agreement especially in relation to grain. Having discovered that Nero was to perform in Naples, the Egyptians insisted that the meeting take place there rather than in Rome.

The two parties met on the day after Nero's appearance at the theatre in Naples. Whenever the talks ended in a stalemate with their demands unmet, the Alexandrians insisted that Nero be personally informed.

The reply by messenger from the Emperor to Rome's delegates left them in no doubt that the Alexandrians were to be given practically everything they'd asked for.

The Romans shook their heads in frustration.

36

Pompeii

The annual Music Festival had finally arrived once more to flood the city with melody. The decision to hold the event despite the recent earthquake was made in an attempt to bolster morale.

Pompeii was saturated with painted advertising posters as well as pamphlets posted up in a flurry one evening on shop fronts, water towers and the walls of buildings, as well as handed out at random to passersby. The runners found themselves the following morning in the unusual position of having earned enough to eat surprisingly well for a few days.

Anyone travelling in the city stopped to look as they passed by, many mentally calculating on which dates they'd be free to attend the advertised events. The last day was always the most popular, when the finals of the lyre and singing competitions were held.

The large theatre was a spectacular venue set into a natural hill formation. It stood beside the gladiator barracks that in the recent past had been a vestibule for the theatre. It had been fortunate to enjoy the patronage of the Holconii family. Their generosity had enabled it to become the most magnificent performance venue of the time in Pompeii or the surrounding region.

The large theatre was not, however, the focal point of the city's Music Festival except for the first night, even though a variety of productions were held there throughout the Festival. That honour belonged to the more suitable, adjacent Odeion theatre, for the male competitors. A villa on Via del Vesuvio was the venue for women. It was not usually acceptable for females to perform on stage. An artistic competition was considered to be on a somewhat different level to a stage farce. Nonetheless, it was still thought more refined and appropriate for women to play and sing at a private venue.

Advertising for the event sought to attract participation from both local and regional musicians. Significant prizes were offered as well the inevitable prestige that winners enjoyed.

First Prize for Lyre and Song

Enter for a chance to win one thousand sesterces

There were surprisingly large numbers of aspiring musicians in Pompeii and the surrounding region. As with any other city, some were downright appalling, never lasting past the first round of competition. That particular circumstance, however, seemed to leave them undeterred from applying when the Festival came around again a year later.

The bulk of the competitors usually fell into the middle group. Generally speaking, they had reasonable technique and about the same level of talent.

The third group, understandably, was much smaller and drew the most interest from other competitors, patrons and public alike. Their standard of talent and performance was high, sometimes, surprisingly so.

Struggling street musicians found a few more coins tossed into their bowls during this time, as the city's inhabitants acknowledged their efforts to entertain pedestrians walking by. Overall, the event brought with it more joy, harmony and a sense of wellbeing than any other public activity, even, and some would have said, especially the games.

Pompeii's Odeion was the perfect performance venue for music competitions. It was a small, exquisite theatre that held an audience of about twelve hundred. It was particularly suitable for speeches and readings or vocal competitions, thus establishing it as the preferred venue each year for the city's Music Festival. It was roofed and so could be used in all weather. Most of all, the acoustics were exceptional, enhancing the performers' talent. The smaller theatre allowed for intimate performances as the audience and performers were closer together.

The Odeion stood off Via Stabiana beside the large theatre and the gladiator barracks. The two theatres formed a wonderful entertainment complex providing offerings of considerable variety. As such, they were a major part of Pompeii's social life. Events began with a mix of poetry readings which were well attended and ranged in content from intellectual to love themes and humour. The classics were also popular as well as more modern offerings.

Because seating was limited in the small theatre, there were always more patrons clamouring tor tickets than actual seats available. The type of animal imprinted on the clay entry tabellas determined the location of each seat.

The city's magistrates had seats in the first four rows, separated from the rest of those attending by a balustrade. Honoured guests were shown to special boxes over the side passageways. The area used by the orchestra had been paved with expensive, coloured marble from the time of Augustus. Its beauty was always remarked upon by visitors. The remainder of tickets were available to ordinary citizens on a 'first come, first served' basis.

———∞∞-⟨⦿⟩-∞∞———

The same committee sat in judgement of the competitors each year causing Valentina, a long term committee member, to come close to pulling out her long, red hair with frustration at their bickering and incompetence. Every year she threatened to resign, but never did. This year, she had a special interest in the results particularly in the female section.

Valentina was going nowhere.

An exciting surprise lifted the spirits of all competitors immediately preceeding the Festival's commencement. The Emperor had decided to attend, in the hope of lifting the morale of the city so recently devastated by ruin from the earthquake. He would reside for several nights at a villa belonging to Poppaea's family. Workmen had just completed repairs so that Nero could be welcomed to accommodations appropriate for royalty.

Lorraine Blundell

Via dell'Abbondanza
The House of Julia Felix

Paris dressed quickly then slipped quietly past the cascade waterfall, down the four steps at the villa's entry and into the deserted street, leaving his lover sleeping. The bed was still warm from where he'd dreamt beside her.

Julia's house stood not far from the amphitheatre. It was huge and luxurious. Although no longer in the first flush of youth, she was still an attractive woman. Her wealth lay in the property she continued to amass. Paris was not her first lover, but had for a considerable time enjoyed her charms. She was not a conventional woman.

He'd always enjoyed being in Pompeii. Audiences were very receptive, he was well paid and there was always the bonus of Julia's eagerness to share her bed with him.

Being famous had its rewards, he thought, as he made his way to the baths on Vicolo delle Terme. Seius, the manager, considered it an honour to have Rome's most famous pantomimist visit the establishment he managed. He happily arrived early, opened up the facilities and heated the water so that his famous guest could enjoy an early, private bathing experience.

'You can't imagine what it means to me to be able to come here,' Paris said, shaking Seius' hand enthusiastically. 'I'm sure this helps my performances!' He slipped one of the small clay theatre entry tabellas into the manager's hand. 'Please come and see me perform tonight.'

As Seius bowed and smiled his appreciation, Paris strolled through to the garden, bypassing the gymnasium. He wasn't one for exercise away from the theatre. He felt that he endured enough physical exertion just performing.

For a while, he sat on a bench in the garden enjoying its beauty and solitude. Eventually he made his way to the indoor facilities. He gave a sigh of pure contentment as he sank into the large, marble labrum. The steaming water soothed and relaxed him. It should, he supposed, given that Pompeii's citizens had paid a whopping 5250 sesterces for it. Still, everyone seemed happy. Not a single complaint had been received.

As he lay admiring the efficiency of the temperature control wall vents, the beauty of the light filled ceiling oculus and the charm of the frieze's cavorting griffins, he had one of the deep thoughts that didn't come to him often.

This was probably the pinnacle of his success.

Reluctantly, after enjoying the solitude of relaxing on a bench in one of the niches in the caldarium, he retrieved his clothes from one of the wall pegs, left the bathhouse and made his way towards the theatre.

Paris was vain, liked the good things of life and was known to be a womaniser. He was also tall, good looking, passionate about his craft and highly professional.

As a pantomimist he was without equal.

37

Via del Vesuvio

The Villa of Gnaeus Poppaeus Habitus
(The House of the Gilded Cupids)

The villa of Gnaeus Poppaeus Habitus on Via del Vesuvio was exquisite. An unassuming entry gave no hint of the richness within. A vain, brilliantly coloured peacock painted on a fresco, enticed visitors through the vestibule in to the rich red landscapes decorating the atrium. The villa was owned by the family of the Empress Poppaea.

On this pleasantly cool, clear night all was quiet as those within, their preparations complete, awaited Nero's arrival. The Empress had declined to grace the event with her presence, saying that she didn't wish to deflect attention away from the female performers. Instead, she would take one of her increasingly frequent visits to the villa at Oplontis.

Not far away Valentina had just finished dressing for the evening. Her long red hair was swept back and caught with a pearl comb. She wore a becoming shade of deep blue and an amber necklace. She'd taken more care than usual with her appearance for what she considered to be a special night.

'The Empress is indeed gracious and thoughtful,' commented her friend, Cassia, when she heard of Poppaea's remark.

'I'm sorry, but that's ridiculous!' Valentina laughed, expressing herself in her usual forthright manner.

'Why?' Cassia demanded, not at all put out at Valentina's comment. They'd been friends for many years, which was just as well.

'Believe me, she's as hard as nails. If you ask me she must have a good thing going at Oplontis,' Valentina quipped. 'The only person she's concerned about is herself.'

'Well, I'm prepared to give her the benefit of the doubt,' Cassia persisted, her gold bangles jingling as she waved her arms emphatically.

'You always were incredibly naïve,' Valentina answered fondly, 'but I wouldn't have you any other way. I must go, though, I'm afraid, or I'll be late to judge the entrants and that wouldn't do at all.'

'I'll see you tomorrow then, and you can tell me how the evening turned out.' Cassia went home leaving Valentina to make her way to Via del Vesuvio.

Those fortunate enough to be invited were required to be seated before the Emperor's arrival. Numbers were limited by the venue, leaving many of the upper elite envious at not having received one of the precious invitations.

———∘∘∘⧙◉⧘∘∘∘———

Claudia and Alessia dressed carefully and in Claudia's case, with as much glamour as possible. Her silver hair was swept back but softened with a gentle wave at her forehead. Her long robe shimmered with golden gems beautifully complemented by an expensive amber necklace. She wore lotus perfume, the fragrance used by the ancient Egyptian queens.

Alessia had been advised by Valentina to dress with seeming simplicity. A soft, white long robe belted in gold, worn with a heavy gold necklace and earrings allowed the natural beauty of her long dark hair and dark eyes to dazzle. Claudia had offered the use of her lotus perfume but there was no dissuading Alessia from her favourite rose perfume.

'I think we're just about ready to leave,' Claudia said. She took one last look at herself and then studied Alessia.

'The only regret I have is that Lucius can't be here,' Alessia sighed.

'I know it's difficult for you, but as he's told us both, he's planning your future and dealing with affairs in Rome. The time will pass more quickly than you realise and he'll be back again,' Claudia reassured her.

'It's just that I miss him.'

'I know, my dear. For now, though, let's just concentrate on this evening. It's an exciting moment in your life. It's a night with memories to cherish.' Claudia smiled at her as they left for Via del Vesuvio with the older woman carefully carrying Alessia's precious lyre.

———∘∘∘⧙◉⧘∘∘∘———

'Good evening Lady Claudia. Alessia, you're competing tonight aren't you?'

'Yes.'

'Helena, take Alessia through to the waiting room to join the others please. Then you may seat Lady Claudia.'

Alessia was led through the vestibule and the atrium to the right then in to a lavishly decorated bedroom. She found all but one of the other five competitors already sitting on couches babbling excitedly. They gathered around her asking her name and offering her a cup of watered wine from a small table.

She looked around at the insets of graceful glass discs etched with cupids painted in gold leaf. The discs were set into the room's ochre coloured walls. Charming, flowing figures full of vitality, they immediately caught the eye of anyone entering. A bronze lamp had been lit to dispel the gloom. Alessia wondered if Poppaea had ever slept here. The final girl arrived moments later and the list of competitors was complete.

Claudia found Fabritio and Tullia already seated in the front row of seats. Having handed Alessia's lyre to a servant to place with the others in the area provided, she seated herself next to them.

'How's Lessi?' Fabritio asked, looking somewhat edgy himself.

'She's fine. I'm sure she'll do well tonight.'

'I do hope so,' Tullia said softly. The few times she'd already met Claudia she'd been somewhat in awe of her. The affect was to dampen her normally exuberant personality to something more subdued.

'Don't worry, Tullia. I'm sure Valentina has prepared her very thoroughly,' Claudia responded.

The audience was small. They were seated around the huge peristyle facing a raised performance area and a small fountain. Due to the recent earthquake it looked a little sorry for itself, as it had no water to allow it to function properly.

The lovely garden was enclosed by small, fluted columns exuding a romantic quality in the half light cast by the wall flares. They also lit the numerous, aesthetic statues and busts placed at random. The assembled elite of Pompeii along with the competitors' families had dressed regally for the occasion. They sat talking and admiring the peristyle with its theatre masks inset into the walls between the columns.

Welcome Ladies and Gentlemen.

I'm told that the Emperor is almost here. Please maintain silence and be so good as to stand when he enters.

Moments later, Nero swept into the garden still beaming from his triumph in Naples. He was escorted to a seat in a prime position in the front row. After a short speech of welcome the first of the competitors was announced.

Perhaps the most stressful facet of the evening for each young woman was the walk from the waiting room, through the portico then up the stairs to the performance area. When her turn came Alessia remembered Valentina's words:

The walk to the centre of the stage to perform seems unbelievably long and stressful. If you believe you are talented enough, however, it need not unduly concern you. You need only to clear your mind and focus on the emotions that you wish to convey to your audience. Remember, you are most of all – a story teller.

Alessia was the third of the competitors to face the adjudicators. Excited and nervous, she sat in the manner Valentina had taught her, with her lyre in the most advantageous position to play well.

Claudia smiled her encouragement.

Alessia's first offering was the sensitive rendition on the lyre of a musical piece about the coming of spring. Then, as taught by Valentina, she began to play and sing a haunting love song. The other judges' heads snapped up from their marking tablets. Valentina sat, head bowed, serenely listening to the voice that she'd come to know so well.

There wasn't a sound in the garden.

The audience hardly seemed to be breathing as they listened to Alessia's voice – surely a gift from the gods. Her playing and especially her singing always produced the same response from an audience. Nero's, however, was extreme. He sat as if frozen in his chair. He heard her pure voice but his pale blue eyes never left her face. He stared at her, entranced. His fingers ran fondly over the small statuette that he carried in his personal belongings, close to him, wherever he went.

He'd just seen the statuette come to life.

———∘∘∘◦◯◦∘∘∘———

Alessia had been led to the front for the presentation and was standing there waiting for the Emperor. Nero stopped as he reached her and whispered something in her ear. Fabritio couldn't tell from the expression on her face what had been said but he feared the worst. Afterwards, Alessia left the stage and joined Claudia, Fabritio and Tullia.

'What did he say to you?' Fabritio asked.

'He said I would be accompanying him when he left here. He's travelling to his villa at Baiae and I'm invited to stay for a few days. Fabritio, I'm afraid. He also said that he's worshipped me for some time as a goddess!'

All three of them were too shocked to speak. Even for Nero the whole thing was bizarre. What could be done? As far as Fabritio could see, his sister had no choice. They sat back in their seats, stunned.

'Fabritio, the best thing we can do is to let Lucius know,' Claudia whispered as they left to return home.

'I agree. Take Alessia home, Claudia. As soon as I've taken Tullia back to Phoebus I'll send an urgent message to Lucius in Rome. Before Alessia leaves, we must give her as much help as we can. She's going to need a great deal of advice on what to do after she sets out with Nero for Baiae.'

The nightingales hid in the trees at Tauromenium.

Nero

The gods have sent one of their own to lighten my load. This girl is surely a goddess in earthly form. My prayers have finally been answered. I will bow down before her and beg her to ease my suffering.

She is pure not only in voice but in herself. I will send ahead to ensure that she receives only the best of everything. As would be expected of a deity it seems she has neither husband nor one to whom she is betrothed.

It is my honour to look upon her. She will be my teacher.

PART III

64 A.D.-65 A.D.

38

Pompeii
The Inn of Euxinus

o home you old soak!

Euxinus closed the door on his last customer as the 'regular,' feeling somewhat cheated, swayed out the door complaining about the inn's early closure. He had never been known as the most genial host, especially since his son had died, but his customers were used to him and liked him that way. His gruffness, they knew, hid a generous heart.

Quickly he cleaned up downstairs and re-made the upstairs beds, providing fresh cups, bowls for washing and wine for the new guests. He anticipated their arrival was imminent. Then, he sat down to wait.

One by one the custodians of Rome's wellbeing drifted into Pompeii through the Herculaneum Gate. Dressed as merchants, they arrived at varying intervals between mid afternoon and dusk. It was a busy market day, a time when they'd calculated they'd be least noticed. Not so much as a glance came their way, as each unremarkable traveller made his way towards the *Inn of Euxinus.*

It had been decided that only a nucleus of the full group would attend the meeting so as not to unduly arouse suspicion. Faenius Rufus, due to his high profile, gave his proxy vote to Seneca rather than personally travelling to Pompeii.

By nightfall everyone had arrived.

Piso, Seneca, Lucanus, Natalis, Scaevanus, Silvanus, Proculus and Proximus would make the decisions that cemented the final plan for Nero's assassination. Euxinus pulled several tables together, placing a cup of wine in front of each place.

The group sat whispering. Euxinus withdrew and stood nonchalantly lounging outside the closed front door, ensuring no customers would try to enter. The warning signal in the event of any real trouble, such as the appearance of soldiers, would be two thumps with his hand on the door behind him.

'Piso, I think it would be unbelievably easy to do the job at your villa in Baiae,' Natalis suggested. 'You said yourself that whenever you're there and Nero's at the royal villa nearby, he visits you without even a bodyguard.'

'I really would rather not do it that way,' Piso frowned. 'I know that sounds easy, but we have to be concerned about how Nero's death will look to the people. It could have the taint of being seen as deceitful and hidden, as if it's a crime. We want it to be seen instead as an honourable action, don't we?'

'I believe that's a good point,' Scaevanus answered. 'After all, if the people aren't with us, we could end up being dragged through the streets and slaughtered.'

'Well, if we're going to get this done at all a decision has to be made now,' Seneca declared firmly.

'If we're agreed with what Scaevanus has just said,' there were nods all around, 'we have to do it somewhere public in Rome. Now we simply need to decide on the place that represents the least danger for us,' Proximus stated.

'What about in the new cryptoporticus?' Silvanus asked. 'Faenius has a good chance of controlling that area with soldiers loyal to us.'

'There's always also an opportunity, limited I grant you, of a few minutes to kill him during one of his visits to the theatre,' Proculus suggested.

'The timing of either of those suggestions could be difficult, though,' Seneca pointed out. 'We won't know enough in advance which theatre productions he'll decide to attend, or exactly what time he's likely to enter the cryptoporticus.'

'There is one place that we do know he will attend and we know when, because it will be scheduled beforehand. It's a place that can be counted upon to ensure we have the benefit of his presence,' Piso said sarcastically. 'I refer, of course, to the Circus.'

There was silence as each conspirator sat thinking.

'On the basis that there seem to be no arguments against Piso's plan,' Seneca stated, 'I propose that we vote on the proposition that Nero will be assassinated at some point on his way to or from the Circus. All those in agreement raise your hands.'

The decision was unanimous.

'I think this deserves a toast to our good fortune and to a better future,' Piso said, refilling the cups.

'To good fortune!'

'I further propose,' Seneca added, 'that we meet here one final time, at an opportune moment in the near future, to choose the exact day that the deed will be carried out. We'll also need to come up with a detailed plan for the assassination itself. Now, we should get some rest. We'll leave the same way we came—singly and secretly.'

The inn was soon in darkness as the conspirators slept the sleep of the just.

———∘o∘━◖◍◗━∘o∘———

The Perfumery
The Next Afternoon

'Where should I put the love potion bottles?' Attice stood with two attractively shaped bottles in her hand. They held coloured liquid, one golden, the other, pink. A cluster of bottles still lay in one of the baskets.

'I think maybe they'd look good on the middle shelf,' Tullia suggested as she came through to the shop from the next room.

'So do I.' Attice reaching up, placed the bottles on display for purchase. 'They look so tempting,' she smiled.

'They do look rather special, don't they!' Tullia looked pleased with herself. The potions would sell well she was sure.

The shop was already open for business again following the earthquake, and customers had begun wandering in looking to buy something inspiring to lift their spirits. Fabritio had been given Phoebus' permission to marry Tullia if she agreed—which she did—emphatically. That meant that she'd be moving out to live with him at his house after they were married.

It was all very exciting!

Attice had thought that her dream would never come true. She couldn't believe it when she'd seen Phoebus down on one knee in her little room, looking somewhat embarrassed, blurting out his marriage proposal. Since then she'd become friends with Tullia, and decided to move into the perfumery once Tullia had gone to live with Fabritio.

Tonight was the young couple's betrothal party. Alessia had arrived early and had been helping with the setting up of the tables and making food all day. Her cooking skills had improved and savoury aromas filled the house. Attice had decided to stay out of the way and see to the shop. Thankfully, there hadn't been many customers, so she'd also been able to lend a hand in the garden, still looking somewhat sad after the earthquake.

Tullia was radiant. Never had she dreamed she could be this happy. If only Alessia had someone too, she thought, it would be just perfect. Tullia had seen her a few times with that nice, good looking senator from Rome, but it seemed they were just friends. Alessia did seem happy anyway, though, so in the end Tullia was sure everything would work out just fine.

—––ooo❧❦❧ooo–––

The Council Chamber
The Municipal Building

'We must plan a city for the future! It must be a city that's an improvement on the one that's been virtually destroyed!' Duumvir Verus argued.

'I don't see the sense in that. What if we have another earthquake as strong as the last one? We can't just keep spending money on public places that will be destroyed again!' countered a council member of long standing.

'Do you know what's in the future?' Verus persisted. 'I don't. I find your attitude unnecessarily pessimistic. I agree, we could have more earthquakes but they don't have to be as bad as the last one, surely. Pompeii may be fortunate and have only slight damage, as we have always had for so many years in the past.'

The youngest of the council members rose to speak. 'I'm inclined to agree with Duumvir Verus. We must remember that Pompeii is a holiday destination. It's also a city of business and commerce. If we don't attract our usual clientele again in those areas—what's to become of us?'

'Does anyone else wish to comment?' Verus asked.

There was no one.

'In that case, I believe it's time that we voted. Please raise your hands to vote *yes* to the following proposal:

Pompeii's forum is to be re-paved in marble—not in tufa.

Of the twelve members, ten voted in the affirmative.

'That's that then,' Verus said, relieved. 'The work will begin next week.'

The council meeting concluded.

Rome

The Wine Shop of Publius
(Below the Caelian Hill)

'I can't give you what I don't have!' Publius threw his arms up in frustration.

'Surely you can do better than that, though!' The woman pointed accusingly at the amphora beside the counter. 'How am I supposed to explain **that?**'

'I don't know and I don't care! Take it or leave it!'

The woman was a regular customer. She served in the house of a wealthy patrician whose villa stood in an elite area on the Caelian Hill. Her master liked to preserve an ordered pattern to his life. A change from his favourite Campania wines to Rome's more tart, local varieties or those from other regions, was hardly likely to maintain that.

She grabbed the amphora of Formianum wine, sniffed with disgust and turned away. Publius sighed. He was sick and tired of the problems since Pompeii's earthquake. That city and the surrounding Campania area usually supplied him with most of the better wines. Imports from places like Crete were often available but inevitably more expensive. He hoped that life would soon return to normal.

213

39

Oplontis
(Near Pompeii)

The Country Villa of Poppaea

S he still couldn't quite believe it!

Farazana had recently found herself caretaker of the most magnificent villa she'd ever seen. Built with the extravagance only an Emperor could indulge in, it stood high on a cliff imperiously overlooking the Bay of Naples.

Fully expecting something 'suitable' as a wedding present, even Poppaea had been stunned by Nero's gift. In the long periods of absence when the new Empress was holding court in Rome, Farzana acted more as an owner rather than a manager of the estate.

Poppaea and Farzana had known each other so long that there were no secrets between them. One day some years earlier, seeing an exotic, beautiful girl selling flowers in a stall in the Pompeii forum, Poppaea had prevailed on her family to allow her to employ Farzana to work at their prestigious city villa. Somewhat to the chagrin of Farzana's father the girl had agreed when approached, becoming over time a close companion to Poppaea. A hefty payment had allowed the girl's father to retire early, thereby helping to smooth the way.

The women were similar in age, the former flower seller being older by a couple of years. As time passed they became close friends. Eventually, they became lovers. It was understood between them that Farzana would remain with Poppaea as she manoeuvred to become Empress.

The liaison was discrete to say the least. It was unknown except to the staff. They were only too well aware of the situation having been left in no doubt that any disclosures of a private nature on their part, would result in their quick dismissal or disappearance. There had sometimes been insinuations about the two women, but in the light of a lack of hard evidence, the rumours went no further.

Farzana's shapely arm hung over the side of the huge pool, her long, slim fingers trailing slowly through the water's delicious coolness, as she lay languorously soaking up the warmth of another sunny, idle day. The rectangular pool, sixty metres long by fifteen metres wide, was so large, it was difficult to fully visualise it without actually having seen it. The pool had recently been re-tiled in expensive tiles the colour of the sea.

Farzana's skin was dusky. She was alluring, with long, wavy dark hair and almond shaped eyes. Her body was lean and her demeanour one of total relaxation. Few would have argued with a description of her as an exceptionally beautiful, young woman.

Her eyes snapped open in response to sudden sounds of commotion from within the villa. She would have the head on a plattter of whoever was responsible for disturbing her leisure, she decided. She frowned in annoyance.

The sound of Poppaea's husky, sensual and quite distinctive voice reached her. Before Farzana could react, Poppaea walked out past the lusciously painted rooms towards the pool.

'Farzana, there you are. How I've missed you!'

'I can't believe you're here,' Farzana squealed. 'You didn't let me know you were coming.'

'Actually, I did, but it seems I've arrived before the messenger.'

The two women clung together in a lover's embrace. Poppaea's beauty was of a different kind from Farzana's. Tight curls framed her face. The rest of her hair was piled towards the back of her head. Her features were pretty, but inclined sometimes to a pouting look when she was upset.

Poppaea placed her arm through her lover's, leading her to a nearby bench in the garden, close to a fountain beside a large, shade tree. The extensive gardens led to the pool. Featuring lemon, olive and pink oleander trees, this place was a haven filled with fragrance and the sound of water.

'I've been worried,' Farzana admitted, looking uneasy. 'I know that becoming Empress was what you wanted,' Farzana squeezed Poppaea's hand, 'but I've wondered lately whether perhaps you might forget me, and turn to another woman. I'm not so foolish as to imagine that there aren't many beautiful women in Rome to tempt you.'

'I'll always love you. You know that will never change.' Poppaea turned Farzana to face her. 'There've been rumours about us in Rome, of course, but I know how to control Nero!' she laughed. 'That's how I got rid of Octavia. You've no reason to be afraid, my love.'

Farzana's relief was obvious.

'You loved me when I was nobody,' Poppaea continued. 'I'd never let you down.'

215

'You've *never* been nobody,' Farazana rebuked her gently, her expression serious. She laid her hand on Poppaea's arm. 'You may be Empress now, but to me you'll always be the same as when I first met you in the forum.'

'I could do with freshening up in a bath, though, you must admit,' Poppaea laughed, 'Will you join me?'

'Just try and stop me!'

The two women left the gardens, walking towards the villa side entry, where they turned into a long corridor, walking past stone benches leading to the internal courtyard.

Poppaea's hard, outer shell fell away when she was with Farazana, allowing her softer side to shine through. Generous, almost to a fault with those close to her, she was loving by nature. Her driving ambition and knowledge of the need to protect herself against others, however, often overpowered her gentler qualities. Farazana brought her back into balance again.

Farazana genuinely adored Poppaea. She'd long ago accepted that she'd never willingly leave her. Poppaea was the love of her life.

'Terene, fill the bath with milk!' Poppaea requested, as her personal maid entered the bedroom. 'And don't forget the rose petals.'

The lovers were soon soaking in indulgence, playfully splashing each other then more sensually stroking and kissing. That afternoon was spent under the nearby stuccoed wall arch, in the soft bed with its luxury pillows and coverings. Servants quickly worked to prepare a welcoming banquet and gave an extra shine to everything from the coloured marble in the great hall, to the silver for the table in the triclinium. The fact that the villa had escaped with only minor damage from Pompeii's earthquake, was considered something of a miracle.

---oo**◦❁❂❁◦**oo---

As evening drew on a glimpse into the dining room would have revealed to a visitor two beautiful women, candelabras throwing a soft light across their faces. The first of many courses was served, decorated with peacock feathers. What the peacock featured on the wall of the adjoining living room with views over the bay would have thought, had it been alive, was anyone's guess.

A few glasses of Vesuvino wine and servings of delectable food later, the two decided to relax in the nearby enclosed garden room, with its scenes of birds and plants enhanced by striking red and black panels.

'There's something going on in Rome and I don't know what it is,' Poppaea said thoughtfully.

'What do you mean something? Can't you find out?' Farzana raised a questioning eyebrow.

'I've been trying to, but it's like whispers and shadows. I can't quite put my finger on it yet, but there's something in the wind.'

'How are things going with Tigellinus?'

'He's a hard one to read,' Poppaea answered. 'He's ruthless and ambitious. There's no way I'd trust him! I don't think it's coming from him, just the same. I wouldn't mind betting there's trouble brewing with the Senate.'

'There's always trouble with the Senate.'

A servant refilled their wine cups.

'Yes, but this has the smell of real danger. I can't explain it. It's just a feeling I have.'

'Trust your intuition,' Farzana advised. 'Sometimes that's better than anything else.'

The two women rose from dinner and arm in arm, took a walk through the white, mosaic floored porticoes, their footsteps echoing hollowly behind them.

'Whatever you do,' Farzana said quietly, her eyes fixed on Poppaea's, 'don't turn your back to anyone. You can't be sure of your safety.'

'My dear, you're right. At the moment, I'll stay clear of any involvement in questionable talk or activities. I intend to hedge my bets until I really know who's likely to attempt to overthrow Nero. Then I'll make a decision. For the moment, I intend to enjoy every moment I have with you in the next few days. Then, I must return to Rome.'

Lorraine Blundell

'Remember Beryllos.'

The young freedman finished scratching his name on to the wall of the passageway near the latrine. He smiled sadly. Perhaps she would see it as she walked past—not that she used that section of the passageway often. It was a desperate attempt to leave a memory of him behind for her.

He'd made the mistake of falling in love with Farzana. Any delusions he'd enjoyed had fallen apart with Poppaea's appearance. He knew he needed to leave. In the morning he'd be gone. Would Farazana even miss him?

Beryllos doubted it.

Handsome and softly spoken, he could have enjoyed the attentions of almost any young woman of his class. His choice to fall in love with Farzana had been foolish. Still, he realised, it really hadn't been a choice at all. It had just 'happened.'

There'd been just that one night to remember. Poppaea had been absent for a long time. He'd thought later that perhaps Farzana had despaired she wasn't coming back.

It'd been a night of torrid passion with Farzana literally ripping the clothes from his body. He'd known at the time that it had been lust, not love, for her, but even that would've been enough for him.

Now, it was over.

40

Rome

*P*estis! The very word conjured up every Roman's worst nightmare. As yet, word of its reappearance in the city had not become general knowledge. Only the physician in an inner city tenement shaking his head over the symptoms of one of his patients, had any clue that the plague was raising its evil head again in Rome. He decided to wait a couple of days before alerting his colleagues in order to avoid appearing idiotic or panic stricken should they not agree with his diagnosis. From what he'd seen, however, the ancient scourge was with them again.

Terentius was worried as he left the man and made his way to the hospital on Tiber Island. There wasn't much point in trying to isolate him. Unless he was very wrong the poor wretch would soon be dead. No one could survive so much fever, vomiting and bowel dysfunction. In any case, the patients at the hospital of Aesculepius wouldn't thank him for subjecting them to the threat of plague.

He peered over the bridge as he crossed to get to the island. The current, as it so often did, was flowing swiftly and the water was higher than usual. The last thing Rome needed, Terentius thought, was a flood as well as plague. The island had been a place of healing for far longer than anyone living could remember. An ancient temple had also made it a place of religious observance.

Terentius' mind zeroed in more on the reason for the return of this monstrous, deadly disease. It seemed that no matter how many times it left the city it always came back. It wouldn't have been quite so bad if it wasn't so deadly. It killed by the thousands.

The cause had to be something in the air or something around them— but what. His glance passed over the marshy, swampy land near the river but he saw only what he had enough knowledge to see. Terentius was young, dedicated and intelligent. He was also compassionate enough to feel a duty to try to stop the carnage.

---∘∘∘⟨◉⟩∘∘∘---

Across town the alluring gardens and fountains enclosed by the colonnades of the Theatre of Pompey, delighted the city's citizens as they strolled along the porticoes in a leisurely fashion before the evening performance. Tonight they'd come to watch what was rumoured to be the best comedy production in years.

At the other end of the gardens the meeting areas of the multi purpose complex, not long ago buzzing with political debate, were quiet and closed for the day. The usual suspects had pushed the patience of Nero's enforcers as far as they dared with their anti Neronian sentiments.

Theatre was a major form of entertainment and had previously been performed in theatres made of wood. The luxury setting and stone construction of this complex was a wonder to behold and would last for many years. It also stood as a tribute to a great past military leader, Pompey.

'That's a good day's work, even if I say so myself!' Claudius Thesius commended himself to his friend Alcimus.

'I'm certainly not going to dispute that,' Alcimus answered. 'I've always wondered thought, you know, why you took to sculpting outside theatre facades and statues for the gardens when you've got the talent to be working on stage scenery. I know how well you paint.'

'Because I don't have the talent in those particular areas to end up as a designer like you are,' Claudius replied. 'Besides, I like to work outdoors whenever I can.'

They stood admiring the grey and rose red columns that loomed up around them and the graceful arches of the colonnades. They lingered, enjoying the last of the day's light before heading home.

'How's Nero been with your stage designs lately?' Claudius asked.

'Not as much of a pain in the backside as usual, actually. He's not around as much at this time of the year. He takes his annual jaunt down to Baiae and elsewhere. Fortunately, he doesn't have time to drive me mad with his suggestions at the moment. The longer he stays away the better, is what I say.'

'I know you have the worst of it,' Claudius agreed, 'but he thinks he knows a thing or two about sculpting, too. What he knows is close enough to nothing!'

They both laughed.

'I'd better be off or Fabia will have my head on a plate instead of my dinner,' Alcimus laughed.

'I'll be lucky of I've got any dinner at all!' Claudius replied.

The two friends hurried away to their loving wives as the theatre goers prepared to enjoy a scintillating evening of entertainment and the plague patient breathed his last.

———◦◦◦◦≫◉≪◦◦◦———

The Vestal Convent

Cornelia's time as a Vestal was coming to an end. Two days ago she'd thought about where she might go and what she might do with her life. She'd walked with steps that were so familiar to her along the porticoes as she'd considered her options. Cornelia felt more nervousness than excitement at the prospect of leaving all she knew and loved. She'd never been the same since the incident involving Rubria, however. The young Vestal's death had taken much of the light and joy from Cornelia's life.

'Drusilla, I believe I may have to stay in bed this morning,' she said as a young Vestal knocked at her door. 'I'm not feeling well. My head feels as if I've been kicked by a horse.'

'May I get something for you?'

'No thank you. I think I'll just sleep a little more.'

When the girl came to check on Cornelia later in the day, concerned that she had still not left her room, she found her superior sweating and vomiting. She was obviously gravely ill.

A priest came to offer sacrifice to the goddess and to pray for Cornelia's recovery. He paused and looked around him at the crowd that had gathered in the Forum. Cornelia's compassion and wise advice had touched many lives, but some of Rome's people came simply out of respect for a much admired chief Vestal. The crowd was varied, united only by their wish to help her. The priest noted the number and variety of supplicants, including a few praetorian guards one of whom stood apart from the rest.

The sacrificial bull, garlanded with red, white and pink roses was led to the place of sacrifice. It was a clean kill. Blood sprayed onto the flowers streaking the petals with crimson.

Cornelia would never find out what life outside the convent might have held for her. The chief Vestal, beloved of all who knew her and devoted servant of Vesta, died two days later. The plague was spreading.

———◦◦◦◦≫◉≪◦◦◦———

Complete and utter panic gripped the city. People huddled inside their houses avoiding public places. The wealthy got out of Rome as fast as possible, travelling to their holiday villas and hideaways to avoid infection. The Via Appia and other city exits were choked with the carts and donkeys of those rushing outside the city walls. Unfortunately for the poor—they had nowhere to run.

Lorraine Blundell

The Forum lay eerily silent. Its grand temples, banking offices, court houses and shopping streets and malls were all closed. People struggled to find sufficient food and left their houses only to scrounge enough to survive on. Inside, they prayed to the gods and spread herbs and healing plants around.

The death carts toiled on their sorry journey towards Mons Vaticanus. In that ancient place the dead were laid to rest with as much dignity and care as was possible. Unfortunately, increasing numbers of bodies took their toll. The burials became more haphazard and the grave diggers more exhausted.

Thirty thousand victims died according to the records of the temple of Libitina. Then the plague left Rome once more.

Mons Vaticanus
(Vatican Hill)

Two graves lay close together in one of the burial grounds after the plague. One,
dedicated to Fabia by her husband, Alcimus, depicted him as an artisan with his
chisel, set square, compass and surveyor's cross.

The second, dedicated to the sculptor Tiberius Claudius Thesius by his wife,
pictured the dead man as he had been in life—sculpting a statue with his dog by
his side.

41

Baiae
(10 miles west of Naples)

Baiae was considered to be the holiday hideaway of the ultra rich. Its wealth and decadence was way beyond that of Capri, Pompeii and Naples. Villas of the elite stood proudly perched on the sloping cliff face overlooking an expanse of sea, while inland, respectable looking building exteriors in the town hid dens of gambling, vice and whoring. The Emperor's holdings extended to a large percentage of Baiae's property and business establishments, adding considerably to his wealth.

Legal offices, wine vendors, medical surgeries, donkey hirers, inns, tanneries, fish farms, pottery factories, hairdressers, fulleries, money lenders and a multitude of other businesses provided for the needs of residents and visitors in Baiae and the nearby major port of Puteoli. One of the largest and most financially rewarding ventures was undoubtedly the sculpture business, creating fake classical statues created from bronze castings. These found their way for extortionate prices to the Saepta or were purchased on the black market for Rome's most luxurious villas, many on the pretence of being an original.

'Baiae is a harbour of vice,' Seneca said, frowning.

'That all depends, of course, on your point of view,' Piso laughed. He'd always known that his companion had a rather narrow point of view and simply ignored it. If there was one thing that Piso liked it was ostentation and extravagance. As far as he could see he'd only live once so he'd better make the best of it.

Piso's villa stood a short walking distance from that of Nero. He lay stretched at full length on a richly gilded couch studying his long legs which were nicely browned from the sun.

'Have you had any second thoughts since the last meeting about getting rid of Nero here? It would only take a push off the cliff or a knife in the back where we're sitting.' Seneca glanced sideways at Piso as he finished the last of his cup of Falernian.

'Not really. It's physically a much easier proposition, certainly, especially sitting here looking at the possibility, but politically, I believe it'd be a disaster.'

'Perhaps you're right,' Seneca murmured.

'When is Nero due here,' Piso asked.

'I'd say, in around three hours. I'd better leave, just in case he's early. What are you going to do?'

'Me—I'm headed to the best sculpture workshop in town. I'd like a good Apollo for the garden. After that I'm going to the casino.'

He laughed at the look of distaste on Seneca's face.

———∞∘◦❋◦∘∞———

'Admire the graceful curve of the arm and the beauty of the face. Surely, one couldn't wish for a sculpture of more exquisite beauty!'

'It's graceful, certainly,' Piso agreed. 'The problem is, I'm afraid, that the price is not.'

The workshop owner looked offended.

'A statue of this quality is worth even more than I'm asking. This is a first class work from a first class sculptor,' he said firmly.

'If this is an original piece of sculpture then I'm Emperor of Rome!' Piso replied sourly.

They stood negotiating in the shabby office of a dusty, sculpture sweatshop, where second rate sculptors reproduced copies from moulds of genuine antique statues. The owner had been through his usual spiel so many times he couldn't count them. This time he was just beginning to realise that he was unlikely to be on the winning end of the argument.

Piso looked down at the scruffy, thin little man in front of him. The contrast between the senator and the sculpture seller couldn't have been more pronounced. Piso was not deluded, however, by the man's appearance. Owners of such workshops in the Baiae area were wealthy men, usually on the backs of the overworked sculptors they employed and the gullibility of buyers.

'If that's your final word on the matter then I'll buy elsewhere.' Piso turned and left the shop.

Within minutes he was being chased down the dusty street by the owner. He soon had his Apollo at the price he'd offered, with free delivery to Rome thrown in as an incentive.

———∞∘◦❋◦∘∞———

Baiae's most classy casino wasn't in the centre of town or in one the narrow side streets. A smart entrepreneur, having done a good deal with a local land owner, built an expensive, exclusive domed casino perched high on one of the cliffs just outside the town centre.

A couple of burly, ex gladiator types standing security at the entrance, looked Piso up and down and admitted him immediately with a nod of their heads. Only those with obvious wealth were welcome. Along with that requirement could be added the necessity to be of a certain social class. Piso met both without difficulty.

The interior was cool and decorated with taste. Marble floors, comfortable couches and heavy crimson curtains, drawn back to make the most of the sweeping sea vista, invited those admitted to sit back, relax and spend their money.

Tables were scattered throughout the large ground floor area for those interested in playing cards. Hostesses in skimpy clothes welcomed newcomers, provided cups of the best wine and willingly sat on the knees of gamblers with roving hands. The girls could be seen randomly heading towards the back of the gaming area to provide more private services as demanded by the clientele.

Piso played a few hands of cards and was then content to simply sit and drink as he watched others spending their money. He was by no means a heavy gambler, for all his love of excess. He always complimented himself that he knew the difference between excess in the pursuit of enjoyment and plain stupidity. He'd been sitting leisurely looking around when one of the hostesses approached him.

'I see that your cup is still full, but is there anything else I can provide for you?' she asked, bending over him provocatively. She was pretty and her smile was inviting. After a moment's temptation Piso decided against a private liaison with her. He'd invited the woman in his life who presently appealed to him, to join him at his villa. He'd wait and not spoil the anticipation of the evening's pleasure.

'No, thanks.'

After a most pleasant afternoon he returned to his villa just as Nero's ship and those of his retinue and 'hangers on' could be seen approaching the royal jetty.

It had taken a long time for Alessia to calm down. She'd tried to take in the advice she'd been given by Fabritio and Claudia, but found herself in a panic, nonetheless. She felt too inexperienced to cope with the situation in which she found herself.

Fabritio had taken her back to the villa on Via del Vesuvio on the morningof departure, ready to leave for Baiae as part of Nero's retinue. She barely saw him for more than a few moments other than at a distance until they boarded the ship.

'Thank you for coming, Lady Alessia.' Nero gave a slight bow as he approached her. She'd been installed in a private room with its own sitting area.

'Divinity.' She bowed low to Nero but he immediately raised her up.

'No. It's not right that you should bow to me. You address me as a god, but I owe you the same deference. So let us not bow to each other for we are truly equals.'

'As you wish, Divinity.'

'Do you have everything you require,' Nero asked.

'I'm very comfortable, thank you,'Alessia assured him.

'Then I'll leave you to relax for the remainder of the voyage until we arrive at Baiae.' Nero departed and Alessia breathed a sigh of relief. It appeared that she was safe at least until the ship docked.

The first time, not long after leaving Naples, that the ship stopped at the shore she thought nothing of it. The second time, Alessia decided to try to see what was happening. She opened the door a chink and peeped out. Seeing no one nearby, she ventured further on to the deck.

A strange sight met her eyes.

'Caesar, please come and enjoy our hospitality!' a woman entreated, beckoning to the Emperor who was already walking closer to her.

The woman was dressed in nothing but a short piece of cloth covering her from the waist to well above her knees, her breasts being fully exposed. Her appearance was that of a common prostitute and her obscene sexual gestures reinforced that belief. Behind her was what could have passed for a small inn, except that it was so ramshackle and flimsy in appearance as to be obviously temporary in nature.

Shocked, Alessia turned to return inside, only to meet the gaze of a praetorian standing beside the door. For a few seconds they stood appraising each other, grey eyes looking into brown.

'May I be of assistance?' the praetorian enquired.

'What is that place?' Alessia pointed to the shack.

'It's one of several places of a temporary nature on this coastline built on the orders of the Emperor. They are for his pleasure as a diversion on the journey to Baiae.'

'Are they what I think they are?' Alessia risked asking.

'Lady, I regret that I'm unable to directly answer you,' the praetorian replied. 'May I simply suggest that you should perhaps believe what your eyes tell you.' He opened the door for her and appeared to be about to say something more but thought better of it. Snapping smartly to attention he gave a slight smile and returned to his post.

Alessia was now more alarmed than she'd been before. She wondered what horrors awaited her at Nero's villa.

The nightingales hid in the trees at Tauromenium.

By Messenger

The Villa of Lucius Diomedes
Caelian Hill
Rome

To: Fabritio Attilius
    The Villa of Diomedes
    Via delle Tombe
    Pompeii

Greetings Fabritio,

I can only echo your concern for Alessia. Thank you for your message. I know that you and Claudia will have used the limited time you had well, to advise her before the trip to Baiae.

I was aware that Nero was to take a holiday there after the competition in Pompeii, but hadn't intended accepting an invitation to attend. Given what's happened, I will certainly go to Baiae immediately, so that Alessia can see me and know that she's not alone.

We must trust to her natural charm and intelligence as well as luck to keep her from harm. If there's trouble, I can promise you that Alessia's safety will be my foremost concern. At least Nero has no idea that there's any link between Alessia and myself. For that, at least, we must be grateful.

Stay positive. Everything may yet be well.

Lucius

42

Nero's Villa

The royal entourage including elite friends of the Emperor as well as senators, arrived at the Baiae villa amidst sweating oxen pulling carts loaded with mounds of baggage. Slaves ran around frantically to meet the demands of their owners as they dismounted from the donkeys that had carried them up the steep cliff from the boats. A detachment of the Praetorian Guard had arrived several days earlier to establish security. They also provided the necessary reinforcements for those already travelling with Nero. They stood ceremoniously at attention to greet him.

He'd brought with him from Naples a select group of advisors. The remainder, including Seneca, Scaurus, Proculus and the poet Petronius, had arrived by land from Rome. Lucius was with them.

'Wait!' Nero beckoned to everyone to stand back. The noise and shouting stopped. He turned to the beautiful young woman beside him. 'My dear, you will have the honour of entering first. Please step down.'

One of the praetorians moved forward to assist Alessia. She took his hand to steady her as she dismounted from the donkey and stood gazing up at the villa's entrance. Nero followed closely behind her.

The whole setting seemed to Alessia like some kind of dream world. Despite her misgivings and considerable fear of the regally garbed figure standing beside her, she couldn't help but be impressed.

'I do hope you like it,' Nero smiled. 'I've ordered that you have the apartment next to mine. The rooms all overlook the sea and I trust will prove comfortable. Should you require anything at all simply tell the house slaves. You have of course, been provided with your own personal attendants.'

'Thank you, Divinity. You are most kind.'

'Your status deserves the best of everything.' Nero inclined his head. 'If anyone displeases you just say so and they will be dispatched.'

Alessia felt a shiver run through her. She managed, however, to walk up the steps into the portico, head held high. The only guarantee of her safety and that of those she loved, was for Nero to continue to regard her as he obviously did—as a reincarnated goddess who had been sent to bring him good fortune. She'd taken a risk when she had initially addressed him as 'Divinity' a title that seemed to delight him, so she continued to use it. Who knew what really went on in his mind, a mind so lost in a dark madness only too clearly on display.

She knew that she must continue to act a part to which she was unaccustomed. Playing a goddess did not come easily to her, but there was no doubt not only her own life but also the lives of those she loved depended on her ability to appear convincing. Fabritio and Claudia had stressed the importance of playing the role expected of her.

Nero turned to her as they entered the atrium. 'Tomorrow night there is to be a dinner. It would please me if you would attend. It will be a special occasion and your presence will enhance the presentation that is sure to be a surprise for everyone.'

He looked enquiringly at her.

'It will, of course, be my pleasure,' Alessia replied graciously.

'Please enjoy visiting the pool and gardens while you're here. Your commands are to be obeyed without question. Now I will have you shown to your apartment.' Nero's expression was that of a child delighted with a new toy.

Alessia turned to find a petite young girl standing beside her. 'Domina, my name is Attia please follow me,' she murmured. Alessia followed the girl out of the atrium.

Attia led the way gracefully across floors so shiny Alessia could have seen her face reflected in them had she chosen to stoop low enough. A marble bathing pool stood in one of the side alcoves. They walked on until reaching the end of the central body of the villa, finally veering to the left into an attached wing closer to the sea.

'This is the apartment reserved for your use.' Attia turned to Alessia, pulling open heavy, wooden doors leading inside.

'This is incredible!' Alessia marvelled. The words escaped her lips before she could stop them. She walked into a small reception area leading into a sumptuous living space overlooking the sea. Lounging couches abounded with vividly coloured cushions and nearby, marble statues of Aphrodite and Apollo watched with disdain. A hallway led to other rooms nearby.

'Domina, welcome to your bedroom!' Attia led the way into one of the rooms off the main hallway.

Alessia was speechless. In front of her was a huge room also overlooking the sea. She could hear the waves as they slapped onto the beach below. A servant had obviously preceded her arrival, providing artistically arranged flowers that filled the room, as well as lit candles. The smell of incense was unmistakable.

The bed was large with expensive linens, and underfoot shone smooth, cooling tiles of imported pink marble. To one side of the room in an alcove, a small shrine had been erected. She saw at its centre a copy of the statuette that Nero had told her he considered to be her likeness. She felt shaken and it frightened her, but she had to admit that the figure certainly did strongly resemble her.

The bathroom held a huge, very deep marble tub. Above it in the centre of the ceiling was an oval, golden disc. To one side with a view of the bed, the bathroom was partitioned from it by a timber wall cut into an intricate lacework design, giving tantalising glimpses into the adjacent room.

There was a knock at the apartment door. Attia admitted a male slave who was carrying Alessia's baggage. He pulled the boxes inside and left.

'Domina, I'm also to be your personal atttendant. Would you like me to put away your garments?' Attia offered.

'That would be wonderful.'

Alessia wondered out onto the balcony outside her room, leaving the maid to unpack. It had not escaped her notice that on the bed lay an array of expensive chitons, tunics, shawls and jewellery. Nero had ensured that she would look her best as an adornment to whatever it was he had planned. No doubt it was also a testament to his respect and fascination for her.

She gazed out at the sea. Always, wherever she went, it seemed to follow her, its never ending progression of waves rolling in and out unceasingly. No matter what her future life held, no doubt the waves would continue forever uncaring of her destiny.

There was another knock at the door. Attia responded and returned to Alessia holding a parchment bearing the Emperor's seal. She opened it and read the contents with mixed emotions.

Greetings!
Compliments to the Divine Alessia.

I would be pleased if you would allow me the honour of dining with you in the garden room of my private apartment this evening. I look forward to your company.
Caesar Nero

Taking a stylus from the desk in her room, Alessia dipped it into an inkwell and wrote an acceptance. She handed it to Attia to give to the bearer of Nero's invitation.

'Attia, I wish to rest now. Please wake me in time to bathe and dress before dinner. I'll also need the services of the royal hairdresser.' Alessia watched as the girl left the apartment, then surrendered herself to the luxury of her bed. Unable to sleep, she tossed and turned restlessly until the maid reappeared.

'Domina, which fragrance would you prefer for your bath?' Attia asked. 'I have lemon or orange.'

'I prefer lemon. Please make the bath very warm.' When it had been prepared she lay soaking, thinking about her situation. Perhaps she should wear one of the Greek chitons tonight. The more like a goddess she looked the better. She had noticed that Nero had a decided preference for Greek clothes and hair styling. At least he would probably approve of her choice.

Nero's invitation was dangerous but she knew she had no option. She must dine with him. Alessia could only pray that she was not to meet the same fate as that of so many other young women before her. Her anxiety level was already rising.

———∘∘∘⟊⟩⟨⟊∘∘∘———

Lucius knew that Alessia had not yet seen him, so she didn't realise he was at the villa. He shared a room with Antonius Natalis in a different wing.

'What are your feelings for Clodia?' Natalis asked unexpectedly as he sat cradling his wine cup.

'She's a wonderful young woman and a real credit to you,' Lucius replied.

'I'm sorry if I appear somewhat blunt, but I've been concerned about her lately. I'm sure she's missing you. Is your answer to my question what it appears to be—a polite way of saying that you have no serious intentions towards her?'

'I regret to say that you are correct.'

'I have to say, Lucius, that I'm somewhat surprised. I thought that you two were getting on so well. Has someone else stolen your heart?'

'I can honestly say, Antonius, that there is no lady in Rome that I believe would make a more suitable marriage partner.' Lucius chose his words carefully. He wouldn't risk making an enemy of the older senator.

'Then why have you put an end to the relationship?' Natalis persisted.

'Antonius, it's purely a matter of personalities. I just wasn't totally sure we were a perfect match. I'm sure you'll agree that Clodia deserves to marry someone she can be happy with forever. I wasn't sure that would have been the case.' Lucius re-filled Natalis' cup.

'Fair enough. At least I respect your honesty,' he relented, answering somewhat gruffly.

Inwardly, Lucius flinched.

———ooo◦❖◦ooo———

Alessia emerged from her apartment that evening dressed in a classic, white chiton caught at the shoulder with a gold fibula. Her hair was piled high on her head and she wore gold sandals as well as heavy gold earrings. A uniformed servant had arrived to escort her to dinner. She was surprised to be led through the hallway to the side door of her apartment, then in the direction of a seldom used door to the adjacent apartment. The evening was fine and warm as she walked along the top of the cliff, the sea swelling below her, and blazing torches attached to the side of the building lighting her way.

'The Emperor is expecting you.' The servant bowed, inviting her to enter.

'Thank you.'

Nero came forward to meet her, directing her towards one of the couches. She settled herself elegantly into its comfort, leaning against a cushion smelling of myrrh.

'A glass of Gauranum, perhaps, Lady Alessia? It's a local wine I think you might like,' Nero beamed at her.

'That would be wonderful.'

A servant was sent to fetch it as Alessia glanced around the room she was sitting in. No wonder it was called the garden room. It was filled with an array of ferns, lilies and other plants, the back wall displaying an exceptional panorama of the starry night sky. The floor was a white mosaic of the highest quality, featuring borders and additional touches of pink and blue, highlighting a giant head of Medusa. How appropriate, Alessia thought. She would probably need a good luck charm tonight. She sipped at her cup of delicious, sweet, white wine. Much milder than the renowned Falernian, she found that she preferred it.

'My lady, how good of you to come. Are your room arrangements and servants suitable?'

'Certainly, Divinity. The apartment is most comfortable.'

'I do hope you'll enjoy the dinner to be served tonight. I have arranged for my chef to prepare some of the superb local fish as well as vegetables, quails eggs and a variety of desserts. Would you care to begin?'

Nero snapped his fingers and the first course of dishes was carried in. Alessia studied him more closely. He really was quite a good looking man, except for a paunch that would no doubt become more evident as the years

234

went by. From what Lucius had told her he was susceptible to flattery and had a cruel, vindictive streak if crossed. She had no intention of finding out if that was true. Over a leisurely dinner they discussed music. His admiration and leaning towards anything Greek was obvious.

For the first time, Alessia realised how truly driven Nero was and the intensity of his ambition. In her opinion, his estimation of his own abilities was misplaced. She considered his talent mediocre. She couldn't help but admire his will to succeed, however, and the work he had done to that end. She also didn't want to be anywhere around if fulfilment of the ambition that drove him was ever thwarted.

'Would you be willing to favour me with your advice in a couple of tutoring sessions during your stay here?' Nero asked. 'I had to let Terpnus go, you understand. He was simply not achieving as much as I'd hoped especially given my level of talent.'

'It would be my pleasure,' Alessia replied. 'Perhaps we should schedule a session for tomorrow?' Inwardly, she wondered if Terpnus had escaped with his life.

Nero seemed as relaxed and happy as she'd ever seen him in the short time she'd known him. Alessia hoped he would stay that way. She had yet to work out exactly how to handle the music sessions she would obviously have to give him. Perhaps she should simply rely on replicating the advice she herself had been given by Valentina.

After dinner they sat leisurely drinking more of the Gauranum. Alessia sipped slowly hoping not to become too intoxicated. Hopefully, the evening was almost over.

Unexpectedly, Nero's mood changed. He came over to her and went down on his knees. Reaching for her hand he held it to his lips, gazing up into her face. She realised with horror that he had tears streaming down his cheeks and into his beard.

'Please, Divinity, it's not appropriate that you should kneel to me.' She struggled to focus on how to handle the situation. Looking distracted, he stood and came to sit beside her.

'Lady Alessia, I need your help,' he blubbered. 'I can't stand the awful nightmares. Octavia and Agrippina pursue me with whips and demons night after night. I don't know how to get forgiveness for what I've done! They will never leave me alone until I do!'

'Divinity, not even those of us who are divine can live our lives without pain,' Alessia answered, turning towards him to take his hand. 'That is the price we pay. Only when you are called to the gods will that pain cease. However, you've been given gifts to use in order to make it bearable. One of those gifts is your music. You must use it to ease your suffering. Also, I'm here to help you.'

Alessia desperately hoped that she had answered wisely. Although she'd heard of Octavia's exile and rumours about her death, she had absolutely no idea what Nero was talking about in relation to his mother. He looked at her with an almost childlike adoration.

'Your wisdom is an inspiration. You are a woman of great beauty, untouchable and a goddess here on earth,' he whispered. I dare only to kiss your hand. Forgive me. I'm grateful for the good fortune and advice you bring me.'

'Divinity, I thank you for your hospitality this evening. I trust your sleep will be restful tonight. It's time I left you.'

Alessia made her way towards the door. Nero hurried to help her out onto the pathway as the servant appeared to guide her to her apartment. His eyes shone with the fervour of madness as he watched his goddess depart.

That night Nero's sleep was dreamless.

Attia

As confided to the slave Anna

I think it's a real shame! I wonder if the Lady Alessia realises how many other young women have come and gone from this apartment that so impresses her. She didn't say much, but I saw the look on her face. She's not like the others. There's something sweet and genuine about her. Nothing seems to have happened at dinner with Nero. She's lucky!

She's out in the garden this morning. She wouldn't feel so peaceful and secure if she realised that that's where Agrippina died a few years ago. I remember that day well because it was the feast of Minerva and we were all running around trying to get everything ready. The night before had been brilliant with starlight and the seas calm. I saw Nero's disappointment when they carried his mother up the cliff after she swam ashore from the boat accident. If that was really an accident I'll eat my sandals!

Agrippina was still alive. That was the problem. One of the legionaries 'finished her off' on the grass out there. Poor lady.

I can't say I was surprised to see one of her servants, Agerinus, blamed for supposedly attempting to assassinate Nero on her orders. The thwarted attempt was reported to have caused Agrippina to commit suicide.

I found out later that the Emperor had ordered his mother's body to be cut into pieces. Then he stopped to have dinner before giving his opinion on how ugly parts of her body were. It's disgusting! But then, what else can be expected from a madman?

Lady Alessia's the only woman who's come here with Nero that I've ever really liked. Not that that counts for anything. I'm only a slave and that's all I'll ever be.

43

Gwauck! Gwauck! The short, raucous screeching sounded like nothing else she'd ever heard, causing Alessia to run quickly back inside the nearest doorway. Deciding to take a walk in the gardens the next morning after successfully giving Nero his lesson, she'd hardly taken a few steps outside when the screaming assaulted her ears.

'Domina, is there anything I can do?' The doorman saw her hurrying inside. He came running from the kitchen where he had taken a few minutes off duty to snatch a stolen kiss from a new female slave.

'What *is* that noise?'

'Have you ever seen live peacocks before, Domina?'

'No, only a few mosaic pictures of them. I'm not sure I want to know more about them either, judging by the din out there.' Alessia could still hear their cries only slightly muffled inside the portico in which she was standing.

'I think you'll find that the peacocks are just around the corner of the building,' the doorman continued. 'It really is quite safe to go and watch them. Might I be so bold as to suggest that I believe you'll find them quite beautiful.'

Alessia looked at him as if he was somewhat 'unhinged.' Still, it wouldn't do she supposed, to appear unwilling to accept his assurances even if he was only a freedman. This was the Emperor's household after all. The servant was hardly likely to risk the physical wellbeing of a guest. She ventured out once again and found herself nearly face to face with some of the most magnificent creatures she had ever seen.

The garden around the corner was flat before eventually sloping down towards the sea. A large area had been fenced off to prevent any of the peacocks straying. A number of them strutted around completely ignoring Alessia's presence. Her eyes were drawn to one in particular. The others all had colours of vivid blue and purple with green eyes on their tails but this one was pure white. As if on cue, it fanned out its stunning tail feathers and began to circle in front of her, dancing as if demanding her admiration.

She stood watching it for some time rapt with its beauty. The peacocks' arrogance was obvious. These creatures were certainly fit for an Emperor's garden.

'It seems you've found the peacocks.' Nero had been watching her, unobserved, for some minutes.

'They're incredible. I wouldn't have believed something so beautiful existed,' Alessia enthused.

'I'm glad you're pleased. I find it interesting and not in the least surprising that you're drawn to the peacocks. Perhaps you don't know, but they are a symbol of divinity and magnificence, so you see, your reaction is highly appropriate. Actually, I've been looking for you to let you know that due to last minute matters needing attention before the presentation dinner tonight, I'm afraid I cannot accompany you to see the bathhouse temple this afternoon as I'd promised.'

'I understand, Divinity. I'm sure I can spend time enjoying the gardens.'

'Rather than have you disappointed, however, I've asked Senator Lucius Diomedes to take you. I trust that is suitable?' Nero looked pleased with himself.

'Yes. I'll miss your company, Divinity, but I look forward to seeing the temple.' Alessia's heart skipped a beat as she realised that Lucius was at the villa. She congratulated herself that she'd managed to keep her composure surprisingly well.

'I've arranged to have one of the praetorians go with you as well for security. However, I doubt you'll need any. Now I'm afraid I must attend to the matters at hand.' Nero smiled, bowed and hurried away.

Alessia could not have been happier. At last, perhaps they would be fortunate enough to have a few stolen moments together. She continued to walk briefly in the gardens before returning to her apartment.

———∘∘∘⦅◈⦆∘∘∘———

One of Baiae's thriving enterprises was the practice of medicine. It catered to the rich suffering from a variety of physical health problems. They visited the many thermal baths hoping for relief, paying enormous sums of money to physicians. These specialists extended their services, when made financially worthwhile, to personally attending patients at the bathhouse of their choice.

There was one thermal bathhouse that stood out from the others. The Emperor had made it known that no one else was to attend on the afternoon he'd planned to go with Alessia. Now she went instead with Lucius.

Known locally as the echo temple, they had the place to themselves when they reached it in the afternoon, with only one of the praetorians trailing behind them. A guard in his early thirties, fit and intelligent, he'd been selected supposedly at random by Tigellinus for this assignment. In reality, it had more to do with the fact that most of the other off duty guards at the time, were already at the whorehouses or gambling dens in town when the Emperor's directive had come through.

The three enjoyed a leisurely stroll, passing through the arched entryway to the bathhouse complex not long after leaving the villa. The approach to the cavern itself had the appearance of a natural garden with ferns and mossy rocks providing a restful setting. The track was well worn and dusty, wildflowers nearby providing a welcoming splash of colour.

'Just watch your step.' Lucius held Alessia's hand as they clambered down the steep incline leading into the main bathhouse chamber.

'Senator, I'll remain on guard out here!' Praxus called out as they disappeared from view. He settled himself on a large rock to enjoy sitting in the sun as he looked forward to a lazy hour or two to follow, tagging along with the two sightseers. The rock cavern in which Lucius and Alessia found themselves was unbelievably huge, with a dome unlike anything she had ever seen. Bathers could enjoy soaking in the steaming water at the bottom of the cave.

'The size of this dome's almost as impressive as the Pantheon in Rome,' Lucius commented, impressed. Alessia clapped her hands with delight. The sound echoed around the cavern as she gazed up at the sunlight shining through the oculus at the top of the dome. It streamed down, bathing her face in an ethereal light. Standing there in her long, yellow robe the colour of sunshine, Lucius thought that she really did look like a goddess. He drew her close to him in an urgent embrace. They clung together their kisses lingering and passionate. When they eventually parted, Lucius sensed someone at his back. He turned to see the praetorian standing behind him.

'Senator, please accept my apologies. I came in to let you know that the Emperor has just sent a message. Dinner is to begin one hour earlier than previously advised.' The guard snapped to attention then turned and marched back outside to the rock.

'Lucius, I'm afraid that if the guard reports what he's seen we may be in great danger.' Alessia looked up at him, alarmed. 'Nero made it plain that he considers me untouchable. Even he dared not touch me except to kiss my hand. It's my only form of protection. You know what he's like. If he considered someone had taken liberties I would be afraid for both of us.'

'Don't worry yet. I'll talk to the guard,' Lucius frowned. 'We should leave now.' Anxiously they re-joined the praetorian at the entrance to the chamber.

'Praetorian,' Lucius addressed him, 'what you saw inside . . .'

Praxus interrupted him. 'Senator, you must be mistaken. I don't know what you mean. I haven't left my post!' He stood stiffly at attention looking into space over Lucius' left shoulder. 'I do need to inform you, however,' Praxus continued, 'that dinner tonight will be one hour earlier.'

'Very good. Come, Lady Alessia, we mustn't be late for the Emperor's dinner.' Lucius acknowledged the guard's words with a brief nod as he led the way past him back up the cliff to the villa. He would discretely find out later who the praetorian was. He was obviously willing for some reason to protect them by keeping their secret.

Praxus hoped that Lucius and Alessia realised the danger the two of them faced if they were caught again in a similarly compromising situation. Today, they'd simply been lucky! Surely they realised that at the end of each assignment the guards were supposed to report anything unusual or that might perhaps be of interest to the Emperor. They seemed to him to be sensible and unlikely to make the same mistake twice. At least he hoped that he was not being overly optimistic. He'd also seen enough to realise that they were deeply in love.

Praxus had no intention of being responsible for carrying out yet another innocent young woman's execution on Nero's orders. Octavia's sweet face was still painfully fresh in his memory.

Count the numerical values
Of the letters in Nero's name,
And in 'murdered his own mother':
You will find their sum is the same

Graffiti – City walls of Rome
(Suetonius)

44

The air was very still. The sun had set leaving the energy sapping heat of the day still very much in evidence. Only the breeze off the sea provided any respite from the oppressive, oxygen depleted air breathed by those listlessly preparing for the evening's activities. Later, it would be said by those who had attended the Emperor's dinner that they had been present at a moment in time that changed history.

Nero's triclinium was filled to capacity with his advisors and the various senators and other dignitaries invited to Baiae. The room was unusually long with ample space to hold large dinner parties. At the very far end furthest from the entry a huge, marble statue of Jupiter stood in magnificence inside a wall niche. It was well lit in comparison with the dim light in the remainder of the dining room.

On entering, all eyes were immediately drawn to Alessia who reclined on the right hand side of the Emperor. Her beauty was dazzling causing Lucius, especially, to catch his breath at the sight of her. He remembered her warning that afternoon and feared that even the Emperor's respect for her as a reincarnated goddess, would not be enough to deter his lechery. Her dark hair was caught in a hairnet embedded with filaments of gold. She was wearing a deep shade of blue and golden bangles on her arms.

'You're a vision tonight. Your beauty can only have been a gift from the gods,' Nero whispered admiringly to her.

'My thanks, Divinity. As you are aware, that is indeed so.'

'I have something for you that I hope you'll like.' Nero beckoned to one of the slaves. He left the room, returning a couple of minutes later.

'This is for you.' Nero leaned so close to her she could smell the wine on his breath. He handed her a fan made of gloriously coloured peacock feathers.

'Divinity, this is a wonderful surprise!' She held it delicately as if afraid to spoil the fragile gift. 'You are most generous.' Nero's delight with her reaction was obvious.

Dinner was a long succession of dishes each more complex than the last. Several musicians on lyres, tambourine and flutes provided background music to which no one paid much attention. A couple of scantily clad dancing girls whirled and gyrated before Nero.

Lucius saw a watchfulness in the faces of Seneca—now retired from the Senate, Piso, who was seated beside him and a couple of other senior senators also sitting with them. He thought that he knew what they were probably quietly discussing.

Eventually, everyone followed the Emperor and Alessia into an adjacent room. The flares and lamps had all been lit and it was obvious that some kind of announcement was to be made.

'Servants, you may leave!' There was an expectant silence as they all left except for those attending to the table. 'Everyone, gather around!' Nero gestured to his guests to surround him. 'I have something important to show you.'

Lucius saw the curiosity on the faces of those present, including Alessia. So he hasn't told her yet what this is about, he thought, studying her as she stood watching. He didn't know if that was a good sign or not and hoped that she could manage to look suitably impressed with whatever appeared on the table.

The covers came off.

There was a gasp of surprise around the room. A huge, detailed model of the city of Rome had been constructed and lay before them in all its detailed complexity. Nero stood watching his guests' reaction, missing nothing.

'Caesar, what is this for?' Seneca moved forward to stand directly beside the table.

'Some of you already know that I've decided to build a new royal palace with gardens, even a lake, that better reflects the glory of the city,' Nero announced. 'I've decided that it will be known as the Domus Aurea. Unfortunately, there's not enough land available in the right location for my project. And so—I've decided to create some. Eventually, I intend that the new, glorious city of Rome will be known as Neropolis.' He looked smugly around him at the shocked faces of his guests.

There was a low murmuring around the group. Surprise was quickly replaced by fear.

'But how, Caesar?' Seneca persisted. 'As you can see, there is no land available.' He waved his hand in a sweeping gesture that encompassed the whole model.

'Do not fear, my noble Seneca. There will be—after the fire.'

'Fire? What fire?' Lucanus stepped up to the table beside Seneca.

'The fire that is being lit as we speak,' Nero said in a matter of fact tone. 'And now, dear guests, in celebration of this great event, I have decided to reward your patience by singing for you. He turned and walked to the nearest couch, clapping his hands for a slave to enter with his lyre. Recognising the danger in anything other than acceptance of the situation, Lucius regained his wits before most and began to applaud while indicating to those around him to do the same.

'Alessia, my dear, please grant me the honour of your company and support. I have chosen 'The Sack of Ilium' for is not Rome as great as Troy? You know how difficult it is even for one as talented as I to give the perfect performance of such a piece. I hope it will be to your liking.'

Nero reclined comfortably, arranging his robes around him. Clearing his throat and looking to the heavens the droning began as he subjected those present to the latest of his long, bizarre performances. Alessia sat nearby smiling encouragement. Inwardly, she prayed only to emerge from the evening alive and unharmed.

———◦◦◦⦓◈⦔◦◦◦———

The Emperor, after pleading from his guests had persuaded him to perform a second time, and having consumed copious amounts of wine, retired to his apartment. Unable to stand upright enough to do so of his own accord, he was carried there by servants. Alessia, after an anxious glance across at Lucius, retired to her own apartment. Quickly, she blew out the candles Attia had lit at her shrine. The whole thing struck her as obscene. The very thought of the fire apparently burning in Rome killing women and children at this very moment, made her sick to her stomach. Eventually, she lay down and tried to sleep.

Lucius made his way into the garden, his mind whirling with the night's implications. As he stood beside an ancient pine tree silhouetted against sea and sky, he sensed rather than than saw someone come up quietly behind him.

'Nero must be stopped! This time he's gone too far. The fire is an abomination. He may well have destroyed the greatest city this world has ever seen,' Seneca hissed.

'Lucius, as you've not approached me, I presume that you've decided not to involve yourself in our endeavours. I respect that decision. I'd simply like to warn you that the place for the attempt has been decided. Now we'll take a decision as to a date. It won't be long before we're rid of that monster.'

Seneca slipped back into the darkness.

As the evening wore on and became early morning, travel weary messengers began to arrive with news of a catastrophic fire in Rome. At two in the morning, not long after he'd retired, Nero was woken with the message. Rather than appearing angry as his attendants had feared, his eyes were almost wild with excitement.

———∘∘∘⟩◯⟨∘∘∘———

Earlier that evening

The bathhouse was empty. Guests had left long before to attend dinner. Lydos was still cleaning up the used towels, strigils and oils left from the bathers. Hearing a slight cough behind him he turned and found himself looking into serious, dark brown eyes in a stately face crowned by silver hair.

'Dominus, I didn't hear you come in.'

'That was my intention,' Seneca replied.

'How may I serve you?'

'Do I understand correctly that your name is Lydos?' the statesman asked.

'Yes.' Lydos wondered what this intense looking man wanted of him.

'Would you like to have your freedom back?'

Lydos simply stared, open mouthed. What was going on here? Was this some sort of a test, or a trick? If so, he wasn't going to fall for it.

Seneca stood watching the slave's reaction, allowing him time to consider the implications. 'I'm here to offer you an opportunity,' he continued. 'I will only offer it once. Either way, if you repeat what I tell you here tonight you will be in a great deal of danger.'

'May I ask what this is all about?' Lydos asked carefully. 'I won't repeat what I'm told.' He'd dropped the bundle of towels he was holding and now stood absolutely still.

'You don't need to know the details,' Seneca answered. 'I need someone to take a message for me to Pompeii. It must be someone who can move quickly and yet carefully. There's an old tunnel that's been dug underground between Baiae and Naples. It's seldom used by anyone. You'll travel through that and then onto Pompeii to an address I give you. There you will wait to be contacted. I need someone I can trust to help out in Pompeii as necessary for a short time. You're not aware of it but you've been watched for several weeks. I believe that you're ideal for this task. In return, after you've completed your assignments, you will be provided with money and your freedom. You can disappear and start a new life.'

Seneca drew a scroll from the folds of his toga. Bearing the official seal of the Emperor, it declared the bearer to be a freedman. On it was written Lydos' name. His gaze was fixed on it.

'Are you interested?'

'Of course,' Lydos replied, his eyes alert, his body tense.

'You must travel tonight. Here is the message you are to carry. Go quickly to your room where you'll find money and a change of clothing. You'll be met at the back kitchen door by a guide who will take you to the mouth of the tunnel. In case you're interested, I can at least tell you that by doing this, you'll ensure that some of the madness is removed from this world. When you reach your destination you will use the code word *Phoenix* to the owner at the following address.'

Seneca handed him a small scroll written in an unknown hand. 'Memorise the information then destroy it.'

The Inn of Euxinus
Via di Castricio
Pompeii

'Good luck! If you're caught I will deny ever having met you. I'm sure you know who will be believed.' Seneca turned and walked quickly away. Lydos hurried to his room. Soon he was trekking with his guide towards the tunnel and eventual freedom—or so he hoped.

———∞∞⊰◉⊱∞∞———

The result of the evening's news was that Nero hurried back to Rome with the Praetorian Guard, leaving his retinue to fend for themselves. They would return in their own time. The Senators, including Lucius, also prepared to hurry back to Rome, fearing the worst in terms of the loss of the city. Before leaving, Lucius went to speak to Alessia as morning rose over Baiae.

'Alessia, I've made arrangements for your return to Pompeii. Nero's gone back to Rome. I'm sorry but I must return with the other senators. Don't worry, you'll be safe. I've also sent a message to Fabritio.'

'Do you have to go, Lucius? I'm afraid for you.'

'I have no alternative,' he replied. 'You'll hear from me again soon. I must leave now before someone sees us talking and becomes suspicious. Take care, my darling.'

Alessia watched him go. It seemed that she had to do that quite often. She felt sick with worry.

Lorraine Blundell

Rome
19th July 64 A.D.

At first it was just a teasing, yellowish red flicker—a small, insignificant 'something' lick, lick, licking at the edge of a rotten, sagging piece of the furniture factory's ancient timber door. It was a tiny pulse of light in the dark night that had already fallen, concealing the squalor of the buildings near the Circus Maximus and their occupants'shady transactions, as well as their more vile human transgressions.

The narrow laneway lay empty, foul and silent except for one old vagrant at its far end, coughing and shuffling on shaky legs as he disappeared from sight around the corner. The transformation when it came was swift and startling. From the rags of decrepit old age emerged a youthful figure, moving fast.

A pile of discarded rags lay strewn on the paving stones. Further up the laneway behind it the tiny, pulsing flicker was also undergoing a transformation. From an existence barely more than nothingness, it eventually became the raging flames of the most relentless, killer inferno that would ever devastate the city.

'I am but a small flickering light in the darkness—yet I will play an important part in changing Rome's history.'

45

Rome

There has to be a way! The Greek muttered under his breath as he walked, unseeing, towards the Circus Maximus. He'd been three nights without much sleep. Perhaps a stroll around what was to him the most exciting of Rome's entertainment venues would help quiet his racing thoughts.

As owner of the *Blues* chariot racing team it was up to him to find a way to take the *Greens* on and defeat them. It seemed an impossible task. He couldn't remember the last time they'd been beaten and the fact that they were favoured by Nero certainly didn't help. The *Green's* popularity brought them wealth the other teams couldn't match.

It was strange, he thought, seeing the huge stadium at night without the screaming crowds. In the dim peace of the darkness it looked almost like a giant, sleeping ghost. Chariot races, crucifixions and even royal celebration dinners had been held there but tonight it lay eerily still.

His tunic needed changing, he was exhausted and he couldn't remember when he'd last eaten. The fact that he could smell the stink of his own body wasn't exactly a good sign, either. If he didn't find an answer to his problems soon, he'd be out of money not just for his own needs but to buy uniforms and feed for the horses. He arrived at his destination and stood where he could just make out the outline of the dolphins on the spina at the centre of the sand track.

Rome's famous chariot racing venue, located at the foot of the lush Palatine, home of royalty and the elite, stood silently waiting for its next big occasion. The huge, high wooden structure with its central spina held thousands upon thousands of screaming spectators whenever races were held.

Tonight could well put an end to all of that.

The tongues of flames were small at first. They began in a furniture shop in a street near the Circus, dancing their way happily towards its vulnerable, wooden walls. The fire moved quickly as if in a hurry to claim its prize. Flames licked at the wooden stands on the eastern side, hungrily devouring the first of the seats. The Greek could barely believe his eyes. He ran for Rome's firefighters.

The Circus'next big occasion had just arrived!

———∘∘∘⦀⦀∘∘∘———

'Don't worry about it. It's bound to be a hoax. The man's lost his senses.' Placidus complacently shrugged at his second in command.

'It looks like it. Maybe he's been drinking.'

The tribune was the senior officer on duty when the Greek stumbled into the vigiles'office mumbling somewhat incoherently. He continued to wave his arms about frantically in an attempt to communicate the urgency of the situation.

'Perhaps we should send a runner over there, just the same. I wouldn't want to be found in dereliction of my duty,' Placidus grinned. 'Hey, Plautus, where's that young urchin that hangs around us?'

Plautus, hearing the din, stuck his head around the door. 'Can't a man even grab a few minutes snooze around here?' he complained irritably. 'What's up?'

'Get that youngster to hike over to the Circus and see if there's any fire there. I want it done now—not next week!'

By the time the boy had reached the Circus its wooden walls had completely turned into leaping walls of flame. They could be seen for miles as they soared above the burning arena, then swept voraciously through the Palatine Hill heading for the Esquiline.

———∘∘∘⦀⦀∘∘∘———

Rome was the most densely populated city in the world. Except for patricians, its people lived cheek by jowl in high rise wooden tenements, usually of shoddy construction. They prayed together at the painted wall images of Rome's deities and unwillingly shared each others' secrets through the thin walls. Arguments and brawls were so common as to be unremarkable. If the building had latrines or water, they were to be found only at ground level.

Streets were narrow, filthy and dangerous. This was particularly true of the Subura which was apartment living for the multitude of the poor. As far as the wealthy were concerned it was located uncomfortably close to the Forum. The streets stank of urine and excrement thrown from top floors onto the alleys below and were robbed of all but a miserly touch of sunlight. The probabily of fire was high with dozens reported in any one week. The firefighters worked hard—usually fighting a losing battle.

Panic set in as the city woke to a blood red sky and the acrid smell of dirty, billowing smoke. The conflagration effortlessly devoured the foundations of tenement after tenement. Fatally damaged, they tumbled and fell headlong like dying giants into the streets and laneways with an ear splitting crash.

Rome's inhabitants ran for their lives, holding makeshift masks over their faces in an attempt to avoid breathing in the suffocating smoke devoid of life giving oxygen. The old were often left to fend for themselves. Many did not escape the flames. With nowhere to run that offered obvious safety, people fled to the open areas of Rome and out of the city walls to the Appian Way and the fields of the countryside.

Most of the city's temples and public buildings as well as her cherished historical monuments, palatial mansions, altars, shrines and priceless art works were incinerated. Even Nero's royal palace, the Domus Transitoria, completed not so long before did not escape damage.

The city burned relentlessly in a scene reminiscent of hell itself. Later, it was said that the fire had killed nine hundred and seventy nine people as it raged on remorselessly. Looters had their way with whatever goods those fleeing had left behind, turning the disaster into a windfall for themselves and additional misery for their victims.

After five days the fire appeared to have burnt itself out leaving a scene of misery behind it. But it had not finished with its prey yet. A highly suspect series of events occurred which saw the fire re-start for another three days. Granaries were destroyed near Nero's new Domus Aurea, and other untouched areas were torched by unknown hands, their owners preventing others from intervening to quell the flames.

'You there! What do you think you're doing?'

A couple of ruffians ran off as a group of Vigiles approached, catching them in the act of setting fire to the grounds of the estate belonging to Tigellinus. The perpetrators' identities remained unknown as did their reasons.

Praetorian tribune, Subrius Flavus, couldn't get the rumours and cries of the dying out of his mind. He sat in his room at the Castra Praetoria, his head in his hands, trying to erase images that he feared would stay with him forever. It never took long for word of unusual orders within praetorian ranks to filter through to those guards still under normal orders. Flavus had certainly heard many such rumours about orders issued to fellow praetorians on the night of the fire.

Praetorians out of uniform were rumoured to have been told to deter those trying to save buildings in certain districts. Force was to be used if necessary.

Official Orders! No Entry! The cry went around.

The buildings were then torched by the enforcers. Could it be that those buildings had been specifically marked for destruction? It was the opinion of Flavus and many like him, that it was not only possible but probable. They lay in the way of Nero's aspirations for his Golden House and gardens.

Sick at heart, Flavus decided to break his oath of allegiance to Nero. Some days later he sought the most respected elder statesman of them all—Seneca. The Pisonian conspirators had gained a valuable convert. Whispers began to circulate in Rome about Nero's complicity in the severity and even commencement of the most destructive fire in Rome's history.

-----ooo❧ooo-----

'Tigellinus, you must do something about it!' Nero stood fuming as his closest courtiers faced him with downcast eyes.

'Caesar, what would you have me do?'

'Get rid of the rumours sweeping the city. There must be a way. They're becoming more wide spread as the days go by.' Nero glowered at the Prefect.

'I believe, Caesar, that there are two ways around this.

First, we must make the people believe that someone else started the fire,' Tigellinus stated firmly. 'Second, you must take measures that show them you care about their plight.'

'They sound like they might work.' Nero stroked his beard as he considered the suggestions. 'Did you have anyone particular in mind to blame?'

'Well, we could always say it was the Christians. No one likes them much,' Tigellinus replied.

'Christians? I've never heard of them. Who are they?'

'They're a small Jewish sect,' Tigellinus explained.

'Caesar, I do believe that Tigellinus may have found the answer to your problem,' Poppaea answered from where she sat nearby being fanned by a slave. She'd been queasy lately and seemed to need to rest often. She wondered what was wrong with her. Perhaps Farzana would have some suggestions.

'Do it—and quickly!' Nero ordered, 'before we have a riot on our hands!'

As the Christians were being rounded up, soldiers began to implement changes to the city drawn up to put in place long term improvements. Handouts of bread were increased and the price of corn reduced to three sesterces a peck. Soldiers were sent into the streets to help clean up the mess and rubble which was then transported down the Tiber and dumped in the marshes of Ostia.

Houses were rebuilt this time using fire proof materials and on broad streets rather than narrow alleyways. They had height restrictions placed on them if they were high rise tenements. Nero paid for the building of colonnades in front of the premises of ground floor landlords. These proved popular as did the high walls erected to enclose buildings. Except for a few complaints about the wide streets being too exposed to the heat of the sun, people were pleased with the outcome.

The tide of public opinion began to soften towards Nero.

Lorraine Blundell

The Royal Palace

Huddled together in small groups they were herded into Nero's gardens as the sightless eyes of marble gods and goddesses looked on dispassionately. Dusk was turning to night as the onlookers gaped at the sight of men and women, young and old and even children being tarred and bound to stakes.

These members of the little known sect of the Jews known as Christians had escaped the day's earlier crucifixions and mauling by wild animals, only to be sentenced to a fate just as painful. All that remained before the final executions was to wait for the darkness of evening and the arrival of Nero.

Finally, all of the palace flares were extinguished. The gardens were lit instead by the bodies of the condemned as the flames burned them alive and their screams rang out in the silence.

46

Misenum
(3 Miles South of Baiae)

The woman walked slowly along the waterfront gazing out at the artificial, rocky outcrops in the sea as she shielded her eyes from the sun's glare. Seating herself on a convenient bench she turned to look not out to the water but towards the land. She was of Greek appearance, tall for a woman, with dark eyes, full lips and a curve to her cheek that made men look twice. Her long, dark hair was whipped away from her face by a stiff breeze.

The scene that met her gaze was typical of a port town. Many run down, slovenly inns had pride of place facing the harbour. A few were scattered through narrow, ill lit back lanes. Drunken brawls, illicit gambling, prostitution, corruption and murder all plagued these establishments.

Epicharis, a freedwoman, lived in a small, respectable house where she'd been renting a room for some months. It was far enough inland to escape the noise endured by those living in or near the inns. Luxury villas had been built in the most elegant, well to do areas of the town, overlooking the gorgeous Bay of Puteoli. They were heavily guarded against intrusion by the less salubrious of Misenum's inhabitants and visitors.

Misenum was the largest base of the Roman navy. It was generally accepted that Rome's military strength did not rely upon her navy. It never had and probably never would, but the importance of a large navy to police the Empire's interests in the Mediterranean, especially the safeguarding of grain shipments, could not be overestimated.

Naval ships of all descriptions sheltered at the port, including quadriremes, triremes and liburnians. The fleet was focused on light, manouevreable, fast capabilities. Its ships were less cumbersone than their predecessors such as the quinqueremes. The crews had considerable periods of 'down' time unless some unexpected event occurred. Their lives were more quiet and predictable than in the remainder of the Roman military forces. Interspersed with the naval fleet a number of speedy merchant ships capable of carrying weapons, animals and provisions lay at anchor.

Epicharis rose as she saw a familiar figure striding purposefully towards her. Volusius Proculus was commander of the fleet and captained the flagship *Taurus Ruber*. The two had met not long after Epicharis' arrival in Misenum several months before. They'd quickly formed a friendship, enjoying each other's company socially and then more intimately.

During a recent visit to Rome, Epicharis, the ex mistress of Seneca's brother, had jokingly confided in Seneca that she'd found herself a new man. Upon hearing of the man's rank his interest had sharpened. The fact that Volusius was constantly openly complaining about the lack of an expected promotion clinched Seneca's acceptance of his importance. Volusius had been involved in Nero's murder of Agrippina. His bitterness at Nero's lack of gratitude was there for all to hear.

Seneca couldn't believe his luck. Taking Epicharis aside privately, he swore her to secrecy, telling her about *Phoenix*. He explained the reason for their decision.

'For the good of Rome we must rid ourselves of Nero before he destroys her,' Seneca told Epicharis emphatically. 'Are you willing to attempt to persuade Volusius and his soldiers to join us? It's dangerous, I know. I'll understand if you refuse.'

'I'll do it!' she told him after a short silence. 'From what I've heard, your group is very slow to take real action. Hopefully, I'll be able to hurry the process along for you.' No more was said and she returned to Misenum.

Epicharis smiled as Volusius joined her on the bench. He was a man in his mid forties, weather beaten and strongly built. His quirky sense of humour and apparent lack of sleeziness or vulgarity had won her over.

'You're looking particularly fetching today,' he complimented her.

'For an old sailor, you're not too bad yourself,' she teased.

They sauntered along the promenade, arm in arm. Epicharis had received a message ealier that day stressing that the matter of Volusius'involvement had become urgent. She couldn't afford to wait any longer. She decided to push ahead with an attempt to recruit her lover to Seneca's cause.

'Why don't we buy a honey pastry at *Alexander's*?' she suggested to him.

'Actually, you've read my mind,' Volusius laughed. 'That's exactly what I feel like.'

Completely at ease with each other, they took their time making their way to the small bakery shop in a pretty square, where they'd discovered what they'd both agreed were the best pastries anywhere. There was no one much around but there would be, later in the afternoon, when the old men came to sit, drink and swap tales of the sea with one another.

They sat on a bench outside the shop stuffing their mouths full of the delicious delicacy. The honey was locally supplied. Its sticky sweetness had many times been credited with a marked improvement in the mood of many of the shop's customers.

'I don't suppose you've had any more news about a promotion?' Epicharis asked Volusius as casually as possible.

'No, and I don't expect to either.'

'It's such a shame,' she persisted.

'It's not so surprising when you really think about it, though,' Volusius commented. 'There's not much gratitude around any more for those of us who try to help someone else—even when they should know better than to just dismiss it afterwards.'

'Have you ever thought about doing something about it?' Epicharis asked ingenuously.

'Of course I have, but there's not much I can do, is there?'

'What if I told you that there's a way not only to make Nero regret his ingratitude, but also to get you that promotion?' she suggested carefully.

'What are you talking about?' Volusius turned to look at her.

'I can tell you in confidence that there's a plot being planned against Nero. It will be going ahead soon. Are you interested?'

'I might be,' Volusius ventured after a short silence. 'Who's involved?'

'I can't tell you that until you've given a commitment.'

'I need time to think. I'll tell you in a couple of days,' he replied, rising from the bench.

They made their way back the way they'd come. Volusius kissed Epicharis goodbye and they agreed to meet again two days later.

Lorraine Blundell

Misenum

The Vigiles Office

'You wish to see me?' The tribune studied the man before him who stood facing him in the small police office.

'I do,' Volusius answered. 'I have news of a plot being planned against the Emperor.'

'I see.' The tribune's interest intensified. 'I understand that you're the fleet commander—is that correct?'

'That's correct.'

'How sure are you about this? I trust that a man of your rank would know better than to waste not only my time, but those of my superiors?'

'One can rarely be sure about these things, of course, but I believe it to be true.'

'Then I thank you for your vigilance. This matter will be reported to Rome with the haste its importance deserves. What is the name of the traitor?'

'Epicharis,' Volusius answered uneasily. The tribune wrote down her name.

Volusius was far from sure of the decision he'd made to report her. He'd tossed and turned all night before realising that if anything went wrong and his name was mentioned, he'd be executed for treason. Also, he wasn't totally sure that this wasn't some kind of a set up. He believed he had no choice.

Unfortunately for Epicharis the report went not to Prefect Rufus, but to Prefect Tigellinus who studied it intently.

47

Pompeii

Gnaeus Allius Nigidius walked briskly towards the Villa Regina rejoicing in yet another real estate coup. His commission on the sale of a property such as this would be substantial. He'd grown wealthy buying and selling for the people of Pompeii over the years, and although values had fallen after the last earthquake he still did well from local deals.

Villa Regina lay not much more than two miles or so from the city walls. It was old but still functioned well as a vineyard, successfully making its own wine from over thirty vines on the property. He'd been a little surprised at the generous price offered up front by the prospective buyer, but that wasn't his concern. The offer had been accepted and the agreement was to be finalised today.

An hour later the deal was done.

Later that day

Claudia and Marcus strolled companionably at a leisurely pace towards the Villa Regina.

'Who came up with the idea in the first place?' Claudia asked.

'Lucius. He's been giving his future a great deal of thought,' Marcus replied, 'especially since becoming betrothed to Alessia.'

'I have to admit that I was a little surprised when he wrote telling me of his plans and asking if I'd be willing to help train him to run the vineyard.'

'I must say that I'm surprised myself, but the more I thought about it the more sense it made,' Marcus admitted. 'Of course, with your experience making your own wine and the knowledge of your people, he knew where to turn for advice. Do you mind if we take a rest for a while here?'

They stopped by a bench beside the track, settling themselves comfortably. The setting was one of sweeping fields on a sleepy day.

'Are you feeling ill?' Claudia asked with concern.

'No, nothing like that. I'd like to talk to you though. We've been close friends now for many years, Claudia, haven't we?' Marcus paused for a few moments as if searching for the right words.

'You're my best friend.'

'Don't you think it's time we made it a little more than that? We're not getting any younger you know,' Marcus smiled and took her hand.

'Oh, Marcus. You're a darling man and you've just paid me a compliment that gives me more joy and honour than I deserve,' Claudia answered softly.

'Then you'll consent to be my wife?'

'No, Marcus, I cannot. I'm afraid that I'm well past that point in my life where I would feel able to commit to anyone, even to you. I could not give the emotional attachment that I'd feel was honest.'

'I'm not going to lose my best friend over my proposal today, though, am I?' Marcus asked anxiously.

'The only way that will happen is when I'm in my grave,' Claudia answered, not totally in jest.

'There'll be no talk like that today, Claudia,' Marcus chided her gently. He kissed her lightly on the cheek. 'We've got a job to do for my son and your daughter—for that is what Alessia is to you, isn't she?'

'Yes she is. I'm a foolish old woman who can't help herself.'

'Old?—Yes. Foolish?—You've never been that,' Marcus replied, receiving a gentle cuff around the ears for his impertinence. 'Now let's go and have a good look around the villa. There's a great deal of work to do, I would think, to get it ready for the most important people in both of our lives.'

'I'm so pleased to have Alessia back here again safely,' Claudia sighed with relief. 'Remember, Marcus, Lucius asked that the purchase of Villa Regina be kept from her until he can tell her himself.'

'You have my word.'

They walked on, arm in arm, a perfect match it would appear. Any more than close friendship, however, was not in Claudia's ability to give.

———◦◦◦)◦|◦(◦◦◦———

The donkey nodded sleepily, snuffling and staring into the mist rising from the nearby stagnant water. An inconspicuous boat sidled slowly towards the bathhouse at the end of the artificial harbour located near the Marine Gate.

The hour was late.

After disembarking earlier at the city's major commercial port, Lydos had offered a generous deal to the boat owner to carry him to the ancient, privately owned bathhouse that stood on the city walls. Seeing the building emerge from the darkness etched onto the canvas of night, he paid the man and stepped ashore onto the lowest of five, slimy steps leading to the bathhouse entry beside the outside cooking area and warehouses.

The Suburban Bathhouse, for men only, provided a brothel at its upper storey, where boat owners, deckhands, tax evaders, minor criminals and others could relieve their needs with a woman of their choice for the night. The visitors sought shelter, food and sex, not necessarily in that order.

Pompeii slept.

Lydos slipped, unobserved, onto the Via Marina, making his way up the short, steep entry to the Marine Gate. Walking past the temple of Venus on his right, to his left he could just make out a large caupona. Its owner had long ago retired for the night to the rooms at the back of the shop. To guide him Lydos risked lighting a flare and followed the white, travertine 'cats'eyes' that had been laid into the centre of the road. This seemed to be a city that catered for strangers, he noticed.

A lone donkey stood tethered to an iron pole, one of many for that purpose inserted into holes gouged out of stones lining the footpath. No doubt the animal had been forgotten or simply left there by a drunken master, gone home to sleep off an over-indulgence in the local wine.

Stopping momentarily, Lydos glanced back at the brothel as its outline receded into the darkness. Temptation gnawed at him. His body craved a woman's sensual curves. Desire coursed through him mercilessly. Regretfully, he turned away, aware that earning his freedom was more precious. He was relieved to find that Seneca's directions were remarkably accurate and in a short time, after passing by the huge basilica, he found the city's major thoroughfare, the Via dell'Abbondanza, the street of abundance. Its very name declared Pompeii's pride in the wealth and business success of the city. He decided to put out his torch in the interest of secrecy.

Now, where was the Via di Castricio? His footsteps faltered as he peered into narrow side streets. Finally, he found the connecting street, then the place he was looking for, the *Inn of Euxinus*. On the left hand side of the wall beside the doorway he could just make out a painted sign.

A phoenix stood proudly above two peacocks facing each other their tails gracefully trailing them. Squinting, he peered at the painted words—

The Phoenix is happy: may you be happy too.

Lydos froze!

He found himself in a vice-like grip from behind and smelt the man's foul breath. For a few seconds there was silence.

'What's your business here?' The voice was suspicious and aggressive.

'I seek the owner of the inn.'

'Why?'

'Are you the owner?' Lydos spat out the words like broken teeth after a fight. He was now not only afraid, but also angry that he'd allowed his guard to slip.

'I might be. What's it to you?'

'I've a word for you, it's *'Phoenix.'*

'Then why didn't you say so before?' Euxinus released his grip on Lydos so fast that he stumbled and fell half on, half off the footpath. Lydos handed the message he carried to the innkeeper after they'd made their way inside.

The final meeting will be in six days. Expect six or seven of us. Keep the messenger there but out of sight as much as possible. Phoenix.

Euxinus grunted. Soon he'd have his revenge. It couldn't bring his son back, but it was better than nothing. Wearily he got to his feet, running his hand across his eyes, glazed from lack of sleep

'I'll give you a room upstairs,' he told Lydos. 'You must be hungry?'

'Thanks. I am. I've been travelling for hours.'

Lydos slept well that night after a plate of hot food. He'd even been given a cup of wine. It appeared that the innkeeper wasn't as bad as he'd first seemed.

Rome

Phoenix

Urgent!

By Messenger

To those who follow the Phoenix. Urgent news has come to hand. Be advised that the one chosen will soon be beyond our capability to contain if we fail to keep to the timeline discussed. His female is pregnant.

Secrecy with regard to our mission is paramount.

48

Rome

The Royal Palace
65 A.D.

Poppaea groaned then ran to the bowl on the table beside her bed where she lent over, retching violently. She'd been pregnant before but had never experienced this terrible nausea and disgusting need to throw up. That's why she hadn't recognised the symptoms at first. She'd thought that the precautions she'd taken would be enough to prevent this pregnancy from happening. Like many women before her, she was shocked to discover that she'd been wrong.

She got little sympathy from Nero. He was probably cursing as he waited for her to arrive in the reception room, she thought miserably. Right now she couldn't care less. She'd arrive when she was good and ready.

Nero had, in fact, become tired of waiting for her. He'd ordered the first case for the day to be brought before him. A tall, dark haired woman, filthy from travelling in a cart more fit for animals than humans, was dragged to the steps where she was firmly pushed down under the boot of the centurian.

'Caesar, this woman's name is Epicharis. She's been accused of treason by fleet commander Proculus from Misenum. He asserts that she tried to recruit him into a group of conspirators to murder you.'

Nero's eyes flashed angrily. He walked over to where Epicharis lay, indicating that she should be permitted to rise.

'Are you guilty of the charge?' he asked her.

'I am not, Caesar. I could never commit an act so evil. I believe that there has been some mis-understanding,'she replied tearfully. 'I refused Volusius when he demanded sex from me,' she added helpfully.

Nero looked across to his right acknowledging the arrival of Poppaea, who settled herself on a reclining couch, her face white and strained.

'Tigellinus, step forward!' Nero ordered. 'What other information is available on this case? Who else is involved?'

'Caesar, Volusius wasn't told anything else. He doesn't know the names of the others.'

'What are their names?' Nero thundered turning to the prisoner, his face only inches from hers.

'I swear by the gods there's no conspiracy. There are no names!' Epicharis began to sob.

'Tigellinus—I'm inclined to believe this woman. Keep her under guard, though, in case we wish to question her further should more information come to hand.'

Nero waved his hand in dismissal and Epicharis was dragged away. She was held in relatively comfortable conditions in a nearby house with cells in its basement. At least she wasn't in the Carcer.

———∘∘∘⋈∘∘∘———

After Epicharis had been locked up and everyone else had gone, Tigellinus sat on a stool outside the cell looking at her through the bars, occasionally inspecting the sharpness of his gladius, which he'd drawn. The silence extended for a considerable time before he chose to speak. So, he was playing games with her, Epicharis decided. Did he really expect her to be dopey enough, she wondered, to fill the silence with either stupid or incriminating babble? Not to mention, of course, the intimidation he was trying on her with his gladius.

Angry, she turned her back on him.

'*I* know your reputation, you whore,' he said menacingly. 'You'll listen to me if you know what's good for you.'

Sources had told him of her shady, previous life as a prostitute, after she'd left her husband and had no other way of surviving. She'd left to escape his cruel beatings.

'Well, if you know so much,' she responded sarcastically, 'why are you still hanging around here?'

'I know you're guilty. I want those names!' Tigellinus snapped. 'If you're smart you'll turn the others in. If you do I can guarantee that you won't be executed. You have tonight to think it over.'

He returned the next morning. One look at the set expression on Epicharis' face told him what her decision was.

Tigellinus shrugged. He could wait.

———∘∘∘⋈∘∘∘———

Flavius Scaevinus felt a new vitality and determination flood through him. He'd asked if he could be the one to strike the first blow against Nero.

Natalis had just left Scaevinus' house having called to tell him that his request had been granted.

They'd both been in a state of raw nerves, knowing that the time that they'd planned and hoped for was growing near. Nothing had been rushed, so plans had evolved slowly. Now all their careful, silent scheming would pay off.

Scaevinus floated rather than walked around the house, so great was his glee at the opportunity to be a second Brutus. History would remember him. His immortality was assured.

'Do you think I'm right or don't you?' Milichus whispered to his wife as they ate their dinner in the kitchen later that evening. He'd been freed by Scaevanus after years of service but still remained as a servant in the household. A dour man with absolutely no sense of humour, he and his wife were a good match.

'Of course you're right,' she answered with determination. 'Otherwise, why would he ask you tonight, to have his gladius blade sharpened? He's also given everyone presents, which is a most unusual occurrence. And, don't forget, he asked for bandages and herbs to stop bleeding to be bought.

Perhaps we should have reported our suspicions about whispers of a conspiracy against Nero earlier. It's never too late, though, you know. Maybe there'll be some kind of reward in it for us.'

'We've got nothing to lose,' Milichus declared. 'I'll do it!'

At dawn the next morning he went to the palace. He pleaded his case with the doorman and then with Nero's personal secretary, Epaphroditus, who was woken and brought out to see him. As he strode through the palace the advisor shook his head at this unnecessary irritation in an already busy life. A freedman himself, he enjoyed a life of ease but due to his close association with Nero, also endured the volatility that came with his position. He was tired and none too pleased to have been woken up even earlier than was normal.

Milichus obviously had a grudge against his master. It happened all the time, he thought, as he impatiently approached the informant.

'Wait here.' Epaphroditus ordered, having heard Milichus' story. Perhaps there was something to this report. He'd let Tigellinus decide.

—∘∘∘—❦—∘∘∘—

At a bathhouse not far from the Palatine, Seneca, Natalis, Lucanis and the Praetorian Tribune, Subrius Flavus, soaked in the water's warmth. The huge, cavernous building was empty of other customers. Anyone else approaching would be easily seen.

As the vaporous steam rose around them, they speculated about the possible ramifications of the latest news about Epicharis. Unfortunately, there was no water or warmth that could alleviate the problems they faced.

Theirs was an early visit to the popular bathhouse which would later be swarming with bathers, those seeking massages or shaves and others enjoying wine with friends along with the latest gossip of the day. The chaos had not yet begun.

'May the gods protect Epicharis,' Seneca said fearfully.

'Surely we're now at risk of discovery?' Natalis grimaced.

'She gave Volusius no names and she'll never break under torture. I know her. She'd die first,' Seneca answered, his face lined with worry.

'It seems to me that this setback, in combination with the news of Poppaea's pregnancy has forced our hand. We can no longer wait for the meeting at Pompeii. We must name the date and time now,' Flavus urged.

'My decision, if everyone else agrees,' Seneca declared with all the confidence he could muster, 'is that the deed should be carried out at the Ludi Cereales when the chariot races take place. The date will be April 19. I'll send a message to Pompeii cancelling our meeting and severing our links there. We need to inform each man who is sworn to our cause about the latest developments. I suggest we do it by word of mouth, one man to another, in places that do not allow for evesdroppers.

There was a murmur of assent.

The nightingales hid in the trees at Tauromenium.

Formiae
(Halfway between Rome and Naples)

Nero's order had been explicit. The fleet, temporarily stationed at Formiae, must return to Misenum immediately. Proculus Volusius studied the sky, the ominously heavy clouds and the frothing waves. He didn't like what he saw.

Hoping for the best, he gave orders for the fleet to proceed to their destination. At least it wasn't a long voyage and perhaps this was as choppy as the seas would become. He had no option but to be optimistic as to the outcome, even though his gut instinct and training told him otherwise.

The waves became more black and malignant as the voyage progressed. The ships rose and fell in mountainous peaks and troughs of unknown depths that threatened to swallow them forever. The violence of the southerly wind had turned into a tempest. Off the coast of Cumae, Proculus knew that none of them would live to see Misenum again.

As his ship and crew fought desperately for survival, a wave higher than he could ever have imagined in his worst nightmares fell upon them. Everything spun in a vortex sucking them down further and further—never to rise again.

Fate had ordained that the chief·witness against Epicharis would face the judgement of the gods—not the further interrogations of man.

49

Nero swung his arm forcefully across the altar sweeping the sacred statuette to the ground, where it smashed into numerous, jagged pieces. 'Destroy this monstrosity!' he yelled at the nearest attendant as he strode from the small chapel.

'What is the problem, Caesar?' Faenius Rufus asked as he endeavoured to keep pace with Nero who was almost running through the palace halls. Rufus was aware of the imprisonment of Epicharis and the commotion earlier at dawn, with the arrival of a freedman alleging a conspiracy against the Emperor. He'd decided to stay as close to Nero as possible, so as to monitor the risks to himself and the rest of the conspirators.

'That woman was supposed to be a goddess who would protect me,' Nero complained. 'Now I'm told there's a conspiracy to murder me. Obviously she was nothing but a deceitful whore. It's incredibly disappointing.'

'Do you wish me to find her, Caesar?' Rufus asked. Having previously been told by Seneca who Alessia was, he sought to protect her with a warning should Nero dispatch an assassin.

'There are more important things to worry about, Faenius, she's not worth the trouble. We must find those who are plotting murder against me.' Nero sank into the nearest chair, wringing his hands nervously.

'Perhaps there's nothing to the accusations,' Rufus suggested soothingly.

'His freedman has implicated Scaevinus. Tigellinus has him here for questioning right now,' Nero replied. 'I thank you for trying to reassure me but I think your optimism may be misplaced.'

---∘∘∘❁∘∘∘---

The sight of the executioner waiting by the palace portico unnerved Scaevinus when he arrived there. He was escorted straight into the presence of Prefect Tigellinus who had a talent for drama, and had set the scene up knowing its probable impact on a guilty man. The minutes passed as Scaevinus continued to deny under questioning, that he had any knowledge of a plot.

'Do you know when the murder is to take place?' Tigellinus turned to question Milichus who was looking considerably more worried than when he'd first arrived. He appeared to have physically wilted and grown smaller under the gaze of Scaevinus who stood nearby.

'No.'

'Then how do you know there's a plot at all?' Prefect Tigellinus persisted.

'It was obvious,' Milichus sniffed, regretting that he'd allowed his wife to persuade him to make the report.

'Nothing is that obvious from what I've heard,' Tigellinus replied.

'Then send for Senator Natalis and ask him. He was always at the house talking to my master,' Milichus suggested.

'I'll do just that.' Tigellinus called for the guards.

———∘∘∘◦◖◗◦∘∘∘———

Natalis, unaware of the drama taking place at the palace, sat in comfort enjoying a well earned rest from his senatorial duties. From his home high on the Esquiline hill he looked out over the city with a sense of contentment. He'd made his wealth from property long ago. All he needed now was to find Clodia a suitable suitor. It was a pity about Lucius Diomedes. He would have been the perfect choice.

When the banging began, he wondered who would be brazen enough to knock on his door in such a manner. A servant went to see.

'Father, there are soldiers here,' Clodia blurted out, her normal, cool demeanour deserting her as they pushed their way into the room.

'Senator Natalis, I have an order for your arrest,' the centurion in charge announced.

'On what warrant?' Natalis demanded.

'Treason.'

'But I've done nothing!' Natalis bluffed, his expression revealing his fear.

'You can tell that to Prefect Tigellinus!'

They marched him briskly from the house and down the hill. Neighbours and those passing by stared curiously at the sight of the wealthy senator being manhandled from his home, and marched across Rome.

The executioner was still lounging in the portico as Natalis and his gaolers arrived at the palace. He straightened as the group approached, an eagerness appearing on his face. If anything, the impact on Natalis' nerves was even greater than it had been on those of Scaevinus.

'Natalis, you can confess now and escape the executioner or you can die with the others,' Tigellinus told him. 'You have only this one opportunity. If you pass it up and you're found guilty later there'll be no mercy.'

Natalis could see no escape. Surely they would find out one way or another about the others. It was only a matter of time before the truth came out. He decided to save himself.

'There was a plot. We decided to act for the good of Rome,' he admitted. He began to shake as his last shred of resolve abandoned him.

'So finally we have the truth at last!' Tigellinus gave a smile of satisfaction. 'Start talking. I want the names of all of them. Who were the leaders?'

'Piso and Seneca.'

The admission surprised even the wily prefect. 'I think it's time you explained yourself to the Emperor,' he declared. 'Take him to a cell!'

———◦∘◦〉◎〈◦∘◦———

Lucius looked back just once as he left the Senate House behind. His life had recently taken twists and turns that he'd never have believed possible. What he did know, was that he no longer wanted to be part of the kind of life on offer to him now in Rome.

His resignation speech had been well received. Senators crowded around him urging him to desist from the final step right up to the end. He left the Senate well respected and with his character intact. That was more than he could say for many others who had turned their backs on it or had been forced out. His old friend, Quintus, had recently sent him a message, having heard that Lucius was considering departing the Senate.

My old and dear friend,
Greetings!
Please accept my assurances that the way of life outside the convolutions of politics will bring you far more joy and peace. You have made the right decision. I wish you well.
Quintus.

Lucius felt a load lift from his shoulders as he departed for Pompeii. Although grieving for Seneca and his lost cause, everything Lucius wanted from life was in Pompeii. Pompeii was the moon to Rome's sun. Which of them he wondered, would be remembered by generations to come. He thought that probably it would be the wrong one.

Lucius looked around him, taking in the ornate decoration of the Senate House, the sight of toga clad senators spilling through its doors, the lictors lined up waiting to do their duty, and heard the babble of the throng in the Forum. Not so long ago, he couldn't even have imagined leaving all of this behind him – certainly, not so soon. He thought, however, that his father would be pleased.

He wondered how many lessons in life he had yet to learn.

His mind wandered momentarily to his friend, Quintus, absent so long from his life. He would need to do something about that!

Lucius Diomedes gladly left behind Rome's intrigue and its cruel and corrupt magnificence. Pompeii's relative peace, especially for a man of his wealth and class, its citizens' zest for living and the opportunity to enjoy a truly meaningful existence was more than sufficient recompense.

There was nothing left for him now in the city that ruled the world.

The Palace Dungeon

It smelled of burning flesh and dead bodies.

The burning flesh was hers. Epicharus was barely conscious as she was dragged from the torturer's dungeon up the steps to the litter. The bleeding welts on her back, the burn wounds on her body, including her breasts and the dislocated bones she'd suffered on the rack made it impossible for her to walk.

She was to be taken back to her cell before enduring further sessions with the interrogator the next day. Despite her pain her face bore the hint of a smile. She had not broken. She'd kept faith with Seneca.

A woman of loyalty, pride and courage she'd played her part. Now it was up to the rest of them. As the litter began its journey, she unwound the scarf that bound her breasts and strangled herself.

50

The Forum
The Temple of Jove (Jupiter)

Nero held the small purple cushion carefully in his hands. A lethal dagger nestled wickedly into its plush folds. The weapon was an unusual sight at the temple except at times of the ceremonial slaughter of a sacrificial animal. This, however, was an occasion of an entirely different nature, requiring a different kind of gift.

As Nero listened to the continuing drone of the priests offering thanks for his safety, he reflected on the plot that had almost ended his life. Action against those responsible had been fast and furious. The one that he couldn't forgive out of the whole bunch of them wasn't Seneca—it was Faenius Rufus. He still couldn't believe it was true. *Faenius Rufus*—the confidant he'd trusted to see him through this crisis. It just showed that there wasn't one person who was totally trustworthy.

We offer our prayers to you, the god Jove, as thanks for the life of our beloved Emperor and ask that you continue to look upon him with favour.

Nero's thoughts were interrupted as the chief priest advanced to accept the dagger from him. Having done so, he placed it on the central altar with due reverence. Nero stood and proceeded to thank those who had presided over the ceremony. He wondered whether the god had heard their prayers and his own, for that matter. He was sure that he was far too young to die. He took one last look at the dagger. Sharp and deadly, it would have struck the first death slash to his body.

The dagger had belonged to Scaevinus. On its blade he'd had an inscription engraved. It sought the protection of Jove.

———oooᚕᚕoooo———

The Royal Palace

Nero settled himself somewhat stiffly on a couch near the window and stared grimly at Tigellinus. After returning from the temple of Jove he'd enjoyed fruit and wine and appeared to be ready to deal with the only remaining matter relating to the conspiracy.

'Should we proceed now? I have the senatorial list,' Tigellinus enquired, unrolling a scroll he was holding.

'Why not!' Nero declared. 'This should clean up the whole nest of vipers. If I have to, I'll wipe out the entire Senate!'

'Bring in Natalis!' Tigellinus shouted. Within minutes the conspirator slunk into the room accompanied by his guards.

Tigellinus glared at him. Natalis seemed to have shrunk in size since the earlier interrogation.

'As I call the names you will answer *yes* or *no* as to whether each senator was involved in the conspiracy,' Tigellinus ordered. 'We'll begin.'

One by one the names were called and each senator's complicity or otherwise confirmed by Natalis.

'*Senator Lucius Diomedes.*'

'No.'

The roundup of the guilty was soon complete.

———∘∘∘❧◉❧∘∘∘———

'Your advice was inspired!' Milichus hugged his wife as they stood in their bright, new apartment.

'Of course it was. Any sensible person could have seen that,' she replied proudly.

Milichus had left the palace with the good wishes of Nero and Tigellinus ringing in his ears. He'd been escorted back to the villa of Scaevinus to get his wife and his belongings then told to follow the two guards. To the couple's surprise, they'd been given the key to an apartment and told to consider it their own. It was located just far enough away from the Subura for them to look down their noses at those worse off than themselves. The villas belonging to Scaevinus and the other conspirators would all, of course, be confiscated by the Emperor.

Milichus gazed with pleasure upon the bags of coins and other gifts from Nero that lay on the table. Their future would be one of comfort.

'Those bastards deserve everything they've got coming to them!' Milichus, who had become to some a local hero, declared boldly. 'The Emperor should be protected. Look at what he's done for us!' He could barely contain his glee.

There were not any two more loyal subjects in all of Rome. Not even the sound of the death carts clanking noisily through the narrow street below could dim their enthusiasm.

————ooo❦ooo————

Outside the Castra Praetoria

'You can't even get the depth of the grave right!' Subrius Flavus sneered at the soldiers in the death squad. They were gathered around a shallow grave in readiness for his execution.

'You won't have to worry about that much longer!' the tribune in charge commented with a wry smile.'

'The way things are going with Nero,' Flavus snapped, 'neither will you!'

'Shut up and kneel!'

The hand of the centurion tasked with Flavus' beheading trembled so much that he botched the job, taking an additional stroke to kill him.

'You're a disgrace!' The tribune glared at him then turned on his heel and walked away.

————ooo❦ooo————

Rome ran red with blood.

A total of nineteen executions resulted from the purge. Additional soldiers including German recruits provided security in the streets and nearby regions.

So called 'suicides' were forced upon those who supposedly died by their own hand. Probable exceptions were two tribunes whose penalty for their treason had been a reduction in rank but who took their lives out of shame. The centurions who had been found guilty were quickly executed.

Scaevinus died with quiet dignity. Lucanis, as he felt his body grow cold with death approaching, wrote and recited poetry. Piso sat inside his house and calmly awaited the arrival of the death message from Nero. It was delivered by new recruits, as the Emperor feared the soldiers who knew and liked Piso would not do their duty. His veins were opened and he died, thereby removing himself as Nero's replacement. Petronius, likewise, awaited the death message at his villa at Cumae. Upon receiving it he gathered his friends around him and opened his veins.

Natalis was pardoned in return for his co-operation.

Only Seneca remained.

Pompeii
The Inn of Euxinus

Euxinus and Lydos sat drowning their disappointment with cups of wine. News of the discovery of the conspiracy and its failure had just reached Pompeii. In houses and on street corners it was the subject of animated gossip and conjecture.

'It was worth a try, I believe,' Euxinus said soberly.

'Yes, it was. So what happens now?' Lydos asked.

Actually, I have something for you,' Euxinus replied. He left the room, returning moments later. 'This came with the last message from our friend. I was to give it to you if things ended the way they have.'

Euxinus handed Lydos a scroll.

Seneca had kept his word. Lydos held in his hand written proof of his free status.

Several days later he returned to Greece.

51

Pompeii

Lady Claudia's Villa

Alessia stared at the crimson figures as if transfixed. Life sized and vibrant they gazed back at her, unmoved. She couldn't have been less prepared than she was for the affect that the room's atmosphere had had on her. It was like being in another world shrouded in mystery.

She'd been given very little information during a talk she'd had with Claudia barely more than a week ago. She remembered how many times in the past she'd walked by the locked room wondering what lay inside and what purpose it served.

'Would you please me by agreeing to belong to a very special sisterhood of women?' Claudia had asked her.

'Of course,' Alessia had replied. 'What does the group do?'

Claudia had said she was unable to give any further information, other than that membership was by invitation only and issued to newly betrothed girls. Alessia must accept or refuse the offer based on trust.

Alessia had made the commitment.

Dressed in a long, white robe she sat watching as Claudia entered. She was dressed in gold and wore a mask. One of the priestesses came and sat next to Alessia. She smiled encouragingly at her as she washed and dried her hands.

Alessia smelled the amber and musk of the incense as a lyre could be heard, softly played. The covering was stripped from her breasts and back. Three priestesses moved towards the centre of the room as Claudia spoke to Alessia about the state of marriage and the need for the purging of her sins. She revealed the sculpture of the phallus.

Alessia was led across to an older matron where she was pushed into a kneeling position, her head held firmly in the woman's lap. As she glanced up her eyes widened at the sight of a whip held in the raised hand of one of the priestesses.

Alessia flinched as twice she felt it strike her.

Then she was being consoled and comforted. She drank the strong, ruby red wine from the silver cup.

'Welcome, daughter!' Claudia's arms held her lovingly.

Alessia felt as if she had come home. She experienced a new emotion she could not yet describe. She only knew that she belonged here and would never leave Pompeii.

———••o—◦◉◦—o••———

The next morning

It had rained during the night leaving the trees dripping but refreshed, as they continued to struggle to fully recover from the affects of the earthquake. The staff had been up early preparing breakfast which was ready when Alessia joined Claudia in the pleasant room where they ate each morning.

'My dear, how are you?' Claudia greeted her.

'I'm a little tired, but that will soon pass,' Alessia smiled as she accepted the dish of fruit Claudia offered her.

'You will be sure this morning to have Julia apply some lavender oil to your back so it heals quickly, won't you?'

'Yes, I'll do that straight after breakfast,' she agreed.

There was a knock at the door and Lucius walked in brushing a light mist of rain from his arms and face.

'Good morning, Lucius. I'll leave you two in private,' Claudia said as she left the table.

After she'd gone, Lucius reached to embrace Alessia. She flinched.

'Alessia, what's wrong?' Lucius was surprised that he'd obviously hurt her.

'Nothing. Really there's not.'

Lucius turned her around and loosening her girdle, gently pushed the robe down from her back. It was just enough for him to see the whip marks. He gasped in surprise.

'What is this? Who's done this to you?'

'Lucius, I understand your concern. Believe me this isn't a problem. It was done with my consent.'

Lucius stood looking at her, puzzled.

She was radiant. Her happiness could be read in everything about her. Whatever she was hiding she certainly didn't seem afraid or upset.

'You must trust me,' she said looking into his eyes. 'I've never been more happy and at peace. I just can't tell you about this.'

Lucius decided to let the matter rest, provided it never happened again. Women and their secrets! Would any man ever really understand them?

279

Lorraine Blundell

Via dell'Abbondanza
A merchant's shop

Claudia stood gazing at the three chests.

'They are all of the best quality ordered for only the most discerning customers,' the somewhat snooty owner assured her.

'I don't doubt that,' Claudia answered.' The prices alone would be confirmation enough, if I needed any.' Once more she carefully lifted each lid, looked inside, then lowered it again.

Which one to choose—that was the question.

Before her stood three large storage chests. These, however, were not just for storage of the usual kind. Each was a "Hope Chest" bought for intending brides to store their special luxuries in before their wedding day.

Claudia sighed. She decided to exclude at least one. That would have to be the iron chest. She thought it was not particularly attractive and of a rather clunky appearance.

Next, she examined the wooden chest. She did like it. It was beautifully carved with birds and acanthus leaves giving it a somewhat classic appearance.

The bronze chest, however, was special. It had a gleam and decoration that was difficult to dismiss. The locks were intricate and the design appealing. She ignored the fact that it was also the most expensive.

'I will have the bronze chest,' she told the pleased shop owner. 'Have it delivered to the villa of Magistrate Diomedes on Via delle Tombe. Now, how much do I owe you including the cartage?'

She was pleased that she'd been told of the secret betrothal of Alessia and Lucius. Having bought the Hope Chest she would now hide it in one of Marcus' villa rooms until closer to the wedding day. It could then be presented to Alessia, at which time it would proudly stand on its base in the atrium of Claudia's villa.

52

Rome

(Outside the walls)
The Farm of Adrastus

The grass was heartbreakingly green and abundant. Adrastus couldn't drag his gaze away from it. And down towards the other end of the fields, the stable building lay strangely silent in the distance, its long roof glinting in the sun. The starting blocks of the new practice laps he'd had built were only three years old. He buried his face in his hands.

How had it come to this?

The property's villa stood on a rise not far from the road to Rome, and as a country residence, was certainly one of the most luxurious. Boasting its own bathing facilities to the main bedroom, its public rooms were decorated with antique furniture and fine busts. A gardener ensured that the villa's main garden, set off a long portico, was kept tended and fragrant.

The tears came unbidden as Adrastus' resolve to remain strong finally broke. Wiping the tears away with the back of his hand, he stood, gave a sigh of resignation, then gathered up the tablets, scrolls and personal belongings that remained on the villa's study table.

The horses were already gone. He was glad of that. He couldn't have said goodbye to them today, of all days. Today, they would all be sold and would no longer be a part of his life. It was a funny thing, that - now he thought about it - Flamma, Electro, Fortuna and Dulcedine. He loved them all like family, and that was hardly surprising, as they were the only family he had. It was many years since he'd left his birthplace in Greece.

The great fire had been the final straw. Struggling financially before the night when he'd watched the flames take hold in the Circus Maximus, it was the final catastrophe that had ruined him. The destruction of the great racing circus had thrown the chariot racing teams into chaos. Even a major team like the *Blues* was not immune to the unavoidable financial loss. It was rumoured that the *Greens*, the team beloved of the Emperor, had received generous financial assistance so that they could continue to meet their costs.

The most distressing part of the whole business, however, was that everything he owned, including the horses, equipment, chariots and the farm itself, would probably end up in the hands of another, rival chariot racing team – undoubtedly the *Greens* with their full coffers.

Adrastus still had nightmares about the night of the fire. He'd done his best to alert the vigiles to the inferno that menaced the Circus Maximus. Even if they'd listened when he first reached them, though, he grudgingly accepted that it would have made little or no difference to the final result.

'Achelous, we're leaving.'

'Yes, Dominus.' The young man, Achelous, Adrastus' only remaining slave, glanced across at him sympathetically. He was unaware that his master intended to free him as soon as today's auction was finished.

Adrastus took one final look around the villa at the still fountain, the rooms stripped of their treasures and the bare windows. It was a fine residence that had taken him years to build, lovingly adding little by little, as he managed to save the money. Resolutely, he shut and locked the heavy wooden door to the vestibule behind them.

This phase of his life was over and done with.

———∘∘∘—◄❈►—∘∘∘———

The Forum

'Hurry!' The Praeco, responsible for all advertising for the auction, gesticulated frantically at the bill posters around him. 'We're late getting these up! If it's left any longer I won't be paid, and obviously, neither will you!' He glared angrily at the motley group gaping at him - who got the message and fled in all directions.

It wasn't long before curious crowds gathered on street corners to gossip excitedly about the news. The precarious financial position of the *Blues* had been kept quiet until today. Anything to do with chariot racing was juicy news to fans, but no one involved in the auction wanted them causing mayhem at the sale.

———∘∘∘—◄❈►—∘∘∘———

Clivus Argentarius

Rome's 'money street' as it was dubbed by those fortunate enough to have anything to do with it, was superbly located by the Forum. It was frequented by those conducting business affairs in the various areas of money transactions. Well heeled patricians, especially senators, visited the pampering, richly appointed offices of their bankers and property advisors. Bidders would also be attending the atrium auctionarium for this day's sale of Adrastus' property.

'The Argentarius said we're not to be at the auction,' Adrastus told Achelous glumly. 'Come on. We'll go for a drink and something to eat.'

'There's a half decent bar at the end of the street,' Achelous suggested eagerly.' He was hungry even though his master seemed to have forgotten to eat at all over the past couple of days.

Lounging over a table inside a relatively clean, welcoming establishment, appropriate to its location, Adrastus and Achelous nibbled at their greasy skewers of lamb, bread and olives in relative silence, as they watched the wealthy go by, on foot or travelling by litter. The afternoon dragged on interminably.

———∘∘∘>◦◦◦———

Adrastus felt his stomach lurch as they eventually entered the nearby auction rooms. The Praeco saw them and hurried over. The empty venue confirmed that the bidders had obviously all gone and the auction was finished. Adrastus felt close to throwing up at the auctioneer's greeting;

'We'd have done better, but unfortunately, there wasn't really anyone to force up the main bidders, especially for the horses,' he declared, unconcerned now that he was assured of his cut of the proceeds.

'Who bought the horses?'

'The owner of the *Greens*,' the Praeco smiled.

Adrastus' main fears had been realised. He didn't like the rumours he'd heard about how horses were treated by some of his opponents' drivers and even trainers. The fact that it was now out of his hands was little consolation.

'What about the villa, farm and stable buildings?' he asked.

'Come in to the office and I'll set all of the figures before you,' the Praeco invited. 'I believe you'll be pleased. The sale actually went quite well. A wealthy senator bought those.'

At the end of the day, Adrastus found himself with more money in his purse and deposited with a banker two doors away, than he'd enjoyed for many a long year. He also had the added bonus of Achelous agreeing to remain with him as a freedman after being offered his liberty. The downside, was that he didn't have his beloved horses, or a home to call his own.

———∘∘∘♦♦∘∘∘———

The Circus Maximus

The ears of those passing by were constantly assaulted, day after day, by the noise of construction works being carried out at the semi-circular end of the Circus. Many fanatical chariot racing fans wept to see the extensive damage to the venerated structure. It had been left in such a state by the great fire, that it would be totally or partially unusable for some time into the future.

Watching the workmen was so popular a pastime, that street food sellers had set up their stalls as close to the action as they dared. As least someone was making a profit from the misery of those who would normally have made their fortunes here.

Fresh from his purchases at the auction house, the owner of the *Greens* team also stood watching. With him was his champion, hero worshipped driver, Alexus.

'Well, what do you think of the new horses, Alexus? I know you've raced against them before, but from now on, they'll have the benefit of better training than Adrastus gave them.'

The team owner, Numerius grinned contentedly at his driver.

Alexus took his time before replying.

'I'm not as sure as you seem to be that we can get much more out of them than Adrastus did. He is good with horses in my opinion.'

'You mean *was*, don't you?' Numerius scowled. 'Adrastus is finished!'

Adjacent to the Circus Maximus

Ancient symbols representing the universe had been cut above the entry to the underground cavern. The air smelt dank and stale in the small space enclosed by white marble, stone and brick walls and a low, hand hewn roof. The feeling inside was one of enclosure and primitive desolation. Rock benches lined both sides of the room, and at its centre, stood a rock carved altar. Cut into the room's floor at the sides, channels had been dug to carry the blood of sacrificial animals to exit holes. The central altar, reached by ascending stairs, depicted an engraving of the god Mithras cutting the throat of a bull.

This dimly lit place, a Mithraeum, was the temple for worshippers of Mithras, a god of Persian origin -the god of Roman soldiers and, increasingly, of a multitude of other Romans. Considered a religious cult acceptable to Rome, the strength of the religion continued to grow and there were several Mithraeums spread across the city.

Untouched by the great fire, this underground gathering place had withstood the devastation of the flames above. The cavern lay adjacent to the Circus Maximus.

It was here that Adrastus walked alone, late in the day, to reflect on his future. He came to a simple conclusion; he could either view the years ahead as lost to any hope of promise and true happiness, or he could consider what had happened as an opportunity.

He chose to embrace the latter.

Lorraine Blundell

The Natalis Villa

Clodia tapped her foot impatiently as she waited for the servant to refill her wine cup. She'd decided that there was little reason for her to care a fig for the views of sour, old matrons and their absolute horror at too many 'tipples' when it happened to be the fairer sex engaged in it.

In fact, there were a great many things about which Clodia had changed her mind since being dumped by Lucius – there really was no other word for it! Her sadness had turned to bitterness that had only hardened with the result of her father's involvement in the conspiracy against Nero. He was considered socially 'unacceptable.'

They'd be very lucky indeed to be left with the family villa. Her friends had all suddenly become invisible, and she'd discovered a new emotion – loneliness.

53

The Domus Aurea

Hinnulus jumped lithely down from the back of the cart, eager to reach his destination. The last thing he needed was to be late.

'Now you can see what I mean,' the farmer gestured ahead of them. 'There's no way you can miss the front entry!' His tone was sarcastic and he looked impatient to be on his way with his cabbages. He grimaced, his partially open mouth displaying the gap from a missing front tooth.

'Thanks for the ride.' Hinnulus waved, then almost ran towards the makeshift barricades erected around what was undoubtedly a giant building site. He got only as far as the outer gate before finding himself faced with a couple of burly soldiers. He noticed that the area was bereft of the usual beggars and hawkers.

'What's your business here,' one barked, looking him up and down as if he was the scum of the earth. That was fair enough. Hinnulus knew that he was hardly dressed to visit royalty.

'I have an appointment with Amulius.' Hinnulus handed over the scroll he'd brought with him.

'Wait here and I'll check.'

Minutes later Hinnulus was allowed past the barricade and led through what would undoubtedly become the front entry portico when construction was finished. They walked quickly along half finished hallways already hinting at their final splendour.

'Amulius, you old crook!' Hinnulus yelled at the toga clad figure balancing precariously on scaffolding. The painter turned at the sound of the interruption.

'Hinnulus!' Amulius scrambled down from his perch with some difficulty, his toga threatening to become tangled around his legs. The two men embraced, laughing.

'I didn't think I'd ever see you again,' Amulius grinned. 'I couldn't believe it when I got your message.'

'It's been a while, hasn't it!'

'Far too long. I can't seem to get the affect I want yet from this painting I'm working on. I'm ready to take a break.' Amulius gestured to the scaffolding behind him. 'Perhaps I'll get you to have a look at it before you go. Hopefully, you'll have some suggestions.'

'I doubt it,' Hinnulus answered. 'You know you were always more talented than I was.'

'Come on. I'll show you around and we'll have a drink before I get on with this again. Nero won't be here today so we don't need to worry about coming across him. You must stay with me for a few nights, won't you?'

'Yes, my old friend. I'd be delighted.'

They wandered together around what was already taking shape as the most incredible place Hinnulus had ever seen. As they walked, they reminisced about their days together at the school where they had learned their trade and become close friends.

'Aquila, this is my best friend, Hinnulus,' Amulius yelled to one of the artisans busily applying gemsones to a stuccoed ceiling.'

'Enjoy your tour!' Aquila grinned, adding another particularly brilliant red gem. 'Just don't take anything,' he advised sardonically. 'They count everything when we finish each day.' He turned back to focus on his work.

Gleaming marble veneers already covered many of the villa's walls with each of the rooms appearing to have its own particular theme. All of the walls were already richly coloured and as they walked the hallways, the two friends passed fountains that would before long have cooling water splashing from them. Some floors had inbuilt pools, and there were mosaics not only on the floors but also on the ceilings.

It was the gold leaf already being applied to the finished areas of the villa, however, that really stopped Hinnulus in his tracks. He stopped, awed by the gold on show. Amulius laughed. He'd worked at the villa for long enough to become somewhat blasé about the ostentation.

'It's not bad, is it?' he joked. 'Neither of us could ever have dreamt of working in a place like this when we first started out. By the way, I heard about your work at the Villa Moregine, I've been told it's first class.'

'I have to admit,' Hinnulus answered, pleased, 'that it's probably my best work so far.'

Amulius nodded.

'There's one more room I'd like to show you.' They walked into the dining room. It was nearing completion. Light streamed from slits around and above its circular structure. At the centre of the domed roof was an oculus. Wall niches competed for attention with vivid frescoes.

'Once Nero moves in here the roof will revolve,' Amulius continued. Panels will open for sprinklers to spray perfume down on the guests. I have to admit, I've never seen anything like it before in my life!'

Hinnulus was too shocked to comment.

'It's too small you know that, don't you!

Severus and Celer, architects and engineers for the building of the Domus Aurea stood in the grounds of the villa discussing aspects of the stables' design.

'No doubt you're right,' Celer admitted. 'We're better to err on the side of building it too large rather than too small.'

'Those horses of his and the chariots are better looked after than most of his people,' Severus commented.

'You know the rules,' Celer rebuked him. 'The less said about that sort of thing the better.'

They were interrupted by the arrival of Amulius and Hinnulus who had begun to stroll through the enormous gardens. The whole estate covered the Palatine and Esquiline hills and part of the Caelian.

'Do you mind if I walk my friend and fellow painter, Hinnulus, around the grounds?' Amulius asked.

'No. That's fine. As long as you're not here tomorrow it won't be a problem,' Celer replied. 'Nero's coming then for another inspection.' Evryone except Hinnulus rolled their eyes knowingly.

Hinnulus found himself looking out on an absolutely enormous pool—it could almost have been called a lake, buildings, plowed fields and trees. Vinyards would eventually yield wine for the villa. He was stunned by the size of the project.

'There's no animals here yet,' Amulius muttered. 'The gods only know what will arrive before long, though. I've heard talk of flamingos and parrots.'

The huge statue of Nero for the entrance hall of the villa had not yet been put into place. The Emperor would be represented as Sol the sun god. The statue would be so high that it would look like it almost reached the sky.

Amulius and Hinnulus returned to the painting that Amulius was currently working on. He beckoned Hinnulus onto the scaffolding. He scrambled up easily, his skinny legs shinning up to the top like a monkey's.

'See what you think?' Amulius asked.

'It's superb. I don't see any problem,' Hinnulus answered, puzzled.

'The problem,' Amulius continued, 'is that I can't seem to achieve one particular affect I want.'

Hinnulus continued to look puzzled.

Amulius bent and whispered in his ear.

Hinnulus' expression reflected his understanding and a slow grin spread across his face. 'Oh, is that all? I can show you how to do that. Step aside and I'll fix it for you.'

A short time later Hinnulus was finished. The eyes of Minerva seemed to follow the two painters when they eventually left the room.

Nero

Finally I have a place where I can live like a human being! The estate's a delight to the eyes. I promised Poppaea that one day I'd build a palace to surpass all others and that's what I've done. Before long I can move in. I must plan a party to surpass all others.

The work's been well fashioned by all of the artists. There is one thing that bothers me though. It's the wall painting of Minerva. It's quite unearthly. I could swear that her eyes follow me wherever I go.

54

The Road to Nomentum

Praxus rode as if his life depended upon it. The only thing was that it wasn't his life but that of Seneca he strove to save. It had taken a long time—probably longer than it should have—he would readily have conceded, but he'd finally reached the end of years of inner turmoil.

His decision had been made.

The horse lathered up and began to struggle as Praxus pushed the animal to its limits. Time was so tight. He had none to spare.

At the palace he'd heard Nero order the death of the elderley statesman, Seneca. That had been one death too many. The gods knew how he'd struggled to hold onto the life that was all he knew—as a praetorian guard faithful to his oath to protect the Emperor.

In the end personal decency had won out over his oath.

Praxus' resignation lay on the desk in his room at the barracks. He'd scrawled it quickly, gathered up his money and a few belongings and mounting his horse, he rode through the guard post never to return.

Surely he must be nearly at the farmhouse! Praxus knew that behind him rode Gavius Silvanus, a tribune of a praetorian cohort. As one of the group of conspirators, he sought to save his own neck by delivering to Seneca the death message from Nero. Apart from any considerations concerning the conspiracy itself, Praxus didn't like the man. He'd found him to be two-faced and a schemer.

After what seemed like an eternity, he reached Seneca's farm and knocked loudly on the heavy kitchen door. Almost immediately it was opened by Seneca's wife.

'It's a matter of life and death! I must speak with Seneca,' Praxus demanded.

'What is the problem, Praetorian?' Having heard the disturbance, Seneca came to the door.

'There's another guard riding close behind me with your death order. 'I've come to warn you. Move now and you'll have a small window of time in which to escape. I'll hold him here for as long as I can.'

'You're obviously a man of conscience and of courage. Please accept my thanks for what you've tried to do. What is your name?' Seneca reached out and placed his hand on Praxus'arm.

'My name is Praxus, sir.'

'Praxus, I'm too old to run. I've lived my life. In a way, death is almost a relief. Now go. Leave before you are found here.'

Sadly, Praxus looked into the old man's weary eyes and saw that his mind was made up. He'd been expecting this death message for some time.

'May the gods protect you,' Praxus told him.

'And you, son.'

Praxus waited, hidden in a copse of trees, until some time later he saw Silvanus ride up and thump on the door. He pounded on it forcefully.

'Open in the name of the Emperor!' He continued until the door was opened by Seneca who studied him, unsurprised.

'You have something to say to me?' he asked calmly.

'I have a message for you from the Emperor. You have only one hour to comply with his order.'

Seneca opened the scroll as Silvanus stood watching him inpassively. He sighed then nodded his head in understanding.

I am of the belief, Seneca, that you will not wish to remain in this life knowing that I have reason to suspect you of treason. You have one hour in which to take action to remove yourself in a statesman-like manner.
Caesar Nero.

'Tell the Emperor that I will embarrass him with my presence no longer.' Seneca gently closed the door leaving Silvanus standing there. He rode off to report to Nero that he'd done his duty.

Sadly, Praxus mounted his horse and rode numbly through the countryside on his way to a new life with his brother in Ostia. He knew that he was fortunate to have family to go to.

Amongst his few belongings he carried Octavia's scroll. He was unsure if some day he'd learn to love again. All he knew was that impossible as it sounded, he'd fallen in love with the sweetest woman that he'd ever been privileged to know. The fact that she'd been Empress of Rome seemed inconsequential.

Ostia

It was growing dark in the walled city of Ostia as a lone horseman made his way onto the Decumanus Maximus. The port city with its trademark lighthouse and naval anchorage usually bustled with life and commercial activity. This was that strange time of day, however, between light and not quite dark, when business of the commercial kind had ceased and business of the flesh had yet to begin.

No attention was paid to yet one more of the many strangers who ventured into the city. The stranger looked tired enough to fall off his horse from fatigue. Even the first of the prostitutes setting up for the evening thought him not worth approaching.

Praxus found his way to Via Gherardo seeking his brother's house. As fate would have it, Sextus Lucceius was standing at his front gate talking to a friend when he saw the horseman approaching. To say he was surprised would have been an understatement.

Praxus fell exhausted into his brother's arms and was carried into his house. The days afterwards passed slowly. Physically, his recovery was quick. Mentally it was considerably slower. Many months went by before he felt able to explain to his brother the circumstances that had befallen him.

55

Oplontis

Poppaea's Country Villa

T he luxurious, private bathing suite was situated towards the back of the villa. Farzana lay soaking in the tepidarium wondering how to spend the rest of the day. It was always lonely when Poppaea wasn't there. Perhaps she'd go into Pompeii for a change. It was market day and maybe she'd see something pretty she wanted to buy.

Farzana's maid stepped forward as she rose from the bath, her naked body dripping wet, her sensuous curves on display. She was a beautiful woman in her prime and she knew it.

'Domina, a messenger has just left this for you.' Terena entered holding a scroll in her hand.

'Just leave it on the bed. I'll read it after I've dressed.'

Farzana took her time being dried off and having oil made with myrrh rubbed into her skin. She loved the smell. Its scent floated her away to imaginary places in the exotic east. Eventually, she made her way alone to the bedroom.

She reached for the scroll.

Moments later a scream rang through the villa. All of the servants ran towards its source—Farzana's bedroom. They found her hysterical on the floor, still screaming, the scroll held tightly in her hand. It took the strength of two of the gardeners to lift and restrain her.

They lay her on the bed while Terena sent for a physician. Finally, he arrived. Heavily sedated with poppy medication, Farzana slept after he'd gone. The physician had taken the liberty of prising her fingers away from the scroll. He glanced at the contents and shook his head.

'Are you her maid?' he asked, turning towards Terena.

'Yes.'

'You'll need to get word quickly to her family. She cannot be left alone or I fear for the consequences. Call me again if necessary. I'll leave more of the sedative with you. I have no doubt she will need it.'

A young gardener was sent to Pompeii to inform Farzana's elderly parents that they needed to care for her. She was taken to Pompeii to live with them and remained in a trancelike condition so long that they feared for her sanity. Eventually, after many months, she recovered enough to return to the villa at Oplontis.

She found herself the owner of the luxury villa left to her in Poppaea's will. The quiet loneliness of the porticoes echoed hollowly around her, as she walked up and down by the gardens mourning her lost lover.

———ooo-❦-ooo———

After Beryllos had left the villa at Oplontis he'd had no real plans for his future. He'd made his way to Rome where he was fortunate enough to gain employment in the royal palace. No matter how many women he took to his bed, however, or how much wine he drank, the vision of Farzana remained fresh and tormenting in his memory.

He was one of the first to hear the news about Poppaea. Quickly writing a scroll to Farzana he despatched it by urgent message to Oplontis. He didn't want her to hear of Poppaea's death, not only late, but perhaps from a complete stranger.

Somewhere, in the back of his mind, Beryllos also harboured the faint hope that when she had grieved enough, Farzana would call for him. Beryllos waited and waited. The summons never came.

Rome

To: Farzana
    Villa of Poppaea
    Oplontis

Domina,

Greetings!

It is with concern for your wellbeing that I write to tell you news of the most devastating kind. I would spare you the additional pain of not knowing for perhaps many weeks, or of hearing this from a stranger.

    The Empress Poppaea died today.

    I believe it is best if I tell you what I understand to be what happened. Already, I fear, other information attempting to hide the truth is being circulated.

    A violent argument took place following the Emperor's return from the games at the Circus. He'd been drinking heavily when he entered the Lady Poppaea's rooms. Her maid was ordered to leave, however, the shouting and foul language continued and was heard by many of the attendants. Lady Poppaea had apparently asked him why he was late.

    It is believed that the Emperor either pushed her causing her to fall and hit her head on a side table, or deliberately attacked her.

    She died and the child was also lost.

    Please accept my utmost sympathy. If there is any way in which I can be of service, please write to me and I will come.

Respectfully,
Beryllos

56

Pompeii

Villa Regina
(Outside the Walls)

Alessia clapped her hands with pleasure, pulling Lucius behind her as she ran laughing through the colonnade. He smiled indulgently at her.

'Slow down, we have all the time we need,' he gently rebuked her.

'We do, don't we.' She stopped and they drew together in an embrace.

Tomorrow was to be their wedding day.

Today had been an absolute delight. As they came over the rise and sighted the villa for the first time, Lucius broke the news to Alessia that he had bought it. They would have their own vineyards and export the finest wines.

They had already agreed that they would live with Marcus. He was growing older and although well served by excellent attendants, Lucius had asked Alessia how she felt about supervising the household. He wanted to ensure that his father was well looked after and not lonely. A woman's touch could also only enhance what was already a beautiful villa.

Villa Regina did not really have full time living quarters as it was more of a working estate. That they should live with Marcus seemed to be an obvious arrangement. Alessia had been exceedingly happy with the suggestion and Marcus even more so. It seemed that everyone would have what they wanted.

Villa Regina slept in its idyllic setting, quiet and unhurried as it waited for the new owner to put it to work. It was very much a rustic, country villa surrounded by thirty two vines. The villa's entrance opened into a small vestibule with rooms on three sides of an inner courtyard. It was colonnaded with red and white painted columns.

'Alessia, why don't we walk through the villa and see exactly what rooms we have and what improvements they need?' Lucius suggested.

'This is going to really be fun,' she answered, her eyes sparkling.

'Maybe for you,' Lucius grinned, 'but for me there's going to be a great deal of work to be done, including learning the wine making business. We really do have to make a success of this. I cannot return to the Senate.' He was pleased to see Alessia so happy. If ever he'd had any doubts about his decision to leave the Senate they'd well and truly disappeared.

'Looks like this is a storage room.'

They passed by a small room into a much larger area with two sections and two functions. One was for treading grapes in a vat, in the other, stood the wooden wine press. The nearby courtyard held eighteen large dolia set into the ground. They would hold the first grapes from their vines, where they would be allowed to ferment in the rain, wind and sun.

Around the corner from the room with the wine press was a tiny lararium. Alessia smiled when she saw that it held a bust of Bacchus. She now not only had her own special deity but was also part of a sisterhood that had become her extended family.

The villa had a kitchen, she was pleased to see, and also a decorated but rather run-down triclinium. Both looked as if they could be more than acceptable once they'd received the attention they needed.

'We'll have to do something about these floors,' Lucius frowned as he studied their run down state.

Someone was banging on the villa's front door.

'Wait here and I'll see who it is.' Lucius hoped it was the person he was expecting, which it was.

Hinnulus stood outside waiting impatiently for the door to be opened. He stepped inside and looked around him.

'This place could do with a bit of freshening up,' he looked askance at its poor condition.

'I know. That's why you're here. Hinnulus, I'd like you to meet Alessia. We're to be married tomorrow.'

Lucius took her hand.

'Alessia, I've a surprise for you. Hinnulus is our fresco painter.'

'Congratulations!' The painter gave what passed for an untidy bow. 'What rooms do you want me to look at today? I can come back and do the painting when you're ready, as long as I know what sort of time it's going to take me and what colours you have in mind.'

'What a lovely surprise. We certainly need you,'Alessia's voice was animated. 'There are two colours in particular that I'd like. One is the Cinnabar red. The other is Cerulian blue.'

They led Hinnulus through the rooms paying special attention to the triclinium, vestibule and courtyard areas. Leaving the painter to his calculations, Lucius and Alessia walked out into the gardens and vineyards. He stopped for a moment and simply listened to the silence interrupted only by the rustling of the trees in a gentle breeze.

Finally, he'd found the peace he most sought.

—ooo◈ooo—

Later, as the last of the sun's rays deserted the sky, Lucius and Alessia headed back towards the Herculaneum Gate to visit Tullia and Fabritio in their new home. As they walked, Alessia came to a sudden stop. Reaching out, she carefully pulled a pink flower from a nearby oleander tree.

You did tell me true, she whispered to it, thinking back to the night she'd sat talking with her brother in the Greek Theatre at Tauromenium. *I did find my true love.*

'What did you say? I didn't hear you,' Lucius asked her.

'You weren't meant to,' she smiled.

The nightingales sang in the trees at Tauromenium.

Epilogue

In September of the year 79 A.D. the city of Pompeii was destroyed by the eruption of Mount Vesuvius. Thousands perished. Many fled to safety.

THE AUTHOR

Lorraine Blundell (Parsons) was born in Brisbane, Australia. She lives in Melbourne and has a daughter, Jenni and a son, Steve.

Lorraine graduated from the University of Queensland with a Bachelor of Arts Degree, majoring in English and History. She holds a teaching qualification in Drama from Trinity College, London.

She trained for six years as a classical singer at the Queensland State Conservatorium of Music, Brisbane. Spanning that period she sang professionally on television as a solo vocalist. Lorraine regularly performed on channels BTQ 7 Brisbane, QTQ 9 Brisbane and HSV 7 Melbourne. She is an experienced performer in amateur musical theatre productions.

Lorraine's interests are singing, ancient history and archaeology. She has travelled extensively.

Author's Notes

Whispers from Pompeii is a work of fiction based on the historical writings of Suetonius and Tacitus, archaeological site excavations, historical records and the non fiction work, *The Complete Pompeii*, by Joanne Berry.

Poppaea forms a link between Rome and Pompeii, as it is thought that she was born in the latter city, where her family owned properties. She received the Villa at Oplontis as a wedding present from Nero. There are also suggestions that she was bi-sexual. The cryptic message 'Remember Beryllos' was found scratched on a wall of the Oplontis Villa.

Descriptions of Nero's singing voice and his teacher, Terpnus, as well as his worship of the statuette of a young woman are historically based.

A wall fresco of Apollo with Nero's likeness was found at the excavation site of the *Villa Moregine*. Few remnants remain of the lovely temple to Bacchus, also outside Pompeii's walls.

I have placed the *House of the Mask Maker* where it may have been, near the theatre complex. In 1749, 15 masks were found in one location, which was not recorded. It is likely that it was the site of an artisan's workshop.

The small, one roomed prostitute's dwelling, can still be seen a few doors from the famous Lupanare brothel. The fresco painter, Amulius, is thought to have painted some of the walls in Nero's Golden Palace. He is credited with a painting of Minerva there, and is believed to have always worn his toga while working.

The *Villa of the Mysteries* and the *Villa of Diomedes* as well as many other locations in the novel, can be visited by tourists today.

Whispers from Pompeii is a peep back through time at people very much like ourselves, who lived at a fascinating and vibrant point in history before their terrible destruction.

Thanks to the dedicated work of archaeologists over 250 years, the unearthing of the city of Pompeii has given us a fascinating, bitter-sweet gift.

Acknowledgements

As always, I have been fortunate to have ongoing support from my family, Steve, Jenni and Lauren. This has taken many forms from photos taken on site and computer assistance to opinions on the novel's content.

Long time friends Carol-Ann and Ken Berndt have given generously of their time to provide encouragement and advice. Thank you to all the friends who have supported me in ways as diverse as simply keeping me functioning physically. Much of the credit for that goes to friend and physiotherapist, Judy Franklin and physician Dr. Harold Cashmore.

Rhonda Willson, an intelligent and talented lady prepared the map and floor plan. I requested that they be simple enough for readers to understand easily, (Pompeii is a very large site), but detailed enough to provide an extra dimension to the novel. I believe she has succeeded admirably.